DIABOLIQUES

DIABOLIQUES

Six Tales of Decadence

JULES BARBEY D'AUREVILLY

TRANSLATED BY
RAYMOND N. MACKENZIE

University of Minnesota Press
Minneapolis · London

Published by the University of Minnesota Press
111 Third Avenue South, Suite 290
Minneapolis, MN 55401-2520
http://www.upress.umn.edu

Library of Congress Cataloging-in-Publication Data

Barbey d'Aurevilly, J. (Jules), 1808–1889.
   Diaboliques : six tales of decadence / Jules Barbey d'Aurevilly ; translated by Raymond N. MacKenzie.
Includes bibliographical references.
ISBN 978-0-8166-9689-5 (hc)
ISBN 978-0-8166-9690-1 (pb)
I. MacKenzie, Raymond N., translator. II. Title.
PQ2189.B32D5513 2015
843'.8—dc23   2015016166

Printed in the United States of America on acid-free paper

The University of Minnesota is an equal-opportunity educator and employer.

20 19 18 17 16 15   10 9 8 7 6 5 4 3 2 1

CONTENTS

INTRODUCTION

Raymond N. MacKenzie

After his death in 1889, Jules Barbey d'Aurevilly seemed destined to remain, at least for a while, an eccentric taste. Rémy de Gourmont called Barbey "one of the most original figures in nineteenth-century literature . . . who will probably remain for a long time one of those singular, subterranean classics that form the real life of French literature. Their altar is at the far end of a crypt, but it is a place to which the faithful descend willingly, while the temple of the great saints is open to the sunlight, revealing all its emptiness and its ennui."[1] Gourmont, an important figure in the symbolist movement and a longtime enthusiast regarding Barbey's fiction, wanted to associate the "subterranean" with the authentic and to suggest that it would take the public a while to catch up with Barbey and to appreciate what is truly unique about him. He was right.

Barbey has meant very different things to many different readers. A close friend to Baudelaire and an enemy to Zola and Flaubert, he was a strong influence on the young Proust and on J. K. Huysmans. With Huysmans, he became associated with the decadence movement, exerting influence on Oscar Wilde, among many others. Proust includes an admiring discussion of Barbey in *La Prisonnière,* and both the conception and the character of Proust's Albertine owe a great deal to Barbey.[2] Walter Benjamin mined his work for background information in *The Arcades Project;* Mario Praz put him in the tradition of "le romantisme noir," and

Deleuze and Guattari used Barbey's "The Crimson Curtain" to define the genre of novella.[3] As a Catholic writer, he was adopted as a master by the volatile, unkempt, and mystical Léon Bloy, and he exerted a strong influence on the generation of Catholic novelists that included Mauriac, Bernanos, and Julien Green. In our time, readers have begun to set him free from those categories—romantic or decadent, symbolist or Catholic—and to recognize a profoundly original, highly poetic talent as well as a compelling set of ideas in his work. In France especially, there has been a resurgence of scholarly and critical interest in Barbey over the past few decades, with a focus on his aesthetics.

Barbey is best known outside France for the six tales collected under the title *Les Diaboliques*. These stories, with their erotically charged and often gruesomely violent content, have always had a certain following among aficionados of the taboo in literature; there has always been something of the lure of the forbidden about them, dating back perhaps to their publication, when the book was seized and prosecuted as an outrage to public morals. But there is much more to these stories than that, and there is much more to Barbey than most Anglo-American readers might suspect. *Diaboliques* are best read as the culmination of the remarkable career of one of the century's most original writers. Barbey stood out in his own time (the era of Napoleon III, the era of capitalist excess and the commodification of everything, of galloping utilitarianism, of secularism and democracy) by virtue of being an aristocrat, a Catholic, a monarchist, and a flamboyant dandy—though each of these terms requires a great deal of qualification. His life work was one long protest against the soul-deadening drift of modernity, against the age of mass man and the worship of money. This protest was by no means passive: Barbey was a poet, novelist, and a highly prolific journalist and critic whose collected essays run to twenty-six volumes. In the rough-and-tumble world of the nineteenth-century French literary marketplace, he was a powerful force to be reckoned with.

Barbey's life and works, then, provide a necessary context for the stories in *Diaboliques*. Jules-Amédée Barbey was born November 2, 1808, in Saint-Sauveur-le-Vicomte in Normandy, a birth with a number of Aurevillien elements: his mother had gone to the town to play her favorite game, whist, and went into labor late in the evening just as a great storm had blown up; the baby was born at two o'clock in the morning, just missing All Saints' Day and instead arriving on All Souls' Day (in French, *le jour des morts*, a more ominous date). The game of whist, the storm, the perilous birth in the middle of the night on an unlucky day—all passed into the legend of Barbey, a legend he cultivated later.[4] A great-grandfather, Vincent Barbey (1692–1770), had been ennobled by Louis XV in 1756, and one of Barbey's uncles, Jean-François Frédéric (1778–1829), began to use the aristocratic surname d'Aurevilly, since the family owned land in and around the tiny village of Aureville. After the uncle's death, Jules Barbey adopted the surname.

The family was therefore legitimately aristocratic but had never been wealthy. Jules's father was a merchant in the region, though he was an "Ultra" during the Revolution and remained bitter about the overthrow of the old order. Jules was never close to his father and for a time was a fervent republican, but he later came to share his father's view and in fact to deepen and broaden that conservatism. Jules's mother came from a family that had had connections to the court of Louis XV, further weighting the family's politics toward the right.

Jules was sent to live with an uncle, Jean Louis François Pontas du Méril, in nearby Valognes, probably to go to school there. But he became close to Pontas du Méril, who was something of a mentor to the boy; he appears, only slightly disguised, as Dr. Torty in the story "Happiness in Crime," and some of his real-life associates appear in other stories, notably "At a Dinner of Atheists." The uncle's tales about families' histories and secrets in the Valognes region stimulated what became a lifelong fascination with the aristocratic population of that town and its environs. Valognes had been a hotbed of antirevolutionary sentiment and action; the *chouans*—the loosely organized guerrillas who fought against the new regime during the 1790s and even later—had a strong presence there, and after Napoleon's downfall many of the emigré aristocrats returned, passing through Valognes, sometimes settling there. The romance of the place and its past intoxicated the boy and continued to inspire the adult, right up to the time of his death.

He attended college in Paris, but when his father got wind of his free and easy social life there, he cut him off. Jules then conceived the idea of a military career, but his father angrily refused permission for his son to serve an "illegitimate" state, and Jules finally attended law school in nearby Caen. There, he began to develop literary inclinations and friendships, the most important of which was with Guillaume Stanislas Trebutien. It would be difficult to overstate the importance of Trebutien to Barbey. Soon after the two met in 1832, they were not only close friends but colleagues in early literary production—editing a journal, seeking out like-minded contributors, and establishing a publishing house. And for decades, Barbey and Trebutien maintained a correspondence that was extremely formative for Barbey; through these letters, Barbey tried out different personae, honed his narrative style, and slowly evolved the self he wanted to be. Trebutien was a scholar and intellectual himself, but he quickly fell under the spell of the more passionate and intense Barbey and ended up serving his friend in many ways—sometimes as a sounding board, sometimes a research assistant, sometimes a publisher, sometimes a kind of superego or moral conscience.[5]

Barbey returned to Paris in 1833 and spent most of the rest of his life there; when he was not in Paris, he was in Normandy, usually Valognes. After receiving a small bequest from a great-uncle allowing him to get himself set up in Paris, he slowly broke off all relations with his family, and even with Trebutien for several years. He began keeping a sort of diary that he called *Memoranda,* and from these and other documents we see him developing the traits of the midcentury Parisian artist—Don Juanism, use of opium and alcohol, depression, and alienation.[6] He began writing in earnest now—fiction, poetry, and journalism, including journalism dealing with fashion. For such articles, he would often use a female pseudonym—Maximilienne de Syrène, among others. By the early 1840s, he was asking Trebutien to gather any information he could about the famous English dandy George

"Beau" Brummell. Brummell had washed up in Caen, more or less destitute, and died in an asylum there. This research would lead to Barbey's first important work, *Du Dandysme et de G. Brummell* (1845). Dandyism is raised to a metaphysical level in this strange but compelling work, which must be categorized as an essay but, as Jessica R. Feldman notes, "scintillates among many generic possibilities: history, biography, autobiography, memoir, eulogy, jeremiad, gossip column, satire, tragic tale."[7]

Barbey's essay on dandyism thus eludes precise definition, as does dandyism itself. It must not be reduced to a matter of appearance, clothes, and fashion, though these have their parts to play. And it certainly is not a matter of living a superficial kind of life. It is, Barbey insists, a way of existing, an inner state more than an outer one. Dandyism, he says,

> . . . springs from the unending struggle between propriety and boredom. . . . Accordingly, one of the consequences and principal characteristics—or rather the most general characteristic—of Dandyism, is always to produce the unexpected, that which could not logically be anticipated by those accustomed to the yoke of rules. . . . [It differs from mere eccentricity, which] is the revolt of the individual against the established order, sometimes against nature: here we approach mania. Dandyism on the contrary, while still respecting the conventionalities, plays with them. While admitting their power, it suffers from and revenges itself upon them, and pleads them as an excuse against themselves; dominates and is dominated by them in turn. To play this twofold and changing game, requires complete control of all the suppleness which goes to the making of elegance, in the same way as by their union all the shades of the prism go to the making of the opal.[8]

Dandyism is the way to remain sane in the modern world, with its "yoke of rules" and its conventions. It is a method of asserting control over life and over the self, of making sense of both—all of which is to say, dandyism is a kind of art, not unlike writing. And while Barbey himself lived the life of the dandy, strolling in impeccable not to say flamboyant dress down the boulevards, being sure to be seen at all the fashionable places like the bar of the Café Tortoni, and while his essay on the dandy was excerpted in a fashion periodical, *La Sylphide,* there was one thing differentiating him from someone like Brummell: his writing. Writing became the mirror that the dandy requires, as Patrick Avrane has argued, and "it was through writing that he avoided the fate of the dandy, having brushed up closely against it."[9] The figure of the dandy appears in nearly all of Barbey's fiction, especially in *Les Diaboliques.*

Charles Baudelaire was also seeking his way in the literary and journalistic world of 1840s Paris, and it is not surprising that the two met and became friends, the topic of dandyism being one of a number of preoccupations they shared. The two met after Barbey had published an enthusiastic article on Edgar Allan Poe, who was an obsession of Baudelaire's. Though both were more or less impecunious (Barbey's inheritance having long since run out), both men were passionate adherents of pre-Revolutionary France, and both identified with the aristocratic, monarchist, and belligerently Catholic thinker Joseph de Maistre (1753–1821). In his journal, Baudelaire declared Maistre to have taught him how to think, and Barbey too had come under his spell. He was delighted to become a regular at the salon of the Baroness Almaury de Maistre (though her husband was only a distant cousin of the philosopher) and to be associated with the name. Maistre's rejection of the modern age was delivered in violent imagery and powerful rhetoric, and it had a strong appeal for late Romantics like Baudelaire and Barbey seeking a philosophy that would let them protest the direction in which the world seemed to be rushing. Maistre detested the complacency and smugness that the Enlightenment had ushered in, and he rejected the glorification of reason and progress, insisting instead on a fallen humanity steeped in its own sin. It is not hard to see the appeal of Maistre to skeptical and idealistic intellectuals living in what Benjamin called the era of high capitalism.[10]

In 1851, Barbey made a calculated splash by publishing two books within a very short period, books so different from each other that they seemed to come from two different people—but of course surprising, even puzzling onlookers is a hallmark of the dandy. First came the novel *Une Vieille maîtresse,* a psychologically intense novel of sexual obsession with sadomasochistic overtones, and this was shortly followed by the collection of essays titled *Les Prophètes du passé.* The latter was a thunderously conservative book, praising monarchist, Catholic thinkers, Maistre foremost among them. They were "prophets of the past" in a dual sense, the larger point being that they tried to make us turn to the past, not to the present or future, for wisdom and guidance not only in art and morality but also in matters of religion and even politics. The contradiction between the two books—a contradiction relished by Barbey, of course—was immediately noticed. One contemporary critic noted that Barbey thought like a Capuchin monk and wrote like a dragoon, a remark that was often quoted.[11]

Both books had a significant afterlife for Barbey, *Les Prophètes du passé* being reprinted and revised several times in the course of the following decades. *Une Vieille maîtresse* from the outset was frequently referred to as indecent, and even the faithful Trebutien could not accept it. Barbey was disappointed and exclaimed, "Ah, the Catholic cannot accept the bohemian, even a baptized one! The Catholic is blocking the artist within you . . . ."[12] Barbey recognized in these readers and in Trebutien a conflict between a chaste, demure Catholicism and the necessary frankness of the novelist, but he continued to think about the issue, and when the book was reprinted in 1865, he added a polemical preface (translated in the appendix to this book) not only justifying his practice but going further and denying that any such conflict could ever exist. He constructs his argument against a generalized enemy, whom he calls by the curiously old-fashioned term *Freethinkers* (*Libres Penseurs,* both words capitalized), and it is clear that by 1865 he has reconceptualized Catholicism for himself:

> What is morally and intellectually magnificent about Catholicism is that it is large, comprehensive, immense; that it embraces human nature in its entirety, in all its diverse spheres of activity, and, above and beyond all it embraces, it deploys always this great axiom: "Shame to anyone who lets himself be shocked!" Catholicism has nothing in it of the prude, the pedant, the worrywart. It leaves all that to the hypocrites, the carefully clipped puritans. Catholicism loves the arts and accepts their audacities without trembling.

It admits their passions and their depictions, because it knows it can learn something from them, even when the artist in question seems not to have done so.

Barbey's argument in the preface is essentially the same one that would dominate discussions of the genre through the twentieth century; we find it rephrased again and again in Mauriac, Graham Greene, Flannery O'Connor. Formulating the argument was important for Barbey's own development as a thinker and artist, and the reader who keeps it in mind will have a richer context for reading the stories in *Les Diaboliques* as well.

Barbey's relationship to Catholicism is a complicated one. He tells us that he was baptized and raised as a Christian but drifted away from the Church early on, returning through a conversion process sometime in the later 1840s, but even after that, he was never anything like a conventional or even orthodox Catholic. Baudelaire wrote that "d'Aurevilly invites you to receive communion with him like someone else invites you to dinner."[13] And a poet and critic from the following generation, Georges Rodenbach, describes Baudelaire and Barbey approaching the altar in Notre Dame as dandies, wondering if it is acceptable to receive communion with hands poised on hips. Rodenbach concludes:

> It would be interesting to write the history of these sorts of Catholics: Barbey d'Aurevilly, [Ernest] Hello, Baudelaire, Villiers de l'Isle-Adam . . . who seem to base their claim to being called believers on their blasphemies, who always have the air, even in their warmest religious practice, of trying to commit sacrilege.[14]

The relationship between belief and blasphemy, God and Satan, is indeed tangled and intertwined in Baudelaire and Barbey, and if its ultimate poetic expression is Baudelaire's *Fleurs du mal,* its finest prose incarnation is in the stories of *Les Diaboliques.* Certainly, Barbey's renewed Catholicism served to strengthen his alienation from the modern age and helped provide a philosophical and theological scaffolding for his deep feeling of distaste for the shallow, smug materialism he saw all around him.

The period of Barbey's conversion is also when his unique imaginary begins to coalesce, that strange amalgam of an aristocratic

dandyism, high conservatism, and a visceral sense of the imma-
nence of evil in human life—not immorality, not wrongdoing,
but evil. During this time he began drafting the story that would
become "Beneath the Cards in a Game of Whist," the first of *Les
Diaboliques* to be completed.[15] He wrote excitedly about it in his
letters to Trebutien, soon declaring that the story would be one
of a set of six, to be titled *Ricochets de conversation,* a title that he
continued to use until abandoning it decades later in favor of *Les
Diaboliques.* The original title signals the form of the stories: they
would be narrated from one character to another and thus have
an oral and social element that was to have been their unifying
force.[16] Barbey was renowned for his conversation in the salons
he frequented; Huysmans called him "the most amazing conversa-
tionalist of our time."[17] A great oral narrator, he tried to transfer
the skill and the feel of oral tale telling to his written work. That
orality creates an atmosphere of ease, or relaxed storytelling,
rather than polished art—but, as Barbey tells us in "Beneath the
Cards," the greatest art "consists in concealing itself." Orality lets
the dandy Barbey exhibit the old Renaissance ideal of *sprezzatura*:
everything must appear effortless. All the stories that eventually
became *Diaboliques* are indeed set up in this way, sometimes using
frames within frames, each frame usually of considerable interest
in itself, often peopled with intriguing, decadent characters. In
this case, the story is set in post-Napoleonic Normandy among
nobles who have returned from their flight during the Revolution, and as such it is a glimpse into a class and a place and time
rarely described, with political and moral situations illuminating
each other. The result of these multiple frames or "ricochets," especially in "Beneath the Cards," is that of an increasingly complex narration along with a diminishing sense of certainty; what
really happened is ambiguous, and the result is a narrative that
resists resolution.[18] That point can be made regarding all six of
the *Diaboliques,* but especially in this story we see a sequence of
mysteries and are never quite allowed to get a firm grip on the
individuals or even the exact nature of the central, horrific crime.

Intriguing as the stories are from the viewpoint of narratology,
though, what will strike most readers far more dramatically is

their content. All are set in the past; in addition to the frames provided by different narrators, there is always the larger temporal
frame. The past continues to haunt the present, to form and shape
it, to be in some way its *dessous des cartes*. Between "Beneath the
Cards" in 1850 and the complete *Les Diaboliques* in 1874, Barbey
wrote three novels, each of which can be seen as a step toward
the culminating vision of the later stories. First was *L'Ensorcelée* (a
woman bewitched) in 1854, a powerful blend of gothic horror
and political resistance in post-Revolutionary Normandy. Around
the time that he returned to Catholicism, Barbey turned his attention to his native region and seems to have wanted to become
to Normandy what Walter Scott had been to Scotland: a kind of
curator of folklore, proverbs, and odd linguistic phenomena, perhaps even some version of an epic poet of Normandy.[19] He went
further, though, burrowing into the history of the region, turning it into his own artistic landscape: he never becomes a mere
regionalist, though his chosen region remained a wellspring of
inspiration for him for the rest of his life. *L'Ensorcelée* is deeply
engaged with Norman history and folklore, and writing it opened
up for Barbey what would become his major thematic concerns,
especially the melding of the Satanic with the divine, here embod-
ied in the hideously disfigured yet charismatic priest the Abbé de
la Croix-Jugan. The priest has sinned first by killing for the *chouan*
cause, and then later by attempting suicide; his demonic aura be-
witches a local woman, Jeanne le Hardouey, touching off a series
of violent, bravura episodes in a complex, swiftly moving plot.
The Abbé is a Byronic figure, with some stock character traits,
but the conception of the character transcends its roots, and the
novel has a highly original power about it.

Next came *Le Chevalier des Touches* in 1864, a more purely political novel, again concerning anti-Revolutionary skullduggery in
the early years of the century; the book resolves itself into a series
of narrated stories within stories and brilliantly deploys the *richo-
chets de conversation* form. Barbey's aim here is in part archaeo-
logical; he refers to himself as a kind of Cuvier, reconstructing a
forgotten whole out of a few words. Set in Restoration-era (the
1820s) Valognes, the novel focuses on a small group of aristocrats

and sympathizers of the ancien régime who meet in a living room and tell stories about the mysterious des Touches (an actual historical figure), who was involved in a great deal of cross-Channel espionage and *chouan* guerilla activity. Much of the novel is narrated by one character to the others, prefiguring *Les Diaboliques*. While *Le Chevalier des Touches* largely avoids the supernatural and fantastic, one could not call it *realist*—at least not in the sense that term was used in the mid-nineteenth century. Barbey's insistence on orality, and on multiple narrators and frames, complicates enormously the "reality" he is depicting. As one critic put it, Barbey's "reality" has always already become a matter of semiotics.[20] Indeed, Barbey strongly disliked most contemporary realism, condemning even masterpieces like *Madame Bovary*.

The third novel between "Beneath the Cards" and the collection of *Les Diaboliques* was the most extreme of them all, one in which any pretense to realism was entirely abandoned in favor of a mode somewhere between the melodramatic and the operatic, the novel that Zola reviewed under the title of *"Le Catholique hystérique."* This was the politico-religious fantasy, *Un Prêtre marié* (a married priest), published in 1865 after a long gestation. *Un Prêtre marié* takes the presence of the supernatural in ordinary life to such an extreme that Calixte, the daughter of the married priest, is born with an upside-down cross on her forehead, a bizarre kind of stigmata, and spends her short, illness-wracked life expiating her father's sin. This motif—that the suffering of one person can atone for the sins of another—is literalized here and has its roots in de Maistre's philosophy.[21] The Norman landscape in which the tale is set is one of moors, ruined castles, and brooding skies; there are omens and prophecies, a world of fatalism that recalls Racine and, before him, the Greeks as much as it does Catholicism. Sombreval, the ex-priest, became obsessed with science—much like Victor Frankenstein—on the path to his sacrilegious apostasy, and as such he seems an embodiment of Enlightenment Prometheanism, convinced that science can provide a cure for his daughter's illness, unable to perceive its emphatically supernatural quality. Barbey had worked on various drafts of the novel for more than a decade, at one point seeing the story of the doomed daughter, Calixte, as a kind of revision of Richardson's *Clarissa* (1748), saying that he was hopeful that Catholicism would lend his story what Richardson's Protestantism could not—the ability to represent "a type of virtue that is as interesting as it is impassioned."[22] Seen in relation to *Clarissa,* or even *Frankenstein,* the novel becomes a kind of dreamlike, or perhaps nightmarish, revision of those works. In its vigorous rejection of positivism, science, and rationalism, *Un Prêtre marié* is Barbey's most extreme novel, perhaps best regarded as a wild experiment in reuniting the supernatural and the real.[23]

Each of the novels Barbey produced between 1850 and 1865 is of considerable interest, and each in very different ways. More important for our purposes is the fact that they all were conceived and drafted almost simultaneously, in a burst of creative effort—amid, of course, Barbey's usual enormous and diverse journalistic output. Immediately after *Un Prêtre marié,* Barbey returned to the idea of a collection of tales, the collection he had envisioned back in 1850 with "Beneath the Cards in a Game of Whist." It is tempting to see the three novels as a kind of preparation for *Les Diaboliques,* which will take up the themes and motifs—even something of the structure—of the novels but in a tighter, more controlled, more fully artistic manner.

For example, the deracinated aristocrats of the novels appear again and again in the stories, as does the topic of *chouannerie,* counterrevolution. The anthropological impulse from *L'Ensorcelée* likewise informs the stories, which are steeped in Norman history, places, and names. The past dominates the present throughout the stories—from the opening phrase of "The Crimson Curtain" to the book's close—and the stories are rich in historical allusion. That past functions as a contrast to a degraded present, and Barbey is at his Maistrean best in the opening sequence of "A Woman's Vengeance," where, in order to show how decadent the present has become, with its "half-witted criminologists" in charge instead of priests, he goes so far as to prefer the age of the Inquisition:

However, crimes in our advanced civilization are certainly more ghastly than those of barbaric eras by virtue of their very refinement, the level of corruption they imply, and the superior level of the criminal intellect. The Inquisition knew all this very well. In an era when religious faith and public morality were stronger, the Inquisition, that tribunal that passed judgment on thoughts, that great institution that twists our modern nerves into knots and causes such alarm to our little birdbrained minds—the Inquisition knew that spiritual crimes were the worst ones, and it attacked them as such. . . .

The point Barbey is making here is perhaps best illustrated by "Don Juan's Finest Conquest," a conquest that reveals what he means by *refinement*. The stories constitute, in their way, the most impressive instance of Barbey's war on modernity. Indeed, the "diabolism" of the stories is practically identical with modernity, and one of the few examples of a morally or spiritually good, nondiabolic action occurs in "At a Dinner of Atheists" when Mesnilgrand turns his back on the present—which, significantly, involves him literally entering the local church. When we see what Barbey has him handing to the priest is perhaps the volume's most poignant moment.

All six stories were substantially written by May 1874, when the publisher Dentu accepted the volume. As the months progressed, rumors about the book's immorality began to circulate, and Barbey began to get nervous. He had been spending much time in Valognes since 1870, just before the disaster of the Paris Commune, and by now he was there more often than he was in Paris. He asked friends, such as Léon Bloy, to keep him informed as to all the gossip about him and the book. *Les Diaboliques* was finally published in November, and it sold well, no doubt benefiting from the rumors about its indecency. Early reviews stressed the immoral content, gleefully pointing out the contradiction between Barbey the so-called Catholic and Barbey the purveyor of unwholesome fiction. On December 5, the police arrived at the publisher to seize the remaining copies, notifying Barbey that his book was to be prosecuted for being an outrage against public morality. They found only one copy at Dentu and could find no others at the bookshops where they inquired; the first edition had evidently sold out.[24]

In a sense, Barbey had been there before. In 1857, when the government prosecuted Baudelaire's *Fleurs du mal*, Barbey worked tirelessly for his friend, contacting everyone he could who might have influence, and gathering and publishing a pamphlet testifying to the book's literary merits. Included was Barbey's own essay on Baudelaire's book, which remains a penetrating piece of literary criticism. Baudelaire's case did not go well; he was found guilty, and a number of his poems were banned, remaining so for almost a century. In late 1874, Barbey would have remembered how painful that experience had been for Baudelaire, and he sought help in his own cause, writing to literary people, to judges, to anyone he thought might understand the book's literary merits. He appeared in court on December 15 to defend *Les Diaboliques,* using arguments similar to those in the preface to *Une Vieille maî-tresse* (see the appendix): the fiction writer must be free to depict the truth, including the truth about passions and about evildoing, but if they are depicted well, they cannot but disgust the reader. He went on to apply the idea to each of the six stories, and his arguments were ultimately accepted: the charges were dismissed in late January 1875, and the book could henceforth be published and sold.

But Barbey did not republish the book until 1882, and there has been much speculation as to why. Jacques Petit suggests that dandy though he was he had a profound aversion to being the center of scandal. Michel Lecureur quotes a letter written during the period of anxiety leading up to the trial in which Barbey exclaims, "It really isn't the condemnation that worries me, instead it's the exhibition of my person (in a courtroom) that makes me vomit."[25] Barbey was enjoying more success than he ever had before: his earlier novels were being reprinted and selling well, and he had greater renown in the literary world than ever; for example, from 1867 to 1871, he had been hired as the literary critic at *Le Constitutionnel,* replacing the great Sainte-Beuve (who, incidentally, had never shown Barbey much respect).

But in 1882 Barbey gave the new edition of *Les Diaboliques* a great deal of care and attention. The book was published this time by Alphonse Lemerre, who had to negotiate with Dentu for the rights, and he put out a very handsome edition, with a frontispiece of the author and a set of extraordinary illustrations by Félicien Rops.[26] Barbey insisted on reading the proofs very carefully with the help of his new assistant, Louise Read, making many corrections.

He continued to write prolifically, and one novel, *Une histoire sans nom* (a story without a name), also published in 1882, was his biggest commercial success.[27] It is a tale that could be printed alongside *Les Diaboliques,* as it involves a wicked priest, a seduction, and a bitter revenge. He also drafted a short piece, "Une page d'histoire—1606" (a page from history), which is included in the appendix. This tale of incest and tragedy from early seventeenth-century Normandy fits perfectly with the other tales in tone, length, and narrative structure; it has a haunting quality as well and is arguably one of Barbey's finest stories. He also published *Ce qui ne meurt pas* (what does not die) in 1883, a novel he had written in his youth, completing the first version in 1833, when he titled it *Germaine.* A story of forbidden love—incestuous, like the love in "Une page d'histoire" and like so many tales inspired by his beloved English model, Byron—*Ce qui ne meurt pas* was apparently translated by Oscar Wilde, under the pseudonym Sebastian Melmoth, who titled it *What Never Dies.*[28]

Barbey's last years were successful, crowded also with many new young friends. Writers like Léon Bloy, J. K. Huysmans, and Paul Bourget formed something of a circle of acolytes around him. Louise Read, nearly forty years younger than he was, had been so moved by his writing that she set out to meet him; she became his secretary and confidante and came to play many important roles, organizing his correspondence and his papers, and publishing a number of posthumous volumes. She and Bloy were with Barbey when he died on April 23, 1889.

Barbey's reputation began to decline soon after his death, in part because he had made many enemies in the literary world. His criticism was often deliberately provocative and overstated, some of which must be attributed to his sense of the journalistic critic having to play a role, to evince a distinct personality. He said in one article that the future of journalism will rely on "the power of what is called Personality—the only power left to us!"[29] Occupying a pulpit in the various *feuilletons* as he did no doubt encouraged some of his more extreme condemnations, especially of any work related to the naturalist movement. He lashed out at Hugo, Flaubert, and especially Zola, and his powerful voice and sometimes thunderous judgments earned him the epithet *le con-nétable des lettres*—the literary high commander. But it is easy to overstate this and to paint him as merely a controversialist who insisted on taking the contrary opinion. His literary criticism has begun to be reevaluated, and scholars are finding a great deal in it worth preserving and discussing. As Malcolm Scott puts it,

> Barbey's literary criticism . . . reveals a finer critical sense than such personalized abuse [of, for example, Zola] might suggest. . . . . His approach was not a crudely moralizing one, but was based on taste, enriched by his ability to reach beyond technical considerations to their philosophical base. He might have said, before Sartre, that a novelist's technique reflects his metaphysics.[30]

The point is certainly true of Barbey's own fiction: the Manda-rin, complex sentences, the ever-expanding tissue of allusion, the insistence on orality and framing devices all serve his own worldview, that blend of traditionalism, high culture, and super-naturalism, all presented with the *sprezzatura* of the dandy.

After his death, it was safe to insult *le connétable,* and some obituaries now mocked his dandyism, even claiming that the aristocratic name of d'Aurevilly was fake—like the *particule* "de" that Balzac had added to his name. And as naturalism continued to dominate the novel, and positivism and secularism came to dominate French culture, Barbey's fiction and his fundamental outlook increasingly came to seem dated. Such is the price an antimodernist inevitably pays, it would seem: modernity gets the last word. Enough time has passed now, though, for us to be able to see Barbey more clearly and to recognize in him not simply an eccentric but an extraordinarily powerful and highly original sensibility.

The ever-faithful Léon Bloy continued to evangelize for Barbey, lecturing and writing about him long after the master's death. He concluded one of those lectures by describing Barbey's last days:

> He lived in a perpetual dream of magnificence and enthusiasm, and when he had finally exhausted that dream, he peacefully dismissed his hippogriff and, readying himself for death, settled himself into the luminous serenity of Christian detachment, as the ascetics had done in ancient times. Without regret, he departed a world that had never possessed his heart, having realized the great truth of this maxim: "The greatest honor one can do to people who belong to the nineteenth century is to suppose that they do not."[31]

It may be that in so vigorously rejecting the assumptions of his era, he can tell us more truth about it than those who embraced it can.

A NOTE ON THE TRANSLATION

The first of the stories in *Les Diaboliques* to be written was "Beneath the Cards in a Game of Whist." It was published in a feuilleton, *La Mode,* in 1850. The story was reprinted in 1855 as an appendix to Barbey's novel *L'Ensorcelée.* All the other stories were written between 1866 and 1870. In 1867, Barbey published "Don Juan's Finest Conquest" in *La Situation.* The six stories were finally published together as *Les Diaboliques* in late October 1874. In December of that year, the book was seized and prosecuted as an offense to public morality; in January 1875 the charges were dismissed, but Barbey did not choose to reprint the book until the edition of 1882. He made a number of corrections in that edition, and it is considered definitive; this translation is based on the 1882 edition.

I have consulted the important modern scholarly editions by Jacques-Henry Bornecque (Paris: Classiques Garnier, 1963) and by Jacques Petit, Pléiade edition, volume II of *Oeuvres romanesques complètes* (Paris: Gallimard, 1966 [reprinted 2003]). I have cited these books when indebted to them for material in the notes.

Barbey's style conforms to the ideal qualities he set for the dandy: it is (a) always surprising; and (b) carefully honed so as to appear effortless. The latter is chiefly achieved through the stories' orality: almost always, someone is telling or retelling a tale to someone else. Barbey was renowned as a raconteur in the salons he frequented, and he demonstrates that same talent on the page in his fiction. But the dandy, and the style, must never be predictable. Thus long, tortuously complex sentences filled with embedded clauses and phrases, firing off arcane allusions and subtle metaphors, sit right beside simple, idiomatic expressions and structures. Barbey somehow makes it all work together and blend into an entertaining, occasionally dazzling whole, and the translator's task is to try to provide something analogous in English prose. That led me to translate rather freely, in search of something that will create an effect like the one Barbey creates in French. Whether I have succeeded, the reader must judge.

DIABOLIQUES

PREFACE TO
LES DIABOLIQUES
(1874)

Here they are, the first six!

If the public takes a nibble and finds them to their taste, the next six will be published, for there are twelve of them, like a dozen peaches—or a dozen sinners![1]

It ought to be clear enough from the title *Les Diaboliques* that this book has no pretention to be a collection of prayers or an *Imitatio Christi.* . . . For all that, they were written by a Christian moralist, but one who prides himself on accurate observation, no matter how painful, and who believes—and this comprises his personal poetics—that the powerful painters can paint anything, and that their painting will always be sufficiently *moral* when it is *tragic* and creates in the viewer *a sense of horror at the things depicted.* The only immoral ones are the indifferent and the sneerers. Now, the present author, who believes in the Devil and in his influence on the world, does not sneer, and he tells these tales to pure souls only in order to terrify them.

After reading these *Diaboliques,* I don't believe there is anyone who will be disposed to turn and begin rereading them, and therein lies the entire morality of the book. . . .

That being said for the honor of the thing, another question arises. Why has the author named these short fully tragic tales with the sonorous name—maybe too sonorous—of *Diaboliques*? Does the word refer to the stories themselves? Or to the female characters in the stories?

These stories are, unhappily, true. Nothing has been invented. The real people have had their names altered: that is all! They have been hidden, and their dirty laundry has been revealed. "The alphabet is mine to use," said Casanova when he was reproached for not using his real name. The alphabet of the novelist consists of all those who have undergone passions and adventures, and it is only a question then of combining the letters of that alphabet, employing the tact that accompanies the deepest art. In any case, despite the sharpness of these stories and the necessary precautions, there are bound to be some excitable types who, whipped up by the title *Diaboliques,* will decide the stories are not nearly as diabolical as the way they want to appear themselves. They will be hoping for the kind of inventions, complications, obscurities, and refinements, for all the chills and shudders of contemporary melodrama that we find everywhere nowadays, even in the novel. But they will be wrong, those charming souls! *Les Diaboliques* are not deviltry; they are *Diaboliques,* real histories drawn from this era of ours, this era of progress, of such delicious and *divine* civilization that when I took it into my head to write them, I felt always as if the Devil were dictating! . . . The Devil is like God. Manichaeism, the source of great heresies during the Middle Ages— Manichaeism is not so stupid. Malebranche used to say that God always *uses the simplest means.* The Devil, too.

As for the women in these stories, why shouldn't they be called *Diaboliques?* Isn't there enough of the Devil in their characters to merit the name? Diaboliques! Not one in this collection fails to deserve the name, at least in some degree. There is not one of them to whom one could seriously say "my angel" without exaggeration. Like the Devil (who was an angel, too, but a fallen one), if they are angels, they are in the same way he is—head hung low and . . . the rest pointing upward! Not one of them here is pure, virtuous, innocent. Monstrous even, in part, what they have in them of good feelings and of morality does not amount to much. They could call each other *Diaboliques* accurately enough. . . . I wanted to create a kind of museum of such women while also waiting for someone to build another museum, a smaller one, of the women who make such a contrast to these in our world, their opposites—for everything is double! Art has two lobes, just like the brain. Nature is like those women who have one blue and one brown eye. Here, that dark eye is drawn in ink—the ink of the *minor virtues!*

We will provide the blue eye at a later date.

After *Les Diaboliques, Les Célestes* . . . that is, if I can find a blue pure enough. . . .

But does such a thing exist?

Paris, 1 May 1874

THE CRIMSON CURTAIN

Really.[1]

Many, many years ago I used to go duck hunting out in the marshlands of the west—and since in those days there was no railroad in the region, I took the *** coach, which passed the crossroads near the Château du Rueil, a coach that, at the particular moment in question, was occupied by a single passenger. This person, a remarkable man in every respect, whom I had often encountered in society gatherings, was a man I will call, with your permission, the Vicomte de Brassard. A futile precaution, most likely! Those few hundreds of individuals known as "society" in Paris are quite capable of determining his real name. . . . It was about five o'clock in the evening. The sun's slanting rays lit up a dusty road, bordered with poplars and meadows, down which we hurtled, drawn by four vigorous horses whose muscled hindquarters we could see twitching at each lash of the postilion's whip—the postilion, that allegory of life itself, always cracking its whip all too vigorously to remind us that the moment of departure is near!

The Vicomte de Brassard had reached that point in life where one rarely cracks his own whip anymore. . . . But his was one of those personalities one could call English (indeed, he had been educated in England), one of those types who could be mortally wounded and conceal the fact entirely, who could positively breathe his last breath while continuing to insist that he was perfectly fine. We all have the habit of mocking, both in life and in books, those individuals who continue to have pretensions to youth though they have gone well past that happy era of inexperience and foolishness, and we are right to do so, because the forms these pretensions take are ridiculous, but when the form is *not* ridiculous, when it is instead actually impressive, inspired as it is by a too-great pride that refuses to be stripped away—in such a case I don't say that it is not nonsense, but it is beautiful in the way that so many nonsensical things are! . . . If the sentiment expressed by the Waterloo guard—*death before surrender*—is heroic, it is no less so in the face of aging, which does not, after all, carry along with it any of the poetry of bayonets. Now, for minds that have a certain military stamp, never to surrender is the whole question, just as it was at Waterloo.

The Vicomte de Brassard, who never surrendered (he is still living, and I shall explain how a bit later on, as it's well worth hearing about)—the Vicomte de Brassard was thus, at the moment when I climbed up into the *** coach, what society—as pitiless as a young girl—hypocritically calls "an old beau." However, it was also true that, for those who pay no attention to certain words and mere numbers when it comes to age, the Vicomte de Brassard could pass for a "beau" *tout court*—for one is only as old as one appears. In any case, at that time the Marquise de V***—who knew her young men and who, playing Delilah to their Samson, had left some dozen of them quite bald—still wore with considerable pride an enameled gold bracelet with the end of one of the Vicomte's mustaches in it, a lock of hair that neither time nor the Devil had managed to fade. . . . But old or not, do not apply to this term *beau* any of the frivolous, thin, airless connotations that people tend to give it, because if you do you won't get the right picture of my Vicomte de Brassard, whose mind, manners, appearance were all large, substantial, generous, steeped in patrician calm, for he happened to be the most magnificent dandy I've ever known—I, who saw Brummel go mad, and d'Orsay die![2]

And he truly was a dandy, this Vicomte de Brassard. If he had been less of one, he would most certainly have been made Maréchal of France. In his youth, he had been one of the most brilliant officers in the waning days of the first Empire. I have heard his comrades in the regiment say, many times, that he combined the bravery of Murat with that of Marmont.[3] With that—and with a straightforward coolheadedness whenever the drum was not beating—he would have been able to speed his way up to the military's highest ranks, if it weren't for that dandyism! . . . If you combine dandyism with the qualities that make up an officer—the sense of discipline, dependability, etc., etc.—you will quickly see just how much of the officer remains in the mixture, and whether even that remainder sooner or later doesn't blow up like a powder keg! If up to that point de Brassard had not exploded, it is because, like all dandies, he was happy. In an earlier age, Cardinal Mazarin would have employed him—as would his nieces, though for quite a different reason: he was superb.

He possessed that beauty more necessary to a soldier than to others, for there is no youth without that beauty, and the army is, after all, the incarnate youth of France! Moreover, it was that beauty that seduces not only women but circumstances themselves—circumstances, those scoundrels—and that beauty was not the only thing protecting the head of Captain de Brassard. He was, I understand, a Norman, of the race of William the Conqueror, and he had, they say, many conquests. . . . After the abdication of the Emperor, he passed naturally to the side of the Bourbons and during the Hundred Days remained almost superhumanly loyal to them.[4] And so, when the Bourbons returned for the second time, the Vicomte was made a knight of Saint Louis at the royal hand of Charles X (then, of course, known as MON-SIEUR) himself. During the entire period of the Restoration, the fine de Brassard never once mounted guard at the Tuileries without the Duchesse of Angoulême addressing some gracious words to him in passing.[5] She, whose graciousness had been dessicated by misfortune, still managed to find some for him. The Minister, observing this favor, would have done anything to advance the man thus distinguished by MADAME; but even with the best will in the world, what could anyone do with this hotheaded dandy who—on a military review day, and in full view of the assembled regiment—had drawn his sword on his inspecting general for having made some comment on his military comportment? It was all they could do to manage to save him from a court-martial. This careless contempt for discipline had always marked de Brassard. Except in battle, where the officer in him really did fully come to the fore, he never let himself be bound by military obligations. Many times people had known him, for example, to slip furtively out of his garrison town, at the risk of ending up imprisoned indefinitely, in order to go amuse himself in a neighboring town and not return until there was a parade or review, warned by some soldier who loved him, for if his superiors did not care to have under their command a man whose nature rebelled against all discipline and routine, his soldiers, on the contrary, adored it. In their eyes, he was excellent. All he demanded of them was to be very brave, fastidious, and well-dressed, and thus to model the old-fashioned type of the French soldier, as he is depicted in the *Permission de dix heures* and in three or four old songs, all masterpieces, that have conserved such a precise and charming image for us.[6] He may have pushed his men a bit too much in the direction of fighting duels, but he claimed that duels were the best thing for developing their military spirit. "I am not a government," he would say, "and I have no decorations to award them for fighting each other bravely; but the decorations I can command for them [he had a tremendous personal fortune] are better gloves, a second cross-belt, anything that might give them a bit more style, so long as there are no regulations against it." And thus the company he commanded was so beautiful in its dress that it outshone all the other companies of grenadiers in the Guard, brilliant as the others already were. In this way he ennobled beyond measure the self-image of his soldiers, soldiers who, in France, are particularly prone to the twin temptations of complacency and vanity, the one arising from the tone one takes, the other from the envy one excites. With all this, it will be readily understood that all the other companies were jealous of his. Men would fight to get into it and fight again to keep from leaving it.

Such had been the quite exceptional position of Captain Vicomte de Brassard during the Restoration. And because he had not been demonstrating heroism in action every morning the way he had during the Empire, no one could predict with certainty how long he could go on like this, this paragon of insubordination who so astonished his comrades and who treated his superiors with the same contempt he would have treated his own life in a battle, when the Revolution of 1830 came along to remove the unpleasant necessity of discharging the imprudent captain, an outcome that had hovered menacingly every single day. Severely wounded during the Three Days, he disdained serving the new regime of the Orléans branch, having contempt for them.[7] When the July Revolution made them the masters of a country they were incapable of maintaining, it found the captain in his bed, laid up with an injury he had sustained to his foot while dancing—as it was alleged—at the last ball given by the Duchesse de Berry. But at the first drumbeats, he nonetheless got up to rejoin his company, and because he was unable to put on his boots due to the injury, he had to go to the riot as he had gone to the ball, wearing polished shoes and silk stockings, and dressed thus he took his place at the head of the grenadiers on the Place de la Bastille, ordered to clear the entire length of the boulevard. Paris, just before the barricades went up, seemed a sinister and frightening place. It was deserted. The sun beat down steadily, like a torrent of fire that would soon be followed by another one, since the shutters of every window were very soon now going to be spitting death at them. . . . Captain de Brassard arranged his soldiers in two ranks, as close as possible to the row of houses on each side of the street, so that each file of soldiers was only exposed to fire from the houses opposite—and he, more the dandy than ever, walked boldly down the middle of the street. In the sights of both rows, aimed at by a thousand guns, pistols, and carbines, he walked all the way from the Bastille to the Rue de Richelieu without being hit, and this despite the size of his chest, of which he was perhaps too proud, for Captain de Brassard swelled out his chest in the face of a battle, the way a beautiful woman will do at a ball when she wants her shape to be noticed—when, having arrived at the Frascati Café at the corner of the Rue de Richelieu, at just the moment when he ordered his troops to mass together to take out the first barricade he encountered blocking his way, he received a bullet in that magnificent chest of his, which had been doubly provocative for its size and for the long, sparkling silver braids he wore stretched from one shoulder to the other, and he had his arm broken by a rock—and yet none of this stopped him from removing the barricade and heading toward the Madeleine at the head of his enthusiastic troops. There, two women in a coach who were fleeing the insurgent city, seeing an officer of the Guard wounded, covered with blood, and collapsing on the blocks of stone that at that time surrounded the church of the Madeleine, still under construction, placed their vehicle at his disposal, and he was taken by them to the church of the Gros-Caillou, where he encountered the Maréchal de Raguse, saying to him in a military manner: "Maréchal, I may have no more than two hours to live, but during those two hours, put me wherever you like!" However, he was wrong. . . . He had more than two hours. The bullet that passed through him did not kill him. It was more than fifteen years after this that I knew him, and he claimed then that in defiance of the doctors who strictly forbade him from drinking anything while he was suffering from fever, he had only avoided certain death by drinking Bordeaux wine.

And how he did drink it! For, being a dandy in all things, he had to be one in his drinking too . . . and he drank like a Pole. He had had a fine Bohemian crystal drinking cup made for him, holding—damn me if I'm lying!—an entire bottle of Bordeaux, and he would drink it off in one gulp! Afterward, he would say that he always drank like that, and it was true. But in an era when all the forms of power and strength find themselves diminishing, perhaps this will seem like nothing to boast about. He was like Bassompierre and could hold his liquor like him.[8] I've seen him go through a dozen of his Bohemian cups, and he seemed unaffected! And I have seen him often at those get-togethers that the decent folk like to call "orgies," and even after the most ferocious drinking he never appeared to be any more than what he termed "a little tipsy," making an amusing little gesture as he said this, adjusting his cap. Now, I want you to grasp the kind of man he was, in the interests of the story that is to follow, so I may as well add that I have known him to maintain seven mistresses at the same time—this fine *bravo* of the nineteenth century, as the sixteenth century would have called him. He referred to them poetically as "the seven strings of his lyre," though I most certainly do not approve of this musical and flippant way of alluding to his immoral behavior. But what can one do? If the Captain Vicomte de Brassard had not been all that I have had the honor of telling you, my story would be less piquant, and probably I would never have even thought to tell it to you.

In any case, it is quite certain that I hardly expected to find him there, when I climbed up into the *** coach at the crossroads near the Château de Rueil. It had been a long while since we had met, and I felt a pleasure at running into him and in anticipating being able to pass several hours with this man who was so much of our time and yet so unlike the ordinary men of our time. The Vicomte de Brassard, who could have worn the armor of François I, and who moved with such easy grace in his blue Royal Guardsman's jacket, did not resemble in the least—no, neither in the way he carried himself nor in his physical proportions— the young men of the present day. The sunset rays of this grand elegance, which had shone upon us for so long, would have made all the little rising stars of our day seem pale and meager! Handsome, with the beauty of the Russian Emperor Nicholas I, whom he recalled in figure but with a less ideal face and a less Grecian profile, he wore a trim beard, still black, as was his hair, through some metabolic or perhaps cosmetic mystery . . . an enigma, and that beard rose up high on his cheeks, which had a vigorous, masculine tint. Beneath his high, noble forehead—a convex forehead, entirely unwrinkled, and white as a woman's arm—rendered even larger and prouder by his grenadier's helmet, which allowed his hair to tumble down like a cap, receding just a little toward the top—beneath that forehead, almost hidden in two recesses, were his two glinting, dark blue eyes. Almost hidden, yet they flashed brightly like two cut sapphires. Those eyes didn't just scrutinize: they penetrated. We shook hands and began to chat. Captain de Brassard spoke slowly, with a deep, rich voice capable of filling the whole Champ de Mars with his orders. Raised in England, as I have told you, it may be that he thought in English; but that slowness of speech, which was in no way embarrassing, lent a certain tone to what he said, and even to his jokes, for the captain enjoyed jokes, even somewhat risqué ones. He had what is called a lively style. The Comtesse de F*** used to say that Captain de Brassard always went *too far*—that pretty widow who, since her bereavement, always wore one of three colors: black, violet, or white. He must have been very good company, for the ladies could certainly have found things to disapprove of in his conversation. But when one is really good company, as you know, the Faubourg Saint-Germain can forgive a great deal![9]

One of the advantages of having a conversation in a coach is that you can break off whenever you have nothing more to say without causing any awkwardness for anyone. In a salon, one has no such liberty. Politeness requires you to go on speaking just the same, and this innocent hypocrisy often ends up as a species of punishment, sentencing you to listen to the vacuous and tedious chatter of fools, even the sort of fools who are naturally silent (and indeed, there are some in this category) and who must labor to dredge up something to say in order to appear amiable. But in a public coach, each person is just as much at home as everyone else is—and you can retreat into silence without any rudeness, and let yourself drift from conversation to reverie. . . . Unfortunately, life being what it is, and in those days (for already, alas, they are "those days") one could get into a coach twenty times—just as today, one could get into a railway coach twenty times—without encountering anyone who could carry on an animated or interesting conversation. . . . At first, the Vicomte de Brassard and I exchanged thoughts about the route, details of the landscape, and memories about some individuals we had both known in the society world, memories aroused by our meeting each other—and then, as the sun began to set, we too settled into our own twilight silence. The night, seeming to fall right down out of the sky—so suddenly does the darkness come in the autumn—felt chilly to us, and we wrapped ourselves up in our cloaks and leaned our temples carefully now against this spot and now against that, seeking the comfortable place that is the traveler's pillow. I don't know if my companion fell asleep there in his corner of the coach, but I remained awake in mine. I was so uninterested in the route, which I had taken so many times before, that I scarcely noticed any of the objects outside the coach, which disappeared as we rolled on, and which seemed to be traveling in the opposite direction. We passed through numerous little towns dotted here and there along that long road that the postilions liken to a long silk ribbon—thinking perhaps of the ribbon that used to tie up their hair behind, when they used to wear it long. The night turned as black as an extinguished stove—and in that obscurity, the unknown towns we were passing seemed to take on strange appearances, giving the illusion that we were coming to the end of the world. . . . The sort of sensations I record here, memories of impressions from a world long disappeared, exist no more and will never be available for anyone again. Today, the railroads, with their stations at the entrances to the towns, do not permit the traveler to take in all at once the fleeting panorama of their streets, along with the sound of the galloping coach horses, always about to be exchanged for new ones so the coach may travel on. In most of these little towns we passed through, street lamps, that recent luxury, were rare, so that one actually could make out less there than in the open countryside. Out there, at least the sky was broad, and the grandeur of that open space created a vague light, whereas here, the approach of the houses so close together, the shadows down their narrow streets, the little bit of sky and stars that one saw passing between the two rows of rooftops— all this added to the mystery of these sleeping villages where the only man one would meet would be standing at the door of the stable with his lantern, bringing out the relay horses, buckling up the harness straps, either whistling to or cursing at his reluctant or overly eager horses. . . . Apart from that, and from the eternal question, always the same one, from some traveler, half awakened from his slumber, who lowers the window and calls out into the night, "Where are we, postilion?"—nothing else can be heard or seen around or within the coach full of sleeping people, stopped in a sleeping village—or perhaps some dreamer, like myself, would stare out through the window of his compartment, trying to make out the indistinct housefronts, and would stop and gaze thoughtfully up at some illuminated window, illuminated at so late an hour for these little towns with their highly regular habits and ways, for whom the night was made solely for sleeping. There is always something impressive about a human being keeping watch through the night—even if it be only a sentinel—when everyone else is plunged into that slumber that is the slumber of the fatigued animal. And one's ignorance of what it was that kept someone awake behind that window, behind those closed curtains, where a ray of light indicates life and thought, adds the poetry of a dream to the poetry of reality. In any case, speaking for myself, I've never been able to see a window—lit up at night, in a village through which I was passing—without projecting a whole world of fantasies upon that screen of light—without imagining intimacies, dramas going on behind those curtains. And even now, yes, after all these years, I can still picture those melancholy windows that will remain forever lit from within, windows that still make me ask, when my reveries lead me back to them:

"What was behind those curtains?"

Well! One of those windows that has remained in my memory for the longest (you'll understand why shortly) is on a street in the town of ***, through which we were passing that night. The window was in the third house past the inn—you see how precise my memory is—where we stopped to relay the horses; but this window gave me more time to ponder than a simple relay would have allowed. One of our wheels had sustained some damage on the way, and they had to send off to awaken the wheelwright to see to it. Now, waking up a wheelwright in a sleeping provincial town, and making him get up to tighten a nut on a coach, and on a coach from a line that has no competition—this is no trifling affair of a few minutes. . . . And if the wheelwright was as fast asleep as the people in our coach were, it would not be easy to awaken him. . . . From the *coupé* compartment, I could hear the snoring of the passengers through the partition, and none of the outside passengers even had jumped down from their seat— those travelers *sur l'impériale,* as it's called, who, as we all know, have a compulsive habit of leaping down the minute the coach has stopped, probably—for vanity flourishes everywhere in France, even on the outside benches of coaches—probably in order to demonstrate their agility in jumping back up to their place. . . . It is true that the inn where we were stopped was closed. There was nothing to eat. We had eaten at the preceding relay. The inn was asleep, just like us. There was no sign of life whatsoever. Not a single sound troubled the deep silence . . . except for the monotonous, weary sound of a broom that someone was sweeping (whether a man or a woman no one knew, and it was too dark to see), sweeping the great courtyard of the mute hotel, whose main gates were always open. The broom dragged across the pavement as if the person who was sweeping were asleep, or very much wanted to be! The inn's façade was as black as the other houses along the street, and there was light coming from only one window . . . precisely that window that I've kept in the very forefront of my memory! The house with the window in which that light could hardly be said to be shining, for it was filtered by a double crimson curtain, seeping out dimly through the thick material, had only one upper story, but a very high one.

"That's very strange!" said the Vicomte de Brassard, as if speaking to himself. "I could swear that it's the very same curtain!"

I turned toward him, trying to see him in our dark compartment; but the lamp beneath the coachman's seat, meant to light the road for the horses, had just gone out. . . . I had thought he was sleeping, but he was not, and he was struck, just as I was, by the atmosphere created by that window; but knowing much more than I did, he knew the reason for the light!

Now, the tone in which he had said that—so simple a thing!— was so unlike the usual one of the Vicomte de Brassard and surprised me so strongly that I was positively seized by curiosity and the desire to see his face, so I struck a match as if to light my cigar. The bluish light illuminated the darkness.

He was pale, not like a dead man . . . but like Death itself.

What had made him turn pale? . . . The window, so striking, the comment he made, and the man going so pale (rarely enough paling otherwise, for he was ruddy, and when emotion moved him he reddened up to the top of his head), the shudder that I sensed coursing down his powerful biceps, resting so close to my arm in that confined compartment—all of this made me suspect there was something hidden. . . . And I, a hunter of stories, might be able to learn what it was, with a little care.

"So you're looking at that window, too, Captain, and you recognize it?" I said to him in the calm, detached tone that implies one is not especially interested in the reply, the tone of that hypocrisy that arises from curiosity.

"My God! Oh yes, I recognize it!" he said, but this time in his normal voice, richly timbred, pronouncing each word slowly.

Calm had already returned to the dandy, the most downright and most majestic of dandies, that group that—as you know!—despises all emotion as beneath them, and not believing, like that idiot Goethe did, that surprise can ever be an honorable state for the human mind.

"I don't pass by here often," he continued, very calmly, the Vicomte de Brassard, "and in fact I even avoid coming this way. But there are some things you simply don't forget. Not many, but there are some: the first uniform one wore, the first battle one fought, the first woman one had. Well—for me, this window is the fourth thing that I will never be able to forget."

He stopped and lowered the coach window. . . . Was it to be able to see that window better? The coachman had gone off to find the wheelwright and had not returned. The relay horses were late in coming and were not yet harnessed. The ones who had hauled us here were immobile with fatigue, exhausted, not freed yet from the harness, their heads hanging down between their legs, too tired even to stamp on the pavement, impatient with the desire to be taken to their stable. Our sleeping coach resembled an enchanted carriage frozen by some fairy wand at some moonlit crossroads in Sleeping Beauty's forest.

"The fact is," I said, "that, for a man with some imagination, that window has a certain character."

"I don't know what kind of character it has for you," replied the Vicomte de Brassard, "but I know what kind it has for me. That's the window of the room where I was billeted in my very first garrison. I lived there. . . . Damn it! It was thirty-five years ago . . . behind that curtain . . . which doesn't seem to have changed at all in all those years, and here I find it lit up, absolutely lit up, just as it was when . . ."

He stopped again, repressing his thought; but I was determined to make it come out.

"When you studied tactics, Captain, in your first days of command as a sub-lieutenant?"

"You do me too much honor," he replied. "It's true that I was a sub-lieutenant then, but the nights I spent there were not nights spent studying tactics, and if I had my lamp lit at a late hour like this, it was not, as the decent folk would put it, in order to be studying the Maréchal de Saxe."[10]

"But," I responded, quick as a ball off a racquet, "all the same, perhaps it was in order to imitate him?"

He returned my volley.

"Oh!" he said. "Those weren't the days when I imitated the Maréchal de Saxe, as you put it. . . . That was much later. In those days I was just a baby sub-lieutenant, all done up in my fine uniform, but quite gauche and timid with women, though they could never believe it, I suppose, because of this damnable face of mine. . . . I never profited from my timidity with them. Besides, I was only seventeen then. I had just come out of military school. We graduated in those days at the age when people are just entering nowadays, because of the Emperor, that terrible consumer of men; if he had lasted much longer, he would have ended up with twelve–year-olds as soldiers, like those Eastern sultans who take nine-year-olds as concubines."

If he keeps on talking about the Emperor and concubines, I thought, I'll never find out anything.

"Still, Vicomte," I said, "I would wager that you wouldn't have retained the memory for all these years of that illuminated window up there if there hadn't been a woman behind the curtain!"

"And you would win your bet, Monsieur," he replied gravely.

"Well, then!" I exclaimed. "I knew it! For a man like you, in a little provincial town that you haven't seen more than ten times since your first garrison, it could only have been some siege you carried out, or some woman you laid siege to, climbing up a ladder to steal her away, that could possibly consecrate the window in that house for you, lit up in just that way in the dark of night."

"But there was no siege . . . at least not in the military sense," he replied, still quite grave; but gravity was often his manner when he was joking. "But when you think about it, can you even call it a siege when the surrender comes so quickly? . . . But as for stealing away a woman, with or without climbing up a ladder, I told you, at that point in my life I was entirely incapable. . . . Also, it was not a question of a woman being taken: I was the one taken!"

I bowed to him—but did he even see me, in that dark *coupé* compartment?

"Bergen-op-Zoom was taken," I said.[11]

"And sub-lieutenants of seventeen," he added, "are not normally at the level of Bergen-op-Zoom in terms of their impregnable wisdom and chastity."

"So," I said cheerfully, "it was some Madame or Mademoiselle Potiphar . . ."

"It was a mademoiselle," he interrupted with such seriousness that it was a bit comic.

"One to add to all the others, Captain! But in this case, the Joseph was military . . . and a Joseph who would not flee . . ."

"No, a Joseph who absolutely fled, on the contrary," he replied, in a very cool tone, "though too late, and overcome with fear! The kind of fear that made me understand what Maréchal Ney said, which I heard with my own ears and which, coming from a man like that, I found quite consoling, I admit: 'I'd like to see the son of a b*** [though he said the word in its entirety] who claims he's never felt fear!'"

"A story that has you feeling such a sensation must be tremendously interesting, Captain!"

"Good God!" he exclaimed brusquely. "If you're curious, I can tell it to you, this story. It was an event that ate into my life like acid into steel, and that has left a black stain on all my pleasures in that particular line. . . . Oh, it's not always an advantage, being a seducer!" he added, with a startling melancholy that struck me forcibly, coming from a rogue like this, one I'd always imagined to be as tough as a copper-plated boat.

He raised the coach window that he had lowered earlier, whether because he feared that his voice would be heard out there, though there was no one anywhere near the coach, which stood immobile and apparently abandoned, or perhaps it was that that regular, back and forth sweeping sound, making its dull scrape across the courtyard's paving stones, seemed to him to be an unhappy accompaniment to his tale. . . . And I listened, all my attention fixed solely on his voice—on the slightest nuances in his voice—since I could not see his face in that closed-in black compartment—and his eyes were fixed more firmly than ever on that window, on the crimson curtain, continuing to shine with the same fascinating glow, the story of which he was about to tell me.

"I was seventeen years old, and I had just got out of military school," he repeated. "Appointed sub-lieutenant in a simple infantry regiment that was awaiting orders to march into Germany, where the Emperor was waging what history calls the 1813 campaign, I scarcely had time to kiss my old father good-bye before joining up with my battalion in this town where we are now. This little town with its few thousand residents more or less could only hold our two first battalions. . . . The other two were stationed in neighboring towns. You, who have no doubt only passed through this place on your way to the west, cannot possibly know what the place is like—or at least what it was like thirty years ago—for someone required, as I was, to live in it. It was certainly the worst possible garrison that chance—which I've always identified with the Devil, who was at that time personified by the Minister of War—could have assigned me for my debut. Good God, what boredom! I can't recall ever experiencing anything as dull and flat as my stay in that town. Fortunately, at the age I was then, and with the intoxication of my first uniform—a sensation you don't know, but one known to anyone who has ever put one on—I suffered very little from the kind of life that in later years I would have found intolerable. And after all, what did this sad little provincial town matter to me? I inhabited it far less, really, than I inhabited that uniform—a masterpiece of tailoring by Thomassin and Pied, really ravishing! I was mad about that uniform, and it either veiled or adorned everything; and you may think I'm exaggerating, but it's true that that uniform was my true garrison! When I grew too bored by this unmoving, uninteresting, lifeless town, I would put on my full dress uniform—with all the braids—and my high stiff collar would chase boredom away! I was like those women who continue to dress and make themselves up even when they're alone and expecting no one. I dressed . . . for myself. I took solitary joy in my epaulettes and the sword knot on my saber, flashing in the sunlight, off in the empty corner of the Promenade where I was in the habit of walking around four o'clock, quite happy with no one else there, and I would puff out my chest the way I would do later on the Boulevard de Gand when I heard someone behind me saying, "Now there is a fine example of an officer." This little town had almost no business activity and very little wealth, with only a few old families, and they would have nothing to do with the Emperor because he had not, as they said, made the thieves of the Revolution cough up their ill-gotten gains, and for that same reason they largely ignored the officers. Thus, no parties, balls, evening gatherings, or dances. The best on offer was the Promenade on Sundays after church, where the mothers came to display their daughters until two o'clock—the hour of vespers; as soon as the bell sounded, all the skirts ruffled away, leaving the Promenade empty.

"By the way, I saw this midday Mass, to which we never go, become a military Mass during the Restoration, which the regiment officers were required to attend; it was at least a live event in this dead garrison town! For lively young men like us, at the age when love and the passion for women are of central importance, this military Mass was a real resource. Except for those on duty, all the officers swarmed into the church and took their seats in the nave. We would usually place ourselves behind the prettiest girls at the Mass, and we would distract them as best we could by talking, just loud enough to be overheard, about the most charming aspects of their faces or figures. Ah, the military Mass! I've seen a great many intrigues begin there. I've seen many a hand slip a note into a girl's sleeve when she was kneeling beside her mother—and they would slip their replies back to us the same way on the following Sunday! But under the Emperor, there was no military Mass. Consequently, there was no means of approaching the respectable girls of the little town; for us they remained hidden, veiled, glimpsed from afar. And there were no other compensations either, to make up for the loss. The establishments that one never names were, frankly, horrific. And the bars where one might drown his sorrows were such that no one who had any respect for his epaulettes would enter one of them. . . . There wasn't even a hotel where the officers could go to make up a table together without being robbed blind by the management, though there is luxury enough here nowadays, like everywhere else; so we had to give up any idea of having a communal life, and instead we were scattered in various boarding houses or the homes of less-than-wealthy bourgeois, who rented to us at the highest possible rate, thus adding a little to their thin tables and incomes.

"I was in one of the latter places. One of my comrades resided in a room at the *Poste aux Chevaux,* which in those days was on this street—there! Just a few doors down from us; in the daylight, you would see the place's sign, with its golden sun half risen out of a lead-colored cloud, inscribed 'The Rising Sun'! Well, this same comrade found an apartment nearby for me—at this place with that high window that seems to me, tonight, still to be my room after all these years! I let him find a place for me. He was older than I and had been with the regiment longer, and he liked taking charge of someone like me, so inexperienced and naïve in his first days as an officer. I've already told you that, apart from my uniform—which I stress because it involves a sensation that your generation, with its peace gatherings and its philosophical and humanitarian absurdities, will soon be entirely unable to grasp—apart from my uniform and my eagerness to hear the cannons roar in battle and to lose my military virginity—please excuse the expression—apart from these things, I really didn't care much. My whole life was in those two ideas, and especially in the second one, because it was something I was hoping for, and we always live more intensely in the life we want than in the life we have. I lived entirely for the future, like the miser, and I perfectly understood those religious zealots who think of earthly life as a kind of slum they must endure for a time. Nobody is more like a monk than a soldier, and I was a soldier! This is how I lived in the garrison. Apart from mealtimes with my landlord and his wife, about whom I'll tell you more in a moment, and apart from daily maneuvers, I stayed in my apartment most of the time, lying on an old devil of a sofa bed, dark blue leather, the coolness of which felt like taking a bath after my military exercise, and I never got up from it except to take my fencing lessons and to join my neighbor across the street for cards once in a while—Louis de Meung, who was less idle than I, for he had picked up a pretty girl from among the town's grisettes as a mistress who served, as he put it, to help kill time. . . . But what I then knew about women did not impel me to try to imitate my friend Louis. What I knew I had learned in a vulgar way, at the place where the Saint-Cyr cadets go to learn such things. . . . And then, some of us are simply slow learners. . . . Did you know Saint-Rémy, one of the worst men in a town famous for the worst? We called him the minotaur, not because of his horns, though in fact he did sport some, for he had killed his wife's lover, but because of how many virgins he had gone through."

"Yes, I knew him," I replied, "but when he was old and past any possibility of reformation, more debauched with every year that passed upon his head. Good Lord, yes, I knew that old 'wreck,' as Brantôme would have called him!"[12]

"He was like something out of Brantôme," the Vicomte replied. "Well—Saint-Rémy, when he was twenty-seven, had not yet touched his first drink or his first skirt. He'll admit it to you, if you ask him! At twenty-seven he was as innocent about women as a newborn baby, and though his nanny no longer nursed him, he never drank anything stronger than milk or water."

"He certainly made up for lost time later!" I said.

"Yes," said the Vicomte, "and so did I! But I found it easier to catch up than he did. My first period of innocence ended soon after I left this town of ***; and though I did not suffer from Saint-Rémy's condition at the time of absolute virginity, I lived as chaste as a Knight of Malta—which I was, incidentally, by birth. Did you know that? I would have even succeeded one of my uncles as a commander in the Order, if it hadn't been abolished by the

Revolution. . . . Abolished as it is, though, I still sometimes wear the ribbon. A piece of vanity!

"As for the hosts I lived with when I rented their apartment," the Vicomte de Brassard continued, "you could not imagine a more bourgeois pair. It was just the two of them, husband and wife, both getting on in years, never at all unmannerly—on the contrary. In their relations with me, they always displayed that politeness that one rarely encounters anymore, and certainly not in their class; it's like the fleeting scent of a time gone by. I was not at the age when one is particularly observant, and they didn't interest me enough for me to even dream of trying to penetrate into the past of these two old people, in whose lives I only figured for two hours a day—at noon and in the evening—for my two meals with them. Their past never came up in their conversation with me; instead, their talk always concerned people and things in the town that they wanted me to know about, the husband with a gleeful tone of malicious gossip, and the wife with more reserve but no less pleasure. I do think I recall the husband saying he had traveled in his youth, but for whom or for what I don't know, and that he had married late . . . and that his bride had waited for him. They were good, honest people who had come to live a good, calm life together. The wife spent all her spare time knitting socks for her husband, and the husband, a music enthusiast, continually scraped away on his violin, favoring the old music of Giovanni Viotti, up in an attic room above mine. . . . Perhaps they had once been better off. Perhaps some financial reversal, which they kept hidden, had forced them to take in a lodger; but apart from the lodger, there was no other sign of it. Everything in their house breathed the comfort of those houses of former times, full of clean-smelling linen, solid, heavy tableware, and heavy, sturdy furniture that seemed to have always been there! I was comfortable there. The food was good, and I had permission to leave the table as soon as I had 'wiped my beard,' as the old servant Olive put it—though it was doing my meager sub-lieutenant's whiskers, still growing in, too much honor to call them a beard!

"I had been there for about six months, as relaxed as my hosts, from whom I had never heard a single word touching on the existence of the person I was about to meet in their home—when one day, as I came down the stairs at the usual time, I saw a tall person off in the corner of the dining room, standing up on tiptoe and reaching up to the clothes rack to hang up her hat by its ribbons, looking as if she were perfectly at home, looking as if she had just come back in. Her back arched in that way to reach up to the high clothes rack, she revealed the superb figure of a dancer making her turn, and that figure was laced up tightly in a bodice, and she wore a fringed green silk jacket over her white dress, one of those dresses from that era that clung tightly to the hips, revealing their shape. . . . Her arms still in the air, she heard me come in and turned toward me, twisting her neck so that I could see her face, but she went on with what she was doing just as if I were not there, ensuring that her bonnet's ribbons were not tangled, and doing all this slowly, attentively, and almost impertinently for, after all, I was standing there waiting to greet her, waiting for her to pay any attention to me; and at that point, she did me the honor of gazing upon me with her cold, black eyes, and her hair, styled in the Titus manner with waves of curls over the forehead, gave to her eyes the depth peculiar to that particular hairstyle. . . . I had no idea who on earth this could be. My hosts had never had any guests. But she had no doubt come for dinner. The table was set, and I saw there were four places. . . . But my astonishment at seeing her was exceeded by my astonishment when I learned who she was. . . . For my two hosts, entering the dining room, introduced her to me as their daughter who had just finished her boarding school and had come home to live with them.

"Their daughter! It was impossible for anyone to be less like them than this girl was! Of course, the most beautiful girls can be born to all sorts of people. . . . I've known some who . . . and you have, too, am I right? Physiologically speaking, the ugliest person can produce the loveliest one. But her! Between her and them there was an abyss, as if they were of two different races. . . . But *physiologically*—and allow me to use that pedantic word, a word from your generation, not mine—what was most remarkable about her was her air, quite singular in a girl like that, a kind of impassive air, very difficult to describe. If it weren't for that air, one might see her and think, 'What a pretty girl,' and think no more about her, or no more than one thinks about all the pretty girls chance places in one's path. But that air of hers . . . it separated her not only from her parents, but from everyone else, for she seemed to have no passions, no feelings, and she stopped you in your tracks, startled. . . . If you know Velasquez's painting *Girl with a Spaniel*, it could give you some idea of that air, which was neither proud nor contemptuous nor disdainful, no! But simply impassive, for a proud, contemptuous, or disdainful air tells men that they do exist, and that someone has taken the trouble to disdain or feel contempt for them, whereas this air said, quite calmly, 'To me, you do not even exist.' I admit that this look of hers raised a question for me that day and many others, a question I still cannot answer: how did that tall girl come from this fat bourgeois with his green and yellow jacket and his white vest, whose complexion was the color of his wife's jam, who had a wart on the back of his neck that peeped out over his embroidered silk cravat, and who stuttered? And if the husband could be dismissed from the problem—since the husband need not really matter in such things—the mother was equally impossible to account for. Mademoiselle Albertine (that was the name of this girl with the attitude of an archduchess, this girl who seemed to have dropped out of the sky into this bourgeois household, as if heaven had wanted to play a trick on them)—Mademoiselle Albertine was called Alberte by her parents to shorten her name just a bit, but her name seemed to fit her figure and her face perfectly, but that figure and face did not at all fit with such parents. . . . At this first dinner, as at those that followed, she seemed a well-brought-up girl with no affectations, habitually silent, but when she did speak, she spoke well and to the point, but nothing beyond that. . . . But in any case, even if she had had all the wit in the world, she would have found no use for it at these dinners. The presence of their daughter forced the two old people to modify their usual gossip. They had to suppress their discussions of all the little scandals in the town. From this time on, we literally spoke of nothing more interesting than whether it would rain. Thus I soon grew tired even of Mademoiselle Albertine or Alberte, with that impassive air that had so interested me at first but with evidently nothing more than that to offer. . . . If I had met her in the level of society I was meant to occupy, that impassibility would have certainly fascinated me. . . . But she was not the sort of girl I could flirt with—even with my eyes. My position with regard to her was delicate, being a lodger with her parents, and the smallest slip could do damage. . . . She was neither close enough to me nor far enough from me to matter much. . . . And I soon, very naturally, began to respond to her and her impassibility with utter indifference.

"And nothing disturbed that indifference either on her side or on mine. There was nothing between us but the politest of words, the soberest of exchanges. She was nothing more to me than an image I hardly noticed—and then, what more could I have been to her? At the table, and we met nowhere else, she paid more attention to the stopper in the water carafe or to the sugar bowl than she did to me. . . . Anything she said, and it was always very correct and very well said, was insignificant, giving me no clue as to whatever her inner character might be like. And anyway, why would I care? I could have passed my whole life without thinking at all about that calm, insolent girl with her regal airs. . . . But a kind of thunderbolt was going to change all that, as I'm about to explain—or rather a lightning bolt that struck with no warning thunder!

"One evening, just about a month after Mlle. Alberte had moved back home, we were sitting down to our dinner. She was sitting next to me, and I paid so little attention to her that I had never really noticed what should have been a rather striking detail: that tonight she was sitting next to me at the table rather than between her mother and father. And when I was spreading my napkin over my knees . . . no, I'll never be able to describe for you the sensation or the surprise! I felt a hand grip mine under the table. I thought I was dreaming—or, rather, I thought nothing at all. . . . All I felt was that unbelievable sensation of that audacious hand seeking mine under the napkin! And it was as unheard of as it was unexpected! All my blood, set afire by that touch, raced from my heart to my hand, as if compelled by her, and then raced back up to my pounding heart! Everything seemed to turn blue before my eyes . . . and my ears were ringing. I must have gone utterly pale. I felt as if I were going to faint . . . that I would simply dissolve in the indescribable voluptuousness of that hand, a little too big, a hand strong like a boy's, that had closed over mine. And you know how it is in youth, when voluptuousness carries with it a certain fear, so I made a movement to withdraw my hand from that mad one that had seized it, but hers held on tighter, as if she were aware of the pleasure she was giving me; she held on with authority, and my will was entirely vanquished, and she gripped more tightly, deliciously warm. . . . This was thirty-five years ago, and please do me the honor of believing that my hand has grown a bit blasé under the grip of women's hands; but whenever I think of it, I can still feel hers holding mine despotically, intensely, passionately! The thousand shudders that hand occasioned in my body—I feared I would inadvertently reveal it to that mother and father sitting there, with their daughter who dared to. . . . But ashamed at being less of a man than this brave girl who was potentially exposing herself to real danger, and whose utter coolness concealed her wild behavior, I bit my lips until they bled in a superhuman effort to control the trembling desire I felt, which could have revealed everything to the unsuspecting couple, and my gaze sought out the other of her two hands, which I had never bothered to look at before, and I saw that it was calmly turning up the lamp on the table, for dusk was coming on. . . . I looked at it. . . . So this was the sister of the hand I felt penetrating my own with a heat like that of a fireplace shooting its warmth in immense waves all through my veins! This hand, a little too thick, but with long, shapely fingers; the lamplight fell on them, giving them a kind of rose-colored transparency, and I saw that they did not tremble as they made their little adjustments to the flame of the lamp but, rather, performed their task with a slow, easy, incomparable grace! But we could not continue like this. . . . We would need our hands to eat with. So Mlle. Alberte's quit mine; but at the instant when her hand withdrew, her foot, every bit as expressive as her hand, pressed up against mine with the same kind of nerve, the same passion, the same despotism, and remained there throughout that too-brief dinner, during which I felt as if I were immersed in one of those baths that are at first unendurably hot, but that one grows used to and eventually comes to find so pleasurable that one imagines the very damned in Hell must come to enjoy their flaming braziers the same way, coming to find them so refreshing and comfortable and natural—like fish in their water! I'll let you guess as to whether I ate much that day, or whether I joined in the chitchat of my respectable, placid hosts, who had no idea of the mysterious and terrible drama playing out under the table. They noticed nothing; but they could very well have noticed something, and I was actually worried for them . . . for them, more than for myself or for her. I had all the moral decency and empathy of seventeen years. . . . I was asking myself, 'Is she completely shameless? Is she mad?' And I looked at her out of the corner of my eye, at this madwoman who never for a moment all during the dinner lost that composure of hers, that air of a princess at some official ceremony; and her expression remained just as calm as if her foot hadn't been saying and doing all the wild things that a foot can do—up against my foot! I admit that I was more surprised by her confidence than by her folly. I had read plenty of those risqué books in which women are not treated gently. I had had a military education. In my own fantasy, I was that fatuous Lovelace type that all young men think they are when they have managed to feast on the kisses of their mother's chambermaid behind the doors and on the staircases.[13] But this overthrew all my little seventeen-year-old Lovelace confidence. This seemed a bit stronger than anything I had read, than anything I had heard said about the deceitfulness of women—about the power of the disguise they can put on to hide their most violent or deepest emotions. And just imagine: she was only eighteen! Or was she even that old? She had come from a school I had no reason to doubt, when I considered that her mother, with all her morality and piety, had chosen the place. This absence of any embarrassment, this—let us use the word—absolute *shamelessness,* this easy control over herself as she did the most imprudent things, the things that are the most dangerous for a young girl who had given no hint, not so much as a gesture or a glance, to the man to whom she was now making so monstrous an advance—all this went through my mind, despite the overwhelming sensations I was feeling. . . . But neither then nor later on did I pause to philosophize about it. I felt no pretended horror about the behavior of this girl, with her frightening precocity in depravity. And then, I was at that age—and it's true when one is much older, too—when you don't see a girl as depraved just because she throws herself into your arms! You're inclined instead to find it all quite natural, and if you say to yourself, 'The poor girl!'—well, it's more out of modesty than pity. And finally, though I was timid, I did not want to be an ass. Not wanting to be an ass! That is the grand French reason for doing the worst things without any remorse. I knew, certainly, that what this girl was feeling for me was not love. Love doesn't go on in such a shameless, impudent manner. . . . But, love or not . . . whatever it was, I wanted it! . . . And when I got up from the table, I had made my resolution. . . . That hand of Alberte's, about which I had never given a moment's thought before, had now left me with the desire, from the depths of my being, to interlace our bodies the way our fingers had been interlaced!

"I went up to my room half out of my mind, and when I had cooled down a bit, I asked myself what I was going to do to clinch this *intrigue*—as they call it in the provinces—with such a diabolically provocative girl. I was more or less aware—like a person who hasn't tried to find out anything more specific—that she was always with her mother, that she worked all day next to her on the same tasks at the same window seat in the dining room, which served also as their drawing room; that she had no friend in town who came to call, and that she hardly ever left the house except for Sunday Mass and vespers with her parents. So, what to do? All this, it wasn't encouraging at all! I began to regret that I hadn't spent more time with the respectable couple that I had treated, not contemptuously, but with that cold politeness one uses toward people in whom one isn't particularly interested; but I said to myself that I couldn't change my behavior now without making them suspect the thing I was trying to hide. . . . The only chances I had to speak privately with Alberte were when we passed each other going up or down the stairs—but on the stairs, we could be seen and overheard. . . . The only opportunity open to me in that house, where everything was so carefully regulated, so routine, where everyone lived so tightly packed in together, was to write; and since the hand of that bold girl was so good at searching out mine under the table, it probably wouldn't balk at accepting a note slipped into it—and so I wrote. It was a note suited to the circumstances—suppliant, imperious, delirious—the note of a man who had tasted one glass of bliss and was now asking for a second. . . . But to get it to her, I had to wait until dinner of the following day, which seemed far too long to me; but finally it came, that dinner! That inflaming hand, whose contact with mine I still felt twenty-four hours later, did not fail to seek out mine below the table, just like the day before. Mlle. Alberte felt my note and took it quickly, just as I had expected. But what I didn't expect was the way she, with that haughty, indifferent princess's air of hers, in a single quick movement slipped the note directly into her bosom, seeming to be straightening a fold in a piece of lace there, and doing all this so nimbly and naturally that her mother, who was looking down at the soup she was serving, saw nothing at all, and her imbecile of a father, who was always humming something whenever he wasn't actually playing his violin, stared straight ahead and only saw the fire."

"Ah, but that's all we ever see, Captain!" I interrupted cheerfully, for his story seemed to me to be turning into one of those common, off-color garrison tales—but then, I didn't know what was yet to come! "Listen, only a few days ago at the Opéra, in the box next to mine, there was a woman who was probably very much like your young Alberte. She was no more than eighteen, but I swear I have never seen such majestic decency in a woman. During the entire performance, she remained as motionless as a statue on a granite pedestal. She didn't turn to the right or the left one single time; but probably she used her shoulders to look around her, because they were very naked and very lovely, for behind me in my box there was also a young man who likewise seemed as utterly indifferent as she was to everything but the opera itself. I can assure you that the young man did none of that playacting that men put on around women in public, those little acts that one can call making advances from a distance. But when the opera was over, amid the general noise and shuffling in the boxes, the young woman stood up straight to button up her mantle, and I heard her address her husband in the clearest, most wifely imperious tone: 'Henri, pick up my hood!' And then, behind Henri's back as he bent down, she stretched out her arm and hand to take a folded note from the young man, as simply and naturally as if she had been taking her fan or her bouquet from her husband's hands. The poor man straightened up, holding the hood—a satin hood the color of a poppy, but less red than his face, having been diving for it under the benches at the risk of an apoplexy. . . . My Lord! I thought to myself that the man ought to hang on to that hood, instead of giving it to her, and wear it himself, to cover up the horns that were going to be sprouting!"

"That's a good story," the Vicomte de Brassard said coldly. "At some other time, I would have enjoyed it more. But do let me finish mine. I admit that I had no doubt whatsoever of my letter's fate with a girl like this. She might well be attached to her mother by her apron strings, but she would easily find a way to read it and to reply to me. I fully expected, in fact, that this would inaugurate a full-scale correspondence with her, carried out under the table—but then the next day, when I came into the dining room, filled with the pleasurable certainty of having an immediate reply to my letter of the preceding day, I thought I must be seeing things: Mlle. Alberte was back where she had been seated before, between her mother and father. . . . And why this change? What had happened? What had I missed? Had the mother or father deduced something? I had Mlle. Alberte directly across from me, and I gave her the sort of intense look that demands an answer. There were at least twenty-five different questions in my eyes, but hers were as calm and silent and indifferent as ever. They looked at me without even seeing me. I have never seen a gaze more frustrating than those long, tranquil gazes of hers that fell upon you exactly as if they had fallen upon some mere thing. I was seething with curiosity, with annoyance, with anxiety, a heap of confused and thwarted feelings. . . . And I couldn't understand how this girl, so

sure of herself that I could have sworn instead of female nerves
she had more muscles beneath her skin than I did, now seemed
not to dare to give me the slightest sign to warn me—to help me
understand—to tell me that we two had an understanding, that
we were accomplices together in the same mystery, that this was
love, even if it really couldn't be love! I had to ask myself if this
was in fact the same girl with her hand and foot under the table,
the one who slipped my note so naturally into her bosom the day
before, as naturally as if she were affixing a flower there! She had
already done so much that she couldn't possibly have been too shy
to give me a responsive look. But no! She gave me nothing. The
dinner passed as I watched for that meaningful glance, the glance
I tried to ignite with mine but could not! 'She must have found
some other method of replying to me,' I thought as I left the table
and went back up to my room, not believing that anyone could
possibly retreat after having made such an incredible advance, not
supposing that she could possibly be afraid or be having trouble
managing a reply, and above all, not supposing that she could possibly have decided she was not attracted to me!

"'If her parents don't suspect anything,' I said to myself, 'if it's
just chance that she was seated with them, then tomorrow I'll
find her next to me again.' But neither the next day nor the following days was I placed beside Mlle. Alberte, who continued to
wear the same incomprehensible expression and to use the same
incredibly indifferent tone as she said the same kinds of things that
were always said at that bourgeois table. You can well imagine that
I observed her as closely as a man could. She seemed as placid
as ever, while I—I was practically in a fury, a fury that was tearing me apart, and that I had to keep hidden! And that air of hers
that never varied, it made me feel so far from her, much farther
than the table that separated us! I was so frustrated that I eventually ceased fearing that I would give her away, and I stared at her
openly, fixing all the strength of my menacing, inflamed eyes on
her large, impenetrable, cold ones. Was this some strategy on her
part? Was it coquetry? Was it a whim that followed upon another
whim . . . or merely stupidity? I have since known women who
at first were in a veritable upheaval of sensuality, but who turned

out to be merely stupid later on. 'Everything depends on knowing the right moment!' said Ninon.[14] But had Ninon's moment
already passed? So I continued to wait . . . for what? A word, a
sign, something risked in a low voice as we got up from the table,
amid the sound of the chairs being moved—and since nothing of
the kind was forthcoming, I began to think of the most absurd,
ridiculous ideas. I took it into my head that, because of the impossibility of communicating within the house, she would write
to me by the post—that she was cunning enough to slip one into
the letter box when she went out with her mother—and under
the influence of that idea, I ate my heart out twice every day for
an hour before the postman arrived. . . . And during that hour I
would ask Olive ten times over in a strangled voice, 'Are there
any letters for me, Olive?' And she would respond imperturb-
ably every time, 'No, Monsieur, nothing.' Eventually my anxiety
became too painful. My thwarted desire turned into hatred. I began to hate that Alberte, and that hatred gave me explanations
for her behavior toward me, explanations that enabled me to feel
contempt for her, because hatred is always hungry for contempt.
'Cowardly slut, afraid of a letter!' I said to myself. I used the
foulest language, insulting her inwardly, believing my insults were
the truth. I forced myself not to think about her, and I spoke in
abusive terms of her to Louis de Meung—for, yes, I spoke to him
about her! The way she had treated me extinguished all chivalric
sentiment in me, and I told the whole story to good old Louis,
who twirled his long blond moustache as he listened to me, and
who then replied—and remember, we were not exactly moralists
in the 27th regiment:

"'Do as I do! One nail drives out another. Take up with some
little seamstress in town, and don't give that damned girl another
thought!'

"But I didn't follow Louis's advice. I was too involved for that.
If she were somehow to know that I'd taken a mistress, I might
have done just that in order to torment either her vanity or her
jealousy. But she would not know. How could I make her know?
. . . Bringing a mistress home with me, the way Louis did at his
Hôtel de la Poste, would involve breaking altogether with my

respectable hosts, who would have insisted I go find other lodg-
ings immediately; and I did not want to give up the possibility of
again encountering, if nothing more than that, the hand or foot
of that damnable Alberte who had begun with such daring but
had now lapsed back into her role as Mademoiselle Impassive.

"'You mean Mademoiselle Impossible,' said Louis, mocking me.

"A whole month passed, and despite my resolutions to forget about Alberte, to be as indifferent as she was, to answer her
stoniness with my own stoniness, I have never in my life lived so
constantly on the lookout—which I hate doing even when I'm
out hunting! Yes, Monsieur, my days were nothing but perpetual
watching and waiting! Watching when I came down to dinner,
expecting to find her alone in the dining room like the first time!
Watching during the dinner, with my gaze constantly on her face,
and her eyes meeting mine with that same infernal calm—neither
avoiding my eyes nor responding to them! Watching after the dinner, for I would stay on afterward a while to see the ladies pick
up their sewing and move to their window seat, on the lookout
to see if she wouldn't let something fall, her thimble, her scissors,
a bit of cloth, anything I could pick up and return to her, and
touch her hand while doing so—that hand that had burned itself
into my brain! Watching when I was back in my room, thinking
that I could hear her step, hear that foot that had pressed against
mine so willfully! On the lookout on the stairs, where I thought
I might encounter her, and where, one day, old Olive surprised
me playing sentinel, to my great embarrassment. On the lookout
at my window—that window you see up there—where I would
plant myself when she would go out with her mother, and from
which I would not budge until she returned, but just as much in
vain as everything else! When she went out—wrapped up in her
young girl's shawl—a shawl with red and white stripes: I've forgotten none of it! And printed with black and yellow flowers. . . .
She would not turn that insolent look of hers back toward me,
not once, and when she came back in, always with her mother,
she never lifted her head or eyes up to the window where I was
waiting! Such were the miserable exercises to which she had condemned me. Of course, I know perfectly well that women always

turn us more or less into their serving men, but not to this extent! And oh, even my uniform no longer made me happy! When I had carried out my duties for the day—after our drills and reviews—I would return home right away, but not to read the piles of memoirs and novels that were my sole reading in those days. I stopped going to visit Louis de Meung. I never picked up my fencing foil. I didn't even have the option of tobacco to deaden the nerves, which you younger men use. One didn't smoke in the 27th in those days or, rather, only the common soldiers did, smoking while they played pinochle on a drum head. . . . I was always both lazy and restless. . . . I didn't feel that good, refreshing coolness anymore of my old sofa bed; I paced up and down my room like a lion cub in his cage when he scents fresh meat nearby.

"And the greater part of the night was just like the day. I went to bed late. I didn't sleep anymore. She kept me awake, that hellish Alberte, by setting my blood on fire and then going away—like an arsonist who doesn't even turn back to see the flames leaping up behind him! At night, I lowered"—and here the Vicomte passed his glove over the coach window next to him, to wipe away the moisture that was accumulating there—"that same crimson curtain, in that same window, more effective than shutters in keeping the neighbors, more curious here in the provinces, from peering into my room. The room was typical of that era—an Empire room, with a Hungarian parquetry floor, uncarpeted, with a bed of cherrywood and bronze with a sphinx head on each corner and lion paws for its four feet; there were also lion faces in cameos on each drawer of the writing desk, each face with a brass ring in its opened mouth, with which you pulled the drawer open. A square table—made of a cherrywood that was lighter in color than the rest of the furniture, with a gray marble top with copper inlay—faced the bed along the wall between the window and the door of a dressing room; and across from the chimney, the great sofa bed of blue leather, which I've already mentioned. . . . The room was high-ceilinged and spacious, with Chinese lacquer brackets in each corner, one of which held an old bust of Niobe, a copy of an ancient work—surprising to find there in this ordinary bourgeois home.¹⁵ But wasn't that incomprehensible Alberte more surprising still? The paneled walls were painted a whitish yellow, with neither pictures nor engravings hung upon them. Using long, gilded copper hooks, I had hung up my swords. When I had rented this great *calabash* of an apartment—as Lieutenant Louis de Meung, who never poeticized, elegantly termed it—I had had a large round table put in the middle, which I proceeded to cover with military maps, with books and papers: it was my desk. I wrote there, when I had occasion to write. . . . Well! One evening or, rather, one night, I had rolled my sofa up to this big table, and I was drawing by lamplight, not to distract myself from my sole obsessive thought but rather to plunge myself more deeply into it, for it was the head of the enigmatic Alberte that I was drawing, that devil of a woman by whom I was possessed, the way pious people say the Devil possesses others. It was late. The street—down which two coaches passed every night, in opposite directions—just like today—one at 12:45 and the other at 2:30 in the morning, both of which make their relay stop at the Hôtel de la Poste—the street was as silent as the bottom of a well. I could have heard a fly; and if by chance there had been one in my room, it would have had to be sleeping in a corner of the window or within one of the pleated folds of the thick silk curtain, which I had loosened from its hook so that it fell heavy, perpendicular, and motionless. The silence was profound, complete; the only sound was the one I made with my pencil and my stump. Yes, it was her face that I was drawing, and God knows with what a caressing touch and what an inflamed desire! Suddenly, without any sound from the lock that would have warned me, my door opened a little, making that flute-like sound a door makes when the hinges are dry, and stopped, remaining half-opened, as if it were alarmed by the sound it had made! I looked up, assuming I had failed to shut it properly and that it had opened unexpectedly this way by itself, with a squeak that could startle anyone still awake and awaken anyone who was asleep. I got up from my table to go and close it, but the door was opening up a bit more, slowly and quietly but with a new repetition of that high-pitched sound that trailed away like a groan in the silent house, and I saw there, once the door was fully opened, Alberte! Alberte who, despite her fearful precautions, had been unable to keep that cursed door from crying out!

"Oh, God above! They talk about visions, the believers; but the most supernatural vision possible would not have dumbfounded me like this one, nor would it have made my heart skip a beat as it did, and as it continued to do in wild palpitations, when I saw coming toward me—through that open door—Alberte, frightened by the sound the door had made, and would make again if she were to close it! Keep in mind, now, that I was not yet eighteen! Perhaps she saw my fear reflecting hers, and she made a quick gesture to cut off the cry of surprise I was about to make—which would certainly have escaped from me without that gesture—and she closed the door, more quickly this time, since the slow opening had made it squeak, trying to avoid the creaking of the hinges—though it was no use, and the squeak was louder and more definite, though briefer; and, the door shut and her ear up against it, she listened for any other sound that might result, a sound more frightening than that of the door. . . . I thought I saw her stagger. . . . I rushed toward her, and I suddenly had her in my arms."

"Well done, that Alberte of yours!" I exclaimed to the Captain.

"You think, perhaps," he continued, as if he had not heard my teasing comment, "that she had fallen into my arms out of fright, or passion, out of her head, like someone being chased, or someone who might be pursued—someone who doesn't know quite what she is doing, as she commits the ultimate of follies, abandoning herself to that demon that all women have somewhere within them—so people say, anyway—the demon that would be in complete control of her if it weren't for two others in her as well, Cowardice and Shame, who put up resistance to the first one! Well, no, it wasn't like that at all! If you had thought so, you would have been wrong . . . She had none of those vulgar sexual fears . . . She took me in her arms more than I took her in mine. . . . Her first movement had been to throw her head against my chest, but then she raised it and looked at me with those wide eyes of hers—those immense eyes!—as if to be sure that it was me she was holding! She was horribly pale, pale as I had never

seen her before, but that princess air of hers was still there. Her
expression was still as composed and firm as a medal. The only
change was that across her slightly pouting lips there wandered
some little hint of distraction, some expression I couldn't quite
read, unless it was the expression of satisfied passion, or passion
about to be satisfied! But at the same time that distraction had
something somber about it, so much so that, in order not to see
it anymore, I pressed my own robust, passionate, and regally triumphant kisses of desire on those beautiful pink, swelling lips!
Her mouth half-opened . . . but those black eyes of hers, those
deep black eyes, whose long lashes nearly touched mine, never
closed—didn't even blink; but deep within them I saw the same
madness that I had read on her lips! Clinging to me in that burning kiss, and as if levitated by the lips that penetrated hers, breathing with my breath, I carried her, cleaving tightly to me, to the
blue leather sofa—my grill of Saint Lawrence during the month
I had tossed and turned on it, thinking endlessly of her—and the
leather creaked voluptuously beneath her naked back, for she was
in fact half-naked.[16] She had left her bed and, to come to me, she
had had—can you believe it?—to pass through the room in which
her father and mother were sleeping! She had crossed the room
on tiptoes, her hands out in front of her to keep from knocking
into some piece of furniture that would have made some noise
and awakened them."

"Ah!" I said. "That's as much bravery as you see in the trenches.
She was worthy to be a soldier's mistress."

"And she was, that very first night," replied the Vicomte. "She
was just as violent as I, and I can assure you that I was! But never
mind . . . the tables were turned! Neither she nor I could forget,
even in our most intense transports, the frightening situation we
were in. Right in the midst of the bliss that she had found a way to
bring to me, she was shocked at the very act she had accomplished
with such a firm will power, and with such determination. I was
not so much shocked at it as stupefied! Without telling her about
it or revealing it to her, I felt the most awful anxiety in my heart
while she was pressing me so closely to hers. I listened, over the
sound of her sighs and her kisses, and within the terrifying silence

that weighed on the sleeping, trusting house, for the horrible thing: for the sound of her mother awakening, the sound of her father getting out of bed! And I kept looking up over her shoulder at that door—with the key still in the lock, left there for fear of making further noise—to see if the door would swing open anew and reveal, standing within it, those two Medusa heads, the pale and indignant heads of the two old parents surging up out of the darkness, images of the hospitality and Justice we were violating! And even the voluptuous creaking of the sofa, sounding the reveille of Love, made me tremble with fear. . . . My heart beat against hers, which seemed to echo the beatings back. . . . It was intoxicating and sobering all at once—it was terrible! Later on, it didn't bother me as much. By dint of repeating the experience— that act of unnamable imprudence!—with impunity, I became comfortable enough with it. By dint of living with the constant danger of being surprised, I ceased to worry about it. I no longer thought about it. I only thought now of being happy. At this first extraordinary meeting, which would have terrified anyone else, she decided she would come to me every other night, since I could not go to her—her bedroom, her childhood bedroom, opened only onto her parents' bedroom—and she did come to me, regularly, every other night, but she never lost the feeling— the astonishment—of the very first night! Time did not produce the same effect on her that it did on me. She never got used to the danger that she faced every time. She would remain a long time resting on my chest, silent, hardly saying anything—for, you might have gathered, she was not much of a talker; and when, later, I grew calmer, seeing that we repeatedly faced danger and repeatedly evaded it, and when I spoke to her the way a man does with his mistress about what had just passed between us—about her inexplicable, mad coldness—when I held her in my arms, after the first boldnesses—when I asked her all those questions the insatiable lover has to ask, which may be ultimately no more than curiosity—the only reply she made me was a long embrace. Her sad mouth remained mute, said nothing . . . except for those kisses! There are women who say to you, 'I ruined myself for you,' and there are others who say, 'You must have contempt for me,' both of which are different ways of expressing love's inevitable destiny. But her—nothing, not a word! A strange thing—and an even stranger person! She gave me the impression of a thick, hard covering of marble that was slowly burning up from a fire beneath it. . . . I thought we would eventually get to the point where the marble would finally crack and break from the heat, but the marble never lost its firmness, its rigid density. The nights that she came, she remained just as uncommunicative, silent, and, if I may permit myself an ecclesiastical phrase, 'difficult to confess' as she had on the first night. I could get nothing more out of her. . . . At best I could tear a syllable from those beautiful lips I was so mad about, all the more because I had seen them cold and indifferent during the day, but that monosyllable didn't shed much light on this girl who seemed more sphinx-like than ever—indeed, she outdid all those other Sphinxes that had proliferated all around my Empire apartment."

"But, Captain," I interrupted again, "there must be an end to all this? After all, you're a strong, sensible man, and Sphinxes are mythological creatures. You must have been able to figure out whatever the secret was that the girl was hiding!"

"An end! Oh yes, there was an end," said the Vicomte de Brassard, as he abruptly lowered the coach's window, as though his monumental chest were having trouble breathing, and he needed more air to finish whatever it was he had to tell me. "But the secret, as you put it, of this singular girl was no more accessible for all that. Our love, our relationship, our affair—call it whatever you like—gave us or, rather, gave *me, me,* sensations that I have never felt with any woman since Alberte, who perhaps did not love me, and whom I, perhaps, didn't love either! I never quite understood exactly what we meant to each other—and this went on for more than six months! But during those six months, what I did know was a species of happiness of which a young man can have no idea. I knew the happiness of those who have to hide. I knew the intense pleasure of being complicit in a mystery that, even while it has no chance at all of success, nonetheless makes the conspirators incorrigible. At her parents' table and everywhere else, Alberte remained the Royal Princess who had so struck me the first day I saw her. Her Neronian brow never showed the slightest blush under those tight curls, so black as to be almost blue, that trailed down almost to her eyebrows. And I tried to be just as impenetrable as she, but I'm sure that I would have betrayed myself ten times over if anyone had been truly observing me; I glutted myself almost sensually with pride to the depths of my being at the thought that all her superb indifference was for me, and that she actually felt for me all the baseness of passion—if passion can ever really be base! No one on earth knew about it, only us . . . and that thought was delicious! No one, not even my friend Louis de Meung, with whom I had been discreet ever since my happiness had come. He could guess the truth, no doubt, since he was just as discreet as I was. He asked me no questions. I had effortlessly taken up again my friendly habits with him, our walks on the Promenade, sometimes in full dress, sometimes less formal, our card games, our fencing, and our punch! Good Lord, when you know that happiness will come to you in the shape of a beautiful girl who has a kind of 'raging toothache' deep inside her, that she will come visit you regularly every other night, at the same hour—it simplifies your days enormously!"

"And this Alberte's parents kept on sleeping like the Seven Sleepers?" I asked teasingly, cutting short the happy reflections of the aging dandy by a joke, in order to appear not terribly interested in the story—for, with dandies, the only way to make yourself respected is to make light of such things.

"So you think that I am fictionalizing, seeking out effects with no basis in what really happened?" asked the Vicomte. "But I am no novelist, I assure you! Sometimes Alberte did not come. My door, the hinges of which were by now well oiled and as silent as cotton wool, did not open at all one night, a night when her mother had heard her and cried out, or one when her father had caught sight of her tiptoeing through their room. But Alberte, with a steely intelligence, always came up with some reason. She was feeling ill . . . she was looking for some sugar without a light, so as not to awaken anyone."

"Those steely intelligences are not as rare as you might think, Captain!" I interrupted again. I was deliberately being contrarian.

"Your Alberte, after all, was not superior to the girl who received her lover every night right in her grandmother's bedroom, the grandmother being asleep behind her curtains and the lover coming in through the window; the girl didn't have access to a blue leather sofa bed, so she settled down right on the carpet, making no fuss about it. . . . You know the story as well as I do. One night a louder moan than usual escaped from the poor girl and awakened the grandmother who, from behind her bed's curtains, called out, 'What's the matter, little one?' which almost caused the girl to faint with fright on her lover's chest; but she replied nevertheless, 'My stay poked me, Grandma, while I was bending down looking for a needle I dropped on the carpet—and I can't find it!'"

"Yes, I know the story," replied the Vicomte de Brassard, whom I had intended to humble a bit by the comparison with his Alberte. "If I recall correctly, the girl you're referring to was one of the Guises.[17] She conducted herself like a girl worthy of her name; but you didn't mention that after that particular night, she no longer opened the window for her lover, who was, I believe, Monsieur de Noirmoutier—whereas Alberte came back the night after these dreadful incidents, exposing herself to even more danger, as if nothing had happened. Well, I was only a sub-lieutenant with no skill in mathematics, a subject I took little trouble to learn; but even to me it was evident that if one were to calculate the probabilities, one would feel certain that some day—some night—there would have to be a *dénouement* . . ."

"Oh, yes, of course!" I said, recalling now the way he had talked about it before beginning his story: "This would be the *dénouement* that led to your feeling that fear you spoke of, Captain."

"Exactly," he replied, in a grave tone that cut right through the light tone I had affected. "You have seen—haven't you?—from the moment she seized my hand under the table up to the moment when she sprang up out of the darkness like some apparition in my open doorway, Alberte had never failed to arouse powerful emotions in me. She had caused more than one shudder to pass through my soul, more than one moment of terror, but up to this point these were the kinds of sensations you would feel when the cannon was roaring and the bullets were whizzing around you: you shudder, but you keep marching forward. Well—this wasn't like that at all. This was fear, real, utter fear, and no longer for Alberte but for myself—really, only for myself! What I felt was the sort of sensation that makes not just the face but the heart go pale; it was the kind of panic that makes a whole regiment break and run. Remember, I have personally seen the whole Chamboran regiment break up and flee, the heroic Chamboran, galloping as fast as they could go, carrying along on their human floodtide their colonel and all their officers![18] But at this point in my life I had not yet seen anything, and I learned—something I had thought impossible.

"Listen, then. . . . It was one night. Given the life we were leading, it could only have been a night . . . a long, winter night. But not one of our most tranquil ones. They were all tranquil, our nights. They had become so because they had been happy. We were sleeping on a powder keg, though. We were not disturbed in the slightest at making love on the blade of a sword stretched out over the abyss, like the bridge that the Turks say leads to hell! Alberte had come a little earlier than usual, in order to be able to stay a little longer. When she came like that, my first caress, my first attentions were paid to her feet, those feet that no longer wore their green boots or their blue ones, two coquetries that gave me such delight, but were naked now in order to make no noise; those feet that had come to me over the cold stone floor, all down the long corridor that led from her parents' to my room at the other end of the house. I would warm them, those feet so frozen just for me, feet that had left their warm bed and might be the means of her catching some horrible cold. . . . I knew how to warm them, how to make those pale, cold feet pink and vermilion again; but that night, my efforts failed. My mouth was powerless to bring back the warm poppy-colored blood to her charming, delicate ankles. . . . Alberte was more silently amorous that night than ever before. Her embraces had a languor and a power that were a language of their own to me, a language so expressive that if I had wanted to talk to her and tell her all my mad, intoxicated thoughts, I would have asked no other answer from her. Those embraces—I listened to them. But suddenly, I heard nothing at all. Her arms ceased pressing me to her, and I thought she was having one of those swoons that she often had—though usually she continued to hold me tightly during those swoons. . . . You and I don't have to be prudish about such things. We're both men, and we can talk to each other like two men. . . . I had experienced those voluptuous spasms that Alberte underwent, and when one of them swept her away with it, I didn't let it interrupt my caresses. I remained as I was, on her breast, waiting for her to return to consciousness, in the proud certainty that she would recover her senses through my touch, and that the bolt that had struck her down would revive her in striking again. . . . But not this time. I looked at her as she lay there on the blue sofa, awaiting the moment when her eyes, hidden now under those large eyelids, would return and reveal again their black velvety fire; when those teeth, which clenched and ground tightly enough to break the enamel at my kisses trailing along her neck and shoulders, would loosen and allow the breath to come through again. But the eyes did not return, and the teeth did not unclench. . . . The coldness of Alberte's feet had mounted up and now reached her lips when I kissed them. . . . When I felt that horrible cold, I half sat up to see her better; I pulled myself up and out of her arms, one of which fell across her body, while the other fell down toward the floor, hanging limply off the couch where she lay. . . . And there was nothing—no pulse in her wrists, her temples, her carotid artery, nothing anywhere. . . . Death had spread all through her, and she was already frighteningly rigid!

"I was certain she was dead, and yet I dared not believe it! The mind can be willfully stupid in the face of such clear evidence, such destiny. Alberte was dead. How? . . . I didn't know. I was no doctor. But she was dead; and though it was clear as noonday that there was nothing I could do, I desperately did everything I could anyway. In my complete ignorance of facts, of instruments, of resources, I emptied every bottle I had moistening her forehead. I slapped her vigorously with my hands, at the risk of waking someone with the noise there in that house where the slightest of sounds could make us tremble. I had heard one of my uncles say, a captain in the 4th Dragoons, that he had once saved the life of a friend who had fallen into an apoplexy by bleeding him quickly with one of those lancets they use to bleed horses. I had plenty of arms in my room. I took up a dagger, and I poked at Alberte's arm to get her to bleed. I massacred that beautiful arm, and the blood wouldn't flow. A few drops oozed out and quickly coagulated. It had clotted. Neither kisses nor sucking nor biting could galvanize that rigid corpse—that body that had become a corpse under my kisses. Not knowing any longer what I was doing, I finally stretched myself out upon her, the method (so the old stories said) of the ancient miracle workers who brought the dead back to life, not believing that I could reawaken her but acting as if I did![19] And it was while I was stretched across that cold body that an idea began to form, an idea that had not quite disengaged itself yet from the chaos into which the overwhelming death of Alberte had plunged my mind, and now that idea appeared clearly to me: and I was afraid!

"Oh, but that fear . . . it was an immense fear! Alberte was dead in my room, and her death would reveal everything. What would become of me? What should I do? . . . At this thought, I suddenly felt the hand, the physical hand of that hideous fear upon me, and my hair stood on end. My backbone felt as if it had turned to freezing mud, and I tried to fight—but in vain—against these dishonorable sensations. . . . I told myself that I had to be calm . . . that I was a man, after all . . . that I was a soldier. I put my head in my hands, trying to reason through the horrific situation I found myself in, but my brain seemed to be spinning like a top under the impetus of all the ideas that rushed in and out, and they all eventually ran up against the fact of this corpse in my apartment, this inanimate body of Alberte who could no longer make her way back to her room, and whose mother would inevitably discover her the next morning *in an officer's bedroom,* dead and dishonored! The thought of that mother, whose daughter I had perhaps killed in the act of dishonoring her, weighed more heavily on my heart than the thought of Alberte herself. . . . There was no way to hide the death, but couldn't some method be found to hide the fact of her dishonor? I asked myself this repeatedly, the one fixed idea in my spinning head. The longer I thought about it, the greater the difficulty grew, and it began to take on the proportions of an absolute impossibility. Ghastly hallucination—at moments, the corpse of Alberte seemed to me to be filling the entire room. Ah, if only hers had not been located behind her parents' room, I would have carried her back to her bed, no matter the risk! But could I possibly get through that room quietly, carrying a corpse, a room I had never entered, where her unlucky parents were sleeping lightly? Yet the state of my mind was such that, with the fear of the morning and the discovery of the corpse in my room galloping through my thoughts furiously, this idea, this boldness, this madness of carrying Alberte back to her room seemed to me like the only means of preserving the poor girl's honor and sparing me the shame of her mother and father's reproaches, the only way for me to get out of this abominable situation. Can you believe it? I can scarcely believe it myself when I think about it. I had the strength to pick up Alberte's corpse and, holding it by the arms, to heave it up over my shoulders. A horrible burden, heavier than the ones Dante describes the damned having to carry in Hell! You would have had to carry, as I did, that burden of flesh that only an hour before had had me burning with desire, and which now horrified me—you would have had to have carried it yourself to know what I am trying to describe! With that burden on my shoulders, I opened my door, my feet bare as hers had been to make less sound, and I stepped into the dark corridor that led to her parents' room at the far end, halting at every step with my weakening legs to listen to the silent house—though all I could hear was the thunderous beating of my heart! It seemed to take a long time—nothing moved—I made one careful step after another. . . . But when I came at last to that terrible door of her parents' room, the door I had to go through, and which she had not quite closed to make her reentry easier, I heard the long, calm breathing of those two poor old people sleeping in utter trust and confidence—and I dared not go in! I dared not cross that black threshold, into the gaping blackness beyond. . . . I turned back; I almost ran, weighted down with my burden as I was! I got back into my room, my terror increasing. I replaced Alberte's corpse on the sofa and, on my knees beside her, I began asking the same questions again: 'What should I do? What will become of me?' . . . In the collapsed state I was in, the absurd and hideous idea occurred to me of throwing the body of that beautiful girl out the window—my mistress of six months!—the idea cut through my spirit like a furrow. Yes, despise me for it! I opened the window . . . I pulled back the curtain you see there . . . and I looked down into the black hole, at the bottom of which was the street, for it was a very dark night. You couldn't see to the pavement. 'They'll think it was a suicide,' I thought—and I picked up Alberte again, and I carried her. . . . But just then a ray of good sense penetrated into my madness! 'How would she have died? Where would they think she had fallen from, if she were found below my window tomorrow?' Realizing the impossibility of the scheme took my breath away! I went to close the window, which squeaked on its hasp. I drew the curtain back across the window, feeling more dead than alive from all the noise I was making. Anyway, whether it was through the window—or on the staircase—or in the corridor—wherever I were to put the corpse, it would be my eternal accuser; the desecration would be futile. An examination of the body would reveal everything, and the eye of her mother, with its cruel instinct, would see everything that a doctor or a judge might try to hide from her. . . . What I was feeling was intolerable, and gazing on my weapons shining there on the walls, the idea of ending it all with a pistol shot passed through my *demoralized* mind (a word the Emperor had used, one I only understood much later). But what can I say? . . . I'll be frank: I was seventeen, and I was in love with . . . my sword. I was a soldier both by inclination and by race. I had never been under fire, and I wanted to experience it. I had military ambitions. In the regiment, we made jokes about Werther, whom many in those days saw as a hero but whom we officers thought of as pathetic.[20] That thought that kept me from making my escape, through suicide, from the humiliating fear I felt led me to another one that seemed to be my salvation, my way out! 'What if I went to see the Colonel?' I asked myself. The colonel, in the military, is like one's father—and I dressed myself as if the general call to arms was beating for a surprise attack. . . . Out of soldierly precaution, I took my pistols. After all, who knew what might happen? . . . I kissed one last time, with all the sentimentality of seventeen—and every seventeen-year-old is sentimental—the mute lips, mute as they had in fact always been, of the deceased Alberte, that Alberte who had overwhelmed me for six months with her most intoxicating favors. . . . I tiptoed down the stairs of that silent house where I was leaving a dead body. . . . Panting like a man running for his life, I spent an hour—it certainly seemed like an hour to me!—unbolting the door and turning the big key in the enormous keyhole, and after closing it up again with all the precautions of a burglar, I ran like a deserter as fast as I could to my colonel.

"I rang his bell as if the house were on fire! I beat on that door as if it were a drum and I were warning him that the enemy was about to make off with the regiment's flag! I knocked everything over, even the orderly who tried to keep me from entering his master's room, and once the colonel was awake from the tempest of noise I had been making, I told him everything. I confessed everything, from beginning to end, rapidly and bravely because there was no time to waste, and I begged him to save me. . . .

"What a man he was, the colonel! He could see immediately what sort of abyss I had fallen into. . . . He felt pity for the youngest of his *children,* as he called me, and I must admit I was in a state to inspire pity! He said to me, cursing in the most patriotically French manner, that the first thing for me to do was to get out of the town immediately, and that he would take care of everything . . . that he would see the parents as soon as I had gone, but that I had to go now and take the coach that would be leaving in ten minutes from the Hôtel de la Poste, and get myself to a town that he named and wait there until he wrote to me. . . . He gave me some money, as I had forgotten to take any along, touched his old gray moustaches to each side of my face, and ten minutes later I was climbing up on the coach's roof—there were no other places remaining—the coach that was making the same circuit we are now, and I passed at a gallop beneath the window (you can imagine the kind of gaze I cast up at it) of that funereal room where I had left Alberte dead, and which was lit just as it is tonight."

The Vicomte de Brassard stopped, his powerful voice seeming to break. I no longer thought of making jokes. There was only a short silence.

"And then?" I asked.

"Well, yes, that's the point," he replied. "There was no 'then'! I've been tormented by an exasperating curiosity ever since. I followed the colonel's instructions to the letter. I patiently waited for a letter that would tell me what happened after I left. I waited about a month; but at the end of that month, it wasn't a letter I received from the colonel, who rarely wrote, except with his sword on the bodies of his enemies; it was instead an order to change regiments. I was ordered to report to the 35th, which was about to go into battle, and I had to arrive at my new post within twenty-four hours. The immense distractions of a campaign, and at that my first—the battles in which I took part, the hardships, and also some adventures with women kept me from writing to the colonel, and also kept me from thinking too much about the cruel memory of Alberte without, however, effacing that memory. It stayed with me, like a bullet that cannot be extracted. . . . I told myself that one day or another I would run into the colonel, who would finally tell me everything I wanted to know, but the colonel was killed leading his troops at Leipzig.[21] . . . Louis de Meung was killed, too, a month before that. It may be a contemptible thing," added the Captain, "but everything wanes eventually, even in the most robust of souls, maybe even more so in the more robust ones. . . . The all-consuming curiosity to know what happened after my departure ended up no longer bothering me. I could have returned to this little town after many years had passed, without being recognized, and I could have found out at least what people knew about it, whatever had leaked out about my tragic adventure. But something—and it certainly wasn't a concern for public opinion, which I've despised my entire life—something like that fear, that fear that I did not want to experience a second time, always prevented me."

He fell silent again, this dandy who had told me his story without the slightest of dandyisms, an all-too-real, sad tale. I mused on his story a while, and I realized that this brilliant Vicomte de

Brassard who had seemed the flower, not of elegance exactly, but the finest flower of all the red poppies of dandyism, the drinker of claret in the chic English manner, was really something very different, a much deeper person than he seemed. I remembered now that he had referred to some "black stain" that had poisoned all his pleasures on that unhappy side of life . . . when suddenly he astonished me even more by grasping my arm tightly.

"Look!" he said. "Look at the curtain!"

The slender shadow of a woman had just passed it, as clear as could be!

"The ghost of Alberte!" said the Captain. "Bad luck is mocking me tonight," he added bitterly.

The curtain had reverted to its usual empty square, red and lit from within. But the wheelwright, who had been working with his tools while the Captain told his story, had just finished the job. The relay team of horses was ready and pawing the ground, their hooves striking sparks. The driver, his astrakhan cap pulled down over his ears and log sheet between his teeth, once he had hoisted himself up to his bench, called out in his clear voice the word of command into the night:

"Let's go!"

And we rolled on, and we soon had left that mysterious window behind, that window that I still see in my dreams, with its crimson curtain.

DON JUAN'S
FINEST CONQUEST

The devil's favorite delicacy is innocence.[1]

I

"What—he's still alive, that old sinner?"

"Good God—still alive indeed, and by the grace of God, Madame," I replied, catching myself as I recalled her religious devotion. "And living in the parish of Sainte-Clotilde no less, the parish of dukes! The king is dead—long live the king!—as they used to say under the old monarchy before it was all broken to bits like so much Sèvres porcelain. Don Juan, though, is one monarch they'll never break down, no matter how many democracies there are."

"It's true, the devil is immortal!" she exclaimed in a tone of reproof.

"Yes, and he has even——"

"Who? The devil?"

"No, Don Juan—dined a few days ago, in the middle of a spree at. . . . Can you guess where?"

"At your hideous Maison d'Or, I suppose."[2]

"Oh no, Madame! Don Juan doesn't go there anymore. . . . They have nothing there to satisfy his grand palate. Señor Don Juan has always been a little like the famous monk, Arnold of Brescia, who, the Chronicles tell us, only dined on the blood of souls.[3] That's what he likes to use to give his champagne a pink tint, and it's been a long time since that was freely available from the common coquette!"

"Next you'll be saying," she replied with irony, "that he supped at the Benedictine convent, with the sisters . . ."

"The Sisters of Perpetual Adoration, certainly, Madame! For once he has inspired adoration—that devil of a man—it will last forever."

"For a Catholic, you seem a bit profane to me," she said slowly, but with a certain tension in her voice. "And I beg you to spare me the details about your suppers and your disreputable women, if you feel you have to invent all this as a way of telling me the news about Don Juan this evening."

"I invent nothing, Madame. The disreputable women at the dinner in question, if they are disreputable, are not mine . . . unfortunately . . ."

"Enough, Monsieur!"

"Allow me my modesty. They were . . ."

"The *mille è tré?*" she asked, her curiosity getting the better of her, leading her to revert almost entirely to her former amiability.[4]

"Oh, not all of them, Madame . . . just a dozen. A perfectly respectable number."

"And yet somehow less than respectable as well," she added.

"In any case, you know as well as I that the boudoir of the Comtesse de Chiffrevas[5] will not hold many people. Great efforts were made to accommodate them; but it's quite small, that boudoir . . ."

"What?" she exclaimed, astonished. "They held the dinner in her boudoir?"

"Yes, Madame, in the boudoir. And why not? Superb dinners may be had on the field of battle. They wanted to give an extraordinary dinner for Señor Don Juan, and it was most fitting to have it in the setting of one of his glorious conquests, in a place where memories blossom like orange trees. A lovely idea, tender and wistful! This was no *bal des victimes*—it was a dinner party for the victims!"[6]

"And Don Juan?" she asked, in the same way Orgon in the play asks, "And Tartuffe?"

"Don Juan took it all in an excellent spirit, and he had a fine dinner—*He, he alone, before all the women!*—as the song goes. He appeared, by the way, in the person of someone you know . . . someone who is no other than Comte Jules-Amédée-Hector de Ravila de Ravilès."[7]

"Him! Oh yes, he makes quite a Don Juan, doesn't he?" she said.

And then, though she had long passed the age of reverie and daydream, this woman with her tooth-and-nail piety, began to fantasize about the Comte Jules-Amédée-Hector—about this man of the race of Don Juan—that eternal, ancient race to whom God has not given the earth but to whom God did permit the Devil to do so.

II

What I had just told the old Marquise Guy de Ruy had been the exact truth. It had been scarcely three days since a dozen women of the virtuous Faubourg Saint-Germain (and let them rest easy, for I will never reveal their names!), each one of whom had, according to the gossiping old hens of the quarter, been "on the closest of terms with" the Comte Ravila de Ravilès—a charming old expression—were taken with the extraordinary idea of giving him a dinner party—*with him the only man invited*—in order to celebrate . . . what? They did not say. It took some bravery, that dinner party, but women, though often cowards individually, are utterly audacious in groups. Not one among them, I suspect, would have dared to offer a dinner at her home alone with Comte Jules-Amédée-Hector; but together, and each helping the other, they did not fear to form a Mesmer-like *baquet* chain around this magnetic, compromising man, the Comte de Ravila de Ravilès . . .[8]

"What a name!"

"A providential name, Madame." The Comte de Ravila de Ravilès who, parenthetically, had always lived up to that imperious name, was indeed the incarnation of all the seducers spoken of in novels and in history, and the Marquise Guy de Ruy—an old malcontent with cold, sharp blue eyes, but eyes less cold than her heart and less sharp than her tongue—agreed that in these days, when women and their concerns are becoming less and less important, if there was anyone who could recall Don Juan, it would surely be he! Unfortunately, it was the Don Juan of the fifth act. The Prince de Ligne said he could not believe that Alcibiades ever was fifty years old.[9] Now, from that point of view, the Comte de Ravila would always be an Alcibiades. Like d'Orsay, that dandy formed from the bronze of Michelangelo, Ravila had the beauty peculiar to the breed of Juan—that mysterious race that does not proceed from father to son like other races but that instead appears now and then, here and there, among the families of humankind.[10]

His was true beauty—insolent, joyous, imperial, *Juanesque* beauty (the very word says it all; one can dispense with description); and—but, had he made some pact with the Devil?—he retained that beauty always. . . . But God was finally beginning to restore the balance; for life's cruel tiger claws had begun to mark that divine forehead, crowned with the roses of so many kisses, and those grand temples were beginning to reveal the first white hairs signaling the invasion of the Barbarians, and the end of the Empire. . . . He wore all this, however, with that impassive pride of his, fueled by his sense of power; but the women who saw these signs looked on with melancholy. Who knows? Perhaps they were seeing on that forehead the warning of what was coming to them, too? Alas, both for them and for him, what was coming was the hour of the terrible supper with the cold Commander of white marble, after which there is nothing left but Hell—the Hell of old age, while awaiting the other one![11] And perhaps this is why, before they would have to share that final, bitter meal, they wanted to offer him one of their own, and to make it a masterpiece.

Yes, a masterpiece of taste, of tact, of patrician luxury, of careful planning, of inspired ideas; the most charming, the most delicious, the most delightful, the most heady, and, above all, the most original of dinners. Did I say *original*? Just think about it! The usual motives for giving such a party are the desire for pleasure or amusement; but in this case it was nostalgia, regret, almost hopelessness, but hopelessness in its best dress, hidden under smiles and laughter, hopelessness that yearned for this one more party, this one last folly, one last escapade for youth's final hour, one more bout of intoxication—and after this one, no more ever again!

The Amphitryonnes of this incredible dinner, so little like the typically timid hosts of their social world, must have felt something like Sardanapalus felt on his funeral pyre, on which he ordered to be heaped upon the pile his women, his slaves, his horses, his jewels, and all the opulences of his life, to perish with him.[12] They were piling up all their own opulences to burn at this dinner, too. They were bringing along with them all that they had of beauty, of wit, all their resources, their finery, and their powers—to throw them all, once and for all, onto this supreme conflagration.

The man for whom they were ready to wrap and dress themselves in this ultimate flame was worth more, in their eyes, than was all Asia to Sardanapalus. They desired him as women never have any single man before or, for that matter, any salon full of men; and their coquetry was intensified by the jealousy they dared not reveal in society but that they didn't need to hide from each other, for they all knew that this man had had every one of them, and when shame is so widely shared it ceases to be shame. . . . The only question was which one of them had made the deepest mark on his heart.

When the evening came, he sat there satiated, sovereign, nonchalant, replete with the feelings of a sultan, or of a confessor of nuns. He was enthroned like a king—like the master—at the middle of the table, across from the Comtesse de Chiffrevas, in that boudoir the color of *hyacinth*—or was it higher sins (I've never been certain how one ought to spell that color)?[13] The Comte de Ravila gazed around him with his blue eyes, an infernal blue that many a poor creature has mistaken for heavenly azure, at the radiant circle of twelve women, all dressed brilliantly and surrounding the table with its crystal, candles, and flowers, spread out around him like an opened rose, or like the sweet amber gold of a grape, hinting at all the subtle graces of ripe maturity.

There were no tender young girls present, the type Byron

detested, like fruits that look ripe but upon tasting are sour and unready—none of those early spring growths; instead, all the women there were splendid, full-flavored like summer, generous like autumn, full-flowering, bountiful, their ample bosoms swelling above low-cut bodices, and their arms, below cameo-colored shoulders, of various shapes and curves, but all of them powerful, like the biceps of the Sabine women who battled with the Romans, strong enough to grip the wheel of life and make it stop turning.

I have mentioned the thought that went into the dinner. One of the most charming was to have all the serving done by maid servants so as not to disturb the harmony of a celebration where the women were all like queens dispensing honors. . . . Señor Don Juan—of the Ravila branch—could therefore bathe his untamed gaze in a sea of flesh as luminous and animated as the type Rubens depicted in his fleshy, heavy paintings, and moreover he could thrust his pride into the more or less limpid atmosphere of the room created by all these beating hearts. The fact is, despite what everyone insists on believing, Don Juan is really quite spiritual! He is like the Devil himself, who loves souls more than bodies and likes to gather and steal them away—the infernal slave trader!

The women were witty, their tone as aristocratic as the Faubourg Saint-Germain requires, but that night they were as bold as the pages in the King's household—in the days when there was a King's household and pages to be found there—and they showed an incomparably sparkling spirit, with a grace, a verve, and a stunning brio to match. They felt themselves superior to even their finest evenings in the past. In this setting they felt a mysterious power arising from their innermost depths, a power they had never felt before.

The pleasure they felt in this discovery, the sensation that their life forces had somehow tripled in strength—and more, the physical stimuli, so essential to high-strung creatures, the glimmering lights, the heady odors of so many flowers swooning in the heat produced by those beautiful bodies, emanations too overpowering for them, and the added spur of provocative wines—all these contributed to the very idea of this dinner party, an idea piquant with sin—like the touch of sinfulness the fair Neapolitan maid asked to have added to her sorbet to make it perfectly exquisite. The thought of this dinner was intoxicating, yes, as was the feeling of complicity among them in their little crime, though it never descended to the vulgarity of one of the Regent's dinners: it remained a party of the Faubourg Saint-Germain and of the nineteenth century, with all those adorable bodices and all the hearts beating away beneath them, hearts that had seen battle and still wanted to take part in one again, for not one of them had lost so much as a hairpin. In short, all these elements combined to tune that mysterious harp that each of these marvelous beings carried within herself, to tune the strings almost to the breaking point, and they found themselves executing sublime octaves, inexpressible diapasons. . . . Strange, isn't it? Will Ravila ever write this particular page of his memoirs? He is the only one who could do it. . . . As I said to the Marquise Guy de Ruy, I was not present at this dinner party, and if I were able to report a few of the details about how it concluded, it is because I heard it from Ravila himself, who, quite faithful to the indiscretion that is traditional and characteristic of the Don Juan race, took the trouble to tell me all about it one evening.

III

It was late—that is to say, it was getting early! Morning was on its way. On the ceiling and on a particular spot on the boudoir's pink silk curtains, which were tightly pulled, one could see a small round opalescent light breaking through, like a slowly growing eye, the eye of a curious new day that wanted to see what was going on in that brightly lit room. Languor was beginning to overtake the Lady Knights of this Round Table, these party hostesses who had been so animated just a moment ago. We all know that moment, when the fatigue and the emotion of the evening past seem to fall on everyone and everything, on the coiffures that droop, the rouged or pale cheeks that now begin to burn, the weary glances of eyes ringed with exhaustion, the moment when even the lights seem to swell and tremble in the candelabras, those bouquets of fire with their stems sculpted in bronze and gold.

The general conversation had been spirited, each one participating as if in a game of tennis, but now became fragmented and dissipated, and no one voice stood out distinctly in the harmonious but general sound of all those aristocratic tones that mingled and babbled like birds at dawn, on the edge of a forest . . . when one of them—a commanding voice, that one's!—imperious, almost impertinent, the way the voice of a duchess ought to be, spoke suddenly to the Comte de Ravila, drowning out all the others; the voice said what was apparently the end of a conversation that had been carried on quietly between the two of them, a conversation that none of the other women, each chatting with her neighbor, had heard.

"You! They call you the Don Juan of our era: you must tell us, then, will you, about the one conquest that most flattered your male pride, the one you would call the finest conquest of your entire life?"

This question, as much as the voice that had uttered it, abruptly cut off the buzzing sound of all the other conversations and plunged the room into silence.

The voice belonged to the Duchess of ***. I will not lift up that mask of asterisks; but you may recognize her when I tell you that her skin is nearly as fair as her hair, and her eyes the darkest under long, amber eyebrows that can be found in the Faubourg Saint-Germain. She was sitting to the right of Ravila, the god of the evening—like one of the Just at the right hand of God—who at this particular juncture had chosen not to reduce his enemies to acting as his footstool. She was slender, ideal as an arabesque or a fairy in her green velvet dress with little glints of silver, its long train twisting around her chair, like the serpent's tail in which the charming derriere of Mélusine terminates.[14]

"What a fine idea!" exclaimed the Comtesse de Chiffrevas, as if to propel the Duchess's idea forward in her capacity as mistress of the house: "Yes! Your ultimate love—whether it was one you inspired or one you felt yourself, the one you would gladly relive if you had the chance."

"Oh! I'd like to relive all of them!" said Ravila with the insatiable tone of a Roman emperor, a tone your more blasé people sometimes use. And he lifted high his champagne glass, which was not the stupid, pagan sort of glass used nowadays, but the slender, svelte glass our ancestors used, called a flute, perhaps because of the celestial melodies it inspires in our hearts! Then he embraced with a circular sweep all the women who formed a lovely sash around the table. "However," he added, setting his glass down in front of him with a melancholy surprising in such a Nebuchadnezzar, who had as yet eaten no more of the grass of the field than is to be found in a tarragon salad at the Café Anglais—"however, it is true that there is one among all the loves of one's life who shines more brightly in memory than the others, and all the more so the older one grows—the one for whom a person would trade them all!"[15]

"The brightest diamond in the jewel case," murmured the Comtesse de Chiffrevas pensively, perhaps as she was gazing deeply into the facets of her own.

"There is a legend of my country," said the Princesse Jable, who was from the region at the foot of the Ural Mountains, "of a famous, fabulous diamond, pink at first but then turning black, though it always remains a diamond, and even more so when it is black . . ." She said this with that unique Gipsy charm of hers—for she is a Gipsy, and the handsomest Prince of the Polish émigré community had fallen in love with her and married her, though she now has just as much the air of a princess as if she had been born behind the curtains of the Jagiellons.[16]

And now there was a real explosion! "Yes!" they all cried. "Tell us the story, Comte!" they added excitedly, all joining in the supplicating tone, trembling with such curiosity that they could feel it in the curls hanging on the backs of their necks. They pressed together, shoulder to shoulder, some resting their cheek in one hand, their elbow on the table; others leaning back in their chairs, their fans spread open and held in front of their mouths, all of them fixing upon him their wide, inquisitive eyes.

"If you absolutely insist," said the Comte, with the nonchalance of a man who knows his casual attitude only inflames their desire all the more.

"Absolutely!" said the Duchess, staring down at the little golden dessert knife she was holding, the way a despotic Turkish sultana might stare at the cutting edge of her saber.

"Well, then, listen to my tale," he said, still entirely nonchalant.

They fixed their eyes and their full attention on him. They drank and ate him with their eyes. Every love story will interest women, but who knows?—perhaps the chief charm of this story was, for each one of them, the hope that it would turn out to be about herself. . . . They knew he was too much of a gentleman and too well mannered to name any names, and to be too specific about any incriminating details; and that thought, that certitude, only made them want to hear the story even more. They felt more than desire: they felt hope.

Their vanity made them suspicious of discovering rivals in this memory of his, the most beautiful episode of his life, the life of a man who had had so many, and such beautiful episodes! The old sultan was going to throw out the handkerchief once more . . . but no hand would reach out to pick it up except that one to whom he had thrown it, and she would feel it drop silently within her heart. . . .[17]

And now, seeing what it was that they all expected, you'll be better able to appreciate the thunderbolt that was about to strike all these attentive, uplifted faces.

IV

"I have often heard moralists say, men with much experience in life"—began the Comte de Ravila—"that our greatest love is neither our first nor our last, as many believe: it is the second. But when it comes to love, anything can be true and anything false, and at any rate this was not the case with me. . . . What you have asked me, Mesdames, and what I am about to tell you this evening, dates from the best period of my youth. I was no longer exactly what would be called a young man, but I was a man and young and I had, to use the phrase my uncle, a Knight of Malta, used to describe that era in my life, 'fought my battles.'[18] In the full flower of my prime, then, I found myself in a 'relation,' to use the charming term they use in Italy, with a woman whom you all know and all admire . . ."

At this point the look that the women all exchanged, the way each one examined every one of the others, the whole group of women breathing in the old serpent's words—it was a look you would have to have seen; it was indescribable.

"That woman was," Ravila continued, "the most distinguished woman you could imagine, in every sense of the word. She was young and rich, she had a most remarkable name, and she was beautiful, witty, with an artist's intelligence—which she showed in an easy, effortless way, the way one does in your world when one has some intelligence. . . . But in any case, she had no other aims than those of pleasing me and devoting herself to me; she seemed to me to be the perfect mistress and the best of friends.

"I was not, I understand, the first man she had loved. . . . She had been in love once before, and it was not with her husband; but she loved virtuously, platonically, Utopically, the kind of love that exercises the heart without fulfilling it, and that builds up one's strength for the next love, which will certainly follow upon it soon; it was the kind of early love that resembles the White Mass of the young priests, who must practice so they won't make mistakes when they come to saying the real Mass, the consecrated one. . . . When I entered into her life, she was still at the White Mass stage. I was to be the real Mass, the one she would say soon with all the sumptuous ceremony required, like a Cardinal."

That last comparison resulted in the prettiest round of smiles flashing across those twelve delicious, attentive mouths like a spreading undulation on the peaceful surface of a lake. . . . It was rapid, but ravishing!

"She was really unique!" the Comte continued. "I've rarely seen more true goodness, more piety, more refined sentiments, even in the throes of passion, which, as you all know, is not always so refined. . . . I've never seen less prudery or less coquetry, those two opposites that are so often united and mixed together in a single woman, like one of those tangled balls of yarn your cats love to get their claws into. . . . No, there was nothing for a cat to do with this woman. . . . She was what the novelists, who poison our speech by their manner of speaking, would call a primitive nature that was only slightly embellished by civilization; all she had taken from civilization were some minor, charming luxuries, none of those little corruptions that sometimes seem even more charming to us . . ."

"Was she a brunette?" interrupted the Duchess abruptly, impatient with all the metaphysics.

"Oh, you're not seeing my point!" said Ravila delicately. "Yes, she was a brunette, her hair as black as jet, the closest thing to true ebony that I've ever seen on that voluptuous, lustrous, convex shape that is a woman's head, but she had a fair complexion—and it is by the complexion that one should say whether a woman is blonde or brunette," the great observer added, for he had not studied women solely for the purpose of drawing their portraits. "She was a blonde with black hair . . ."

All the blonde heads at the table—all those who were blonde only in terms of their hair—made an imperceptible movement. It was clear that the interest of the story had, for them, already diminished.

"She had the hair of Night," continued Ravila, "but it was combined with the face of Dawn itself, for she glowed with incarnadine freshness, striking and rare, a face that had resisted the nightlife of Paris where she had lived for years, which burns up so many roses in the flames of its candelabras. Her own roses seemed only to have grown stronger, more radiant, as the tint on her cheeks and lips was practically luminous! The double splendor of hair and complexion was well complemented by the rubies she wore on her forehead, for in those days women dressed *en ferronnière,* which, combined with her flashing eyes whose intensity prevented one from seeing their color, gave one the impression of a triangle of three rubies![19] Slender, yet robust and even majestic, formed to be the wife of a cavalry colonel—though her husband was at the time only a squadron leader in the light-horse division—she had, elegant lady though she was, the health of a peasant girl who drinks in the sun through her skin, and she had all the ardor of the sun, too, in her veins as in her soul—yes, always present, and always ready. . . . But this is where the strange part comes in! This creature, so strong and simple, this nature as pure and unspoiled as the rosy blood that lent its tint to her lovely cheeks and arms, was—would you believe it?—clumsy and awkward when it came to lovemaking . . ."

Here, some eyes were lowered, but they were soon raised up again with a malicious glow in them.

"Awkward in her lovemaking just as she had been imprudent in her life," continued Ravila, giving no further detail on that particular point. "The man who loved her had to be continually trying to teach her two things, which she would never learn: first, not to forget that society is always watching and always armed, and second, to practice those great arts of love that keep passion alive. She had love, but she would never learn the art of love. . . . It was just the opposite from most women, who have only the art! Now, to understand and apply the politics of *The Prince,* you need to be something of a Borgia. Borgia comes before Machiavelli: the one is the poet, the other is the critic. She had nothing at all of the Borgia in her. She was a good, decent woman in love, naïve despite her magnificent beauty, like the little girl in the picture who is thirsty and tries to drink from the fountain with her hands; she tries to pick up the water, but it trickles through her fingers, and she remains confused. . . .

"Still, there was something delightful about the contrast between that confusion and awkwardness, on the one hand, and the sight of that fully grown, impassioned woman on the other, who, if you were to see her in society, would have deceived every observer—who knew love to the point of bliss but who was unable to return the love given her. But unfortunately I was not of a sufficiently contemplative outlook to content myself with admiring this lovely, artistic study in contrast; hence, on certain days, she became angry, jealous, and violent—all the things one becomes when one is in love, and oh, she was in love! Yet jealousy, anger, violence all died out soon enough in her inexhaustible goodness of heart at the first sign of pain she thought she might have caused—as awkward in wounding others as she was in lovemaking! She was like some unknown species of lioness that imagined having claws but, when she wanted to extend them, found nothing but velvety softness in her paws. She scratched at you with velvet!"

"Where is this going?" the Comtesse de Chiffrevas asked her neighbor. "Because this really doesn't seem at all like Don Juan's finest conquest!"

All those complicated women were unable to believe in such simplicity!

"And so we lived," Ravila continued, "in an intimacy sometimes darkened with clouds but with no serious pain, and that intimacy was no mystery to anyone in that little village they call Paris. The Marquise, after all . . . was a Marquise."

There were three with dark brown hair at the table. But they did not so much as bat an eyelid. They knew only too well he was not speaking of them. . . . The only velvet any of them had was on the upper lip of one—an upper lip bearing a voluptuous, faint trace—an upper lip, which at the moment, I can assure you, curled in quite evident disdain.

"And a Marquise three times over, just as pashas can be three-tailed!"[20] Ravila said, the relish he was taking in his story beginning to grow. "The Marquise was one of those women who didn't know how to keep anything hidden and who, even if they wanted to, would be unable to. Even her daughter, a girl of thirteen, could, despite her innocence, see only too well the sort of feelings her mother had for me. Has any poet ever asked what they think of us, the daughters of those women we have loved? A profound question! And one I often posed to myself whenever I happened to catch the spying gaze, dark and threatening, directed at me from the big, somber eyes of that girl. The girl, ferociously shy, who usually left the room as soon as I entered it, and who kept the greatest possible distance between her and me whenever she was forced to stay on, seemed to feel an almost convulsive horror of my person. . . . She tried to hide it, but it was stronger than she was and it betrayed itself. . . . It revealed itself only in the smallest of details, but I did not miss a one of them. The Marquise, who was not at all observant, would often say to me, 'Watch out, dear. I think my daughter is jealous of you . . .'

"But I was far more careful than she was.

"I would have defied this girl, had she been the Devil himself, to fathom my game and my strategies. . . . But her mother's game was entirely transparent. You could see everything reflected in the mirror of her face, so often troubled! With regard to this hatred her daughter felt, I could not help thinking she had found out her mother's secret through some little emotional outburst, some loving gaze held a little too long. She was, in case you're interested, a puny girl, quite unworthy of the mold from which she had been made, so ugly that even her mother admitted it, though she only loved her the more for it—a small topaz, a rough one. . . . How can I put it? A kind of sculptor's mock-up in bronze, but with two of the darkest eyes . . . magical! And yet, later . . ."

He paused at this point, as if he had wanted to stop himself but had already said too much. . . . His listeners' level of interest now began to rise again, which was evident in the expression on every face, and the Comtesse herself could not keep from letting an impatient phrase escape from her lips: "At last!"

V

"In the early days of my affair with her mother," the Comte de Ravila began again, "I had shown the girl all the little caressing familiarities one does with children. . . . I had brought her little bags of sugared almonds. I would call her 'little dark eyes,' and often while I was conversing with her mother, I would toy with the little curls that hung by her temples—thin, sickly little curls that looked like kindling shavings—but the 'little dark eyes' whose great mouth had a smile for everyone would seem to collect herself and withdraw, her smile for me fading away, her eyebrows furrowing; her face took on the expression of a shamed caryatid seeming to feel an unbearable weight when my fingers passed over her brow, the weight of a great entablature.[21]

"Observing this continuing sullenness, this apparent hostility, I eventually left the sensitive little flower alone, seeing it contract so violently whenever it came into contact with the slightest caress from me . . . and I even ceased speaking to her! 'She thinks you are stealing something from her,' the Marquise explained to me. 'She instinctively feels you are taking away some of her mother's love.' And sometimes she would say directly, 'This child is my conscience, and her jealousy is my remorse.'

"One day, having tried to question her on why she felt so deeply estranged from me, the Marquise got nothing out of her but broken, stubborn, stupid replies, the kind all children give you when they don't want to answer. . . . 'There's nothing wrong . . . I don't know.' And seeing how resistant the little bronze sculpture of a girl was, she stopped asking questions and gave up, worn down. . . .

"I forgot to mention that the bizarre child was very pious—with a somber, Spanish, medieval, superstitious kind of piety. She twined all sorts of scapularies around her scrawny body and stuck a heap of crucifixes onto her chest—which was as flat as the back of my hand—and hung images of Blessed Virgins and Holy Spirits all around her neck. 'You are, unfortunately, an unbeliever,' the Marquise said to me. 'You might have said something one day that scandalized her. I beg you, be very careful of what you say in front of her. Don't make my sins even worse in the eyes of that child—in whose sight I am already so guilty!' Then, when the child's behavior did not change in the slightest, she said uneasily, 'You will end up hating her, and I won't be able to blame you.' But she was wrong: I felt nothing but indifference to the girl, apart from some impatience.

"I maintained that politeness between us that adults do when they do not like each other. I used exaggerated courtesy with her, always addressing her as 'Mademoiselle,' and she always replied with a glacial 'Monsieur.' She didn't want to do anything in front of me that might show her worth or even make her stand out in any way. . . . Her mother could never talk her into showing me one of her drawings, or playing a piece on the piano. When I came upon her once playing with ardor and with concentration, she stopped short, got up from the stool, and refused to play anymore. . . .

"Just once, her mother insisted (there was company that night), and she placed herself in front of the instrument with one of those *victimized* airs, which, I can assure you, had nothing charming about it, and she began to play from some score that demanded abominably difficult fingering. I was standing by the fireplace and was able to watch her from the side. She had her back turned to me, and there was no mirror or glass before her in which she could have seen that I was gazing at her. . . . All of a sudden her back (she had dreadful posture, and her mother always said to her, 'If you keep on carrying yourself that way, you'll end up with some disease of the lungs')—all of a sudden her back snapped up straight, as if my gaze had struck her like a bullet; and violently shutting the lid of the piano, which made a tremendous crash when it fell, she raced out of the room. . . . They went off to find her, but no one could persuade her to come back to the room that evening.

"Well, it would seem that the most conceited men are not that way always, for the conduct of that tempestuous child who interested me so little seemed to have nothing whatever to do with me and gave me no hint of the feeling she had for me. Nor did her mother guess it. Her mother, who was jealous of all the women who frequented her salon, was in this case not jealous enough, just as I was not vain enough. But the truth came out, and the Marquise, incapable of keeping a secret from her intimates, had the *imprudence* to reveal it to me, still pale from the terror she had just undergone, but laughing out loud at having felt such fear."

His inflection underlined the word *imprudence* as effectively as the most skilled actor would have done it, and as a man would who knew that the entire interest of his tale depended on that very word!

And it was apparently sufficient, for now the twelve lovely female faces were once again as enflamed with feeling as those of Cherubim before the throne of God. Isn't it true that the curiosity in women is as powerful a feeling as adoration is with the Angels? . . . As for him, he gazed upon them all, those Cherubic faces (and beneath them, the expanse of bare skin stretching down from the shoulders), and finding that they were all fully readied for what he had to tell them, he immediately returned to his tale without further pause.

"Yes, she broke into laughter, the Marquise, at the very thought of it!—or so she told me a bit later, for she had been in no laughing mood at first! 'Just picture it,' she said to me (I'm trying to recall her exact words)—'I was sitting right here, where we are now.'

"We were in one of those little sofas called *back-to-backs,* the best piece of furniture ever designed for people to quarrel, sulk, and then make up, all without changing their place.

"'But you were not sitting where you are now, fortunately!—when I was told that someone had come—can you guess who had arrived? . . . You'll never guess. . . . Monsieur le Curé de Saint-Germain-des-Prés. Do you know him? No! You never go to Mass, which is very wicked. . . . How could you know this poor old saint of a priest, who never sets foot in the home of a female parishioner unless it's a question of looking for money for his poor or for his church? At first, I assumed that is what he had come for.

"'He had instructed my daughter when the proper time had come for her First Communion, and she, a frequent Communicant, had kept him as her confessor. For that reason I had invited him many times to dinner, but always in vain. Now, when he came in, he was clearly troubled, and I could read on his face, normally so placid, an embarrassment so little dissimulated and so great that I could not attribute it to his timidity, and I could not help exclaiming to him—in fact it was the first thing I said to him: "Oh, good God! What's wrong, Monsieur le Curé?"

"'"There is"—he said to me—"Madame, you see before you the most embarrassed man in the world. I have been a minister of the Lord for fifty years, and I have never had such a charge as this, nothing as delicate, nothing I understood less than what I have to tell you . . ."

"'And he sat down, asking me to close the door while we spoke. As you can imagine, all this seriousness had me a bit upset. . . . He perceived it.

"'"Don't let yourself be too upset, Madame," he said. "You're going to need all your strength and calmness to hear me out and to help me understand the unheard-of thing of which I must speak, and which, to be frank, I cannot believe. . . . Your daughter, on whose behalf I have come to you, is, you know as well as I, an angel of purity and piety. I know her soul. I have had it in my keeping since she was seven years old, and I am convinced that she is mistaken . . . perhaps due to her very innocence. . . . But this morning, she came to tell me in confession that she was, and you will not believe this Madame, nor do I, but I must say the word . . . *pregnant!*"

"'Involuntarily, a cry escaped me . . .'

"""I cried out exactly the same way, Madame, in my confessional this morning," the Curé went on, "at this declaration of hers, made with every mark of the most sincere and ghastly despair! I know this child's heart. She knows nothing of life or of sin. . . . Out of all the girls who confess to me, she is the one I would most readily answer for to God Himself. And that is all I can tell you! We priests are the surgeons of the soul, and like doctors we must deliver all the little shameful acts they try to hide, using all our delicacy neither to wound nor to pollute the girls. I took, therefore, every possible precaution as I questioned her, pressed her with questions, that despairing child, but once she had vocalized the thing, admitted her guilt, which she called a crime and her eternal damnation, the poor girl!—after that, she would give me no further information and she stubbornly closed herself up in a silence that she has not broken except to beg me to come to find you, Madame, and to apprise you of her sin—'for Mama must know of it,' she said, 'and I would never have the strength to admit it to her!'"

"'I listened to le Curé de Saint-Germain-des-Prés, and with what a combination of stupefaction and anxiety, you can imagine! Like him, even more than him, I was convinced of my daughter's innocence; but the innocent sometimes do fall, and due to their very innocence. . . . And what she had said to her confessor was not impossible. . . . I did not believe it. . . . I did not want to believe it; but nevertheless, it was not impossible! . . . She was only thirteen, but she was a woman, and her precocity had unsettled me before. . . . I was seized with a fever, a transport of curiosity.

"""I want to find out, and I will find out!" I exclaimed to the good old priest, sitting there in a daze before me, anxiously plucking at the brim of his hat. "Leave me now, Monsieur le Curé. She won't speak in front of you. But I am sure she'll tell me everything . . . or I will drag everything out of her, and then we will finally comprehend this thing that is now incomprehensible!"

"'The priest went on his way, and the minute he was gone I went up to my daughter's room, not having the patience to send for her and have to wait for her.

"'I found her in front of her crucifix, not kneeling but prostrate, as pale as a corpse, her eyes dry but very red, eyes that had wept a great deal. I took her in my arms, had her sit down beside me, then put her on my knees, and I told her that I could not believe what her confessor had just told me.

"'But she interrupted to assure me, with heartbroken gestures and looks, that it was true, what he had said, and that was when, growing more and more disturbed and surprised, I asked her the name of the man who . . .

"'I could not finish the sentence. . . . Ah, it was a terrible moment! She lowered her head and pressed her face against my shoulder. . . . But I could feel the feverish heat on the back of her neck, and I felt her shudder. The silence she had maintained with her confessor she maintained with me. She was as impenetrable as a wall.

"'"It must be someone very much beneath you to give you such a sense of shame? . . ," I said to her, thinking I could make her talk by disgusting her, for I knew how proud she was.

"'But she stayed silent, and her head remained pressed down on my shoulder. This went on for what felt like an infinity, when all of a sudden she said, without raising her head, "Promise me you'll forgive me, Mama."

"'I promised her, at the risk of perjuring myself later; and I was worried about it, too! I was impatient. I was boiling . . . I felt like my forehead was about to burst . . .

"'"Well, then—it's Monsieur de Ravila!" she said in a low voice, and she remained still in my arms.

"'Oh, the effect that name had on me, Amédée! I felt a blow directly in my heart, as if this was the punishment for the greatest sin of my life! You are, with regard to women, so frightening a man, and you've made me fear so many rivals that the phrase "And why not?" rose up within me, why not the man I love, the man I fear. . . . I had to hide what I was feeling from that cruel child, who had perhaps divined her mother's love affair.

"'"Monsieur de Ravila!" I exclaimed, with a voice that I feared revealed everything—"But you never even talk to him! You flee from him!" And as the anger rose in me, and I could feel it rising, I almost added, "So you've both been false to me?" But I repressed it. Would I not have to learn the details, one by one, of this horrible seduction? . . . And I asked her for them, in a gentle voice that nearly killed me, when she suddenly released me from that crushing vise, that torture, by saying naïvely:

"'"Mother, it happened one evening. He was in the big easy chair in the corner by the fireplace, across from the loveseat. He stayed there a long time, then he got up, and I had the bad luck of going over and sitting in the chair where he had been. Oh, Mama!—it was as if I had fallen into a fire. I wanted to get up, but I couldn't move. . . . My heart just stopped! And I felt that. . . . Oh, I felt, Mama . . . that what it was inside me . . . was a baby!"'"

The Marquise had laughed, said Ravila, when she told him the story; but not one of the twelve women surrounding the table even dreamed of laughing—and neither did Ravila.

"And there, Mesdames, if you will, there you have it"—he added by way of a conclusion—"the finest conquest of my life!"

He stopped, and they were silent, too. They were pensive. . . . Had they understood?

When Joseph was a slave in the household of Madame Potiphar, the Koran tells us, he was so handsome that when he waited on the table the women there slipped into a reverie and cut their fingers with their knives, gazing at him.[22] But we do not live in Joseph's time any longer, and our preoccupations over our desserts are less formidable.

"But for all her cleverness, your Marquise was such a fool, to say something like that to you!" exclaimed the Duchess, who permitted herself to wax cynical, but who cut nothing at all with the knife she continued to hold in her hand.

The Comtesse de Chiffrevas gazed attentively into the depths of a glass of Rhine wine, a glass of emerald crystal, as mysterious as her thoughts.

"And the little dark eyes?" she asked.

"Oh! She was dead, dead quite young, and married to someone out in the provinces, when her mother told me this story," Ravila replied.

"Ah—if it weren't for that," said the Duchess, pensively.

HAPPINESS IN CRIME

In this delicious era of ours, when you hear a true story,
you have to assume that the Devil dictated it.

One morning last autumn, I was walking in the Jardin des
Plantes with Doctor Torty, who is among my very oldest
acquaintances.[1] When I was only a child, Doctor Torty practiced
in the town of V***; but after some thirty years of that agreeable
life, and when all his patients had died—his "tenant farmers," he
called them, and indeed they brought in more for him than all
the tenants do for their landlords throughout Normandy—at that
point he decided to take on no new patients.[2] And having reached
a certain age and going just a bit mad with that sudden awareness
of independence, like a horse who has always had the bit between
its teeth and who, eventually, snaps it and runs free, he came
to immerse himself in Paris—close by, too, near the Jardin des
Plantes, on the Rue Cuvier, I believe. He no longer practiced
medicine except for his own enjoyment, but he did that often
enough, for the man was a doctor through and through, and a
good doctor, and a great *observer,* too, a man who observed a great
deal beyond the physiological and the pathological. . . .

Have you ever met him, Doctor Torty?[3] He was one of those
tough, vigorous types who, so to speak, never wear gloves, for
the good, proverbial reason that "a cat in gloves will never catch a
mouse," and he had caught an immense number of them, and he
wanted to go on catching them; a wily type, the type I've always
liked, and for the very traits that make others dislike him. In fact,

most people did dislike this brusque, eccentric man when they were healthy; but the ones who most disliked him, as soon as they fell ill, began salaaming to him like the natives when they heard Robinson Crusoe's gun go off, but for a different reason than the savages: not because he could kill them but because he could cure them! And without that important consideration, the doctor would not have earned twenty thousand livres a year in that little aristocratic town—that pious, prudish town, the chief inhabitants of which would have kept him firmly on the outside of the carriage gates of their grand homes if they had been motivated solely by their opinions and antipathies.[4] He talked about the fact with equanimity and even joked about it. "They had to choose," he said mockingly, regarding that thirty-year period in V***, "between me and Extreme Unction, and, pious as they were, they tended to prefer my presence to that of the Holy Oils." As you can see, he speaks his mind freely, the doctor. He enjoys his slightly sacrilegious humor. A genuine disciple of Cabanis in his medical philosophy, he belonged, like his old comrade Chaussier, to that terrifying school of absolute materialism; and like Dubois—the first Dubois—he was cynical about everything, a man who would use the familiar *tu* form with Duchesses and maids of honor, calling them "my little mothers" as if they were common fish merchants.[5] To give you some idea of Doctor Torty's cynical humor: just before a dinner where some one hundred and twenty society people were about to gather, he looked over the vast expanse of place settings with a proprietary air and said, "I made every one of them!" Moses himself would not have been prouder, showing you the rod with which he had turned rocks into fountains.[6] But what can I tell you, Madame? He lacked, phrenologically speaking, the bump of respect, going so far as to say that where other men's skulls had such a bump, his had a cavity. He was old, having passed his seventieth year, but solid, robust, and as tough and gnarled as his name,[7] with a sarcastic expression beneath his chestnut-colored hairpiece—smooth and lustrous, that hairpiece, cut quite short; his sharp, penetrating eyes had never needed glasses, and he dressed always in gray or in that brown that is called "Moscow smoke," looking utterly unlike the gentlemen doctors of Paris,

always correct with their white cravats, the color of their patients' shrouds! This was a different kind of man. He wore buck-
skin gloves, which, along with his thick-soled boots resounding
firmly as he walked along, gave him the brisk, attentive look of
a horseman—and horseman he was, for he had put on leather
leggings and rode a beast for those thirty years over roads that
would have broken a centaur in two. You could tell all that from
the way he still arched his broad back and twisted his torso atop
his powerful legs that had never known rheumatism, though they
were as bowed as a postilion's. Doctor Torty was something of a
Leatherstocking on horseback, living on the frontier of Cotentin, like James Fenimore Cooper's Leatherstocking in the forests
of America. A naturalist who scorned social convention, like the
heroes in Cooper, but one who, again like Cooper's, had not replaced convention with the idea of a God, he had become one
of those pitiless observers who cannot help but become misan-
thropes. It is inevitable. And he did. But he had had the time,
while inhaling the dust and mud of country roads on horseback,
to meditate on other kinds of dust and mud. He was not at all a
misanthrope like Alceste.[8] He showed no righteous indignation.
He did not get angry. No—he despised mankind with as much
equanimity as he would take a pinch of snuff, and he took more
pleasure in the snuff than in the despising.

Such was Doctor Torty, with whom I was taking a walk that day.

That autumn day was one of those sunny, clear ones that keep
the swallows from departing. The Notre Dame bell rang out noon,
and the solemn sound seemed to spread out in a long, luminous
shudder all down the green, moiré surface of the river to the pil-
ings of the bridges, and we could even feel it passing above our
heads, so vibrant and clear was the air! The russet leaves on the
trees around us had slowly emerged from the blue fog of those
October mornings, and a fine, late-season golden sun warmed
our backs, the doctor's and mine, as we stopped to look at the
famous black panther (which died the following winter, incidentally, like a young girl, from a disease of the lungs). Here and
there around us were the usual sorts of people who frequent the
Jardin des Plantes—soldiers, nannies, and the like, people who

take pleasure in tossing little bits of walnut shells or orange peels into the cages where the animals were drowsing behind their bars. The panther, to whose cage we had wandered up, was of the species peculiar to Java, the country where nature is at its most intense, seeming itself to be a great tigress, untamable by man yet fascinating to him, swallowing him up slowly into its terrible and splendid soil. In Java, the flowers have more scent, the fruits greater savor, the beasts greater beauty and power than anywhere else on earth, and nothing can give a better idea of the violence of life in that both enchanting and poisonous country than saying it is like a combination of Armida and Locusta![9]

Sprawled out with her elegant paws stretched in front of her, her head erect, her emerald eyes immobile, the panther was a magnificent specimen of that country's awe-inspiring productions. Her black velour fur was without the slightest tawny patch; its blackness was so deep and so rich that the sun glistening on it did not so much illuminate it as become absorbed by it, the way water is absorbed into a sponge. . . . When you turned your gaze from this ideal form, this supple beauty, with its power terrible even in repose, with its imperial, impassive disdain, to look at the humans surrounding it and gawking at it timidly with their wide eyes and their gaping mouths, it was certainly not humanity that impressed you as the more beautiful. And she was so superior that it was almost humiliating! I was saying this quietly to the doctor when two people parted the crowd in front of the panther's cage and planted themselves directly in front of it. "Yes," the doctor replied, "but look now! The equilibrium between the species has just been restored!"

It was a man and a woman, both of them tall, and from my first glance at them I concluded they were from the upper reaches of Parisian society. Neither of them was young, but they were nevertheless perfectly beautiful. The man must have been somewhere in his midforties or more, and the woman around forty or more. . . . They had, therefore, as the sailors returning from South America put it, "crossed the line," the fatal line, the line far more formidable than the equator, the line that, once passed on the ocean of life, no one ever crosses again! But they seemed unconcerned about the circumstance. There was no melancholy about them at all. . . . The man was slender and patrician in his black coat, buttoned up correctly in the manner of a cavalry officer; if he had been wearing the kind of costume Titian gives to his characters, he would have resembled one of the courtiers of the era of Henri III, with his haughty yet feminine air, his mustaches as pointed as a cat's whiskers, and the points beginning to whiten; and to make the resemblance complete, he wore his hair short, so that one could see the glitter of two dark blue sapphire earrings, which reminded me of the two emeralds that Sbogar wore. . . .[10] Except for that *ridiculous* detail (as the world would have termed it), which suggested a disdain for the tastes and ideas of the moment, everything about him was simple and *dandy* in the sense Brummell understood dandyism, that is, the man's clothing was utterly *unremarkable* and attracted no particular attention beyond that which the man himself commanded, and indeed he would have attracted universal attention if it were not for the woman on his arm. . . . This woman in fact attracted more stares than the man accompanying her, and she held them longer. She was tall like him, nearly the same height. Dressed entirely in black like him, she reminded one of the great black Isis in the Egyptian Museum by her shape, her mysterious pride, and her strength. A strange thing: with this fine-looking couple, it was the woman who had the muscles and the man who had the nerves. . . . At that point I still could see only her profile, but that profile seemed to be beauty in its most dangerous form, or at least in its most startling. Never, I believe, have I seen a purer or nobler face. I could not judge her eyes, fixed as they were on the panther, who no doubt found her gaze magnetic and disturbing, for the creature, though immobile before, now seemed to retreat into a state of pure rigidity the longer the woman stared at it; and—like a cat blinded by sunlight—without moving its head in the slightest, without its whiskers trembling at all, the panther blinked several times and then, as if it could take no more, it slowly lowered its eyelids over its green eyes. The panther simply shut itself away.

"Look there—panther versus panther!" the doctor whispered to me. "But satin is stronger than velvet."

The satin was the woman, who was wearing a dress of that shimmering material—a dress with a long train. And he was right, the doctor! Black, supple, just as powerful and just as regal looking—in her own way, just as beautiful and with a somehow more disturbing kind of charm—the unknown woman was like a human panther, standing there in contrast to the animal whom she eclipsed; and the beast knew it, and that was why she had closed her eyes. But the woman—if she was a woman—was not content with this triumph. She was no generous victor. She wanted her rival to see her own humiliation and wanted her to open her eyes to see it. So, she undid the twelve buttons on her violet glove without saying a word, baring her magnificent forearm, took off the glove, and audaciously slipping her hand between the bars of the cage, she used it to slap the short muzzle of the panther, who only made a single movement . . . but what a movement!—and flashed her teeth, as quick as a bolt of lightning! A cry went up from the crowd around us. We thought her hand had been bitten off: but it was only the glove. The panther had swallowed it. The frightening beast was outraged, and she rolled her hideously dilated eyes, her nostrils flaring and trembling. . . .

"Fool!" said the man, seizing the beautiful wrist that had just escaped the most powerful of bites.

You know how people sometimes say that word, *fool!* That is how he said it, lifting up and kissing her wrist passionately.

And since he was standing on our side, she turned three-quarters toward him to see him kissing her naked wrist, and I caught sight of her eyes . . . the kind of eyes that fascinate tigers, and that were at the moment fascinated by a man; her eyes were two large black diamonds, big enough to express all of life's pride, but now, gazing at him, expressing nothing more than an absolutely adoring love!

Those eyes were poetry, and they spoke poetry. The man had not released her arm, which had just felt the hot breath of the panther, and holding it tight against his heart, he led the woman off with him down the Jardin's broad promenade, indifferent to the murmurs and exclamations of the crowd—still excited by the danger they had watched the woman risk—and he walked calmly away. They passed close by us, the doctor and me, but their eyes were on each other, pressed closely together, side by side, as if they each wanted to penetrate the other, he into her, she into him, and make a single body out of their two, seeing nothing in the world but each other. Seeing them pass by, one would assume they were superior creatures who didn't even feel their feet touching the ground, who passed through the world wrapped in their own cloud, like the gods in Homer, like Immortals!

Such sights are rare in Paris, and for that reason we stood there and watched them walking off, that master-couple—the woman letting the black train of her dress spread out in the dust of the walkway, like a peacock disdainful of its own plumage.

They were superb, passing along like that in the noonday sun, so majestically interlaced together, those two beings. . . . And soon they had reached the gates of the Jardin and ascended into their waiting carriage with its brass-harnessed horses.

"They ignore the whole universe!" I exclaimed to the doctor, who understood my thought.

"Oh, what do they care about the universe!" he replied in his sarcastic voice. "They see nothing in all of creation, and, what's even more stunning, they walk right past their doctor without seeing him."

"What—are you their doctor?" I cried. "But in that case you must tell me who they are, my dear Doctor."

The Doctor paused, wanting to make an effect, because he is always crafty, my old friend!

"Well, they're Philemon and Baucis," he said, very simply.[11] "That's all."

"Damn!" I exclaimed. "A Philemon and a Baucis with a great deal more hauteur than the ancient ones. But, Doctor, that isn't their name. . . . What are their names?"

"What!" he replied. "In the society in which you move, and in which I have no place, have you really never heard the Count and Countess Serlon de Savigny spoken of as models of marital love?"

"Heavens, no," I said. "People speak very little about marital love in the world I frequent, Doctor."

"Hmm! It's possible," said the Doctor, more in response to his own thought than to my comment. "In that society, which is also theirs, many things that are more or less correct take place. But apart from the reason they have for not going into society, and apart from the fact that they live nearly the whole year round at their old chateau in Savigny, in the Cotentin region, there were also some rumors about them circulating in the Faubourg Saint-Germain, where the nobility still retain some solidarity, and it's better to be silent than to speak."

"And what were those rumors? . . . Oh look, you've got me hooked now, Doctor! You know perfectly well that the Savigny chateau is not far from the town of V***, where you were the physician."

"Oh, those rumors," said the Doctor, pensively taking a pinch of snuff. "Ultimately, they were believed to be false! All that is over now. . . . But nevertheless, though marriages based on love and the happiness they bring are considered the ideal among all the mothers in the provinces, generally romantic and virtuous women, they couldn't very well—at least the ones I know—hold this one up as an example to their daughters!"

"But didn't you just call them Philemon and Baucis, Doctor?"

"Baucis! Baucis! Hmm! Monsieur—" Doctor Torty interrupted, crooking his finger and passing it down the length of his nose (one of his typical gestures)—"wouldn't you say that fine woman looks less like Baucis and more like Lady Macbeth?"

"Doctor, my good, amiable Doctor," I replied, with all the coaxing tones I could get into my voice, "are you going to tell me the whole story of the Count and Countess de Savigny?"

The Doctor said, "The physician is the confessor of these modern times," with mock solemnity. "He has replaced the priest, Monsieur, and he is just as much obliged to keep the secrets of the confessional as the priest. . . ."

He gave me a sly look, for he knew about my respect and my love for the things of Catholicism, which he saw as the enemy. He winked at me, thinking he had caught me.

"And he is going to keep those secrets . . . just the way the priest does!" he added with a burst of his most cynical laughter. "Come over here. We're going to talk."

And he led me over to the grand, tree-lined promenade that forms a border between the Jardin des Plantes and the Boulevard de l'Hôpital. . . . There, we sat down on one of the green benches, and he began:

"My friend, finding the beginning of this story is like looking for a bullet after the flesh has closed over the wound; for, you see, forgetting is like the flesh of living creatures that re-forms itself and covers events up, keeping us from seeing anything there at all, or even suspecting that there is anything there. It was during the first years following the Restoration.[12] A regiment of the Guard was passing through the town of V***; and having been obliged to stay there for two days for who knows what military reason, the officers decided to put on a swordsmanship exhibition, an 'assault of arms,' as an honor to the town. That town truly deserved such an honor from the Guards, as a matter of fact. The place was, as they put it back then, more royalist than the King. Given its size—a population of only five or six thousand—it positively abounded in nobility. More than thirty young men from the best families were in the military then, whether in the Gardes-du-Corps or with Monsieur, and the officers of the regiment passing through V*** knew them all.[13] But the main reason for putting on this martial exhibition for the town was the reputation of the place, which had been nicknamed 'the swashbuckler' and which was in fact still the premier swordsmanship town in France. While the Revolution of 1789 had taken away the right of the nobility to wear their swords, in the town of V*** they showed that, if they no longer wore them, they still knew how to use them. The exhibition given by the officers was outstanding. It attracted all the region's best swordsmen and even some amateurs, a generation younger, who had not cultivated the complex art of fencing as they had done in the past; and everyone showed such enthusiasm for the right wielding of an épée, which had been the glory of our forefathers, that an old provost-marshal of the regiment, who had served his term of duty some three or four times over, and whose sleeve was covered with chevrons, thought that the town of V*** would be a good place to retire and open a fencing school. The colonel to whom he presented his plan approved of it and gave him his discharge. This old provost's real name was Stassin, but his nom de guerre was Saber-tip; his idea for the school was a stroke of genius. There had been no proper fencing school for many years in V***, which was often lamented by the nobles who were obliged to teach their children themselves, or to find some friend who had recently left the military to do it for them, someone who might not in fact have been much of a swordsman or a teacher. The inhabitants of V*** prided themselves on being very particular. They really had the sacred fire. It was not enough for them to kill their man: they wanted to kill him in a learned way, artistically, in accord with the best principles of the art. Above all, they insisted on demonstrating grace and elegance in combat, and they had nothing but contempt for those rough and tough but clumsy types who were called *duelists* but by no means merited the term *fencers*. Now, Saber-tip had been a fine fellow in his youth and was so still. When encamped in Holland, he had soundly defeated all the other provosts and had carried off the prize of two silver foils and masks—he had been in fact one of those swordsmen that no school can produce if nature has not done her part first by endowing the man with exceptional qualities. Naturally, he was the admiration of all V*** and soon something even better. There is no social equalizer like the épée. Under the old monarchy, kings would ennoble the men who taught them how to use it. Didn't Louis XV, if I recall correctly, give his fencing master Danet—who has left us a book on the subject—for his coat of arms four of his fleur-de-lis between two crossed épées?[14] These country gentlemen, stuffed to the gills with monarchical ideas, very quickly became friends with the old provost, as if he had always been one of theirs.

"Up to that point, everything was going well, and all one could do was congratulate Stassin, nicknamed Saber-tip, on his good luck; but unfortunately, the heart of padded red morocco leather sewn on his breast, which he wore while giving his magisterial lessons, was not his only one. . . . As it turned out, there was another one underneath it, one that began seeking for a mate in the town of V***, a safe harbor in which he could rest. It would seem that a soldier's heart is always made of gunpowder. Now,

when time has dried out the powder, it is all the more susceptible
to catching fire. At V***, the women are generally so pretty that
stray sparks were everywhere, ready to ignite the dry powder
of our old provost. And so, his story ended the way so many old
soldiers' do. After having knocked around all the countries of Europe, and after having had experiences with all the girls that the
Devil had put in his path, this old soldier from the first Empire
concluded his final love affair by marrying, at the age of fifty, and
with all the formalities and sacramental rites, of both the munici-
pality and the Church—a young flirt from V***. Now this particular flirt—and I know them all in that part of the country; I've
attended at the deliveries of enough of them!—this one gave him
a child precisely nine months later to the day; and that child, who
was a girl, is none other, my friend, than that goddess-like woman
we just watched pass us by, the one who insolently brushed us
with her dress, and who paid no more attention to us than if we
hadn't been there at all!"

"The Countess de Savigny!" I exclaimed.

"Yes, the Countess de Savigny through and through! Ah! One
should not inquire into origins, either of nations or of women;
never look into anyone's cradle. I recall having seen the cradle
of Charles XII in Stockholm, and it looked like the manger of a
horse, crudely painted red, sitting on four uneven legs. But that
was where that whirlwind of a man had his beginnings. But then
all cradles are like cesspits, and one is obliged to change their lin-
en several times a day, and even for those who believe in poetry, it
is never poetical—except for when the child is no longer there."

And to support his axiom at this point in his story, the doctor
slapped his thigh with one of his doeskin gloves, which he held by
the fingers; and the doeskin resounded in such a way as to prove
to one who knows something about music that the good doctor
was still muscular enough.

He waited. I said nothing to contradict his philosophy. Seeing
this, he continued:

"Well, like all old soldiers, who love even other people's children, Saber-tip was delighted with his own. There is nothing surprising in this. When an older man has a child, he loves it even more

than he would have when young, for vanity, which always doubles everything, also doubles paternal affection. All the vain old men who I've observed having children late in life adore their offspring and show such a fierce pride that you'd think it was some great feat that they'd managed to accomplish. They become persuaded that they're young again, a folly nature plants in their heads just to laugh at them! I know of only one joy more intoxicating, only one pride more comical: and that's when an old man, instead of producing one child, manages to produce two at once! Saber-tip did not have the glory of fathering twins; but it's true that his child was big enough to make two. His daughter—you've seen her; you can tell how well she's lived up to her promise!—she was a wonderful child, outstanding for her strength and her beauty. The old provost's first concern was to seek out a godfather from among the nobles who haunted his fencing school; and from all of them, he picked the Count d'Avice, the oldest of all those connoisseurs of the épée, a man who had, during the forced emigration of the nobles, served as a fencing master himself in London, charging a good many guineas per lesson. The Count d'Avice de Sortôville-en-Beaumont had been a knight of the order of Saint Louis and a captain of dragoons before the Revolution—at that time he had to have been at least seventy years old—but he could still 'button' the young men and, to use the term they used, he showed superb attack.[15] He was an inveterate talker when he fenced, tossing off sarcastic remarks right along with his ferocious swordplay. Thus, for example, he liked to put his blade in a candle's flame, and when by this method it became very stiff, he called his old sword—which now would not bend when it thrust up hard against your sternum or your sides—he called his sword by the insolent name of 'scoundrel-pusher.' He liked Saber-tip very much and was on familiar terms with him. 'The daughter of a man like you'—he said to him—'should have a name like that of a valiant knight's sword. Let us call her Hauteclaire!'[16] And that was the name he gave her. The priest of V***, true, grimaced a bit at this name that had never been heard at the baptismal font of his church; but since the godfather was the Count D'Avice, and despite the liberals and their constant whining, there was and will always be an indestructible bond between the nobility and the clergy; and, since, as it happens, there is a saint named Claire in the Roman calendar, the name of Olivier's épée was therefore given to the child, without the town of V*** being much disturbed by it. A name like that seemed to announce a destiny. The old provost, who loved his profession almost as much as his daughter, resolved to teach her all he knew, and to leave her his talent as her dowry. Pathetic dowry! Meager pittance! Especially when one considers modern ways, which that poor devil of a fencing master could not foresee! As soon as the child was able to stand upright, he began giving her lessons in fencing, and since this girl was a tough little one, with joints and tendons like thin steel, he was able to develop her in such a strange manner that when she was ten, she seemed to be fifteen, and she already held her own with her father and with the best swordsmen of V***. . . . Everyone was talking about little Hauteclaire Stassin, who, a bit later, had to be called Mademoiselle Hauteclaire Stassin. And it was above all, as you might guess, among the young ladies of the town—into whose society the daughter of Stassin, called Saber-tip, could not venture, no matter how close her father was to theirs—that an incredible or, rather, a perfectly credible curiosity grew up, mixed with feelings of spite and envy. Their fathers and brothers spoke about her in front of them with surprise and admiration, and they would have liked to get a good close look at this female Saint George whose beauty, it was said, was the equal of her swordsmanship. But they only saw her at a distance. I had recently come to live in V***, and I often witnessed that burning curiosity. Old Saber-tip, who had served in the Hussars under the Empire and who, with his fencing school, was growing rich, bought a horse to give his daughter riding lessons; and because he agreed to the task of breaking in other people's horses at any time during the year, he was often seen riding with Hauteclaire out on the roadways both in and around the town. I ran into them many times as I was making my rounds as a doctor, and it was during these encounters that I was able to take the measure of the extreme interest that this tall young girl had aroused among all the other girls in the neighborhood. I was always out on the roadways and pathways in those days, and

I would often cross paths with them, in their parents' carriages, off paying their visits to the various chateaus in the neighborhood. Let me tell you, you cannot imagine the eagerness, even the imprudence, with which I saw them rush up to their carriage windows whenever Mademoiselle Hauteclaire Stassin would appear, trotting or galloping down a road in the distance, riding side by side with her father. But it was always a bit futile; the next day, when I called upon their mothers, all I heard were expressions of disappointment and regret, for all they had been able to see was the general shape of that Amazon-like girl, holding herself like—well, you've seen her, so you can imagine—and keeping her face hidden under a too-thick blue veil. It was only the men of V*** who knew Mademoiselle Hauteclaire Stassin. . . . All day long, her foil in her hand, and her face protected by her fencing mask, which she rarely removed, she hardly ever left the fencing school of her father, who was beginning to grow older and feebler. She was very rarely seen out in the street—but any women who wanted to see her would have to see her there or at Mass on Sunday, and at Sunday Mass and out in the street she was almost always just as fully masked, the lace of her black veil being even darker and less penetrable than her fencing mask. Was there some affectation in this way of presenting herself—or, rather, of hiding herself—was it all just a method of exciting others' curiosity? . . . It was entirely possible; but who knows? Who could say? And was it not true that this young girl who went from mask to veil had a character at least as impenetrable as her face? What was to follow proves that only too well.

"You must understand, my friend, that I am forced to pass rapidly over all the details of that era in order to get more quickly to the moment where this story really begins. Mademoiselle Hauteclaire was around seventeen. Her father, Saber-tip, had evolved into a contented bourgeois; he had lost his wife, and then the July Revolution came like a mortal blow to his spirit, as it forced all the nobles back home to their chateaus in mourning, emptying his classrooms, and on top of all that his gout was hurrying him off to the cemetery.[17] For myself as his doctor, the diagnosis was all too clear. I had given him only a short time to live when, one morning, a young man was brought to his school—by the Viscount de Taillebois and the Chevalier de Mesnilgrand—a young man brought up far from there, who had returned to live in the chateau of his recently deceased father.[18] It was the Count Serlon de Savigny, the 'intended' (as the townspeople of V*** put it, speaking the language of small towns everywhere) of Mademoiselle Delphine de Cantor. The Count de Savigny was certainly one of the most promising of all the up-and-coming young men of the region, in that era when they all were up-and-coming, both at V*** and everywhere else. Nowadays, they're all gone. People had spoken to him about the famous Hauteclaire Stassin, and he had wanted to get a look at this miracle. He found her to be just what she was—an admirable girl, striking to look at, and devilishly provocative in her silk hose, which showed off a figure like that of Velletri's Pallas Athena, and in her jacket of black morocco leather, which fit her robust form tightly, her irresistible form— one of those figures that the Circassians create by imprisoning their daughters in tight leather belts that can only be broken by the growth and development of the body.[19] Hauteclaire Stassin was as serious as a Clorinda.[20] He watched her as she gave her lesson, and he asked for the chance to cross swords with her. But he was not to be the Tancred of this situation, the Count de Savigny! Mademoiselle Hauteclaire Stassin bent her épée in a half-circle many times against the breast of the handsome Serlon, and his foil never once touched her.

"'You are untouchable, Mademoiselle,' he said to her with a perfect grace. 'Is this an omen?'

"Could it be that the young man's self-esteem was overcome by love?

"In any case, after that evening, the Count de Savigny came back for lessons every day at Saber-tip's school. The Count's chateau was only a few leagues away. He could ride or take his carriage in with nobody paying any attention in that little town where, although the tiniest things were enough to arouse gossip, the love of fencing explained everything. Savigny took no one into his confidence. He went so far as to schedule his lessons for times when no other men would be there. That Savigny—he was a clever sort. . . . What passed between him and Hauteclaire, if anything did pass between them, nobody knew, and nobody even suspected. The plans for his marriage to Mademoiselle Delphine de Cantor, which the parents of both families had decided upon years before, were by now too advanced not to take place, and indeed the wedding was held three months after the Count's return; it was even a chance for him to spend a whole month living in V***, so as to be close to his fiancée, whose residence he passed every day, as regularly as clockwork, on his way to take his fencing lesson. . . .

"Like everyone else, Mademoiselle Hauteclaire heard the marriage banns for the Count de Savigny and Mademoiselle de Cantor announced at the parish church of V***; but there was nothing in her attitude or her physiognomy to indicate that she took the slightest interest in those public declarations. Of course, it is also true that no one was on the alert for any such thing. Those who might have been observers were not yet keyed into the possibility of a liaison between Savigny and the beautiful Hauteclaire. When the marriage had been celebrated, the Countess moved into her chateau very contentedly along with her husband, who did not alter any of his daily habits and continued to come into town every day. And in any case, many of the other nobles in the neighborhood did exactly the same. Time passed. Old Saber-tip passed away. His school was closed for a few days, and then Mademoiselle Hauteclaire Stassin reopened it, announcing that she would continue giving lessons as her father had; and far from losing students after his death, she actually gained more. Men are all the same. They dislike strangeness among themselves and even find it painful; but if strangeness wears skirts, they are delighted with it. In France, a woman who does what a man does, even if she does it quite poorly, will always have a marked advantage over the man. Now what Mademoiselle Hauteclaire Stassin did, she did far better than a man. She had become even better than her father. Her demonstrations during her lessons were incomparable and, in terms of the beauty of her style, splendid. She executed irresistible strokes with her foil—the kind of strokes one can neither teach nor learn any more than the *coups d'archet* or wrist movements of a violinist. . . . I did a little fencing in those days, like everybody else in the place I lived, and I must admit that some of her passes had a real charm about them. Among others, she had a way of disengaging from a *carte* to a *tierce* that seemed like magic.[21] It wasn't a foil that struck you—it was a bullet! The man with the swiftest parry was left whipping his foil in the air, even when she had warned that she was about to disengage, and inevitably he felt her foil striking his shoulder and chest. Her sword simply seemed to disappear from sight! I've seen swordsmen fly into a rage at this stroke, which they called witchcraft, ready to swallow their swords in their fury! If she hadn't been a woman, they would have found some devilish way of forcing her into a duel over that stroke. A man like that would have had to fight twenty duels.

"But quite apart from that phenomenal talent, which was so unsuited to a woman, and yet which she carried off so nobly, she was quite an interesting person, this young girl who had no wealth nor resource apart from her sword and who, as a result, found herself mixing with the richest young men in town, among whom were some shady types and some egotistical fools—and yet her reputation never suffered. No one gossiped about her and Savigny, or about her and anyone else. . . . 'It would appear that she is an honest woman,' said all the correct, proper women, speaking of her the way they would have spoken about an actress. And as for myself, since I've introduced myself into the story, I piqued myself on my insight into people, and I was on the same page with the rest of the town with regard to the virtue of Hauteclaire. I sometimes went to the fencing school, and both before and after the marriage of de Savigny I had never seen so serious a young girl who went about her business with such simplicity. She was, I must say, too, an imposing person, and she had the respect of all, never being too familiar with anyone. Her expression was very proud, and at that time she did not carry that passionate look you found so striking, and it showed no anxiety, no preoccupation, nothing at all that would make one predict the remotest chance of the stunning event that, in that little town's tranquil, routine atmosphere, had the same effect as a cannon going off and breaking all the windows. . . .

"'Mademoiselle Hauteclaire Stassin has disappeared!'

"She has disappeared? What? How? Where did she go? No one knew. The only thing for sure was that she had disappeared. First there were exclamations—then silence—but the silence did not last long. Tongues started wagging. Tongues that had long been restrained, like water held up behind a sluice gate: but when the gate is finally lifted, the water streams out and sets the mills to working furiously; like the foam lifted up by waves, all the gossip turned on this unexpected, sudden, unbelievable disappearance, for which there was no explanation, for Mademoiselle Hauteclaire had disappeared without saying a word to anyone. She had disappeared the way a person does when he or she really wants to disappear, not leaving behind some clue that people can seize on for an explanation. She had disappeared in the most radical manner. She had not 'done a moonlight run,' as they sometimes say, for she left no debts behind; she had instead vanished into thin air. The winds blew, but they did not blow her back to town. The great mill of tongues began working again, even though there was nothing for it to work upon, and instead ground cruelly upon that reputation that had heretofore been so spotless. The subject was taken up again and again, run through the sifter, turned to powder. . . . How, and with whom, did that proud girl run away? . . . No answer available for that one. It was enough to render a small town mad, and in fact that is what happened to V***. How many motives there were for its righteous indignation! In the first place, whatever the facts in the case might have been, there was the matter of what they had lost. Then, they wasted their time in making guesses about that girl whom everyone thought they had known, but whom none of them had really known, for they had all assumed her incapable of running away *like that*. . . . Then they considered how they had lost a girl who by rights should have grown old or married, like all the other girls in the town—who should have stayed in her position on the chessboard of a country town, waiting for the call, like a horse in a stable. Finally, they considered that in losing Mademoiselle Stassin, who now was always and only 'that Stassin,' they were also losing a celebrated fencing school, one that had been the distinction, the ornament, the honor of the town, its proud cockade, its unique flag. Oh, this loss was a hard one! And all these were reasons for hurling the maximum amount of mud at the memory of the irreproachable Hauteclaire! And much mud was hurled. . . . Except for a few of the greater squires who were too lordly to do so, who, like her godfather the Count d'Avice, had known her from infancy and who found it entirely natural that she had found some shoe that fit better than that of a fencing master; but apart from them, no one defended the disappearance of Hauteclaire Stassin. Her disappearance had wounded everyone's self-esteem; and it was the younger men who retained the most bitterness for the longest time, because she had not chosen to disappear with one of them.

"It was their great grief and their great anxiety for a long time. With whom had she run away? . . . Many of these young men went every winter to Paris for a month or two, and two or three of them claimed to have caught sight of her there—at a play—or on horseback on the Champs-Élysée—alone, or with someone else—but they could not be sure. They could not swear to it. It was she, but then again it might not have been she; but their preoccupation with her did not flag. . . . None of them could stop thinking about her, this girl they had so admired and who, in disappearing, had plunged the entire town's fencing population into mourning, that population of which she had been the great artist, the special diva, the star. And after that star had burned out, that is, after the disappearance of the famous Hauteclaire, the town of V*** fell into the same lassitude and pallor that marks all small towns that have no center of activity where passions and tastes can converge. . . . The love of arms began to weaken. Lately so animated with all its martial youthfulness, the town of V*** became a sad place. The young men who, when they were in residence at their chateaus, used to come in every day to fence, now turned to firearms. They all turned into hunters and spent all their time on the grounds of their estates or in their woods, the Count de Savigny like all the others. He came less and less into V***, and when

I did encounter him, it was at the home of his wife's parents, who were patients of mine. Having no suspicion whatsoever that there could be anything between him and that Hauteclaire who had so abruptly disappeared, I had no reason to speak to him about her, and silence began to fall upon the topic, as the tongues had grown tired—nor did he speak about Hauteclaire and the times we used to see each other at her school, not making the faintest allusion to those times."

"I can hear your wooden sabots coming," I interrupted, using an expression they used in that district, which was my home region, too. "He was the one who ran off with her!"

"No—not at all!" said the doctor. "It's much better than that! You won't be able to guess what really happened. . . .

"Besides the fact that a secret elopement is not easy to pull off in the country, the Count de Savigny had never budged from his Savigny chateau.

"He lived there, as everybody very well knew, in a marriage that seemed like an endless honeymoon—and since everything is endlessly discussed and gossiped over in the country, Savigny was endlessly discussed and gossiped over, like one of those husbands who ought to be burnt alive (country humor) and his ashes thrown over all the others. God knows how many times I myself was duped by that reputation of his, and I would have gone on being duped if it hadn't happened that one day—more than a year after the disappearance of Hauteclaire Stassin—I had been called, in urgent terms, to come to the Savigny chateau, for the wife was ill. I set off immediately and, as soon as I arrived, I was shown in to the Countess who was indeed suffering from some vague and complex illness, the kind of thing that is far more dangerous than a severe attack of some more commonplace sickness. She was one of those women who come from a very old family—worn out, elegant, distinguished, haughty—one of that kind who, beneath their surface pallor and their thin frame, seems to be saying, 'Time has vanquished me, as it has all those of my race; I am dying, but I still despise you!' And the Devil can take me for feeling this way, but complete plebian that I am, and something of a philosopher, too, I can't help but see something beautiful in that. The Countess was lying on a daybed in a kind of parlor with black beams and white walls, a very large, high room, decorated in such a way as to do great honor to the taste of the counts of Savigny. A single lamp illuminated the vast room, and its light, rendered more mysterious by the green lampshade that veiled it, fell upon the face of the Countess, her cheekbones aflame with fever. She had been ill for several days now, and Savigny—in order to watch over her more carefully—had had a little bed brought into the parlor and placed next to his well-beloved better half. It was when the fever showed itself to be more powerful than his attentions that he sent for me. He stood there, his back to the fire, with a somber, anxious air, leading me to believe that he passionately loved this woman who was now in such danger. But the anxiety that marked his brow was not for her, but for another, one whom I did not guess was there at the Savigny chateau, and the sight of whom shocked me to the point of amazement. It was Hauteclaire!"

"The devil you say! He risked that!" I exclaimed to the doctor.

"Such a risk," he continued, "that I thought I was dreaming when I saw her. The Countess had asked her husband to ring for her chambermaid, who she had asked to prepare the very concoction that I was now on the verge of prescribing for her—and a few seconds later, the door opened.

"'Eulalie, do you have my drink?' she asked with some impatience.

"'Here it is, Madame!' said a voice that I recognized, and I saw emerging from the dark perimeter of the parlor, coming into the illuminated circle around the bed, Hauteclaire Stassin—yes, Hauteclaire herself!—holding a silver tray in her lovely hands, upon which steamed the cup the Countess had asked for. It took my breath away to see her! Eulalie! . . . Fortunately, that name of Eulalie, articulated so naturally, told me everything, and was like a blow with a hammer of ice to shock me back into my normal calm demeanor—which I had very nearly lost—and back into my role as the impassive, observing physician. Hauteclaire, turned into Eulalie, and the chambermaid of the Countess of Savigny! . . . Her disguise—insofar as a woman like that can disguise herself—was complete. She was dressed like one of the servant girls of V***, with that hairdo of theirs that looks like a helmet, with those long corkscrew curls trailing down the side of their cheeks—curls that preachers of the day called serpents to discourage pretty girls from wearing them, but with no effect. And underneath all that she had a beauty marked by reserve, a nobility in her cast-down eyes, which proves that these she-devils can do anything they like with their bodies, these female snakes, when they have something they want, no matter how small. . . . Having caught myself just in time, and in renewed control of myself now, like a man who has just bitten his lips to keep from crying out with surprise, I nonetheless was weak enough to have the desire to let this audacious girl know that I recognized her; and as the Countess drank, the cup obstructing her view, I looked her straight in the eyes, as directly as if I were pounding two nails in there; but her eyes—looking as soft as those of a doe that evening—were as controlled as those of the panther you just watched her stare down. She did not blink. A tiny trembling, almost imperceptible, passed through her hands as they held the serving tray. The Countess drank very slowly, and when she had finished she said: "'Very good. Take it back.'

"And Hauteclaire-Eulalie turned back and walked away with that movement I would have recognized anywhere—I could have picked her out from even among the twenty thousand gaits of the daughters of Ahasuerus—and she returned the cup and tray.[22] I confess that I avoided looking at the Count de Savigny for a moment, for I sensed what it would have meant to him to have met my gaze just then; but when I did risk looking at him, I found him staring fixedly at me, and the expression on his face passed from one of the most horrible anxiety to one of deliverance. He saw *that I had seen,* but he also saw *that I intended to pretend to see nothing,* and he let himself breathe again. He felt sure of my invincible discretion, which he probably explained to himself (not that I cared) as that of a doctor who didn't want to lose such a client as himself, whereas it was really the discretion of an inveterate observer, who didn't want to say something that would result in the door being closed to him—the door of a place with so many fascinating things going on, quite unknown to the rest of the world.

"And I left, my finger against my lips, fully resolved not to breathe a word to anyone of a thing that no one in the region suspected. Ah, the pleasures of an observer! The impersonal, solitary pleasures of the observer, which I've always ranked above all the others, and how I was going to enjoy them now, here in this obscure corner of the countryside to which, in my role as doctor, I had entrée whenever I felt like it. . . . Relieved of one anxiety, Savigny had said to me, 'Until I tell you otherwise, Doctor, please come every day.' I could therefore study—with as much interest and care as I would study a disease—the mystery in this situation, which, if it were told to someone else, would have seemed impossible. . . . And since, from the very first day, this mystery had aroused my analytic faculties, which are to the learned man and especially to the doctor what his cane is to the blind man, I immediately began thinking about this situation in order to understand it. . . . How long had it been going on? Was it ever since Hauteclaire's disappearance? Had Hauteclaire Stassin been chambermaid to the Countess de Savigny for a whole year? How was it that no one else besides me had seen it—and how was it that I had so easily been allowed to see it? All these questions leaped up on horseback along with me and accompanied me as I rode to V***, along with many others that I picked up along my route. The Count and Countess de Savigny, who seemed to adore each other, lived, it was true, largely isolated from all society. But certainly a visitor must from time to time show up at the chateau. And it was true that, if the visitors were men, Hauteclaire would not have to show herself. And if the visitors were women, well, the women of V***, by and large, had never had a good unobstructed view of that girl who kept herself in her fencing school, and who, when she did go out, seen from afar on her horse or in the church, would always be wearing a thick veil on purpose—for Hauteclaire was, as I've told you, among the proudest of the proud, the type to whom too much curiosity is an offense, the type who would hide herself in direct proportion to the degree of curiosity others had about her. As for Savigny's staff, with whom she would have to live, even if they came from V***, they would not have met her, and perhaps they were hired from elsewhere. . . .

Thus I spoke to myself as I trotted along, devising answers to these first questions, and before I got down out of the saddle I had constructed a whole edifice of more or less plausible hypotheses to explain what, to a less analytic thinker than I, would have been inexplicable. The one thing that perhaps I could not explain quite so well was Hauteclaire's extraordinary beauty, which ought to have been an obstacle to her being hired to serve the Countess de Savigny, who loved her husband and who, therefore, had to be jealous. But then, I considered that those patrician ladies of V***, as haughty as the wives of Charlemagne's paladins, would never suppose that even the most beautiful of chambermaids could ever possibly be to their husbands anything more than a handsome lackey could be to them (a grave error—but then they had not read *The Marriage of Figaro*!), and I concluded as I took my foot out of my stirrup that the Countess de Savigny must have her reasons for believing herself loved, and that that rascal Savigny no doubt had his methods of adding to those reasons."[23]

"Hmm!" I grunted skeptically to the doctor, unable to keep myself from interrupting. "All this is well and good, my dear Doctor, but still, you'd have to say the situation is highly imprudent."

"Not at all!" he replied. And then that great connoisseur of human nature added, "And what if it were that very imprudence that created the whole situation? There are certain passions that can only be ignited by imprudence, passions that, without the danger they provoke, would not exist at all. In the sixteenth century, as passionate an era as there ever was, the most magnificent incentive to love was the very danger of loving. As he left the arms of his mistress, a man was in danger of being poniarded; or the husband might put poison in his wife's sleeve, which you would kiss and act the fool about as lovers do; and all this, far from making love affairs frightening, all this danger only increased the appetite and made love irresistible! In the flat dullness of our modern day, in which law has dethroned passion, it is clear that the article stating, in the law's gross, unlovely language, its condemnation of the husband who 'introduces a concubine into the conjugal household' is an ignoble enough danger to run; but for the noble soul such a danger, perhaps because it is so ignoble, is all the more grand—and Savigny, in exposing himself to it, found there, perhaps, the sole anxious voluptuousness that can intoxicate a great mind.

"The next day, as you might imagine," Doctor Torty continued, "I was at the chateau first thing in the morning; but neither on that day, nor on the succeeding days, did I see anything that was at all unlike any other household. Neither on the part of the patient nor on that of the Count, nor even on that of the false Eulalie, who went about her work as naturally as if she had been born for nothing else, did I observe anything that could give me any further information about the secret I had stumbled upon. The one thing that was certain was that the Count de Savigny and Hauteclaire Stassin were playing out the most staggeringly imprudent of dramas with all the naturalness of consummate actors. But what was less certain, and what I was most curious about, was whether the Countess was really their dupe, and if she were, how long she could possibly remain so. And therefore I concentrated my attention on the Countess. It was very easy for me to see her since she was my patient and her illness made her the natural focus of my observations. She was a true lady of V*** in this one particular respect: *she knew nothing about anything* beyond the fact that she was noble, and that outside of the nobility, life offered nothing worthy of her attention. Among the women of V*** of the higher classes, the sense of their own nobility is the only thing that impassions them. Mademoiselle Delphine de Cantor was raised among the Benedictine nuns and, having no religious vocation, was horribly bored there; she left, only in order to be bored among her own family, up until the moment she married the Count de Savigny whom she loved, or believed she loved, with all the alacrity that bored young girls have when it comes to falling in love with the first man introduced to them. She was a pale woman, soft of skin but hard of bone; her skin was the color of milk, but milk into which some bran has been mixed, for the little red freckles that dotted it were certainly darker than her hair, which was a lovely russet. When she held out her pale arm to me, with its pearly blue veins and its thin, aristocratic wrist through which a pulse beat as languidly as normal, she gave me the impression of having been created and placed in the world solely in order to be a victim . . . to be trampled under the feet of the fiercely proud Hautclaire, who pretended to bow before her as a servant. But that impression, which arose from one's first look at her, was contradicted by the upraised chin at the extremity of that thin face—a chin like Fulvia's on Roman coins, looking quite lost on such a pretty little face—and also by the bulging forehead beneath her fringe of lusterless hair.[24] Altogether, it made me doubt my analysis. As for the trampling feet of Hauteclaire, perhaps that was the difficulty—for it was impossible that a situation like the one I was observing in this presently tranquil household could continue without some frightful explosion. . . . And so, with a view to that future explosion, I redoubled my efforts at examining that tiny woman, who could not remain a closed book for long to her physician. When you know the body, you quickly come to know the heart. If there were moral, or immoral, causes for the current illness of the Countess, she could try to roll them up tightly and hide them from me, but sooner or later she would have to reveal them. That is what I told myself; and believe me, I kept her in my medical grip and turned her every way I could. But it was clear to me after a few days that she had not the slightest suspicion of her husband's and Hauteclaire's complicity in the domestic crime being played out in the silent, discreet theater of that house. . . . Was it a weak intelligence on her part? A repression of her jealous feelings? What was it? . . . She had maintained a proud reserve toward the entire world except her husband. With the false Eulalie who served her, she was commanding but gentle. That might seem contradictory. But it isn't at all. It's the simple truth. She gave her orders curtly, but she never raised her voice, the voice of a woman created to be, and confident of being, obeyed. . . . And she was obeyed, admirably. Eulalie, that frightening Eulalie, insinuated herself into the room silently and, I don't know how, enveloped the sick woman with so much care that it was just short of being tiresome, and her service showed such a finesse and a knowledge of her mistress's character that it seemed to reflect her own good will and intelligence. . . . I soon brought myself to speak to the Countess about this Eulalie, whom

I watched circling around her bed so naturally during my visits, and who made a chill run down my spine, as if I had come upon a serpent unawares—and watched it unroll itself, and extend itself, without the slightest sound, and slither toward the bed of a sleeping woman. . . . One evening when the Countess had told her to go fetch something, I forget what, I took advantage of her rapid, light-footed exit to hazard an observation that might bring something to light.

"'What velvet footsteps!' I said, watching her leave the room. 'Madame Countess, you have an extraordinary maid there, I would say. May I ask where you found her? Is the girl by any chance from V***?'

"'Yes, she's been a good servant to me,' the Countess replied in an indifferent tone as she continued to gaze into her hand mirror, framed with green velour and decorated with peacock feathers, in that impertinent tone one adopts when one is entirely occupied by something other than what one is saying to you. 'I couldn't be happier with her. She is not from V***, but I really don't know where she comes from. Ask Monsieur de Savigny if you want to know, Doctor, for he is the one who brought her to me, shortly after our wedding. She had been a servant—he told me in introducing her to me—at the home of some elderly cousin of his who had recently died, and she was left without employment. I trusted him implicitly, and I was wise to do so. She is the perfect lady's maid. I don't think she has a single fault.'

"'Well, I can think of one, Madame Countess,' I said, in a pretended grave tone.

"'Oh? And what is that?' she said languidly with that same complete indifference, as she continued to study her pale lips in the little mirror.

"'She is too beautiful,' I said. 'She is really too beautiful for a lady's maid. One of these days, someone will run off with her.'

"'Do you think so?' she asked, continuing to gaze into the mirror, still distractedly.

"'And it will be, perhaps, some man from your level of society who will become infatuated with her, Madame Countess. She is beautiful enough to turn the head of a duke.'

"I carefully observed the effect of my words as I spoke them. It was an attempt to sound her; but if there were no result, I couldn't try it a second time.

"'There is no duke in V***,' the Countess replied, her forehead remaining as placid as the glass into which she gazed. 'And anyway, all those sorts of girls, Doctor,' she added, smoothing one of her eyebrows, 'when they want to leave won't be held back by any affection you have for them. Eulalie does charming work, but she would abuse my affections just like all the rest, so I'm very careful not to grow attached to her.'

"And there was no more discussion of Eulalie that day. The Countess was entirely taken in. And who wouldn't have been? Even I—who had known Hauteclaire, seen her many times with her épée in her father's fencing school—even I had moments when I was tempted to believe in Eulalie. Savigny was far less natural and easy in his lying than she was, but she! Oh, she lived and moved in it like the supplest fish in water. She certainly must have loved him, and loved him in a strange way, to do what she was doing, to have planted herself here in this bizarre existence when she could have had her vanity flattered every day by having the eyes of every man in town upon her—that little town, a universe to her—where later on she would have found her admirers and worshippers and from among them picked out one to marry, and then moved up into a higher level of society, a level of which so far she had known only the men. Her lover certainly had less at stake than she did. In terms of devotion, he was the inferior. His masculine pride must have suffered at being unable to spare his mistress the indignity of so humiliating a situation. There was even something that didn't quite fit with the impetuosity of character people attributed to Savigny. If he loved Hauteclaire to the point of sacrificing his young wife, he could have carried her off and taken her to live with him in Italy—a thing that was easily done in those days—without making her go through this abomination of being a concubine. Did he, then, love her less? . . . Did he passively let himself be loved by Hauteclaire, more than actively love her himself? . . . Was it Hauteclaire on her own who had broken through the defenses of the conjugal home? And did he, finding the thing audacious and stimulating, welcome this new version of the Potiphar story into his house to provide him with constant, rekindled temptation?[25] What I could see told me little about Savigny and Hauteclaire. Accomplices—they were certainly that!—in some kind of adultery, but what were the feelings at the base of the adultery? This was the unknown variable in my algebra; this was what I needed to solve. Savigny was irreproachable when he was with his wife; but when Hauteclaire-Eulalie was present, I could see out of the corner of my eye that he made little adjustments suggesting he was not at peace inside. When, in the course of ordinary daily life, he would ask his wife's maid for a book, a newspaper, some object or other, he had a way of taking the object from her that would have revealed everything to anyone other than this schoolgirl raised by the Benedictines, this woman he had married. . . . I could see that he was afraid to let his hand touch that of Hauteclaire, as if in touching it by accident he should find himself unable to let it go. Hauteclaire didn't show any such hesitations and needed to take no nervous precautions. . . . A temptress, like they all are, willing to tempt God Himself in His heaven, if there is one, and the Devil in his hell, she seemed to want to make it all more tense just to enhance the danger and, thus, the desire. I saw this once or twice—on a day when my visit coincided with their dinnertime, which Savigny always spent piously by his wife's bedside. It was Eulalie who did the serving, the other domestics never entering the Countess's rooms. In order to place the dishes on the table, she had to bend over Savigny's shoulder, and in doing so the folds of her dress caressed the neck and ears of the count, who went entirely pale . . . and who glanced up to see if his wife had noticed. By God, I was young in those days, and the agitation of the molecules in the organization of the body, well, that seemed to me to be about the only thing worth living for. So I imagined that there must be quite a thrill in that concubinage disguised as a false servant, right in front of the abused wife's eyes, when she could guess the truth at any moment. Oh yes, concubinage in the conjugal home, as our delightfully proper law puts it—at that moment, I understood it!

"But, apart from the going pale and the passing, near-trance states of Savigny, I saw no evidence of the drama the two were playing out, or of its impending catastrophe . . . which I saw as inevitable. What were the two of them up to? That was the secret of their story, and finding it was my goal. It gripped my thinking like the claw of a sphinx, so much so that I went from observation to *espionage*—which is another word for observation at any cost. Ha! A strong hunger or thirst will often enough deprave us. . . . To uncover some facts, I permitted myself any number of low, base actions, quite unworthy of me—which I recognized at the time, yet I went ahead and did them anyway. It's the habit of observation, my friend! I observed everywhere. When I arrived at the chateau, taking my horse to the stable, I would get the servants to gossip about their masters, without seeming to be interested in the topic. I *sneaked* around—oh, I won't spare myself the word!— to satisfy my curiosity. But the servants were taken in just as much as the Countess. They took Hauteclaire-Eulalie on good faith as one of theirs, and I would have had nothing at all for all my pains if it had not been for chance, for an accident that, as it usually does, told me more than all my spying did.

"I had been coming to see the Countess for more than two months, and her health had not improved; instead, it had worsened into that condition, so common today, that the doctors of this neurotic age call *anemia*. Savigny and Hauteclaire continued to play, with the same perfection, their roles in the very difficult drama that my arrival had done nothing to disturb. Nevertheless, one might have been able to perceive just a bit of fatigue in the actors. Serlon had lost weight, and I had heard people talking in V***: 'What a model husband Savigny is! His wife's illness has changed his appearance so much—what a fine example of love and sympathy!' Hauteclaire, in her changeless beauty, kept her eyes lowered, the way one does when one has been crying— though those eyes of hers had perhaps never in her whole life shed so much as a single tear; but now they looked the way eyes look when one has gone too often without sleep, yet this only made those eyes shine all the more ardently from within the dark violet circling them. Savigny's loss of weight and the rings around Hauteclaire's eyes might have had some cause other than the highly compressed lives they had imposed on themselves. They could have arisen from any number of things, living on top of a volcano as they were! I took note of those telltale signs on their faces, continuing to wonder without coming to any conclusion, when one day, out making my medical rounds in the neighborhood in the evening, I found myself on Savigny's land. My intention had been to proceed to the chateau, as I usually did, but a very difficult childbirth in the countryside had made me quite late, so that when I came to pass the chateau, it was already too late for me to go in. I'm not even sure what time it was. My hunting watch had stopped. But on the great dial of the sky, the moon had passed midnight, having begun its descent down its curved path, just touching the tops of the tall pines of Savigny, behind which it was soon going to disappear. . . .

"Have you ever been to Savigny?" asked the Doctor, interrupting himself suddenly and turning toward me. When I nodded, he said, "Yes. Well then! You know that one has to enter the forest of pines and pass along the walls of the chateau, that you have to double around it like a cape, in order to get to the road that leads directly to V***. . . . All of a sudden, in the thick blackness of that forest in which I saw not a glimmer of light nor a whisper of sound, I heard a noise like that of someone beating clothes—probably the work of some poor woman who had been busy in the fields all day, and who was taking advantage of the moonlight to launder her linen in some spring or some ditch. . . . But as I advanced toward the chateau, that regular sound mixed with another one, which finally explained the original sound. It was the clicking sound of fencing swords crossing, rubbing, and rattling together. You know how, in the clear night air, you can hear the slightest sounds with the greatest precision! I listened, and I could not have been mistaken—it was the lively sound of clashing steel. An idea crossed my mind; and when I had come out of the chateau's pine forest, in the white moonlight, where a window was open:

"'Well!' I said to myself, admiring the power that tastes and habits have over us. 'This must be their way of making love!'

"Clearly, it was Serlon and Hauteclaire at arms at that hour. You could hear the épées as well as if you were seeing them. What I had taken for the sound of beating clothes were the *appels du pied,* the footwork, of the fencers. The opened window was in the pavilion farthest, of the four, from the Countess's bedroom. The sleeping chateau, dreary and white in the moonlight, was like some dead thing. . . . Everything apart from this carefully chosen pavilion, where the window, ornamented by a balcony, was partly obscured by half-open Venetian blinds—everything else was silence and shadow; but through those zebra stripes of light coming through the blinds came the double sound of those *appels du pied* and their clashing foils. I could hear it so clearly that I guessed, correctly as you'll see in a moment, that since the evening was so warm (this was in July), they would have opened the half-door under the Venetian blinds that gave onto the balcony. I had stopped my horse at the edge of the woods, listening to what sounded like a very vigorous match, finding it highly interesting, this armed assault between two people who had fallen in love while armed and who continued to love each other in that manner, when, after some time had passed, the clicking of the foils and the beating sounds of their footwork ceased. The blinds above the balcony door were opened, and to avoid being seen in that bright moonlight, I barely had time to get my horse back under the shadows of the pines. Serlon and Hauteclaire came out and rested their elbows on the balcony's iron railing. I could see them wonderfully. The moon descended behind the little forest, but the light of a candelabra behind them threw them both into high relief. Hauteclaire was dressed, if you could call it that, as I had so often seen her when she gave her lessons in V***, in a tight leather jacket that served as a cuirass, and her legs in skintight silk hose revealed their muscular contours. Savigny was wearing a similar costume. Both of them svelte and robust and standing framed in that luminous niche, they looked like beautiful statues representing Youth and Power. You admired the proud beauty of both of them just now in this garden, so you can see that the years have not destroyed it yet. Well, try to add to the magnificence of this couple by imagining how they looked to me then, standing on that balcony in those tight clothes suggestive of nudity. They were speaking, leaning on the railing, though their voices were too low for me to hear what they were saying; but their bodies spoke clearly enough. At one point, Savigny let his arm passionately encircle the waist of that Amazon who seemed capable of resisting all advances yet did not resist. . . . And the proud Hauteclaire responded by putting her arms around Serlon; the two of them formed something like that famous, voluptuous sculpture by Canova that everyone remembers,[26] and they remained sculpted like that, lips touching lips, for a long time, long enough, my God, to drink a whole bottle full of kisses! It lasted a total of sixty pulses—which I counted on this pulse that was pounding far more rapidly than it is at present, and which the spectacle was causing to pound even faster. . . .

"'Oh! Oh!' I said as I came out of my hiding place under the trees once they had gone back in, still wrapped around each other closely; they went back in and lowered the curtains, the thick, heavy curtains. 'One of these days they will have to confide in me. And it won't be just the two of them that they'll have to hide then!' As a doctor, I foresaw the consequences of those caresses and that all-revealing intimacy. But my prophecy turned out to be false, probably due to their very ardor. You know as well as I that when people love too much" (here the cynical Doctor used another term) "they don't make babies. The next morning, I went to Savigny. I found Hauteclaire turned back into Eulalie, sitting in a window seat on the long corridor that led to her mistress's room, a pile of linen and chiffon in front of her, which she was busily trimming and mending—she, the swordswoman of the night before! Could it be? I asked myself, seeing her there in her white apron, thinking of the forms I had seen, almost nude, framed on the balcony, half-drowned here in the folds of a dress, but not entirely hidden. . . . I walked past her without speaking, for I spoke to her as little as possible, not wanting to seem to know what I knew, which might have filtered through my voice or my glance. I felt much less capable as an actor than she was, and it made me nervous. . . . Normally, when I came down this corridor, where she was usually working when she wasn't serving the Countess directly, she was so sure that it was I that she would not even raise her head. She remained looking downward, under her starched cap, or under her horned coiffure that resembled that of Isabel of Bavaria, her eyes fixed on her work and her pale, oval face partly hidden by the long bluish-black curls that hung down, so that all I could see was a curved neck with thick curls, a neck that arched itself like the desires to which it gave rise.[27] It was the animal aspect of Hauteclaire that was superb. No other woman, I suspect, has her kind of beauty. . . . The men, who say everything to each other in private, often made the same point. At V***, when she was giving her fencing lessons, the men privately called her Mademoiselle Esau. . . .[28] The Devil teaches women their true natures—or, rather, they teach them to the Devil, if by chance he doesn't know already. . . . Hauteclaire, scarcely what one would call coquettish, nonetheless had a habit of twisting those long, thick curls on her neck around her fingers when one spoke to her, the rebel curls that had escaped the chignon, a single one of which was enough to 'ravish the heart,' as the Bible puts it.[29] She knew very well the effect this gesture had, and the ideas to which it gave rise! But now, in her role as lady's maid, I never once saw her indulge in the gesture, as powerful as the flame is to the moth, even when looking at Savigny.

"My friend, this has been a long parenthesis, but I needed to give you as much information as I could if you are to understand Hauteclaire Stassin and my story. . . . On that day, she was obliged to quit her work in the corridor and let me see her face, for the Countess rang for her and told her to bring me some ink and paper for the prescription I wanted to write, and she came. She came, her little steel thimble still on her finger, and she had stuck her threading needle in her dress against her provocative breast, where she had stuck a great many others, pressed tightly together and looking like a steel ornament. Even the steel of those needles seemed to go well with the diabolic nature of this girl, made for steel, who in the Middle Ages would have worn a cuirass. She continued to stand there in front of me while I wrote, offering me the writing tablet with that same noble, smooth motion of the forearms that her habit of swordplay had taught her. When I had finished, I raised my eyes and looked at her, so as not to seem unnatural, and I saw in her face the fatigue from the night she had spent. Savigny, who had not been there when I arrived, now suddenly came in. He seemed even more fatigued than she did. . . . He spoke with me about the Countess's condition, which was not improving. He spoke like a man impatient with this nonrecovery. His tone was the bitter, violent, abrupt tone of an impatient man. He paced back and forth as he talked. I watched him coolly, thinking this act was a bit overdone, and a bit annoyed with the Napoleonic tone he was taking with me. 'But if I cured your wife,' I thought, insolently, 'you wouldn't be able to go fencing and making love all night long with your mistress.' If I wanted to, I could have brought him back to reality and to the manners he was forgetting by putting the smelling salts of a sharp reply under his nose. But I contented myself with looking at him. He was growing more interesting than ever now, for it was perfectly obvious at this point that he was acting."

The Doctor stopped here for a moment. He plunged his thick thumb and index finger into his engraved silver snuffbox and pulled out a pinch of Macoubac, as he pompously called his tobacco.[30] He seemed so interesting to me that I made no remarks at all, and he took up the story again, after having absorbed his pinch of snuff and run his crooked finger over his birdlike beak.

"Oh, as for being impatient, that he really was; but he was not at all impatient for his wife to recover, that woman to whom he had been so determinedly unfaithful! What a devil! If he was going to cheat on her with a servant in her own house, he could hardly be impatient for her to get better! Or was it that her cure would make the adultery more of a challenge? But it was true that carrying the wickedness on for so long had worn on his nerves. Had he expected it to go on this long? And then the thought crossed my mind that, if the idea of having it over had occurred to either him or her, or to both of them, since neither the illness nor the doctor was going to finish her off, perhaps this was the time . . ."

"What? Doctor, but did they—"

I couldn't finish my sentence, for it took my breath away, the idea he had just suggested!

He lowered his head and looked at me, as tragic as the statue of the Commendatore when he accepts the supper.[31]

"Yes!" he said softly, in tune with the soberness of my thoughts. "Anyway, a few days later, everyone heard with horror that the Countess had been poisoned and was dead."

"Poisoned!" I exclaimed.

"By her maid Eulalie, who had mistaken one bottle for another, and had given her mistress a bottle of printing ink instead of the medicine I had prescribed.[32] Such a mistake was, of course, possible. But I knew that Eulalie was Hauteclaire! I had seen the two of them, making that Canova statue, on the balcony! No one else had seen what I had seen. Everyone else simply assumed it had been a terrible accident, at first. But when, two years after this disaster, people learned that the Count Serlon de Savigny was publicly marrying *Stassin's daughter*—for it had to *explode,* at last, the real identity of the false Eulalie—and that he was going to put her in the still warm bed of his first wife, Mademoiselle Delphine de Cantor, oh, then there was a thunderous rumbling of suspicions voiced at first quietly, as if people were afraid to say out loud what they were thinking. But ultimately, no one knew for sure. All they knew about for sure was this monstrous misalliance, which ostracized Savigny and isolated him like a leper. And that was enough. You know what a dishonor such a thing is or, rather, was (for things have greatly changed in that region since those days), to say of a man, 'He has married his servant!' The dishonor stuck to Serlon and remained on him like a stain. As for the horrible gossip about the crime they suspected him of, it fed on itself for a while and then died off, like an engorged horsefly falling dead in a rut. But there was somebody, nonetheless, who did know and who was sure . . ."

"And that could only be you, Doctor?" I interrupted.

"Yes, it was I," he continued, "but not only I. If I were the only one who knew, I would never have had those vague glimmerings, which are worse than ignorance. . . . I would never have been sure, and"—he emphasized his words now with absolute certainty—"I am sure!

"And let me tell you how I am so sure!" he added, clutching my knee with his gnarled fingers, which felt like a pair of pincers. But his story had pinched me even harder, gripped me more tightly, than the crablike joints of his formidable hand.

"You would assume," he went on, "that I was the first to know about the Countess's poisoning. Guilty or not, they had to send for me, for I was the doctor. They didn't even take the time to saddle a horse. A boy from the stable came bareback and at full gallop to find me in V***, from which I followed him, also at full gallop, to Savigny. When I arrived—had they planned on it?—it was too late to arrest the ravages of the poison. Serlon, wearing a devastated expression, came into the courtyard to meet me, telling me quietly as I disengaged from my stirrups, as if he were afraid one of the domestics would overhear:

"'A servant has made a mistake.' (He did not name Eulalie, which everyone knew by the next day.) 'But Doctor, is it possible? Can printing ink be a poison?'

"'It depends on its composition,' I replied. He brought me to the Countess, who looked wrung out with pain, her twisted, tightened face looking like a ball of white thread that had fallen into green dye. She looked frightening. She smiled hideously at me with her blackened lips, with the sort of smile one would use to imply, 'I know what you're thinking. . . .' I glanced quickly around the room for Eulalie, who was nowhere to be found. I wanted to see her face at such a moment. She was not there. Courageous as she was otherwise, was she afraid of me? Oh, at that moment, I had only uncertain ideas. . . .

"Seeing me, the Countess made an effort and raised herself up on one elbow.

"'Ah, there you are, Doctor,' she said, 'but you've come too late. I'm dying. Serlon, don't send for the doctor—send for the priest. Go now! Order him to come and have everyone leave so I may have a moment alone with the Doctor. These are my wishes!'

"She said, '*These are my wishes*' as I've never heard it said before— like a woman with the chin and the forehead that I've described to you.

"'Even me?' asked Savigny in a weak voice.

"'Even you,' she replied. And she added, in a caressing tone,

'You know, my dear friend, that women have certain modesties to uphold in front of their loved ones.'

"As soon as he was gone, there was a horrible change in her. From sweetness she changed to savagery.

"'Doctor,' she began in a hate-filled voice, 'this death of mine is no accident but a crime. Serlon is in love with Eulalie, and she has poisoned me! I didn't believe you when you said the girl was too beautiful to be a chambermaid. I was wrong. He loves that creature, that execrable girl who has murdered me. He's even guiltier because he loves her and he betrayed me for her. For the past several days, the glances they've exchanged with each other across my bed have alerted me to it all. And then there is this horrible taste of the ink they've used to poison me! . . . But I drank it all, I took it all, despite the hideous taste, because I was perfectly ready to die! Don't tell me about any antidotes. I don't want any of your remedies. I want to die.'

"'But then why did you have me come, Madame Countess?'

"'Well, then—here is why,' she said, breathing with difficulty.

"'It was in order to tell you that they have poisoned me, and to have you give me your word of honor that you will not reveal it. All this will make a terrible scandal. But it doesn't have to. You are my doctor, and people will believe you when you tell them about this lie they've invented, and when you add that even if it hadn't been for the poison, you could not have saved my life, for my state of health had become so poor. Swear it to me, Doctor . . .'

"And when I did not immediately reply, she saw what I was thinking. I thought that she loved her husband to the point of wanting to save him. That was the idea that came to me, an idea perfectly natural and perfectly vulgar, for there are some women so steeped in love and its self-denials that they would not fight back against the blow that killed them. But the Countess de Savigny never seemed to me to be remotely like such women!

"'Ah, it's not what you think, Doctor, that makes me ask you to swear to this! Oh, no! I hate Serlon too much right now, but despite his betrayal, I could love him again. . . . But I'm not so cowardly as to pardon him! I leave this life feeling jealous of him and feeling implacable. But it's not just about Serlon, Doctor,' she continued energetically, showing me a whole new side of her character, a side I had missed because it was hidden so deeply. 'It's about the Count de Savigny. I don't want the Count de Savigny, after I am dead, to be called the murderer of his wife. I don't want for him to be hauled into a courtroom, accused of complicity with an adulterous, poisoning servant! I wore the name of Savigny, and I don't want that stain on the name. Oh, if it were only about him, he would be worthy of gracing any gallows in the country! Oh, him, him—I could eat his heart! But it's about all of us, including the respectable people! If we were still the way we used to be, I would have had that Eulalie thrown into some forgotten hole of a dungeon in the chateau, and she would never be spoken of again! But nowadays, we are no longer our own masters. We no longer command our own swift and silent justice, and I don't want the scandal and the publicity of yours, Doctor; I would rather leave them in each other's arms, happy together and freed from me, and die in a state of rage than to think, as I die, that the nobility of V*** would have the disgrace of counting a poisoner among their ranks.'

"She spoke with an unheard of intensity despite her shivering, which made her teeth chatter and grind hard enough to break them. I recognized her, but I was still learning who she was! Clearly, the aristocratic woman was at the core of her being, and here in death it trumped the jealous wife. She died a death worthy of a daughter of V***, the last noble town in France! And moved by the spectacle more, perhaps, than I should have been, I promised, I swore that if I could not save her, I would do as she wished.

"And I did, my friend. I did not save her. I could not save her: she stubbornly refused every remedy. After her death, I said what she wanted me to say, and I was persuasive. . . . It's been twenty-five years now. . . . Now, everything about that frightening adventure is calm, silenced, forgotten. Many of the contemporaries have died. New generations, ignorant and indifferent, are making their way to their own tombs; and the first person I've told about this whole sinister story is you!

"And we had to have seen what we've just seen for me to be able to tell it to you. We had to have seen those two creatures, unchangingly beautiful despite the years, unchangingly happy despite their crime, strong, passionate, absorbed in each other, passing just as superbly through life as they just did through this garden, looking like two altarpiece angels who have come to life and risen, united in the shadow cast by their four golden wings!"

I was paralyzed with horror. "But," I said, "if what you've told me is true, Doctor, there has to be some hideous disorder in creation if it allows those people to be happy."

"A disorder, or perhaps an order, whichever you prefer," replied Doctor Torty, a thoroughgoing and tranquil atheist, like the people whose story he had told. "But in any case, it's a fact. They are exceptionally happy, offensively happy. I'm an old man, and I've seen many happinesses that failed to last; but I've never seen one so profound, one that endures forever!

"And believe me, I've thought about it, studied it, analyzed it, thought about it some more! Believe me, I've looked everywhere to find the little crack in the wall, the tiny flaw in that happiness! Pardon the expression, but I might say I have combed through and deloused that happiness. . . . I've looked into the lives of these two creatures as deeply and as carefully as I could to see if there wasn't some rupture or gap somewhere in their shocking and revolting happiness, even some very small one, hidden away somewhere; but I've never found anything but an enviable felicity, a fact that would give the Devil a fine and triumphant little tale to tell God about, if there were a God and a Devil! After the death of the Countess, I remained, as you can well imagine, on good terms with Savigny. Since I had done all I could to support the story they had concocted about the poisoning, they had no reason to want to avoid me, and I had every reason to want to find out what was going to happen next, what they were going to do, what they were going to become. I was horrified, but I overcame my horror. . . . What came next was, first, the mourning period for Savigny, set at the usual two years, during which he confirmed the public opinion of himself as having been the most excellent of husbands past, present, and future. . . . During those two years, he saw no visitors at all. He shut himself up inside his chateau so completely that nobody knew that he had kept Eulalie on, she who had been the inadvertent cause of his wife's death, she whom he should have thrown out immediately, if only for appearance's sake, even if he had been convinced of her innocence. This imprudence in keeping such a girl with him in his home after such a catastrophe demonstrated to me the irrational passion that I had suspected drove Serlon. And so I was not at all surprised when, one day upon returning from my doctor's rounds, I ran into a servant on the Savigny road and, when I asked him for news about what was going on in the chateau, he told me that Eulalie was still there. He said it with such indifference that I could tell no one among the Count's domestics suspected that Eulalie was his mistress. 'They're taking a real risk,' I said to myself. 'Why don't they leave the country? The Count is rich. He could live on a grand scale anywhere he wished. And why not take along this beautiful she-devil (and when it comes to she-devils, yes, this is one that I do believe in) who, in order to knit herself more closely to him, preferred to live in her lover's house, risking everything, instead of being his mistress in V*** and living in some out-of-the-way place where they could meet discreetly?' There was something going on there that I could not fathom. Their madness, the way they greedily devoured each other—were they, then, so great that they were above the necessary prudence and caution that life requires? Hauteclaire, whose character was, I thought, stronger than that of Serlon, Hauteclaire, whom I took to be the man in their relationship—did she want to stay in that chateau where she had been seen as a servant so that she could now be seen as its mistress, and in staying on there, did she consider the scandal of it, and the even greater scandal that would come from marrying the Count de Savigny? If the idea had occurred to her, it had not occurred to me, at that point in the story. Hauteclaire Stassin, daughter of that old mainstay of the fencing school, old Saber-tip, whom we had all seen in V*** giving her lessons and *se fendre à fond* in her tight hose—this girl, the Countess de Savigny![33] Oh, impossible! Who would have believed such a turnaround, such an end-of-the-world event? Oh! Well, by God, what I believed was that these two fierce beasts would privately drag their affair on, and that they would come to see that they were both of the same species and that they had dared to carry on their adultery right before the eyes of the Countess. But a marriage, a marriage performed boldly in the sight of God and of other people—such a defiance hurled in the face of the entire country's opinion, such an outrage upon the sentiments and mores—I swear, I was a thousand miles from believing it would happen when, at the end of the two-year period, the thing did suddenly take place, and it struck me like a thunderbolt, as if I were one of those country imbeciles who never expects anything that's obviously about to happen and then, when it does happen, goes whining around like a whipped dog, moaning and whimpering at every crossroads.

"In any case, during those two years of Serlon's mourning, so strictly observed but, when people saw how it all turned out, so furiously accused of hypocrisy and baseness, I didn't go to the Savigny chateau very often. . . . What would I have done there? . . . They both seemed to be healthy, and until that moment when I would be summoned on some night to take care of a childbirth that I would then be asked to conceal, they had no need of my services. Nevertheless, from time to time I risked a visit to the Count. Politeness, you see, but fueled by redoubled curiosity. Serlon would greet me in this place or that, wherever he happened to be, when I arrived. He exhibited not the slightest embarrassment around me. He had recovered his kindly manner. He was serious. I've often noticed that the happiest people are serious. They carry their heart attentively within them, like a full cup that the slightest movement might cause to spill or break. . . . Despite his gravity and his black mourning clothes, Serlon's eyes revealed an expression of immense felicity, an expression that cannot be counterfeited. It was no longer the expression of relief and deliverance that I had observed on that day in his wife's room when he saw that I recognized Hauteclaire and saw also that I would pretend not to recognize her. No, not at all! This was a fine, handsome, truly happy expression. Although we only talked, during these brief formal visits, about superficial things, the Count de Savigny's voice, in saying such things, was not the same voice he had used when his wife was alive. It revealed now, in the warm fullness of its intonations, that he had to struggle to contain the feelings within him. As for Hauteclaire (still Eulalie and, as the servant had told me, still at the chateau), it was a long time before I encountered her again. When I walked down that long corridor, she was no longer there as she had been during the Countess's time, working in her window seat. Yet the little heap of linen in the same spot, the scissors and the sewing kit and the thimble on the windowsill, all implied that she must continue to work there, on that empty seat, still warm perhaps, that she had quitted upon hearing me coming. You'll recall that I was stupid enough to believe that she feared my penetrating gaze; but now she had nothing to fear. She did not know that I had received the terrible confidences of the Countess. With her audacious and haughty nature, she would have been happy to brave anyone's gaze, anyone's insights. And I knew this for a fact, for the day when I finally did see her again, her state of happiness was written so clearly on her expression that you could not have effaced it if you had poured over it that whole bottle of printing ink she had used to poison the Countess!

"It was on the great staircase of the chateau where I finally encountered her again. She was coming down as I was going up. She was descending rapidly, but when she saw me, she slowed down—no doubt with the intent of looking me directly in the eyes; but if her gaze could close a panther's eyes, it could not close mine. Coming rapidly down the steps of her staircase, her skirts floated behind her, creating the impression that she had just descended from heaven. Her happiness made her sublime. Oh, her air was fifteen thousand times more intense than Serlon's! But nonetheless, I passed by her without making any polite nod, for if Louis XIV was said to have greeted his chambermaids on the staircase, at least his were not murderers! Chambermaid—that's what she still was on that day, wearing the clothes and the white apron of that rank; but now the air of the most joyful, the most triumphant and despotic mistress had replaced that of the impassive slave girl. And she has never lost that air. We've just seen her, and you can judge for yourself. That expression is more striking than the actual beauty of the face it illuminates. That superhuman air, that air of pride in a happy love affair that she must have given to Serlon who at first did not show it—they have it still, after twenty years, and I've never seen it diminished or even veiled for an instant on the faces of these two Privileged Ones. They respond to everything with that same air, victoriously, to being ignored, to slander, to the contempt of outraged public opinion, and with that air they convince everyone who encounters them that the crime of which they've been accused must be an atrocious calumny."

"But you, Doctor," I broke in, "with all that you know, you haven't been fooled by them, have you? After all, you haven't followed them everywhere, and you haven't seen them at every hour of the day."

"Not in their bedroom at night, no, but I'm quite sure they're not unhappy there," said Doctor Torty jokingly, but seriously at the same time. "I've observed them, I would say, at all the points of their lives since their marriage—which was performed who knows where, in order to avoid the uproar that the general populace of V*** would have raised, just as furious in their way as the nobility were in theirs. When they returned married, she authentically the Countess de Savigny now, and he absolutely dishonored by having married a servant, they took up residence there, in their chateau. People turned their backs on them. They could feed on each other as much as they wanted. . . . But they were never tired of such feeding, apparently; even today, they hunger only for each other. As for me, I don't want to die until I've written a treatise on teratology, and these two interest me . . . like a pair of monsters, so I will by no means join the crowd that shuns them.[34] When I saw the false Eulalie become the Countess, she received me as if she had been one all her life. It didn't matter to her that I could still picture her in her white apron, carrying her serving platter! 'I am no longer Eulalie,' she said to me. 'I am Hauteclaire, Hauteclaire happy to have been servant to him. . . .' I thought to myself that she had been something else as well; but since I was the only one who continued to visit the chateau when they had returned there, I swallowed my shame, and I ended up visiting there often. I will say that I persevered, though, and kept trying to pierce through to the truth about the intimacy between these two beings whom love had made so completely happy. Well, you may believe me or not, my friend, but this happiness, grounded as it was in a foul crime of which I was certain, was never so much as clouded, let alone tarnished. A dirty, cowardly crime, one that did not even have the courage to be bloody—and I never saw so much as a spot on the perfect azure sky of their happiness! It's enough to hurl to the ground, wouldn't you say, all the moralists' theories, and all their fine axioms about vice being punished and virtue rewarded! Abandoned and isolated as they were, seeing no one but me, their doctor who had become almost a friend, still they didn't even bother to be on their guard around me. They forgot about me and continued to live very well, with me present, swept up in the intoxication of that passion beyond comparison, I tell you, to anything I've ever seen in life. . . . You witnessed it yourself just a moment ago: they walked past us and they never even noticed me, though I was right at their elbow! And for most of the time I spent with them, they never noticed me either. . . . Polite and affable but usually distracted, they behaved toward me in such a way that I would never have come back to Savigny if I hadn't been determined to put that incredible happiness under a microscope, in order to find, for my own personal edification, the tiny grain of sand of ennui, or of pain, or of, let me say it, the grand word, *remorse*. But nothing! Nothing! Love dominated everything, penetrated everything, swallowed up everything, including morality and conscience—as you would say, you others; and it was in observing them that I was reminded of something my old friend Broussais[35] liked to say about the conscience: 'I've been dissecting bodies for thirty years, and I've never uncovered so much as a trace of any such little animal!'

"And don't misunderstand me," continued that old devil, Doctor Torty, as if he had just read my mind. "What I'm telling you here is not to prove some thesis . . . proving some doctrine that I believe to be true having to do with the conscience that Broussais denied. No, there is no thesis here. I am not trying to undermine your opinions or change your mind. . . . These are only facts, and they've stunned me as much as they've stunned you. It is a phenomenon only, an uninterrupted happiness, a soap bubble that continues to grow and never cracks or bursts! When happiness is uninterrupted, that's already quite a surprise; but this happiness in crime, this is amazing, and I've been in that state of amazement for twenty years now. The old doctor, the old observer, the old moralist . . . or, rather, *immoralist*" (he added this, seeing my smile) "feels disconcerted by the spectacle he's been watching for all those years, and which he can't relate to you in concrete detail, for as the old truism—and how true it is!—has it, happiness has no history. No more description is possible. You can't paint happiness, that infusion of a higher, superior life into this life, any more than you could paint the circulation of the blood in the veins. The beating of the arteries attests to the fact that it is circulating, and in the same way I'm attesting to the happiness of the two beings you've just seen, that incomprehensible happiness whose pulse I've taken for so long now. The Count and Countess de Savigny replay every day that magnificent chapter of Madame de Staël's *Love in Marriage,* or the even more magnificent lines in Milton's *Paradise Lost.*[36] As for me, I've never been very sentimental, much less poetical, but in realizing the ideal in the way that they have, they've shown me how distasteful are all the very best marriages I've known of, the ones society calls charming. I've come to find them by comparison inferior, colorless, and cold. Fate, or their stars, or chance—how would I know?—made it so they can live for themselves only. Wealthy, they've been given that gift of idleness without which love cannot exist, but which just as often kills the love to which it gives birth. . . . As the exception that proves the rule, though, idleness has not killed theirs. Love simplifies everything, and love has made a sublime simplification of their lives. There are none of those big things people call 'events' in these two spouses' lives, and they seem to live as if they were the proprietors of the whole world but removed from that world and asking nothing of it, concerned neither for its respect nor its contempt. They are never apart. Where one goes, the other follows. The roads around V*** again see Hauteclaire on horseback, as in the days of old Saber-tip, but now it's the Count de Savigny who is with her, and the local women who, just as in the old days, pass by in their carriages, now stare perhaps even harder than when she was the tall, mysterious girl in the somber blue veil whom they never quite saw clearly. Nowadays, she lifts up her veil and boldly shows them the face of the servant girl who learned how to get herself married, and they go back home indignant but thoughtful. . . . The Count and Countess de Savigny never travel; they come to Paris now and then, but they only stay a few days at a time. Their life is centered entirely in the Savigny chateau, which was the theater of the crime that they have perhaps forgotten altogether, the memory of it buried somewhere deep in the abysses of their hearts . . ."

"And they never had children, Doctor?" I asked him.

"Ah!" Doctor Torty exclaimed. "You think that's it, that's the crack, the payback from Fate, or God's vengeance and justice? No, they never had children. Remember, though! Once the thought did occur to me that they would have none. They love too much. . . . The fire that devours them consumes but does not produce. One day, I said to Hauteclaire:

"'It doesn't sadden you to have no children, Madame Countess?'

"'I don't want any!' she replied imperiously. 'I would love Serlon less. Children,' she added, with a certain contempt, 'are good for unhappy wives!'"

And with that, Doctor Torty abruptly finished his story, which he thought a profound one.

It had interested me. "Criminal as she may be," I said, "this Hauteclaire is interesting. Apart from her crime, I can understand Serlon's love for her."

"And maybe even with her crime!" said the Doctor. "So can I!" he added, the good old man.

BENEATH THE CARDS
IN A GAME OF WHIST

"You don't care, Monsieur, for stories like this?"
"Isn't there a kind of tulle fabric, Madame,
that they call tulle illusion?*"*
——AN EVENING WITH PRINCE T . . .

I

One evening last summer, I was visiting the Baroness de Mascranny, a Parisian woman who still loves the kind of witty, sparkling conversation that used to be in fashion, and who opens the
double doors of her salon (though only one door nowadays would
be more than sufficient) to the little bits of it that still exist among
us.[1] It's true, isn't it, that Wit has undergone a change and has
become what we now call Intelligence? . . . The Baroness is, on
her husband's side, descended from a very old and very illustrious
family, originally from the Grisons region. Her coat of arms is, as
everyone knows, *gules with three fasces, gules with an eagle displayed*
silver, a key silver dexter, a helmet silver sinister; the shield charged with
an escutcheon azure and a fleur-de-lis or. This coat of arms and all
the details on it were grants given by many different European
sovereigns to the Mascranny family in recompense for the services they had rendered in different historical eras. If the sovereigns of Europe were not otherwise occupied with many other
matters today, they might consider granting another device to a
shield already so nobly complex, as recompense for the efforts

to maintain the arts of conversation made by the Baroness, that example of the dying breed of leisured aristocrats and absolute monarchs. With the wit and the manners befitting her name, Baroness Mascranny has made her salon into a delicious sort of Koblentz where refuge is still afforded to the conversation of yesteryear, that glory of the French mind now forced to emigrate by the utilitarianism of our modern age.[2] It sings its swan song there every night, until the day when it dies out forever. There, just as in those few other homes in Paris that still maintain the tradition of good conversation, fine phrases are never heard, and still less the boorish monologue. Nothing reeks of the newspaper article or of political discourse, those two molders of vulgar thought in the nineteenth century. Wit is allowed to shine in sentences sometimes charming, sometimes profound, but never tedious; from time to time, even a simple intonation or gesture is the hallmark of genius. Thanks to this happy salon, I have come to know better a power I never really doubted—the power of the monosyllable. Many times I've heard one launched, or simply dropped, with a talent superior even to that of Mademoiselle Mars, the queen of the monosyllable on the popular stage.[3] But even she would have been dethroned by the Faubourg Saint-Germain,[4] if she had been allowed to enter there; for the women there are too high in the world to bandy phrases, when they are at their finest, like some actress playing Marivaux.

Now on that particular evening, however, the general drift was not toward the monosyllable. When I entered the Baroness's salon, I found a number of the people there who she calls "her familiars," and the conversation was as animated as usual. Like the exotic plants in jasper vases that dotted her various tables and desks, the Baroness's familiars come from many different countries. Among them you will find English, Poles, Russians; but all of them are French in their language, and in that turn of mind and quality of manners that is always the same when one ascends to a certain level of society. I don't know how the conversation had arrived at that point, but when I came in the talk concerned novels. When people "talk about novels," they are actually speaking about their own individual lives. And do I even need to say that, in a group of society men and women, there is no question of literary pedantry in such a conversation? Their interest was in the depths of things and not in their form. Every one of those superior moralists, those practitioners, in varying degrees, of passion and of life, all concealing the depth of their serious experiences behind light comments and a detached air—every one of them saw in the novel only matters of human nature, social customs, and history. Nothing more. But then, isn't that everything? . . . In any case, they must have been discussing the subject for quite a while, for their faces had that expression that denotes an interest that has been stimulated for some time. Each one delicately honed by the others, every wit was sharpened. But a few of the liveliest spirits—I counted three or four in the room—kept their silence, some with their faces lowered, others with their eyes fixed as if in reverie, gazing down at the rings on a hand that rested on a knee. Perhaps they were searching for a way to embody their thoughts, something that can be as difficult as spiritualizing one's sensations. As the discussion continued, I slipped in unnoticed behind the stunning, velvet-smooth back of the beautiful Countess de Damnaglia, who was absentmindedly biting the tip of her folded fan between her lips as she listened intently, as they all were listening, for the art of listening is also a charm. The sun was descending, creating a kind of pink sky that gradually shaded into black, just like happy lives. We were sitting in a circle in the twilit drawing room, forming a garland of men and women in diverse poses, casually attentive. It was a kind of living bracelet, in which the mistress of the house, with her Egyptian profile, on the couch she always occupied like Cleopatra, formed the clasp. An open window showed a patch of sky and the balcony with several people on it. And the air was so pure, and the Quai d'Orsay so profoundly silent at that moment that even those on the balcony did not miss a syllable of what was said, despite the thick draperies on the window, which should have deadened the sonorous voice and buried its vibrations within their thick folds. When I realized who it was who was speaking, I was no longer surprised at the attention everyone paid—which was, after all, no more than the graciousness paid to grace. . . . Nor was I surprised at the audacity of someone holding the floor for so much longer than it was customary to do, especially in a salon with so exquisite a tone as this one.

The speaker was in fact the most brilliant talker in this kingdom of talk. Though that is not his name, of course, it is his title! Excuse me: he had another one as well. . . . Gossip and calumny, those Menaechmi who look so much alike no one can tell them apart, and who write their reports backwards as if they were Hebrew (and aren't they, often enough?), had scratched out their message that he had been the main character in more than one adventure of the kind that he would certainly not be recounting tonight.[5]

"The best novels in life," he was saying, as I established myself on some cushions, comfortably sheltered behind the Countess de Damnaglia's white shoulders, "are the ones that call up the realities one has brushed past with one's elbow, or perhaps stumbled over with one's foot. We've all seen this. The novel is more ubiquitous than history. I don't mean the ones with striking, dramatic events and catastrophic outcomes, those dramas played out with all the audacity of the most exalted sentiments and flying in the majestic face of Public Opinion; quite apart from those rare cases that cause such a scandal in societies like ours, which was hypocritical yesterday and is nothing more than cowardly today, we have all witnessed those mysterious outbursts of feeling or passion that destroy an entire destiny, those breaking hearts that make only a muffled, low sound, like the sound of a body falling into the abyss of obscurity, those cases to which the world adds either its thousand voices or its silence. We can say of the novel what Molière said of virtue: 'Where the devil will it show up next?'[6] Where you least expect it, there it is! I personally saw when I was a child—no, *saw* isn't the word! I sensed it, had a premonition of it, of one of those cruel, terrible scenes that are not played out in public, though the public sees the main actors every day, one of those 'bloody comedies' in Pascal's phrase, but one acted behind closed doors, behind an artfully placed veil, the curtain shielding the private, intimate life.[7] What results from these hidden, muffled dramas, which I would call something like 'blocked-up perspiration,' is more sinister and has more of an effect on the imagination and on memory than if the drama had been played out before our eyes. What we don't know makes a hundred times greater impression on us than what we do. Perhaps I am mistaken, but it seems to me that if you saw Hell through a small window, it would be far more horrific than if you were able to see the place in its entirety."

Here he paused for a moment. He had described a sentiment so human that for anyone who had even a little imagination, there could be no contradicting him. Every face expressed the greatest curiosity. Young Sibylle, who was sitting crouched almost double before her mother's sofa, turned and reached out to her in fright, as if someone had slipped a snake down between her flat chest and her corset.

"Stop him, Mama," she exclaimed, with the familiarity of a spoiled child, one being raised to be a despot: "Make him stop telling these horrible stories that make me shudder."

"I'll stop if you wish, Mademoiselle Sibylle," replied the man she had not even named but simply called "him" out of a naïve and almost tender familiarity.

He, who lived close to the young girl, knew both her curiosity and her fearfulness; she was the kind of girl who reacted to things with intensity, as if she had plunged her feet into cold water and had to catch her breath until she grew used to the temperature of the water.

"Sibylle has no right that I'm aware of to impose silence on my friends," said the Baroness while caressing the hair of her daughter, so prematurely pensive. "If she is afraid, she has available to her the resource of the frightened: she can leave the room."

But the capricious girl, who was perhaps just as interested in the story as her mother was, did not flee but instead straightened her meager body up, trembling with a timid fascination, and cast her dark, deep eyes onto the narrator, looking as if she were perched on the edge of an abyss.

"Well, then—tell your story!" said Mademoiselle Sophie de Revistal, turning on him her great brown eyes bathed in light, yet moist, as if the Devil shone within them. "Look around you!" she added, with an almost imperceptible gesture. "Everyone is waiting."

And he went on to tell the story that follows. But can I possibly retell it without enervating it, nuanced as it was by his voice, his gestures? Can I possibly create the impression he did that evening upon every one of us in the sympathetic atmosphere of that salon?

"I was raised in the provinces," said the narrator, setting off on the journey of his narrative, "in my family's house. My father lived in a small town with its feet in the water, at the base of a mountain, in a district I will not name, and close to a little town that you will all recognize when I tell you that it is, or at any rate it was in the time of my story, the most profoundly, most fiercely aristocratic in France.[8] In any case, I certainly have never seen its equal in that regard. Neither our Faubourg Saint-Germain, nor the Place Bellecour in Lyon, nor the three or four large cities that are often cited for their exclusive, proud, aristocratic spirit—none of them could give you the idea of this little place of six thousand souls with, before 1789, some fifty carriages with coats of arms rumbling proudly up and down its streets.

"It was as if, in shrinking and withdrawing from the rest of the earth's surface, driven away by an invading, insolent bourgeoisie, the entire aristocracy had become concentrated here, as at the bottom of a crucible, with a glow like that of a heated ruby, a glow that will only perish when the stone does.

"The nobles in this nest of nobility would die, and perhaps are dead as we speak, rather than abandon a single one of those prejudices, which I call not prejudices but sublime social truths; they were as incapable of compromise as God Himself. They were not acquainted with that which brings ignominy to all nobilities, the monstrosity of misalliances.

"The daughters, ruined by the Revolution, died stoically, old and unmarried, supported to the end by their escutcheons, which carried them through everything. My early manhood was kindled by the sight of these beautiful and charming young girls who knew the futility of their beauty, and who knew that the hot blood that their hearts were pumping, the blood that dyed their pensive cheeks red, was flowing through them in vain.

"When I was thirteen, I dreamed of finding a way to show the most romantic devotion to these poor girls, whose fortunes now consisted of nothing more than the circular crowns on their coats of arms, those majestically sad girls taking their first steps in a life that was already doomed. That noble class kept itself pure, like a spring in the mountains, and saw no one outside its own circle.

"'What do you want from us?' they would say. 'Do you expect us to mix with those bourgeois whose fathers once waited upon ours at table?'

"And they were right; it was impossible because, in the case of this small town, it was literally true. One can understand the idea of enfranchisement at a certain distance; but in a neighborhood the size of a handkerchief, the classes are separated by their very proximity. Each class saw only other members of the same class, apart from a few English inhabitants.

"For the English were attracted to this little town, which reminded them of certain regions in their own countryside. They liked its silence, its rigidity, the cold formality of its manners, its being not too far from the sea that had brought them there, and they liked its low cost of living, which allowed them nearly to double the purchasing power of the mediocre incomes they received from their homeland.

"The descendants of the same piratical ancestors as the Normans, in their view this place was a kind of Continental England, and they spent lengthy sojourns there.

"The young English misses learned their French while they pushed along their hoops beneath the spindly linden trees in the Place d'Armes; but when they reached eighteen, they were sent back to England, for this ruined aristocracy could not give itself the dangerous luxury of marrying girls who would bring only a small dowry with them, like the English. So off they went, but other migrations would bring new ones to occupy their deserted houses, and the quiet streets with the grass growing in them, as it does at Versailles, always saw more or less the same number of girls promenading in green veils, checked dresses, and Scottish plaids. Apart from these sojourns, which tended to last from seven to ten years per English family, with a complete turnover after a long enough interval, nothing broke the monotonous existence of the little town in question. That monotony was horrible.

"People often speak—and it's exaggerated far too often!—about the narrow circles of life in the provinces; but that life here, utterly devoid of incident, was even narrower and poorer because the antagonism between the classes, the rivalries that spring up, built on vanity and pride, the kinds of conflicts and tensions that flourish in other places, were entirely absent here. Such jealousies, such nursed hatreds, such wounds to one's self-esteem keep up a low level of ferment that will break out now and then into scandal, into some dark deed, or one of those little acts of spite for which there is no legal remedy.

"But here, the demarcation was so profound, the line so thick and unbreakable between that which was noble and that which was not, that any conflict between the nobility and the commoners was quite impossible.

"For such a conflict to exist, there has to be some common ground and some engagement between the parties, and there was neither. Still, the Devil probably didn't end up the loser.

"And that is because, buried deep within the hearts of these bourgeois, whose fathers had waited on the tables of the nobles, in the depths of these children of domestics, now enfranchised and enriched, there were cesspools of hatred and envy, and from time to time these sewers would let their stench rise up against the nobles, who had put the bourgeois entirely out of their minds once they ceased to wear livery.

"But all that never quite rose to the notice of the patricians, all their attention focused within their chateaus, keeping their gates closed to all except their peers, as if there were no life at all beyond the boundaries of their caste. What did they care about anything that inferior people might be saying? . . . They never heard it. And the younger men, who might have heard the insults and chosen to fight back, would under no circumstance be found in public areas, those places that are like arenas heated red hot with the admiring gaze of women.

"There were no plays. There was no theater for them, and no actors. The cafés, ignoble as they always are in the country, scarcely saw anyone at their billiard tables apart from the most debased of the bourgeois, a few good-for-nothings, and a smattering of officers, the exhausted debris of the Empire's wars. Moreover, though half-enraged with a wounded sense of social equality (that feeling that, by itself, accounts for the horrors of the Revolution), these bourgeois retained, despite themselves, a superstitious but unacknowledged respect for social rank.

"The respect of the people resembles the Holy Ampulla, which so many have mocked with so little wit.[9] When it is empty, there is always more. The son of the village toymaker declaims against the inequalities of rank; but on his own, he would never dare to cross the public square of his native town, where everyone knows him and has known him since childhood, to accost and insult, say, the son of a Clamorgan-Taillefer walking along with his sister on his arm.[10] The whole village would rise up against him. Like so many hated and envied things, one's birth operates physically upon those who detest it in a way that is the surest possible proof of its rightness. In times of revolution, people struggle against it, which is a way of submitting to it; but in times of peace, the submission is complete.

"Now, it was during one of those peaceful periods, in 1 8 2*. . . . Liberalism, which had been growing steadily in the protective shade of the Constitutional Charter, as were its watchdogs in their borrowed kennels, had not yet strangled altogether the enthusiastic royalist sentiments that the return of the Princes from their exile had aroused.[11] But whatever one wants to say about it, this was a superb moment for a convalescent France, edging back toward monarchy; the cleaver had hacked deep into her bosom, but now she was full of hope, felt herself coming back to life again, and felt no longer the painful throbbing of that cancer within her that had brought her so close to death.

"And for the little town I'm trying to describe for you, it was a time of deep, concentrated peacefulness. A religious mission that had just ended had succeeded in shutting down the last vestiges of liveliness, bustle, and amusements open to the nobility. There was no more dancing. Balls were proscribed as one of the roads that led to perdition. The girls wore mission crosses on their bosoms and formed religious groups under the direction of a female president. Everyone strove mightily to look as grave as they could, which was enough to make you laugh, if anyone had dared to laugh. When the four whist tables were set up for the dowager ladies and the old gentlemen, with two tables set off to one side for the young people, the young ladies arranged themselves into groups as they would have done in church, within their own little chapels, separated from the males, and there they sat, off to one corner of the salon, in silence . . . or at any rate, as silent as possible considering their sex (for everything is relative), whispering more than speaking, stifling their yawns with such effort that the tears came to their eyes, their rather rigid poses contrasting enticingly with the pliant suppleness of their young bodies, the pinks and lilacs of their dresses, and the light playfulness of their capes and ribbons."

I I

"The only thing," continued the narrator of this tale, in which everything is true and just as *real* as the small town in which it occurred, and which he described so accurately that someone less discreet than I had just spoken its name—"the only thing that looked remotely like, I won't say a passion, but that looked like animation, interest, desire, intensity of sensation in this extraordinary society in which the young women had twenty-four years of ennui bottled up within their limpid, untroubled souls, was gambling—that last infirmity of an exhausted soul.

"Card playing was the great obsession of these old nobles, who had been cut to the pattern of the great lords of the past but were as idle nowadays as a set of old blind women. They played like true Normans, the ancestors of the English, the most card-crazy nation on earth. Their kinship with that people, the time they spent there during the emigration, and the dignity of the game, which was played with all the discretion and secrecy and seriousness of high-level diplomacy—all these things made them adopt the game of whist. They hurled themselves into whist playing to fill up the gaping, empty abyss of their days. They played after dining every evening until midnight or one o'clock in the morning (which, for provincial life, amounts to a real Saturnalia). The card party at the Marquis de Saint-Albans's was the great event of the day. The Marquis seemed to be the feudal lord of all the local nobles, and they surrounded him with a reverence that was like a halo, considering that those who showed that respect all deserved it themselves.

"The Marquis was very good at whist. He was seventy-nine years old. Was there anyone with whom he had not played whist? . . . He had played with Maurepas, with the Count d'Artois himself, who knew whist as well as he knew tennis, with the Prince de Polignac, with the Bishop Louis de Rohan, with Cagliostro, with the Prince of Lippe, with Fox, with Dundas, with Sheridan, with the Prince of Galles, with Talleyrand, with the Devil back in the days when he was closest to the Devil, during the dark days of the emigration.[12] He needed, therefore, worthy adversaries. Usually, the English who were received by the nobility furnished a contingent to the card party, of which they spoke as if it were an institution, referring to 'Monsieur de Saint-Albans's whist' the way at court they would have spoken of 'the King's whist.'

"One evening, at Madame de Beaumont's, the green card tables were set out and ready; they were awaiting an Englishman, a Mister Hartford, to play with the great Marquis. This Englishman was some sort of industrialist who had set up a cotton mill at Pont-aux-Arches—parenthetically, one of the first to be established in that region that has always been so hostile to innovation, not due to ignorance or to a failure to understand things, but out of that excessive prudence that is the defining trait of the Norman race. And permit me one more parenthesis: the Normans always remind me of the fox in Montaigne that was so good at logic. Wherever they put their paws down, you can be assured the river is sufficiently frozen to cross.[13]

"But to return to our Englishman, Mister Hartford—who the younger ones all called simply Hartford, though the silver time-piece of his hair suggested that he was at least fifty; I can still see that closely cropped hair of his, looking like a tight skullcap. He was a favorite of the Marquis. Nothing surprising in that: he was one of the great players, a man whose life (quite a phantasmagoria, incidentally) had no meaning, no reality apart from cards, a

man for whom the highest happiness was winning at cards, and
the next best was losing—a magnificent axiom that he had borrowed from Sheridan, but one that he so thoroughly lived that
he was excused the plagiarism.[14] But apart from this gaming vice
(and in consideration of that vice, the Marquis de Saint-Albans
would have forgiven him anything, even the very greatest virtues), Mister Hartford seemed to have all those pharisaical and
Protestant qualities that the English group together under the
complacent heading of 'a respectable man.' People thought of him
as the perfect gentleman. The Marquis invited him for weeks at a
time to his chateau at La Vanillière, and he saw him most evenings
in town as well. Thus, on this particular evening, it surprised everyone, including the Marquis himself, to see the punctilious, exact foreigner arrive late. . . .

"It was during August. The windows were open onto one of
those beautiful country gardens, and the girls, grouped closely
together, their heads bent over their sewing, were chatting among
themselves. The Marquis, seated at the card table, was pursing his
long white eyebrows into a frown. He was leaning on the table
with his elbows. His hands, handsome in their very aged way,
were joined together beneath his chin, supporting that great face
of his with its expression of surprise at having been expected to
wait, looking rather like Louis XIV and just as majestic. A servant
at long last announced Mister Hartford. He appeared, in his customary, irreproachable dress, his shirt dazzlingly white, rings on
every finger, in the style of Monsieur Bulwer, an Indian handkerchief in his hand, and between his lips—for he had just finished
dining—a peppermint lozenge that veiled the scent of anchovies,
Harvey sauce, and port wine.[15]

"But he was not alone. He greeted the Marquis and presented,
like a shield against any reproach, a Scottish friend of his, Mister
Marmor de Karkoël, who had burst like a bombshell into his dinner, and who was the best whist player in the Three Kingdoms.

"That circumstance—being the best 'whister' in all of Great
Britain—gave rise to a charming smile on the pale lips of the
Marquis. The game was quickly set up. In his haste to begin play-
ing, Mister de Karkoël failed to remove his gloves, which in their

perfection recalled the celebrated gloves of Beau Brummell, cut by three special craftsmen, two working on the hands and one on the thumbs. He was the partner of the Marquis de Saint-Albans. The dowager Madame de Hautcardon ceded that place to him.

"Now, ladies, regarding this Marmor de Karkoël's appearance: he was a man of about twenty-eight, but it may have been the effect of sunlight, or perhaps some inner fatigue, or perhaps the passions themselves—but whatever the cause, it had given his face the mask of a man of thirty-five. It was not a handsome face, but an expressive one. His hair was black, thick, straight, and somewhat short, and his hand constantly brushed it back from his temples. This repeated gesture had a kind of sinister eloquence about it. He seemed to be brushing away some remorse. It was striking at first and, like all genuinely profound things, it continued to be striking.

"I had known this Karkoël for several years, and I can testify that this somber gesture of his, repeated ten times an hour, always produced its effect, and among a group of a hundred different onlookers, it would always produce the same effect on each one of them. His forehead was regular but a bit low, expressive of audacity. His clean-shaven upper lip (no one wore a mustache in those days, unlike our time) was immobile enough to drive mad a Lavater, or anyone who believes that the truth of a man's nature is revealed more by the expression of his mouth than that of his eyes.[16] When he smiled, his eyes did not, and he revealed pearl-like teeth, common enough among the people of his island, but then they usually go on to lose them or blacken them, like the Chinese, due to their excessive tea drinking. His face was long, and his cheeks hollow, his skin an almost olive color that seemed natural to him, but bronzed by the rays of a sun that, to have done this much damage, could not have been the dull sun of foggy England. His nose, long and straight, was nonetheless more curved than his forehead, and it divided two black Macbeth-like eyes, the most somber possible and set close together, which is, they say, the sign of an eccentric character or perhaps of some variety of insanity. His clothing was carefully chosen. Sitting there nonchalantly at the whist table, he seemed larger than he really was, due to an odd disproportion of the torso, for he was a small man; but despite this defect, he was strong, with a force that seemed only asleep within him, like a tiger's strength lying latent beneath his soft, velvety fur. Did he speak French well? His voice, that golden chisel with which we sculpt our thoughts in the minds of our listeners, with which we shape our seductions—was his voice in harmony with that repeated gesture of his, which I cannot mention without imagining it afresh? Well, one thing is for certain: on that evening, his voice struck no fear in anyone. The only words it uttered were the sacramental ones of whist, words like *tricks* and *honors,* the only expressions that come at regular intervals to interrupt the holy silence in which the players plunge themselves.

"Thus, in that large salon full of people for whom the arrival of an Englishman was no significant event, no one apart from those at the Marquis's table paid any attention to this unknown whister that Hartford had towed in behind him. The young ladies did not so much as turn their heads to glance at him. They were in the midst of discussing (everyone was starting to *discuss* back in those days) the composition of their religious society's committee and one of their vice presidents who was absent from Madame de Beaumont's that evening. This was just a bit more important, thank you, than looking over some Englishman or some Scotsman. They had become rather blasé about the eternal importation of English and Scots. Just another man whose only interest in women concerned the Queen of Diamonds or the Queen of Clubs! A Protestant, to boot! A heretic! Why couldn't it ever be a Catholic lord from Ireland? As for the older people playing at the other tables when Hartford had been announced, they gave a distracted glance to the stranger following him and then plunged back into their play, like swans plunging their long necks back into the water.

"Monsieur de Karkoël having been chosen as partner to the Marquis de Saint-Albans, the person playing across from him was the Countess du Tremblay de Stasseville, whose daughter Herminie, the sweetest flower of all the young girls filling up the window seats, was talking with Mademoiselle Ernestine de Beaumont. By chance, her gaze happened to fall upon the table where her mother was playing.

"'Ernestine, look there,' she whispered. 'Look at the way that Scotsman deals!'

"Monsieur de Karkoël had just removed his gloves. He had pulled from those scented kid gloves a pair of white, perfectly sculpted hands, enough to inspire worshipful care in any fashionable lady, were she gifted with hands like those, and he was dealing the cards the way one does in whist, one by one, but with so rapid and sure a circular movement that one couldn't help being reminded of the fingering of Liszt. The man who managed cards like that must surely be their master. . . . Ten years of gambling life were revealed in that stunning, magisterial style of dealing.

"'He's master all right—a master of bad taste,' said Ernestine, curling her lip in disdain.

"A severe judgment for so young a girl, but then, for that pretty Ernestine, having 'good taste' was more important than having all the wit of a Voltaire. She had missed out on her destiny, Mademoiselle Ernestine de Beaumont: she would end her life in bitterness at never having become the *camerera major* of a Spanish queen.[17]

"The way Marmor de Karkoël played was every bit the equal of the marvelous way he dealt. He revealed a superiority that delighted the old Marquis, and he raised the level of play for this man who had once been the partner of Fox. Any superiority has a seductiveness to it, fascinating you and carrying you off into its orbit. But that is not all. In carrying you off, it also enriches you. Look at the great conversationalists! They demonstrate for you the best ways to reply, and they inspire your own replies. As soon as they leave the conversation, the fools, deprived of the illumination that surrounded them, return, floating up into the conversation drab and dull like dead fish, belly up, their scales beneath the water. Monsieur de Karkoël did much more than simply give a new sensation to an old man who thought he had exhausted them all; he actually improved the self-esteem of the Marquis, adding yet another gem to the crown that this king of whist imagined himself wearing in his proud solitary reveries.

"But despite the pleasure he felt, the Marquis carefully observed the stranger during the game, keeping a discreet eye on him from the cover of the *crow's-feet* (the ugly term we give to the spots scratched by the talons of Time, to pay him back for his insolence in putting them there) that surrounded his keen eyes. The Scotsman could only be appreciated, really savored, by a truly great player. He had that profound, thoughtful attention that only deepens as the game proceeds, and he veiled it behind a superb impassiveness. Compared with him, the sphinxes crouching on their basaltic lava looked like allegories of openness and expansiveness. He played as if he had three pairs of hands, without bothering to look at what each was holding. The last breezes of that August night were breaking in perfumed waves over the thirty or so coiffures of the young ladies at the windows, and they came in to break on that large, low, forehead of his, that reef of human marble without a single wrinkle. He never even felt it. His nerves were muted. At a moment like that, one had to admit he merited his name of Marmor![18] Needless to say, he was winning.

"The Marquis retired each evening at about midnight. He was escorted by the obsequious Hartford, upon whose arm he leaned as he walked to his carriage.

"'That Karkoël plays like a god!' he exclaimed, in a tone of enchanted surprise. 'See to it that he doesn't leave us soon.'

"Hartford promised, and the old Marquis, despite his age and his sex, prepared to play the role of a veritable Siren of hospitality.

"I've dwelt upon this first evening of a stay that lasted many years. I was not there; but one of my older relatives told me about it, a card player like all the young people in that town, for whom play was their only diversion in that era of the famine of the passions; he, like all the others, pledged his allegiance to the god of tricks. Looking back on it now, our retrospective impressions cast their magic over the evening, though it would have seemed prosaic and ordinary enough then; but that game of whist came to take on a significance that may perhaps surprise you. Well—the fourth person in the party, the Countess de Stasseville, my relative also told me, lost her money with the aristocratic nonchalance with which she did everything. Perhaps her fate was settled during that game of whist, wherever it is that human fates are decided. Who can understand any part of the mystery of life? . . . At that time, no one had any reason to observe the Countess closely. The only mutterings in the salon were the sounds of the counters and tokens used in the games. . . . It would be curious to go back and determine if anyone could have seen in that woman, at the time considered a polished and perfect block of ice, any of the things that have been believed and whispered since; it would have been something to have been able to see it all beginning that evening.

"The Countess du Tremblay de Stasseville was a woman of forty, in poor health, pale and thin, though with a kind of pallor and thinness I've never seen elsewhere. Her Bourbon nose, a little pinched, her light brown hair, her very thin lips, all proclaimed her a thoroughbred aristocrat, and one whose pride could easily slip into cruelty. Her sulfur-tinted pallor gave her a sickly look.

"Mademoiselle Ernestine de Beaumont, who rummaged everywhere, even deep into Gibbon, for material for her witty sayings, liked to say that if the Countess had been named Constance, one could have called her Constantia Chlora.[19]

"For those who knew the type of wit Mademoiselle de Beaumont employed, they would have been able to read the correct level of cruelty into it. But despite the pallor of the Countess du Tremblay de Stasseville, despite her lips the color of wilted hydrangea, the careful observer would have noted precisely in those thin, tight lips, vibrant as a taut bowstring, the frightening physiognomy of repressed fire, of a powerful will. The society in this provincial town did not see it. Indeed, they saw nothing behind that narrow, murderous lip; they only saw it as the steel bowstring on which the barbed arrow of an epigram was forever ready to fly. Her blue-green eyes (for the Countess showed *sinople, étincelé d'or* in her gaze as well as on her coat of arms) crowned her face like two fixed stars, though without warming it. Those two emeralds with their yellow glints, set beneath the arched blonde eyebrows, were as cold as if they had come from the belly of Polycrates's fish.[20] Only her wit—a wit damascened and sharpened like an épée—her brilliant wit sometimes lit up that icy gaze with a fire like that of the 'fiery flashing sword' in the Bible.[21] The other women hated that wit of the Countess du Tremblay as if it had been a species of beauty. And in fact her wit was her beauty! Like Mademoiselle de Retz, of whom the Cardinal has left a portrait—a portrait painted by a man who has abandoned all his youthful illusions—she had a certain defect in her figure that could, strictly speaking, be considered a deformity.[22] Her fortune was quite considerable. The death of her husband had left her with the light burden of two children: a little boy, stupid but charming, who had been entrusted to the care of an old abbé who taught him nothing, and her daughter, Herminie, a girl whose beauty would have been admired even in the most demanding and most artistic circles of Paris. She had brought up her daughter irreproachably, at least with regard to her official education. But the irreproachable, with Madame de Stasseville, always had something in it of impertinence. There was impertinence in her very virtue—and who knows, perhaps that is the only reason she had been able to maintain it. And she was always virtuous; her reputation defied calumny. No serpent's tooth had ever bitten into that fruit. Thus the gossips, frenzied at having nothing with which to undermine that virtue, wore themselves out instead in accusing her of frigidity. This was no doubt the result, they said (ah, what scientists people can be!), of anemia. With a little judicious encouragement, her best friends would have said of her that she suffered from that same hereditary bar that had been invented to calumniate a charming and celebrated woman of the preceding century in order to explain that she had had all of elegant Europe at her feet for ten years, while permitting no one to mount up so much as an inch higher."

The narrator's gaiety of tone saved him from causing serious offense with this last remark, though it did occasion a certain bustle of affronted prudery. I say *prudery* without meaning to be pejorative, for the prudery of well-born women who lack affectation has something quite graceful about it. Moreover, darkness was falling, so that one sensed this movement without really seeing it.

"My word, you're exactly right in your description of this Countess de Stasseville," stuttered the old Viscount de Rassy. He was both hunchbacked and a stammerer, but witty enough that he might as well have been a cripple, too. Who in Paris does not know the Viscount de Rassy, that walking memorandum of all the little corruptions of the eighteenth century? With a handsome face in his youth like that of the Marshal de Luxembourg, he had, also like him, his other side of the coin.[23] But nowadays, the better side of the coin was gone. . . . When the young men of the era found him doing or saying something anachronistic, he would say that at least he was not dishonoring his white hairs—for he always wore a brown wig, parted down the middle, with the most incredible, most indescribable side curls!

"Ah! You knew her?" asked the narrator. "Well, then! You know, Viscount, whether I am exaggerating in the slightest."

"It's as true as if you traced it from the life, that p-p-portrait of yours," replied the Viscount, giving himself a light slap on the jaw in impatience with his stutter, though at the risk of dislodging some dried flakes of the rouge he applied there, which he did just the way he did everything else, entirely without shame. "I knew her slightly a l-l-little time after your story. She used to come to Paris for several days every winter. I would run into her at the Princess de C-C-Courtenay's, who was related to her. She served up that wit of hers on ice; you could catch a cold just being around her."

"Now, apart from those several days spent each winter in Paris," continued our audacious narrator, who did not allow his characters even the half-mask of Harlequin, "the life of the Countess du Tremblay de Stasseville was as rhythmically regular as that tedious piece of music that is the life of a proper lady. For six months out of the year, she buried herself in her town house—in that town that I've described to you in such detail—and then she traded that for burying herself in her chateau for the other six months, a pretty little place about four leagues distant. Every other year she would take her daughter to Paris—and she would leave her with an old aunt, Mademoiselle de Triflevas, when she went there alone—at the beginning of the winter; but not once did she go to Spa, to Plombières, to the Pyrenees! She was never seen at any of the watering places. Did she fear malicious gossip? In the provinces, when a woman like the Countess de Stasseville goes on her own to such places, who knows what people will say? The envy of the ones who stay at home avenges itself on the pleasure of those who go. Bizarre winds come to ruffle the purest of waters. Which one is it, the Yellow River or the Blue, where they go to expose their infants in China? . . . Well, the watering places in France are a bit like that river. If it's not an infant, there's always something exposed to the eyes of those who stayed at home. The sarcastic Countess du Tremblay was far too proud to sacrifice some caprice of hers to opinion; but watering places were not one of her passions, and her doctor much preferred to have her close by rather than two hundred leagues away, because it's much harder to make endless, unnecessary ten-franc house calls at such a distance. In fact it was questionable whether the Countess had any caprices or passions at all. Wittiness is not the same as imagination. Hers was so dry, so trenchant, so decided, even when she was joking, that the very idea of caprice seemed to be excluded. Even when she was feeling cheerful (which was rare), her wit smacked of that sound that you hear from the ebony castanets or tambourines of the Basques, all tight, stretched skin and harsh little metal bells, so that one could not imagine that anything within that dry, rational mind could possibly fit into the category of fantasy, or of curious dreams, nothing that could engender the need to get up and travel some place new. During the ten years that she had been both widowed and rich, and thus entirely her own mistress, she could have at any time picked up and left that little burrow of nobles, where her evenings were an endless round of card games with old women who could remember the *chouan* uprisings, and of old chevaliers, unsung heroes who had helped save Destouches.[24]

"If she had wanted to, she could have done like Lord Byron and gone wandering all over the world with a library, a kitchen, and a birdhouse in her carriage, but she had no interest in such a thing. She was not just indolent: she was indifferent, as indifferent as Marmor de Karkoël when he was playing whist. But the difference was that Marmor was not indifferent to whist itself, whereas she had no whist in her life: she was indifferent to everything! Hers was a stagnant nature; the English would have called her a

woman-dandy. Apart from her witty sayings, she existed in a kind
of elegant larval state. 'She belongs to the class of cold-blooded
animals,' her doctor used to whisper into certain people's ears,
as if you could explain a person by means of a metaphor, the way
you explain an illness by citing its symptom. Though she looked
ill, the doctor always denied that there was anything wrong. Was
this supreme discretion on his part, or did he really not see anything? She never complained, though, about any physical or spiritual malady. She didn't even have that almost physical shading of
melancholy that stretches across the lined foreheads of women of
forty. Her days fell away from her rather than being violently detached, and she saw them fall away with the same satirical glance
from her sea-green, Undine-like eyes that she bestowed upon all
things.[25] She seemed to want to contradict her reputation as a wit
by refusing to indulge in any of those personal habits that we call
eccentricities. She performed—naturally and simply—exactly
what all the other women in her society did, no more and no less.
She seemed to want to prove that equality—that chimera so beloved by villains—only existed among the nobility. Only among
them are there true peers, for their birth, and the four generations of nobility required to form a gentleman, put all on the
same level. 'I am but the first gentleman of France,' Henri IV liked
to say, and with that saying he managed to lower the ambitions
of each nobleman while raising the status of them all. Like the
other women of her caste (and she was too much the aristocrat
to wish to surpass them), the Countess carried out her religious
and social duties with the greatest sobriety, which is the supreme
convention of that world in which all enthusiasms are severely
forbidden. She neither fell behind nor tried to go beyond her
peers. Had she succeeded at last in subjugating herself entirely
to the monotony of life in this provincial town—had she buried
what was left of her youth here, like the still, dormant pools that
sleep beneath the water lilies? The inner springs that moved her
to action, her motives of thought, conscience, instinct, tempera-
ment, taste—all those inner torches that illuminate our acts cast
no light upon hers. Nothing from the interior illuminated the
exterior woman. Nothing from the outer world found any echo

within her! Fatigued by having watched for so long without having learned anything about Madame de Stasseville, the people in her neighborhood, who had displayed all the patience of a fisherman awaiting a tug on his line in hopes of discovering something, eventually gave up on the whole puzzle and turned their backs, the way one tosses behind a chest some manuscript that has proven impossible to decipher.

"'We've all been fools,' said the Countess de Hautcardon in a definitive tone one evening—and this was after several years—'to have made such a fuss about learning what's at the bottom of that woman's soul. Most likely, there's nothing at all!'"

I I I

"And everyone accepted that opinion from the dowager de Hautcardon as final. It had the force of law for all those upset and disappointed people who had carried out such lengthy but futile observations, and who were now only too glad to have a reason to go back to sleep. It still held sway, but rather in the manner of the *rois fainéants,* when Marmor de Karkoël, just about the least likely man in all creation to show up in the life of the Countess du Tremblay de Stasseville, came in from the far corners of the world to take a seat at that table where a partner was needed for the whist game.[26] He had been born, said his traveling companion Hartford, in the foggy hills of the Shetland Islands. He was from the country where Walter Scott had set his sublime story of *The Pirate,* a story Marmor was going to reenact, with some alterations, in a forgotten little town on the coast of the English Channel.[27] He had been raised on the shores of that ocean sailed by Cleveland, and as a young man he had danced the dances of young Mordaunt with the daughters of old Troil. He remembered them, and more than once I saw him dance them on the polished oaken parquet floors of that little, prosaic, respectable town, so incongruous with the wild, bizarre poetry of those northern dances. When he was fifteen, his parents bought him a commission in an English regiment bound for India, and he spent twelve years there fighting in the Maratha wars.[28] All this was learned about him from Hartford, as

well as the fact that he was a gentleman, a descendant of the great
Scottish hero Douglas 'of the bleeding heart.'[29] But that was all
that was learned; nobody knew anything more, and they evidently
never would. The stories about his adventures in India, that grand
and terrible country where men learn to breathe so deeply that
Western air is never good enough for them thereafter—he said
nothing about all that. Yet those stories were traced in mysterious
characters on his bronzed forehead, which revealed no more than
does one of those jeweled boxes with Asiatic poisons in them,
which are kept in reserve for the day of the Indian sultan's defeat and disaster. They flared out, though, in moments when his
black eyes flashed, a flash he could stifle the way one snuffs out a
candle when one does not want to be observed, and in those oft-
repeated gestures of sweeping the hair back from his temples during a rubber of whist or a game of écarté. But apart from those
hieroglyphics of gesture and physiognomy that the keen observer
knows how to read, and that, like real hieroglyphics, employ only
a very small vocabulary, Marmor de Karkoël was indecipherable,
just as much so in his way as the Countess du Tremblay was in
hers. He was a silent Cleveland. All the young nobles of the town
where he was living—and there were many clever ones among
them, curious as women and subtle as serpents—were positively
consumed with the desire to hear him narrate the secret memoirs
of his youth, preferably accompanied by a few cigarettes from
Maryland. But their hopes ran aground every time. That Hebri-
dean sea lion, burnt brown by the sun of Lahore, would not let
himself be tricked by their salon-mousetraps, would not take the
bait of vanity, the very snare into which French stupidity wanders
like a peacock, losing all its feathers for the pleasure of getting
to show them off. The difficulty could not be overcome. He was
as sober as a Koran-believing Turk. Silent as a mute guarding the
sultan's harem of his thoughts! I never saw him drink anything but
water or coffee. And the cards, which seemed to be his passion:
were they really his passion, or were they simply a passion he had
willed himself to have? For one can will oneself into a passion
just as easily as into an illness. Did the cards serve as a kind of
screen to hide his mind and heart from view? I often wondered

that, when I saw him playing the way he played. He enveloped, deepened, rooted the passion for cards in that little town to the extent that when he left, a hideous ennui, the ennui of betrayed passions, overwhelmed the place like some accursed sirocco, making it resemble an English town more than ever. At his place, the whist table was set up already in the morning. His typical day, when he was not at La Vanillière or some neighborhood chateau, had all the simplicity of the day of a man in the grip of an obsession. He arose at nine, took tea with some friend who had come for whist, began to play at once, and did not stop until five in the afternoon. Since there were always many people at these gatherings, the groups changed after each rubber, and those who were not playing placed bets on the games. Moreover, it was not the young and idle who frequented these parties, but the gravest, soberest men of the town. It was the *family men,* to use the term women of thirty-something liked to use, who dared to pass their days in this gambling den, and such women went on to cast the foulest aspersions and throw the blackest mud at this Scotsman, as if he had infected the whole countryside, and especially their husbands, with the plague. They were perfectly accustomed to seeing their men play, but never with this level of stubbornness and ardor. The party would break up at five, and the same people would encounter each other that evening at one or another social occasion, and there they would—to all appearances—conform to the official game and the accepted approach to it that had been set by whichever hostess was involved, but in reality they would surreptitiously continue playing the game they had begun that morning, playing 'whist à la Karkoël.' You can well imagine the level of skill these gentlemen attained, seeing that they did nothing else but play whist. They elevated whist to the level of the highest, most difficult fencing. There were, no doubt, considerable losses; but what prevented the downright catastrophe or ruin that gambling always brings with it was precisely the ardor and the superior skill of the men playing. All the competition ended up by creating a kind of equilibrium among them; and given the narrowness of the field, everyone ended up being everyone else's partner from time to time, and there was no way to avoid paying up when one had to.

"Despite the town's decent women balking and working against it in secret, the influence of Marmor de Karkoël not only did not diminish but actually continued to grow. And one can see why. It was not so much Marmor himself or the force of his personality as it was a passion that he had found already there when he arrived, a passion that he shared and that his presence helped intensify. The best way, and perhaps the only one, of governing men is to take control of them through their passions. Why, then, did Karkoël not take power? He had what a government needs, but he had no desire at all to govern. And that is why he became so popular that he might have been taken for a sorcerer. People fought to spend time with him. He always received the same welcome for the whole time he spent in that town, and it was always a rapturous welcome. The women, who feared him, much preferred seeing him at their houses to knowing that their sons or husbands were at his, and they welcomed him the way women welcome a man they may not like but who is the center of attention, the focus of an obsession, almost the head of a movement. In the summer he went to spend two weeks or a month in the country. The Marquis de Saint-Albans had taken him under his special protection, though *protection* is too weak a word. In the country, just as in the town, it was whist all the time. I recall attending (I was a schoolboy, home on vacation at the time) a superb salmon fishing party in the sparkling waters of the Douve, while Marmor de Karkoël sat in a boat playing double dummy whist with one of the local gentlemen. If he had fallen into the river, he would have kept right on playing! . . . There was only one woman in that group who never invited the Scotsman to her place in the country, and scarcely ever in the town. That was the Countess du Tremblay.

"And who would find it surprising? No one. She was a widow, and she had a charming daughter. In the country, and among that envious, faction-oriented group in which everyone plunges into the details of everyone else's life, one cannot take too many precautions against the kind of cheap inferences that people so easily make from what they see to what they have not seen. The Count-ess du Tremblay took the precautions of never inviting Marmor to her Stasseville chateau and never receiving him in town except on the most public and most populated of occasions. She was polite to him, but in a cold and impersonal way. It was the kind of po-liteness one owes to everyone, not so much for their sake as for one's own. He responded with the same kind of politeness; and it was all so natural, so unaffected between the two of them that it took four years for people to catch on. As I've already said, apart from card playing, Karkoël seemed not to exist. He spoke little. If he had had something to hide, he would have been covering it up very nicely by his habitual silence. But the Countess, as you will remember, had a very outgoing, biting wit. For those sorts of people—always social, always brilliant, always aggressive—holding oneself back, keeping something hidden is a difficult thing. Hiding oneself away—isn't that a kind of self-betrayal? But if she possessed the shiny scales and the triple tongue of the ser-pent, she also had its cunning. Therefore, there was no change in her fierce wit and her customary jesting. Often, when the subject of Karkoël came up in her presence, she would take a shot at him in such scathing, piercing terms that Mademoiselle de Beaumont, her rival in epigrams, was jealous. If this was just another kind of lie, then never was lying carried out so daringly. Did her dry, tightly wound personality give rise to this ease with dissimula-tion? But why did she bother to dissimulate at all, since she was the very embodiment of independence, in addition to being such a proud and satiric person? Why, if she loved Karkoël and he loved her, did she hide it under those sarcastic gibes that she launched so many times, those betrayals, those traitorous, impious insults that degraded the adored idol . . . the very greatest sacrileges in matters of love?

"My God—who knows? Perhaps on some level she took plea-sure in it. . . . Now, Doctor," said the narrator, turning toward Doctor Beylasset, who was leaning on a Bulle cabinet, his fine, bald head reflecting the light from the candelabra that the ser-vants had just lit over his head. "If you were to give the Countess de Stasseville one of those 'physiological' glances that you medical men can give, the kind that the moralists ought to borrow from you—it would be evident to you that all the impressions that woman had were bound to be held inside, bottled up tightly, just like the faded hydrangea line of her lips when she closed them so tight together—like those nostrils of hers, that contracted rather than expanding, that never trembled—like those eyes that, at certain times, shrunk back so far under the arcades of her brows that they seemed to be retracting all the way into her brain. Despite her apparent delicacy and that physical weakness that showed itself in every aspect of her appearance, weakness you could trace in her the way you would trace a crack in some too-dry substance—despite all this, she was the most striking image of sheer will power, of that inner Volta battery within us that powers all of our nerves.[30] That temporarily slumbering will power, circulating within her veins like *potential* energy (forgive me the term—it's overly pedantic, I know)—this power revealed itself even in her hands, aristocratic, even regal in their whiteness, elegance, and opalescent smoothness, but which, in their thinness, in the swollen cords of bluish veins that crisscrossed them, and above all in the sudden shocking way in which they would grab hold of things, resembled those fabled claws that the startling poetry of the Ancients would attribute to certain monsters with the face and breasts of a woman. When, after she had spat out one of her witticisms, as sharp and sparkling as the poison arrows used by savages, she would flick her viper-like tongue across her hissing lips, and at such a moment you would believe that this woman, both so frail and so strong, would have the supreme strength she needed in the moment of ultimate necessity, the power they attribute to the Negro, of being able to swallow her own supple tongue to bring on her own death. Looking at her, you would be certain that she belonged to that type of organism found at every level of nature, one of those that, whether out of instinct or preference, always look not to the surface but to the bottom of things; one of those creatures destined for mysterious, occult relations, the type that plunges deep down into life the way the great swimmers dive down into the water, like the miners who find a way to breathe deep underground, the type who love mystery for its own sake because of the depths in it, spinning it all around themselves and loving it to the point of loving lies—because the lie is a redoubled mystery, a thick veil passed over the truth, shadows cast at any price! It may be that organisms of this sort love the lie for lying's sake, the way some love art for art's sake, the way the Poles love battles. . . ." (Here the doctor nodded his head gravely in a sign of agreement.) "You have seen the type I'm describing, have you? Yes, I'm convinced that for certain souls there is happiness only in imposture. They find a frightening yet intoxicating happiness in the idea of lying and successfully deceiving; in thinking that *only they know,* and that they are playing a role in front of society, which is their dupe, an expensive role but one that compensates itself in that sense of contempt they love to feel toward their dupes."

"But it's horrible, what you're saying!" interrupted the Baroness de Mascranny, appalled to hear of such dishonesty.

All the women in the audience (and it may very well be that among them were some connoisseurs of hidden pleasures) had felt a kind of shiver go through them at the narrator's last words. I could see it in the naked back of the Countess de Damnaglia, sitting so close in front of me. That kind of nervous shiver is familiar to everyone; everyone has felt it. It has sometimes been poetically called "the angel of death brushing past." Or was it truth that was brushing past?

"Yes," the narrator replied, "it is horrible; but is it true? Those people who wear their hearts on their sleeves can have no idea of the solitary pleasures of the hypocrite, the person who prefers to live and breathe behind a mask. But when you stop to think about it, isn't it easy enough to understand that such pleasures have all the intensity, all the fiery depth of hell itself? Now, hell is simply the inverse of heaven. The words *diabolical* and *divine,* when applied to intense pleasures, mean exactly the same thing—that is, they both refer to sensations rooted in the supernatural. Was the Countess de Stasseville one of that race of souls? . . . I don't want to condemn her or to justify her. I am only telling her story as best I can, a story nobody else knows, and one I'm trying to analyze and clarify scientifically, the way Cuvier approached his subjects. That's all.

"Anyway, the analysis I'm trying to perform now on the Countess du Tremblay, on the image of her I carry within me, imprinted onto my memory like the seal an onyx ring makes on wax, was by no means one I performed at the time. If I do understand this woman, it's an understanding to which I only arrived much later. . . . That all-powerful will that I only discovered in her upon later reflection, after experience had taught me to what extent the body is sculpted and shaped by the soul, had not yet whipped up and stimulated her life, thus far closed-in and kept calm by her unchanging habits—just as the swollen ocean wave does not trouble the inland lake, serene and calm within its borders. If it hadn't been for the arrival of Karkoël, the British infantry officer that his colleagues had sent out to 'live on his half-pay' in some Norman town—a town that might just as well have been English—the pale, weak, sarcastic creature the locals sometimes called 'Madame Ice' would never have learned what a powerful, imperious will lay hidden beneath all that snow, as Mademoiselle Ernestine de Beaumont would have put it—snow on which ideas of morality had made no more impression, however, than they would have on the hardest hillocks of the polar regions. And when he did finally come onto the scene, what did she feel? Had she ever learned that for a person like herself, deep feeling was a matter of will? Did she manage, by sheer will power, to attract to her side a man who seemed to have no love left for anything other than cards? . . . And how did she manage it, carrying off an intimacy like that in a provincial town where all eyes were always upon everyone? . . . Mysteries, all mysteries, and they always will be; but though there were suspicions later, there were none then, at the end of the year 182*. . . . And yet, at just that time, in one of the most peaceful-seeming mansions of that town, where card playing was the only thing happening every day and night, behind the heavy, silent blinds and the embroidered muslin curtains, behind those pure, elegant, and often half-raised veils on a serene life, a novel that one would have called impossible must have been playing itself out for a long time. And yes, the novel was that correct, irreproachable life, so highly regulated, so satirical, cold almost to the point of illness, that life that seemed all mind and no soul. It was really there, gnawing away beneath the surface of appearances and reputation, like worms beginning to gnaw a man before he was actually dead."

"What an ugly comparison!" exclaimed the Baroness de Mascranny again. "I'm beginning to think my little Sibylle was right in not wanting to listen to your story. You certainly have an appalling imagination tonight."

"Would you like me to stop?" asked the narrator, with a sly courtesy and the cunning of a man confident of the interest he has aroused.

"Stop now?" replied the Baroness. "Can we possibly stop now, when your story is only half-done, and we're all on tenterhooks?"

"Oh, that would be just too much!" said Mademoiselle Laure d'Alzanne, winding one of her long, deep black curls around a finger, and presenting the most languid image possible of happy idleness, though somewhat startled by the idea that the story would be broken off and her nonchalance with it.

"And just too disappointing!" the doctor chimed in with a smile. "Wouldn't it be like going to a barber for a shave, and having him stop after doing half your face, put away his razor, and explain that it would be simply impossible for him to go any further?"

"Well, I'll continue, then," said the narrator with all the simplicity of the greatest art, which consists in concealing itself. "In 182*, I was in the drawing room of one of my uncles,[31] the mayor of that small town that I've been describing to you as the place most antipathetic to the passions and to adventure, and although it was a solemn occasion, the King's Day, Saint Louis's Day, which is always elaborately observed by those 'ultras' from the time of the emigration, those political quietists who have invented a slogan of the most mystical, purest love—'Long live the King, all the same'—in that drawing room, one did just what one did every other day. We played cards, in other words. I apologize for bringing myself into the story; it's in bad taste, I know, but I'm afraid it's necessary. I was an adolescent at the time. However, thanks to an exceptional education, I suspected more about the passions and about the world than most people do at that age. I resembled less some awkward schoolboy who's seen nothing of life beyond what's in his textbooks, and more a curious young girl who's always insisted on eavesdropping at doorways and then goes off and ponders deeply about what she's heard. The whole town was there that evening, in my uncle's drawing room, and as usual—for there was never any change in that eternal world of mummies who shook off their bandages only in order to play cards—the group was divided in two, those who were playing and those who were not. Mummies, too, were the young girls, who had no choice but to take their places, some here, some there, in the catacombs of the celibate; but their faces, striking in their futile youth and freshness, were enchanting to my eager gaze. Among them perhaps only Mademoiselle Herminie de Stasseville had enough of a fortune that she could possibly dream of a love-marriage without descending in rank. I was not yet old enough, or maybe I was already too old, to go over and mix with that swarm of young ladies, whose whisperings were now and then interrupted by loud, open laughter or barely suppressed giggling. A prey to that overheated self-conscious adolescent timidity that is sometimes a pleasure and sometimes an agony, I took refuge by seating myself next to the king of whist, the great Marmor de Karkoël, who was something of a hero to me. Of course, there was no question of any friendship between us. But the feelings have their own secret hierarchy. It is not at all rare to see, in underdeveloped natures, certain sympathies arise with no intelligible foundation, a phenomenon that leads one to conclude that young people simply need their heroes, just as all people (who, whatever their age, are always more or less children) need their leaders. My leader, my hero, was Karkoël. He often visited my father, who was a fanatical card player just like everyone else. He had often joined my brother and me in our athletic games, and he showed a vigor and an ability that was nothing short of miraculous. Like the Duke of Enghien, he could jump and clear a seventeen-foot-wide river.[32] That alone would have been enough to fascinate boys like ourselves, who were being raised to become soldiers; but that was not the reason I was so obsessed with Kar-koël. He must have worked on my imagination somehow, with that power that exceptional beings have over other exceptional beings (for vulgarity is immune to higher influences, in the same way that a bag of wool is good protection against a cannonball). I cannot tell you how fascinated I was by that brow of his, sculpted in the color that painters call 'Sienna earth'—or by those sinister eyes of his, with their short lids—or by all those various marks that unknown passions had left upon the Scotsman's body, like the four lashes the executioner gives a man being tortured upon the wheel—and above all, by that man's hands, soft and civilized from the wrist to the fingers, but savage from the wrist upward, those hands that could deal the cards with such velocity and rotation that it reminded one of the twisting and turning motions of a flame, hands that had made such an impression on Herminie de Stasseville when she had first seen them. Now, on that particular night, in the corner where the whist table was, the blinds were half-open. The group playing was as somber as the half-light illuminating them. It was a game of the very best. The Methuselah of the marquis rank, Monsieur de Saint-Albans, was Marmor's partner. The Countess du Tremblay had chosen the Chevalier de Tharsis, officer of the Provence regiment and a Knight of Saint Louis as her partner, one of those old men no longer above ground nowadays, whose military career bestrode two centuries—yet who were no Colossus figures for all that.[33] Now during the game at one particular moment, the Countess du Tremblay de Stasseville happened to lean forward to pick up her cards, and in doing so, one of the points of the diamond sparkling on her finger happened to cross the shadow that the blind cast over the green table, and a ray of light intersected with the diamond's light in the kind of sudden encounter that transcends all human artistry, throwing out a white, fiery shaft of such brilliancy that it almost blinded the players' eyes, like a bolt of lightning.

"'Oh—what is it that's shining like that?' exclaimed the Chevalier de Tharsis, in a high-pitched voice as thin and reedy as his old legs.

"'And who's coughing?' asked the Marquis de Saint-Albans at the same moment, having had his rapt concentration on the game interrupted by a loud hoarse cough, and turning to look at Herminie, who was sewing a frilled collar for her mother.

"'It is my diamond and my daughter,' said the Countess du Tremblay with a thin-lipped smile, replying to both at once.

"'Good Lord, how beautiful it is, that diamond of yours, Madame!' the Chevalier replied. 'I've never seen it sparkle quite like it does this evening; it would force the blindest of men to notice it.'

"And with that, they had come to the end of the game. The Chevalier took the Countess's hand, saying, 'May I?'

"The Countess languidly slipped off her ring, tossing it to the Chevalier across the card table.

"The old émigré examined it closely, turning it this way and that like a kaleidoscope. But light is capricious in its own way. Turning the ring's facets every way he could, he could not produce a second flash like the one that had so stunned them before.

"Herminie got up and raised the blind, so that the declining sun fell more directly on her mother's ring so that they might better appreciate its beauty.

"She sat back down and leaned on the table with her elbows, gazing at the prismatic ring along with the others; but her cough came back, a wheezing cough that injected a redness into the pearly whites of her lovely blue eyes, normally moist and pure.

"'Where did you pick up that cough, my dear child?' asked the Marquis de Saint-Albans, more occupied now with the girl than the ring, with the human diamond than the mineral one.

"'I don't know, Monsieur le Marquis,' she replied, with the lightness and ease of youth that believes it will live forever. 'Maybe from walking in the evening, along the edge of the pond at the Stasseville chateau.'

"I was suddenly struck by the group that they formed there at the open window, those four.

"They were immersed in the red light of the setting sun. The Chevalier de Tharsis was looking at the diamond; Monsieur de Saint-Albans, at Herminie; Madame du Tremblay, at Karkoël, who in turn was looking idly at the Queen of Diamonds that he held in his hand. But what struck me most was Herminie. The 'Rose of Stasseville' was pale, paler even than her mother. The dark purple of the dying day, striking her pale cheeks, made her look like a sacrificial victim, as if she were reflected in a mirror of blood.

"All of a sudden, a chill went through me, and through who knows what furious and involuntary evocation, I was seized with a memory, one of those thoughts that assault the mind brutally but at the same time make it fertile.

"About two weeks before, more or less, I had gone to visit Marmor de Karkoël at his home. It was early. None of the players who usually frequented the place had yet arrived. When I went in, he was standing in front of his desk, seeming to be involved in something that required the utmost delicacy and attention. I could not see his face; his head was bent downward. In his right hand, he held a little bottle with a black, shiny liquid in it, a bottle about the size and shape of the tip of a broken dagger, and he was carefully pouring whatever the liquid was into an opened ring.

"'What the devil are you doing there?' I asked, as I approached the desk. But he called out in a commanding tone:

"'Don't come over here! Stay where you are; you'll make my hand tremble, and what I'm doing is more dangerous and delicate than trying to break a corkscrew at forty paces with a pistol that could explode at any moment.'

"That was a reference to something that had actually happened to us a short while before. We had been amusing ourselves, out shooting with the worst pistols we could lay our hands on, so that the marksman's skill would stand out better due to the weakness of the instrument, and we had very nearly blown a hole in our skulls with one pistol that exploded on us.

"He managed to insinuate the mysterious liquid into the ring, letting the small drops fall slowly from the opened mouth of the bottle. When he was done, he closed the ring and slipped it quickly into a drawer in the desk, as if he wanted to hide it.

"I noticed that he was wearing a glass mask.

"'Since when have you become a chemist?' I asked him jokingly. 'And are you mixing some potion for when you finally lose at whist?'

"'I'm not mixing anything,' he replied, 'but what's in here' (and he pointed to the black bottle) 'is a remedy for everything.' And he added, with the grim humor of the country of suicides, his native land, 'This is the marked deck with which you're sure to win the final game with Fate.'

"'What kind of poison is it?' I asked him, picking up the bottle, whose strange shape attracted me.

"'It's the most wonderful of all the Indian poisons,' he replied, removing his mask. 'Breathing it can be lethal, and no matter how it's absorbed into the body, it doesn't kill immediately, but you only need to wait: its effect is as certain as it is hidden. It attacks the body slowly, almost languidly, but infallibly, going after the sources of life, penetrating, taking root down in the organs, masking itself behind the symptoms of well-known maladies completely familiar to medical science, eliminating all suspicion of poison, if there had been any such suspicion. They say that the mendicant fakirs in India mix it up from extremely rare substances that only they know, and that are only found in the high plateaus of Tibet. It dissolves the cords of life rather than rupturing them. In that respect it reflects the Indian character, so apathetic, so gentle; they look upon death as a sleep, and let themselves sink into it as if they were lying down on a bed of lotus. In any case, it's very difficult, almost impossible, to get hold of. If you only knew what I had to go through to get this bottle from a woman who was supposedly in love with me! . . . I have a friend, an officer in the English army like myself, who, also like me, returned from India after seven years there. He hunted for this poison with all the fury of an Englishman's obsession—and later, when you're a bit older, you'll know what I mean by that. Well, he never did find it! He bought, at steep prices, cheap counterfeits. In despair, he wrote me from England and begged me to send him a few drops of this death nectar. And that's what I was doing when you came in.'

"What he said didn't particularly surprise me. It's just the way men are: without any evil thoughts or plans, they simply like to have some poison around them, the same way they like weapons. They like to stock up and hoard means of extermination, just as misers like to hoard money. The ones say, 'Just in case I wanted to kill . . .' while the others say, 'Just in case I wanted to buy . . .' They're both the same infantile idealism. And being infantile myself in those days, I thought it was perfectly natural that Marmor de Karkoël, who had been in India, would feel that kind of curiosity about a particular poison that could be found nowhere else, and that among his souvenir daggers and arrows, buried down at the bottom of his officer's trunk would be that bottle of black liquid, that pretty trinket of destruction that he had shown me. And when I had carefully looked the toy over, polished as marble, like something an Almée might have worn between the two topaz-brown globes of her bosom, and might have impregnated its porous substance with her own golden drops of sweat, I tossed it aside into a cup on the mantel piece, and thought no more about it.[34]

"Well, can you believe it? The memory of that little bottle came back to me now! . . . The spectacle of the suffering Herminie, her pallor, that cough that sounded as if it came from deep within spongy, unhealthy lungs, where there were perhaps already some of those deep lesions that the physicians call—have I got the right word, Doctor?—using an all-too-vivid image, *caverns*. And that ring that, through some inexplicable coincidence had sparkled so brightly and strangely at just the moment that the girl had coughed, as if the glinting of the homicidal stone had expressed the murderer's glee; and the circumstances of a morning that I had almost forgotten, but that came back vividly to me now: all this came flooding over me, like a wave of thoughts! What link there might be between that memory and the present, I did not know. The connection I had involuntarily made in my mind seemed insane. I was afraid of my own thoughts. So I forced myself to stifle them, to extinguish that false blaze I had allowed to be lit, that flash that had passed through my soul just the way the glint of that diamond had passed over the table! . . . In order to regain my wits and to crush out that criminal idea within me, I gazed attentively at Marmor de Karkoël and the Countess du Tremblay.

"The posture and the facial expression of each proved to me that what I had imagined could not be possible! Marmor was always Marmor. He continued to look at his Queen of Diamonds as if she were the sole, definitive, ultimate love of his life. As for Madame du Tremblay, her brow, her mouth, the look in her eyes all spoke of that calmness that so defined her, that never left her even when she was firing off one of her satirical epigrams—for her witticisms were like bullets, the only weapon that kills without passion, unlike the épée, for instance, which shares the passion of the hand that wields it. She and he, he and she—they were two abysses placed in front of each other. The one, Karkoël, was dark and shadowy like night; the other, that pale woman, was light and inscrutable like space. She always kept her indifferent eyes on her partner, though they gleamed with an impassive light. However, since the Chevalier de Tharsis *would not finish* examining her ring, she had taken a large bunch of mignonette from her belt, and she started breathing in its scent with a frank sensuality that I never would have expected from a woman like her, so unlikely to indulge in voluptuous daydreaming. Her eyes turned upward and then closed as if she were swooning inside from some inexpressible emotion and, with an avid passion she seized a few of the flowers' fragrant stalks between her thin, colorless lips, and she began to grind them between her teeth, as her face took on a savage, idolatrous expression and she stared directly at Karkoël. Was this some kind of sign between them, some kind of shared understanding, some complicity like lovers share, these flowers chewed and devoured in silence? . . . Frankly, it seemed like it to me. She languidly slipped the ring back onto her finger when the Chevalier had finally admired it sufficiently, and the whist game started up again, self-enclosed, mute, somber, as if there had been no interruption."

Here the narrator paused again. He had no need to hurry. He had us all on the edges of our seats. It may be that the entire worth of his story lay in his manner of telling it. . . . When he paused, as now, we all continued listening, in the silence of the drawing room, to his very breathing. As for me, peering up over my alabaster ramparts, the bare shoulders of the Countess de Damnaglia, I could see the intense interest stamped in its diverse forms on every face. Involuntarily, I looked around for the young Sibylle, that wild young girl who had balked at the very beginning of the story. I would have liked to watch her fall under the trance of the tale, to see it in those black eyes of hers, which made me think of that black, sinister Orfano canal in Venice, because more than one heart will drown in them someday. But she was no longer seated by her mother's sofa. No doubt feeling some disquiet about where the story would be going, the Baroness had probably made some subtle sign for her daughter to withdraw quietly, and she was gone.

"But when you think about it," the narrator continued, "what was there in all that to move and disturb me so, to engrave it all in my memory as precisely as an etching? For, in fact, time has not erased so much as one detail from the scene. I can still see the figure of Marmor, the calm, crystal-like expression of the Countess, broken for one moment when she inhaled the scent of those mignonettes and then ground them between her teeth with an almost voluptuous shudder. All of that has stayed with me ever since, and I'm going to explain why. These facts, the connection between them as yet unclear to me, these facts so abruptly lit up by an intuition of which I felt ashamed, were all tangled up in a skein in which the possible and the impossible were hopelessly confused, but they later received a spark of light, which eventually clarified everything and led my mind up and out of that chaotic state.

"I believe I've already told you that I was late in beginning my formal education. And the last two years of my schooling passed by without my coming home at all. So I was away at school when I learned, through letters from my family, of the death of Mademoiselle Herminie de Stasseville, the victim of a wasting disease that no one had suspected until it was in its final stages and quite incurable. The news, which they had transmitted to me without comment, froze my blood; it was the same sensation I had experienced that evening in my uncle's drawing room, when I had first heard that cough that was the harbinger of her death, and that had started up in me so many frightening suspicions. Those of you who have had experience of profound matters like these will understand me when I say that I did not dare ask a single question about this sudden death of a young girl, stolen away from her loving mother and a life filled with the best possible expectations. It seemed entirely too tragic for me to be able to speak about it with anyone. When I returned to my parents, I found the town of *** very much changed; for, after a few years, towns change, just as women do: they are no longer recognizable. This was about 1830. Since the time when Charles X passed through the place on his way to take ship at Cherbourg, most of the noble families that I had known since my childhood lived close to each other in semi-retirement within their chateaus.[35] The political events had fallen even harder on these families because they had all believed that their side was going to be victorious, and thus the collapse of their hopes was all the harder to bear. And in fact they had seen the glorious moment finally arrive when the right of primogeniture was restored by the only genuine statesman of the Restoration, and this was going to reestablish the greatness of French society once and for all on its only true basis, its only true power: monarchy.[36] But then, all of a sudden, this idea, just as sensible and right as it was just and true, which had shone in the eyes of these men, the sublime dupes—dupes through their very devotion to the monarchy—this idea, which had held out to them one last ragged scrap of fur and ermine, just enough for them to line their coffins with and soften their last sleeps, this idea itself perished at the hands of public opinion, an opinion, and a public, that had never known enlightenment or discipline. The little town that has featured so often in this story was now little more than a desert of closed blinds and doors that no longer opened. The July Revolution frightened away the English, and they all abandoned the town whose mode of life had received such a repudiation by events. My first concern was to ask what had happened to Monsieur Marmor de Karkoël. I was told that he had been ordered by his government to return to India. The person who told me that was none other than the same old Chevalier de Tharsis, one of the four who had made up that famous diamond ring whist group (famous to me, at any rate). But in telling me this, he stared at me in the way a man does when he wants you to interrogate him further. So, involuntarily—for the will is often late in such matters, and the understanding has already raced ahead—I questioned him.

"'And the Countess du Tremblay de Stasseville?' I asked him.

"'Have you heard something?' he replied, mysteriously, as if there were hundreds listening to us, though we were quite alone.

"'No,' I replied. 'I haven't heard anything.'

"'She died,' he said, 'of a chest malady, just like her daughter, one month after the departure of that devil, Marmor de Karkoël.'

"'Why one month later?' I exclaimed. 'And why do you talk about Marmor de Karkoël that way?'

"'So it's true,' he replied, 'that you don't know anything! Well, then! My young friend, it would appear that she had been his mistress. At least that's what they say around here, though they keep their voices down. And nowadays, no one dares to speak about it at all. That Countess was a hypocrite of the first order. The way some women are blonde or brunette, she was *that,* and born that way. She practiced lying to the point where you couldn't tell it from the truth, so simple and natural she seemed, so unaffected in every way. Her skill at deception was so profound that no one ever suspected a thing, but some rumors began, though they were so horrific that they were stifled by the very people who would have spread them. . . . To listen to them, that Scotsman, who loved nothing but card playing, was not only the lover of the Countess, who never received him at her home the way everybody else did and, wicked as a demon, would wax more sarcastic and satirical about him when the occasion presented than she ever did about anyone else. . . . But good God, all that would be nothing if that were all there was to it! The worst of it is that the "king of tricks" played a "trick" on the whole family. That poor Herminie silently adored him. Mademoiselle Ernestine de Beaumont will tell you all about it if you're interested. It was like fate, unstoppable. As for him, did he love her? Did he love the mother? Did he love both of them? Or didn't he love either one? Did he think that the mother would make good cover for what he had in mind? . . . Who knows? . . . The real story isn't clear, not at all. The one thing that everyone is sure of, though, is that the mother—whose soul was as dried up as her body—was overcome with hatred for her daughter, which contributed not a little toward making her die.'

"'People are saying that!' I said, feeling more frightened at having suspected it all along than at the thing itself. 'But who could possibly know it? . . . Karkoël is no braggart. He wouldn't have confided in anyone. No one ever managed to learn much about his past life. He wouldn't have started taking on confidants, or becoming indiscreet, with regard to the Countess de Stasseville.'

"'No,' replied the Chevalier de Tharsis. 'The two hypocrites made a perfect pair. He left the way he came, and none of us could have said that he was anything more than a master whist player. But despite the Countess's perfect control and irreproachable behavior, her chambermaids (for whom there is no such thing as a heroine)[37] have told stories about her shutting herself up with her daughter for long hours alone together, and when they came out, each seemed deathly pale, but the daughter was always the worse, and it was obvious that she had been crying.'

"'You have no better witnesses than that, Chevalier?' I said to him, trying to push him to see things more clearly. 'After all, this is the testimony of chambermaids, remember. . . . I would rather hear from Mademoiselle de Beaumont.'

"'Mademoiselle de Beaumont!' exclaimed de Tharsis. 'Ah, they had no love for each other, the Countess and she, for their personalities were too similar! And now, the surviving girl never speaks of the dead woman but with a look of hatred in her eyes and with a kind of reticence, as if she could say much more than she will. There's no doubt that she would like us all to believe the very worst, the most hideous things . . . though she really only knows of one, that Herminie loved Karkoël, and that's not so hideous.'

"'And that's not knowing so very much, Chevalier,' I replied. 'If one could eavesdrop on all the confidences between girls, the subject of who fantasized that she was in love with whom would be the one constant topic. And you'll have to admit that a man like Karkoël was just the type to inspire love fantasies.'

"'That's true,' admitted old de Tharsis, 'but this is more than a matter of chitchat between girls. You'll remember—no, you were too young!—but many people saw it and commented on it in our society . . . that the Countess de Stasseville, who had never been in love, neither with a person nor even with flowers, and I defy anyone to say what that woman's tastes really were, later in her life took to carrying a bouquet of mignonettes tucked into her belt. And, while playing whist, and anywhere else for that matter, she would pluck off the stems and chew on them, to the point where one day Mademoiselle de Beaumont asked Herminie, with a delighted tone of mockery in her voice, how long it had been since her mother had turned herbivore. . . .'

"'Yes, in fact I do remember that,' I replied. 'And I've never forgotten the wild, savage way that the Countess would breathe in and then eat the flowers from her bouquet, almost as if it were some form of cruel lovemaking, during that game of whist that made so lasting an impression on me.'

"'Well, then!' said the good old man. 'Those mignonettes came from a magnificent flower stand that Madame de Stasseville kept in her drawing room. Oh, the time was long gone when strong scents made her ill. We could remember a time when she couldn't tolerate them, during her last pregnancy; she would say, languorously, that some tuberoses had practically killed her during her delivery. But now she loved flowers, loved them almost madly. Her drawing room was so thick with scent that it was almost asphyxiating; it was like a greenhouse in there, with the windows not being opened till noontime. Because of it, there were two or three sensitive women who would not come to her home anymore. All this was quite a change! But people attributed it to illness, or to nerves. After her death, the salon was to be redone—for her son's tutor had managed to get the little imbecile sent off to boarding school, as rich a little imbecile as you'll find, by the way—and they wanted to take those lovely mignonettes and replant them outdoors . . . and what do you think they found in the bottom of that flower stand? The corpse of a baby, who had been born alive! . . .'"

The narrator was interrupted here by a very real cry of horror from two or three women in the audience, though they were not the sort usually to have much to do with the natural emotions. They had turned their backs on such things for many years but, good heavens, they came back now! The others, who had better self-control, only permitted themselves a little jump, but that jump was convulsive.

"'Quite the dungeon for a dangerous little prisoner!' quipped that amiable little piece of scented rottenness known as the Marquis de Gourdes, whom we all called 'the last of the marquises,' one of those people who would crack jokes behind a coffin, or even inside one. His light tone in saying it made everyone laugh.

"The Chevalier de Tharsis continued, as he kneaded the contents of his snuffbox: 'Where did this child come from? Whose was it? Did it die a natural death? Did someone kill it? . . . Who killed it? . . . Impossible to answer all these questions, but they give rise to horrifying suspicions and whispered guesses.'

"'You're right, Chevalier,' I replied, repressing within myself what I thought I knew. 'It will always remain a mystery, and I hope it will grow even more mysterious, until the day when no one mentions it again.'

"'In fact,' he said, 'there are only two people in the whole world who know the truth—and it's not likely that they will ever reveal it,' he added with a sly smile. 'One is Marmor de Karkoël, who's gone off to India, his trunk heavy with the gold he won from us. We'll never see him again. The other . . .'

"'The other? What other?' I asked, astonished.

"'Ah! The other,' he said with a wink that he thought was highly subtle. 'For the other, there's even greater danger. I mean the confessor to the Countess. You know him, that fat Abbé de Trudaine, who, by the way, has just been nominated for the See of Bayeux.'

"'Chevalier,' I interrupted, struck by an idea that suddenly shed a great deal of light on that secretive woman. The Chevalier de Tharsis, along with all the other myopic observers, called her a hypocrite, when in fact perhaps she had put that strong will of hers above her passions precisely in order to enhance them, to redouble the strength of her stormy pleasures. 'Chevalier, you're wrong. The nearness of death itself would not have broken open that walled-in, sealed-tight personality of hers, that woman more suited to sixteenth-century Italy than to our times. The Countess du Tremblay de Stasseville died just as she had lived. The voice of the priest would have been like a breeze blowing on a rock; her impenetrable nature kept her secret till the end. If in fact she had ever repented and opened her heart to the minister of eternal mercy, there never would have been anything found in the bottom of that flower box in her drawing room.'"

The narrator had finished his story, the novel he had promised us, and he had only shown us what he knew, that is, the extremities, the externals. Emotion prolonged the listeners' silence. We were all lost in our own private thoughts, using what imaginative powers we each had to fill in the gaps in this novel of real life. In Paris, where wit is so quick to toss feeling out the nearest window, such a long silence in such a clever salon was the greatest possible mark of success.

"What a sight you've shown us beneath the cards at your whist parties!" said the Baroness de Saint-Albin, as enthusiastic a card player as any ambassador's aging wife. "And what you were saying is very true. Giving us just a glimpse makes more of an impression than if all the cards were turned face up and we could see exactly what each person had been holding."

"Reality is more fantastic than fiction," said the Doctor with great seriousness.

"Ah!" Mademoiselle Sophie de Revistal exclaimed. "It's just the same with music and life. What makes the greatest impression in both are the silences, more than the notes."

She looked at her close friend, the haughty Countess de Damnaglia, she of the unbending torso, who continued to nibble on the gold-tipped ivory of her fan. What did she see in the blue-steel eyes of the Countess? . . . I could not see, but her back, pearled ever so slightly in perspiration, seemed expressive to me. People say that the Countess de Damnaglia, much like Madame de Stasseville, keeps her passions and her pleasures locked away from view.

"You've ruined some flowers for me that I was quite fond of," said the Baroness de Mascranny, turning halfway toward the novelist. And breaking the neck of a perfectly innocent rose that she had plucked out of her corsage, scattering the petals in a kind of pensive horror, she said:

"No more, then! I won't wear mignonettes ever again."

AT A DINNER OF ATHEISTS

This is worthy of godless men.
—ALLEN

Night was just falling in the streets of ***.[1] But inside the
church belonging to that small, picturesque town in the
west of France, night had fully come already. Night almost always
falls first in the churches. It comes there more quickly because
of the effects of the dark, stained-glass windows, when there are
windows, and because of the many crisscrossing pillars, so often
likened to a forest of trees, and because of the shadows cast by the
arches. But the doors are not yet closed, though night has fallen
inside, anticipating the definitive nightfall outside. Generally they
remain open until the Angelus has rung—and sometimes much
later than that, on the eve of a major feast day in a pious town, for
example, when great numbers of people want to confess before
the next day. At no other hour of the day are provincial churches
more frequented than this twilight time, the hour when the day's
labor has ended, when the light begins to die, and when the Christian soul begins to prepare itself for the night—the night that so
resembles death, and during which death could well come. This
is the hour when one realizes anew that the Christian religion is
the child of the catacombs, and that it still keeps something of the
melancholy of its cradle. This is the time, in fact, when those who
still believe in prayer like to come and kneel, elbows propped on
the pew ahead of them, their faces hidden in their hands, in these
mysterious nights, these empty naves that respond somehow to

the deepest of human needs—for if we others, we worldly ones, we creatures of passion, find a solitary, secret meeting with a beloved woman more exciting at such an hour, why shouldn't it be the same way for the religious souls with their God, when the tabernacles are dark and they can speak to Him, lips against His ear, in the shadows?

Now, that is just how they seemed to be speaking to God in the church of *** on that particular day, those pious souls who had come there to pray, as was their custom. Though the town itself was still gray in its foggy autumn dusk, the street lamps had not yet been lit—nor had the little wire-mesh lamp before the statue of the Virgin, which used to be seen on the façade of the convent of La Varengerie but has since been moved—and it was now two hours since Vespers had been said—for it was Sunday, this particular day—and the cloud of incense that always forms a bluish dome over the choir after the service had not yet evaporated. The thick, dark night had already unfurled within the church, like a sail unfurled from a mast. Two thin candles attached to two of the nave's pillars, but far apart from each other, and the sanctuary lamp, a motionless little star shining in the greater darkness of the choir, together threw not so much a light as a phantasmagoric gleam on the shadows in the nave and the side aisles. That highly filtered light made it possible to make out people indistinctly, but not to recognize them. . . . One could make out, here and there in the dim light, small groups that seemed denser than the shadows, and that detached themselves from them—glimpses of a bent back, of a woman's white cap, of some people kneeling on the floor—two or three capes, their hoods thrown back—but that was all. One could hear much more easily than see. Mouths were praying in low voices in that great silent, sonorous nave, its silence making it even more sonorous, creating a strange whispering sound like that of an anthill of souls, visible only to the eye of God. Only the sound of a sigh interrupted, from time to time, that low, continuous whispering, the murmuring of those lips—a sound to strike the imagination in the shadows of a silent church.

The only variation was the occasional sound of a door opening in one of the side aisles, groaning on its hinges and then closing again behind the person who had come in; the sharp, clear sound of a wooden sabot walking down past the side chapels; the clatter of a chair knocked over somewhere deep in the shadows; or the sound of a cough or two, that kind of cough that the pious use, when they try to stifle the sound, making it sound almost musical, out of respect for the holy echoes in the house of the Lord. But all these noises were passing ones, sounds that came and went rapidly without really interrupting the attentive, fervent believers or the eternal whisper of their daily prayers.

And that is why this group of the faithful, assembled as they were every evening in the church of ***, paid no attention to the arrival of a man who would surely have surprised many of them, had there been daylight or candlelight enough to be able to recognize him. He was not the sort who was typically seen in a church. In fact, he was never seen there. He had not set foot in the place since he had returned, some years back, to take up temporary residence in the town where he had been born. Why, then, had he come in on this evening? . . . What emotion, what idea, what scheme had induced him to cross the threshold of this place, a threshold he passed by several times each day as if it did not even exist? . . . He was a man of high stature in every respect, and he must have had to bend his pride as well as his back to pass in through that little low-arched door, stained green by the incessant dampness of the climate there in the West. That fiery head of his did not lack for poetry. Therefore, when he came into this place, which he had probably forgotten entirely, was he struck by the tomb-like appearance of the church, constructed so as to resemble a crypt, with its floor on a lower level than the street outside, and its doorway, standing at the head of a set of steps, higher up than its main altar? He had not read Saint Bridget.[2] If he had, he would have been struck, upon entering this nocturnal atmosphere, full of mysterious whisperings, by its similarity to her vision of Purgatory, a vast dormitory, somber and terrible, where no one can see anyone else, but only hear their low murmurs and their sighs emanating from the walls. . . . But whatever his reflections might have been, the fact is that he stopped, seeming unsure of himself and his memories, midway on the side aisle down which he had been striding. If anyone had been observing him, it would have appeared that he was looking for but not finding someone or something in the shadows. . . . However, once his eyes adjusted and he could make out the contours of things around him, he finally caught sight of an old beggar woman, more heaped up than kneeling, saying her rosary at the far end of the so-called pauper's bench, and he touched her shoulder and asked her where the chapel of the Virgin was, and where the confessional of a particular parish priest was. Once informed by the old tenant of the pauper's bench, who had herself formed part of the church's furniture for some fifty years now, and was as much a part of the place as its gargoyles, the man made his way, with some difficulty, through the chairs scattered about in disarray since the end of the day's services, and came to stand in front of the confessional at the far end of the chapel. He stood there with his arms crossed, in the pose adopted by men who have not come to pray but are trying to look suitably grave. A number of ladies from the Congregation of the Holy Rosary were praying in the chapel, and if they had noticed the man, they would have noticed what I would not call the impiety but, rather, the nonpiety of his posture. Normally, on evenings when there was confession, there was a twisted candle of yellow wax standing just beneath the Virgin's statue, illuminating the chapel; but since such a large number of people had taken communion that morning, and there was no one waiting for confession, the priest had come out of the confessional and extinguished the candle; he then returned to his little wooden cell to continue his solitary meditation in that total darkness that eliminates all distraction and enriches contemplation. Was that the reason—or was it chance, or caprice, or simply a sense of economy—that led the priest to take this step? The one sure thing is that it preserved the man's incognito status, if that was what he wanted to preserve during the short time that he was there. . . . The priest, who had snuffed out the candle before his arrival, had caught sight of him through the bars on the window of his confessional door, and he swung open the door without getting up from the spot where he sat inside. And the man, uncrossing his arms, handed some small object that he drew out from his shirt.

"Take it, Father!" he said in a low but distinct voice. "I've been carrying it with me a long time!"

He said nothing more. The priest took the object, just as if he knew what it was all about, and calmly closed the confessional door. The ladies of the Congregation of the Holy Rosary expected that the man who had just spoken to the priest would go on now to kneel down and confess, but they were astonished in the extreme to see him nimbly step out of the chapel and return to the side aisle from whence he had come.

But if they were surprised, he was even more surprised when, right in the middle of that side aisle, which he was following to find his way out of the church, he felt himself abruptly seized by two strong arms and heard a loud laugh, scandalous in a holy place like this, bursting out not more than two inches from his face. It was a lucky thing for those laughing teeth that he recognized the laugher, standing so close to him.

"Good God!" said the laughing man in a low voice, but not so low as to keep others from hearing his profanity. "What the hell are you doing here, Mesnil, in a church at this hour? We're not in Spain anymore, like the times when we used to rumple the habits of a few nuns in Avila!"

The man he had called Mesnil made an angry gesture.[3]

"Shut your mouth!" he said, in the tone of a man used to commanding. "Are you drunk? You're swearing in a church as if you were in a barracks. Come on—no more stupidity out of you! Let's leave the place quietly and decently."

And he quickened his pace, followed by the other, and made his way back out of the little low door. When they were finally outside in the open air of the street, they could speak in their normal voices again.

"May all the lightning bolts of Hell fry you, Mesnil!" the other continued, seeming enraged. "Are you going to turn monk?

. . . Are you going to swallow those Masses of theirs? . . . You, Mesnilgrand, you, captain of the Chamboran regiment, in a church, like a priest-lover!"

"You were there, too," Mesnil said calmly.

"I was there because I followed you in. I saw you go in, and I swear it shocked me more than if I had seen somebody raping my own mother. I said to myself, what the devil can he be doing in that priest sty? . . . Then it occurred to me that there must be some damned skirt involved somehow, and I wanted to see whether you were meeting up with some little grisette or some great lady of the town."

"I was here strictly for myself, my friend," said Mesnil, putting an insolent iciness into the last phrase, a tone of utter contempt and complete indifference to what the other might think of it all.

"Come on—you're being more damned shocking to me now than ever!"

"My friend," Mesnil repeated, coming to a stop. "Men like me . . . were destined from all eternity for one thing only . . . shocking men like you."

And turning his back and striding off like a man who has no intention of being followed, he walked up the Rue de Gisors and back to the Place Thurin, in one corner of which he lived.

He lived there with his father, the old Monsieur de Mesnilgrand as the townspeople called him, whenever they spoke of him. He was a rich, miserly old man (they said), a bit slow on the uptake—again, the phrase they used—who had lived in complete isolation for many long years, seeing company only during the three months out of the year when his son came back from Paris to visit him in ***. At those times, old Monsieur de Mesnilgrand, who wouldn't invite in so much as a cat at other times, invited and hosted all his son's old friends and regimental comrades, putting on sumptuous dinners for all—miser's dinners, the more Rabelaisian guests said, but unfairly, for the food was really very good (the kind that's often called 'peasant food').

To give you some idea, in those days there was a well-known tax collector in *** who had arrived in town with all the éclat of a man clattering into a church in a coach and six. He was a fat man but not so expansive when it came to money matters. Nature had amused herself by making him a superb chef. The story had it that in 1814, when Louis XVIII was fleeing toward Ghent, the tax collector had brought the king a cash box with his district's taxes in one hand and a truffle purée in the other; the latter seemed to have been concocted by the seven devils of the seven deadly sins, so delicious it was! Louis XVIII had, as was only proper, accepted the cash box without comment; but in recognition of that purée, he ornamented the broad stomach of the master chef, sprung from the ranks of the tax collectors, with the great black ribbon of the Order of Saint Michael, normally awarded only to scholars or artists. With that wide, moiré-silk ribbon forever displayed across his white waistcoat, and its gold star sparkling on his paunch, this Turcaret[4]—actually, his name was Monsieur Deltocq—who, every Saint Louis Day, would go out sporting a sword and a velvet coat, as proud and insolent as any thirty-six English coachmen in their white powdered wigs, believing that everyone should bow down before him, as emperor of sauces— well, the man was a figure of almost superhuman pomp and pride in the town of ***. . . . My point is that this man of mammoth proportions, who boasted of being able to make some forty-nine different clear soups, but was not sure of how many meat soups he could make—probably the number was infinite!—had as his chief competitor or rival old Monsieur de Mesnilgrand's cook, and she gave him plenty to worry about during those months when the old man's son came to stay in ***!

He was proud of his son, the old man, but he felt sad for him as well, and he had good reason! His "young man," as he continued to call him, though he was by now more than forty years old, had had his future destroyed by the same blow that had smashed the Empire to bits and reversed the fortunes of Him who forever more was only called the Emperor—as if his very name had been dissolved in the grandeur and the glory! He had left home at eigh- teen and was made of the stuff of which great military men were made in that era; the younger Mesnilgrand had fought in all the Empire's wars, his battle helmet plumed with hopes—but the thunderbolt of Waterloo had razed all his ambitions down to the ground. He was one of the soldiers who were not called back into the army after the Restoration, because he, like so many others, had been unable to resist the siren song of the return from Elba—which had made so many forget their oaths of allegiance, almost as if they had had no wills of their own![5] The men of Mesnilgrand's Chamboran regiment—that romantically heroic regiment—liked to say, "You can try to be as brave as Mesnilgrand, but to be any braver is impossible!" He saw many of his old comrades, men with far less experience and distinction than himself, promoted into colonelships in the Royal Guard, and though he was not an envious man, such sights were misery to him. . . . He had an intensely sensitive nature. The almost Roman military discipline of that era was the only thing capable of keeping his emotions in check—passions so inexpressibly powerful that, before he had turned eighteen, they had horrified his native town and nearly killed him as well. Even before eighteen, his excesses with women had left him with a nervous malady, a species of tabes dorsalis, for which he had had to have his spine burnt with moxas.[6] This terrifying operation frightened the town of *** as badly as his behavioral excesses had done; the fathers in town forced their sons to watch as a kind of lesson, teaching them morality by means of terror. They brought the young ones to "watch Mesnilgrand burn"; the young man only survived the trial by fire by dint of a constitution that was strong as hell. And *hell* is exactly the word. That constitution got him through the moxas treatment, and later on it got him through all the fatigue, wounds, and scourges that befall a warrior. Now, Mesnilgrand saw himself come to full maturity without the great military career that he had hoped for, his sword rusting in its scabbard, his feelings swelling up into the bitterest kind of rage. . . . If, in order to make his character clearer to the reader, we were to look into history for someone to whom he could be compared, we would be obliged to go to Charles the Bold, Duke of Burgundy.[7] An ingenious moralist, preoccupied by how illogical our destinies appear to be, once explained it by hypothesizing that men are like portraits: the ones who have only their head and shoulders depicted seem larger than they could really have been in life, while others practically disappear, shrunken and reduced to looking like dwarves by the absurd size of their portrait's frame. Mesnilgrand, the son of a mere Norman squire, was going to have to live and die in the obscurity of civilian life, having missed out on the great historic glory for which he had been born, and yet he was also a man who possessed—but for what possible purpose?—a frightening level of endless, ongoing rage, the poisonous, ulcerating fury that plagued Charles the Bold, whom history also calls Charles the Terrible. Waterloo, which had ended up throwing him out on the pavement, had been for him in a single battle what the battles of Granson and Morat had been for that human thunderbolt who was finally extinguished in the snows of Nancy. However, there was no snow and no Nancy for Mesnilgrand, the erstwhile captain of his squadron who had been *unseated,* to use the vulgar term that irreverent men used. Back then, people thought he would either kill himself or go mad. He did not kill himself, and his mind stayed whole. He did not go mad. But then, that was because he was mad already, said the jokers—for there are always jokers. But although he did not kill himself—and, given his nature, his comrades chose not to ask him why he did not—he was not the kind of man to let his heart be eaten by a vulture without at least trying to break the vulture's beak. Like Alfieri—that incredible man, Alfieri who, knowing nothing in the world except breaking horses, at the age of forty taught himself Greek and began writing poetry in Greek[8]—Mesnilgrand threw himself into painting, or, in other words, the one activity most opposite to everything he knew and was, exactly like the way a man drags himself up to the seventh floor to throw himself out the window—so that he will have farther to fall. He did not know the first thing about drawing, but he became a painter like Géricault, whom, I believe, he had known when he was in the Musketeers.[9] He worked furiously—as furiously as a man retreating from battle, he said with a bitter smile—showed his work, achieved some notice, showed no longer, tearing up his canvases after finishing them and then returning to work relentlessly. This officer, who had always lived with sword in hand, whose horse had carried him all across

Europe, now spent his time standing in front of an easel, slashing at the canvas as if his brush were a saber, and so disgusted with war—the disgust that is only felt by those who have adored it!—that what he primarily painted were landscapes, landscapes like those he had ravaged. While he painted, he chewed some kind of opium compound, mixed with tobacco, which he also smoked day and night, and he had invented a new kind of hookah that he could continue smoking even while he slept. But neither the opiates nor the drugs, nor any of the poisons with which men paralyze themselves and commit slow suicides, could put to sleep the raging monster within him; it was always awake, and he called it the crocodile in his fountain—a phosphorescent crocodile in a fountain of fire! There was some talk that he had secretly joined the Carbonari, but those who knew him better dismissed such rumors, for there was too much high-sounding rhetoric and vacuous liberalism among the Carbonari for a man like Mesnilgrand, and he would have looked upon them with the cool rational judgment of his caste and race.[10] And it was quite true that, apart from his oversized and sometimes overwhelming passions, he had the solid, unshakeable sense of reality typical of Normans. He could not let himself be seduced by the false allure of conspiracies. He predicted General Berton's fate to him.[11] And the democratic ideals espoused by the Imperialists during the Restoration repelled him instinctively. He was profoundly aristocratic, and not just in terms of his birth and the class into which he was born: he was an aristocrat *by nature,* in the same way that he was himself and no one else, and that is what he would have been even if he had been the lowliest shoemaker in town. In short, he was an aristocrat, as Heinrich Heine put it, "through his grand manner of feeling," and decidedly not in a bourgeois manner, like those social climbers who seek out external signs of distinction.[12] He did not wear his decorations. His father, seeing that he was about to be made colonel, just when the Empire collapsed, had acquired a baronage for him, but he never used the title, and his card simply read "The Chevalier de Mesnilgrand." Titles, emptied of all the political privileges with which they had once been full, were meaningless in his eyes—as meaningless as the rind of an orange when the fruit has been sucked out of it—and he mocked them, even in front of people who respected them. He proved it one day in that little town of ***, infatuated with nobility, where the old landed gentry, ruined and sacked by the Revolution, were marked, perhaps as a way of consoling themselves, by an inoffensive mania for assuming titles such as Count and Marquis, which their families, which were very old ones and hence quite sufficiently dignified without any such titles, had never held. Mesnilgrand, finding their claims to such titles ridiculous, came up with a bold way of putting a stop to it all. One evening, at a party at one of the most aristocratic mansions in town, he told the servant: "Announce the Duke de Mesnilgrand." And the bewildered startled servant announced, in his most stentorian voice, "Monsieur the Duke de Mesnilgrand!" The assembled guests all started. "Good heavens," he said, seeing the effect he had produced, "since everybody else is giving themselves a title, I thought I'd pick up that one!" There was absolute silence. And then slowly, in one or two corners of the room, among the guests who had a sense of humor, a few quiet bursts of laughter were heard. But that was the end of the mania for fake titles. There are always some knights errant abroad in the world. They no longer right wrongs with lances but ridicule them with wit, and Mesnilgrand was one of those kinds of knights.

He had the gift of sarcasm. But that was not the only gift that almighty God had given him. While character was the dominant force in his constitution, wit occupied the second place and was a real strength for him to use against others. There is no doubt that if the Chevalier de Mesnilgrand had been a fortunate man, he would have been a great wit; but as an unfortunate, he had the opinions of a desperate man, and when he was in high spirits, which was rare, there was something desperate about him; and nothing will shatter the kaleidoscope of wit more readily, preventing it from twisting and casting ever new splendors, than a fixed, steady unhappiness. But one other gift he had, to accompany those passions of his that always simmered just below the surface, was an extraordinary eloquence. What people say about Mirabeau, and what could be said about all the orators—"If only you

could have heard him!"—applies even more to him.[13] You ought
to have seen him, in even the most trivial conversation, his breast
swelling like a volcano, his face going paler and paler, his brow
furrowing—furrowing like the ocean in a storm, when he got
angry—his eyes seeming to start from their sockets, as if to reach
out and assault the listener, like two flaming bullets! You ought to
have seen him, breathless and throbbing, his voice becoming even
more emotionally powerful the more often it broke, the intensity
of his irony bringing trembling flecks of foam to his lips, which
continued to vibrate even after he had finished speaking—and his
exhaustion after these outbursts itself made him even more sublime, like Talma playing Orestes, killed magnificently yet not dying, his fury ready to leap back to life the next day, or in an hour,
or in a minute, a phoenix of rage, always being reborn from its
own ashes! . . .[14] And in fact there were certain chords within him
that, no matter when you touched them, were taut and ready to
vibrate with a power that would astonish anyone unwary enough
to have struck them. "He visited our house yesterday evening,"
a young lady said to one of her friends. "My dear, he ranted the
whole time. He acts like he's possessed by a demon. One of these
days, people won't let him in their homes anymore." If it weren't
for those rants—the *wrong tone* for certain salons and the sort of
people who frequent them—he might have been of interest to
the young ladies who spoke of him with satiric severity. This was
around the time when Lord Byron had begun to be all the rage,
and when Mesnilgrand was quiet and reserved, he had something
of the Byronic hero about him. His was not the regular, perfect
beauty that women with cold souls are always searching for.
He was frankly ugly; but his pale, ravaged face beneath that still
youthful chestnut hair, his prematurely furrowed forehead like
that of Lara or the Corsair, his nose, flat like a leopard's, his greenish eyes, edged with thin lines of blood like those of champion
racehorses—all this made an impression to trouble and disturb
the thoughts of even the most satiric of the young ladies of ***.[15]
When he was around, the ones who were always giggling giggled
no more. A large man, strong and well built, though he did slouch
a little as if he were going through life wearing too heavy a suit of

armor, the Chevalier de Mesnilgrand, in his modern clothes, had the out-of-place air you see in some old family portraits. "He's like a walking painting," said another young lady, upon seeing him enter her drawing room for the first time. In any case, Mesnilgrand crowned all his advantages with one supreme one, at least in the eyes of the girls: he was always impeccably dressed. Was this one last echo of his long-standing flirtatiousness, of his earlier years as a ladies' man? Was it one last flourish from a failed life, a little hint of what used to be emanating from the burial of the ruin that was his life now, like the last rosy ray of light the setting sun casts over the clouds before it sinks away altogether? . . . Was it a final touch of the sultan-like luxury that the former captain of the Chamboran regiment had once displayed? (For he had made his old miser of a father cough up twenty thousand francs once just in order to pay for tiger skin to put beneath his saddle and to line his red boots!) Anyway, the fact is that no young man from Paris or London outdid the elegance of this misanthrope, who no longer even mixed in society and who, during the three months he spent at his father's house in ***, scarcely ever paid any visits and never repeated the ones he did.

He lived there the same way he did in Paris, busy with his painting until nightfall. He didn't do much walking in that proper, charming little town with its dreamlike aspects, that place built for dreamers, for poets—though it was unlikely that so much as a single poet actually lived there. But sometimes he would be seen passing through the streets, and the shopkeeper would say to the stranger who had asked who that haughty-seeming man was, "That's Commandant Mesnilgrand," as if everyone on earth would know who Commandant Mesnilgrand was! Those who did get a glimpse of him never forgot him. He made an impression, like all men who no longer ask anything of life; for whoever asks nothing of life stands above life, and then life does your dirty work for you. He never went to the café with the other officers who had been crossed off the military rolls by the Restoration, though he never failed to stop and shake hands with them when he encountered them. Provincial cafés were repugnant to his aristocratic spirit. It went against his basic sensibilities to enter one, which caused no scandal, of course. His comrades were always sure of running into him at his father's place, which became, during the months of the son's stay, a place of magnificence and generosity, though it was a miser's lair the rest of the year; the others called the feasts he put on Balthazars—though none of them had read the Bible.[16]

At these feasts, the father sat facing his son, and though he was old now and looked like a character out of a comedy, one could see that in his day he would have looked quite worthy of having produced such a son, and his pride in him was obvious to all. . . . He was tall and thin, as straight as the mast on a ship, resisting the onslaught of age nobly. Always wearing a long, dark coat that made him seem even taller than he was, he had the austere look of a philosopher, of a man for whom the world's pomps and works held no attraction. He wore, and had continued to wear for years now, a white cotton nightcap with a lilac stripe; but none of the local jokers would have dared to comment on this headgear, traditionally associated with *Le Malade imaginaire*.[17] The elder Monsieur de Mesnilgrand aroused the comic spirit in no one. The sight of him would have wiped the smile off Regnard's lips and made the pensive Molière even more pensive.[18] Whatever the youth of this almost majestic Géronte or Harpagon might have been like, it was so long ago that no one could remember.[19] People said he had been on the side of the Revolution, though he was related to Vicq d'Azir, physician to Marie Antoinette, but he soon shifted allegiance. The man of some means, the landowner, soon enough came to the fore and overthrew the man of ideas. But he emerged from the Revolution an atheist in politics, just as he had gone into it an atheist in religion, and the two atheisms combined made him the kind of firebrand denier that would have frightened even Voltaire. But he didn't talk much about his opinions except at those dinners he gave to celebrate his son's visits when, finding himself surrounded by people with opinions and ideas, he let some thoughts escape that would have fully justified what people in town said about him. For the religious types and for the nobility, of which the town was full, he was just an old reprobate they wouldn't dream of inviting to their homes, a solitary old miser who did everyone a favor by staying in isolation. . . . His life was a very simple one. He never went out. The borders of his garden and courtyard were the limits of his world. During the winter, he would sit in a corner by the kitchen fire, where he had had a big reddish-brown Utrecht velvet easy chair rolled in; he would sit there silently, to the annoyance of the servants, for they felt they had to whisper around him as if they were in a church. During the summer, he delivered them from his constant presence and spent all day in the dining room, where it was cool, and sat there reading newspapers or some old books he had bought at an auction from an old monastery's library, or he would sort and organize his receipts at a little maple desk with copper corners that he had had brought down there, so as not to have to walk upstairs when his tenant farmers came, even though this was hardly the kind of furniture one would have in a dining room. And if anything other than interest calculations ever passed through his mind, no one would know it. His face, with its short, somewhat flat nose, white as chalk and pitted from smallpox, showed nothing of his thoughts, which remained as enigmatic as those of a cat purring by the fireside. The smallpox, which had riddled his face, had also reddened his eyes and made the lashes grow inwards, so he had to trim them, and that horrible operation, which had to be repeated frequently, had affected his eyes, making him blink constantly, so much so that when he spoke to you, he had to put his hand up over his eyes to shade them, a gesture that made him seem insolent and proud. There is certainly no pair of eyeglasses that could create so insolent an effect as old Monsieur Mesnilgrand with his trembling hand poised up over his eyebrows, trying to get you into focus so that he could see who he was talking to. . . . His voice was that of a man used to commanding others, a voice that came more from the head than from the chest, as if he had more head than heart; but he didn't make much use of it. He was as miserly with his voice as he was with his coins. He economized, and not just the way Fontenelle did when he had reached a hundred years of age, by breaking off what he was saying when a coach passed by, and only picking up the thread after the noise had passed, so as to save his breath.[20] Old Monsieur de

Mesnilgrand was not, like the elderly Fontenelle, a delicate old piece of porcelain, perpetually busy in examining all his chips and cracks. Instead, he was like an ancient dolmen, solid as granite, and if he rarely spoke, well, that was because dolmens don't speak much, like the gardens in La Fontaine.[21] When he did find himself having to speak, he was concise, like Tacitus.[22] In conversation, he chose his phrases with care. It was as if his words were to be graven into stone—and he did stone you with them, for he was born sarcastic, and when he tossed a stone into someone's garden, it never failed to hit someone. In the past, like many fathers, he had shrieked like a cormorant over his son's extravagances and follies; but ever since Mesnil—and he had taken to calling him by that abbreviated name—had been imprisoned like an ancient Titan under the overturned mountain of the Empire, he felt respect for his son, the respect of a man who had weighed life in the scales of contempt and had concluded that there was nothing finer, after all, than the spectacle of human strength being crushed by the stupidity of fate!

He demonstrated his respect to his son by his manner, a highly expressive manner. When his son spoke, a look of rapt attention would come over his cold, pale face, which looked like a moon drawn on gray paper with a white pencil, with some red chalk dots to indicate the smallpox-reddened eyes. But the greatest proof of the respect he felt for his son Mesnil was how, when his son came to stay, he utterly forgot his miserly habits (and avarice is a vice that rarely lets a man out of its cold grip). The evidence was in those famous banquets he put on, the ones that made Monsieur Deltocq lose sleep and feel his laurels slipping away. . . . Those were the kind of dinners that only the Devil knows how to put together for his favorites . . . and, come to think of it, weren't the guests in fact all good friends of his? "Every rogue and scoundrel in the district can be found there," murmured the royalists and the religious types, who still felt the passions they felt in 1815. "They must say hideous things there—and probably do them, too." The servants, who were not dismissed after the dessert, as they were at the Baron d'Holbach's suppers,[23] gossiped about all the abominable things that went on at these blowouts, and they were so widely believed in the town that old Monsieur Mesnilgrand's cook found herself surrounded by her friends, who warned of the dire things that were in store for her, the worst of which was that the priest would forbid her to take the Sacrament during the months that the son was visiting his father. In fact, the town of *** felt almost as much horror in hearing about these banquets in the Place Thurin as the medieval Christians did in hearing about the Jews' banquets, at which the Host was profaned and children's throats were slit. True, this horror of theirs was tempered somewhat by an obvious and sensual envy, which was evident when mouths began to water whenever the talk turned to the dinners at old Monsieur de Mesnilgrand's. In the country, and in a small town, everyone knows everything about everyone else. The market in such a place is worse than the proverbial Roman glass house: it's like a house with no walls at all. Everybody knew, right down to the last partridge or snipe, what was going to be served or what had been served at every weekly dinner at the Place Thurin. These meals, which usually took place on Fridays, snapped up the best fish and best shellfish in the market, and sumptuous heaps of both fish and meat would be served so that the Church's rule of Friday abstinence and mortification might be all the more effectively transgressed. . . . And that really was the goal of old Monsieur de Mesnilgrand and his Satanic guests! It added spice to their food to eat well on a fast day, and only to abstain once they were full—to fast like a cardinal, in other words. They were like the Neapolitan girl who said that her sorbet was good but that it would have been better if it had been a sin to eat it. But what am I saying—a sin? It would take a multitude of sins to satisfy this godless group, for every one of them who came to sit at this dinner table was ungodly, every one a fully fledged and scarlet-topped sinner, every one a mortal enemy of priests, symbols of the hated Church, every one an atheist—an absolute, furious atheist—the way people were in that era, when there was a particular type of atheism going around. It was a period filled with men of action, men of the most immense energies, men who had lived through the Revolution and the wars of the Empire and who had experienced all the excesses of those terrible times. So theirs was not the atheism of the eighteenth century, though that was where it originated. Eighteenth-century atheism had pretensions to truth, and to thought. It was rational, sophistical, declamatory, and, above all, insolent. But its insolence was nothing compared to that of these veterans of the Empire, these apostate regicides. We who have come along after these men, we too have our own brand of atheism—absolute, focused, erudite, cool, hate-filled, implacable!—and hating everything related to religion with the hatred of the termite for the beam he is gnawing. But neither our modern nor eighteenth-century atheism can give any idea of the ferocity of the atheism of these men earlier in the century, who were bred like dogs by their Voltairean fathers, and once having reached manhood, having had their arms plunged up to the shoulders in all the horrors, all the double corruptions of politics and of war. After two or three hours of howling blasphemies from those drinking and eating, the dining room of old Monsieur de Mesnilgrand had quite a different atmosphere and quite a different look from that sorry little room in a restaurant where some of our grand literary mandarins recently held a little anti-God orgy at five francs a head.[24] No, these were quite a different kind of feast! And since they will probably never happen again, at least not in the same way, it's both interesting and necessary for the history of mores to recall them.

Those who took part in those sacrilegious dinners are dead, long dead; but they were alive then, and that was the time in which they lived most intensely, for life is at its best when the faculties have not yet declined but some misfortunes have amplified it. All those friends of Mesnilgrand, all the habitués of his father's house, had their maximums of strength and power, and all the more because they exercised their powers, drinking deeply of all desire's excesses, all life's pleasures without being overwhelmed by them. But the plug of the barrel from which they drunk was no longer clenched in their teeth or clutched in their hands—like Cynegirus, hanging on to the boat to hold it back.[25] No, circumstances had torn away the breast on which they suckled but before they were done, and now they were all the more thirsty for having suckled. For them, and for Mesnilgrand, it was the time of rage. They did not have the grandeur of soul of Mesnil, that modern Orlando Furioso whose Ariosto, if he had had an Ariosto, would need the tragic genius of Shakespeare to depict him. But on their own levels, their individual levels of spirit, passion, and intelligence, they were like him in that their lives also were over before they were dead—for death is not the end of life but often comes long after the end. They were disarmed men still able to bear arms. They were not only officers who had been dismissed from the Army of the Loire: they had been dismissed from life and hope. The Empire was lost, and the Revolution had been crushed by a reaction that had not been strong enough to keep it under control, the way Saint Michael keeps his foot on the dragon's neck, and all these men, discharged from their employment, from their ambitions, from all the benefits of their past lives, had drifted back to their hometowns powerless, defeated, humiliated, crawling back "to die like miserable dogs," as they said in their rage. In the Middle Ages, they would have gone on to become shepherds, or perhaps soldiers of fortune; but one does not choose the age one lives in—still, here they were, their feet caught and stuck in the grooves of a civilization that insists imperiously on geometrical precision in all things, tossed aside and expected to remain tranquil, to accept the bit in their mouths, to eat their own heart and drink their own blood, and simply to swallow their disgust! They often turned, naturally enough, to dueling; but what is the good of a few saber slashes or bullet wounds, when what they needed was so much more, vast floods of bloodshed, enough to drown the very earth, in order to calm their apoplectic fury and resentments? You can pretty well imagine, then, the kind of *oremus* these men addressed to God when they spoke of Him—for, if they didn't believe in Him, there were others who did—their enemies!—and that was enough to make them curse, blaspheme, and assault anything and everything that men called holy or sacred.[26] One night Mesnilgrand looked around his father's table at them, their faces lit by an enormous bowl of flaming punch, and said, "This would make a good pirate crew!" And he added, nodding at the two or three defrocked priests mixed in among these soldiers out of uniform, "Nothing would be missing, not even chaplains—if pirates took a notion that they needed chaplains!" But after the lifting of the continental blockade and the peace-obsessed era that followed, it wasn't pirates who were lacking but shipowners.

Well! These Friday guests, who provided a weekly scandal to the town of ***, came, as they always did, to dine at the Mesnilgrand house on the Friday following the Sunday when Mesnil had been so rudely accosted in the church by one of his old comrades, shocked and angry to see him there. This old comrade was Captain Rançonnet, of the 8ᵗʰ Dragoons, who, incidentally, was one of the first to arrive at the dinner that day, not having seen Mesnil at all in the intervening week and still unable to make sense of that visit to the church, and of the way Mesnil had reacted to him when he asked for an explanation. He fully intended to come back to this astonishing business that he had witnessed, and to get it cleared up in the presence of all the Friday group, to whom he would narrate the whole thing. Captain Rançonnet was by no means the worst man in this Friday crowd of bad men. But he was one of the noisiest, a blusterer, and the one who was most naïve in his impiety. Though he was no fool, he had become downright stupid on this topic. The idea of God was continually buzzing around in his brain like a fly. He was an officer from that era from his head down to his toes, with all the faults and virtues of the age, steeped in war for war's sake, believing in nothing else, loving nothing else, one of those dragoons who make their spurs ring as they stride along—as the old dragoon song has it. Of the twenty-five who were dining that evening at the Mesnilgrand house, he was probably the one who most loved young Mesnil, though he felt he had "lost the thread" of "his" Mesnil since he'd seen him entering a church. The majority of the twenty-five guests—do I need to say so?—were officers, but there were nonmilitary men as well. There were doctors—the most this-worldly of the town's doctors; a few ex-monks, fugitives from their abbeys and in violation of their vows, contemporaries of the elder Mesnilgrand; two or three priests who claimed to be married but were in fact living with mistresses; and to top the group off, an erstwhile representative of the people, a man who had voted for the King's execution.[27] . . . *Bonnets rouges* or shakos, the former fiery revolutionaries and the latter furious Bonapartists, always ready to squabble and claw each other's guts out, but all of them atheists, united on this one point, the negation of God and contempt for all the Churches of the world—a most touching unanimity.[28] This Sanhedrin of devils with many styles of horns was presided over by the one in the cotton nightcap, the father Mesnilgrand, his face so pale and terrible that there was no comic quality in that headgear. He sat in the middle of the long table, like the mitred bishop at a Black Mass, across from his son Mesnil, whose fatigued face was like that of a lion in repose, the muscles beneath its muzzle always ready to ripple into life and attack.

One would have to say that he stood out—imperially—from all the others. Those officers, erstwhile *beaux* of the Empire, a time when there were so many *beaux,* certainly had their good looks and even elegance; but their handsomeness was conventional, purely physical (or, rather, impurely so), and their elegance was the elegance of the soldier. Though dressed in civilian clothes, they maintained the rigidity, the stiffness of the uniform that they had worn for so long. To use an expression of their own, they were a little too "dressed up." The other guests, the men of science like the doctors, or the turncoats like the ex-monks, who took considerable pains about the clothes they wore (though they had willingly enough thrown off and trampled under foot the sacred, splendid habits of their orders)—their outfits made them look like so many worthless curs. . . . But young Mesnilgrand was—as the ladies would have said—superbly dressed. Because it was still morning, he was wearing a gorgeous black frock coat and a cravat (for people still wore cravats then) that was white with ecru accents, speckled with almost imperceptible gold stars, hand-embroidered. Since he was at home, he was not wearing boots. His feet—so fine and delicately shaped that beggars called out "My Prince!" when they caught sight of them—were clothed in openwork silk socks and low-slung high-heeled shoes, the kind that Chateaubriand affected, the man who gave more attention to his footwear than anyone in Europe, with the exception of the Grand Duke Constantine.[29] He wore his coat (tailored by Staub) open, revealing his sloe-colored trousers with a slight iridescent glint, and a plain black cashmere waistcoat with no watch chain; for on that day, Mesnil had no need of jewelry of any sort, except for an antique cameo of very great price, depicting the head of Alexander, affixed to his cravat, which he wore in an almost military style. No one seeing him dressed in this way, with so confident a taste, could fail to infer that the artist in him had overtaken the soldier, and that this man was not of the same type as the others there, though they continued to speak to each other with the familiar *tu*. This patrician by nature, this man "born wearing epaulettes" as they said in their military language, stood out and made a strong contrast to these hardy, energetic, valiant, but ultimately vulgar soldiers who were clearly unsuited to higher levels of command. He was only the second master in the house, for his father did the honors at the table; Mesnilgrand spoke only rarely at these raucous dinners, unless some topic pulled him up to attention by the hair, like Perseus gripping the Gorgon's head, causing him to vomit forth one of those streams of fiery eloquence of his. The tone of these meetings was not quite his style, and when, after the oysters had been served, the voices were raised in such a cacophony that it would have been impossible to add one voice more, the ceiling—the cork of the room—looked as if it were about to pop, just like all the other corks.

The guests gathered at the table precisely at noon, which was the ironic custom of these irreverent mockers, who seized on the smallest of things to express their contempt for the Church. People in this pious western part of France somehow have the idea that the Pope sits down at the table at noon, and that before eating he offers his blessing on the whole Christian world. Well, that august benediction seemed comic to our group of freethinkers. Thus, the better to jeer at it, old Monsieur de Mesnilgrand never failed, when the first strokes of noon pealed from the village clock tower, to declaim in a loud voice, and with that Voltairean smile that occasionally creased his moon-shaped face, "To the table, gentlemen! Christians like ourselves must not miss out on the Pope's benediction!" This phrase or its equivalent was like opening a door for every sort of impiety that gentlemen such as these could come up with. Now, generally speaking, it's true that all male-only dinner parties, without even a single female hostess to preside over them, where there is no calming, graceful womanly influence, where no woman can serve as a kind of caduceus around which can twine all the gross vanities, the outrageous pretensions, the violent and stupid passions to which even men of wit and spirit are inclined—all such parties are generally likely to turn into mere squabbling and are just as likely to end the way the feast of the Lapiths and the Centaurs ended (and there were probably no women present there either).[30] At these sorts of dinners, uncrowned by the presence of women, even the most refined and best bred of men lose all their polite charm and their distinction, and who would wonder why? . . . They no longer have a gallery to try to please, and they immediately start to become ill mannered, and this becomes worse with the slightest encouragement, at the slightest friction among them. Egotism, that never-really-banished egotism that society's art has managed to conceal under attractive forms, soon comes to the fore and leads to elbows leaning on the table, and then to their digging into your ribs. Now, if it is thus for the most Athenian, the most cultured of men, what must it be like for these guests at the home of Mesnilgrand, these one-time warriors and gladiators, these denizens of Jacobin clubrooms and military barracks, who seem to think they are always in either a club or a barracks, and often enough in even worse places? . . . It may be difficult to imagine, if you haven't heard it for yourself, the conversation—including the snapped officers' batons, the broken windows, the broken glasses—of men like these, great eaters and great drinkers, stuffed full of hot food, enflamed by heady wines, men who even before the third course have let their tongues run free on any topic and cast off all inhibitions. Their conversation wasn't all impieties, however, though impiety formed its flower—and one could say that there was no vase without its flower! . . . Imagine! This was the era of people like Paul-Louis Courier, who incidentally would have fit right into a group like this; Courier tried to whip France up into a rage by writing, "The only question now is whether we are all going to be monks or lackeys."[31] But that was not all. After talk of politics, of hatred for the Bourbons, of the dark specter of the Congregation, and of regrets for the past that these defeated men had lived through, all those avalanches of words that roiled and boiled from one end to the other of that steaming table, there were other conversational topics, too, other things to raise a racket about.[32] For example, there was always the topic of women. Woman is the eternal subject when men converse with each other, especially in France, the most conceited nation on earth. There was woman in general and women in particular—the universal woman and the woman next door—the women from the countries that these soldiers had passed through, showing off in their fine victorious uniforms, and the women of the town of *** whom they never actually went to see, but whom they insolently referred to by their given names, as if they knew them intimately, for heaven's sake, and observing no decency, peeling away their reputations at dessert the same way they would peel a peach before cracking its pit. Everyone took part in these assaults on women, even the eldest ones, the toughest, and the ones who cynically claimed they were through with women—for a man may give up illicit love but never self-love in talking about women, and even when they're tottering on the edge of their opened graves, they're still always ready to dip their snouts into the swill of conceit!

And on this day they plunged them right in, all the way up to their ears, for the language at this dinner turned out to be the coarsest of any of the dinners that old Monsieur de Mesnilgrand had yet given. Within that dining room, silent today, but with so much to say if only its walls could talk—for walls have that kind of impassivity, that habit of silence that I myself lack—at that point, the hour of bragging that always follows an all-male dinner had arrived, first reasonably decent, then progressively less so, then uninhibited, and then stripped absolutely naked. Each one of them had his anecdotes to relate. . . . It was like a confession of demons! All those insolent railers, who couldn't have found enough scorn to heap upon some poor monk making his confession to his abbot in front of all the brothers in his order, were doing exactly the same thing, only not in order to humble themselves like the monk but to engorge themselves with pride and boasting about the abominations in their lives. All of them, so to speak, spat out their souls toward God—but the spittle blew back on their own faces.

Now in the midst of this tide of braggadocio of every sort, there was one that was more . . . *piquant,* shall I say? No, *piquant* isn't a vivid enough word—more peppery, more spicy, more suited to the palates of these wild men who, when it came to stories, would have happily swallowed even vitriolic acid. But the man who was narrating it was the coldest of all these devils. . . . He was like the backside of Satan, for Satan's backside, despite the heat in Hell, is very cold—or so report the witches and sorcerers who kiss it at the Black Mass. It was a certain ex-Abbé Reniant—a prophetic name!—who in this society on the wrong side of the Revolution, seeking to undo all the Revolution had done, had changed himself from a priest who lacked faith to a doctor who lacked science, clandestinely carrying out procedures that were at best suspicious, and at worst—who knows?—possibly murderous.[33] Among educated people, he did not admit to his business. But he had convinced the lower classes of the town and the neighboring region that he knew far more than the doctors with all their certificates and diplomas. People whispered that he knew secrets for curing illnesses. *Secrets!* A fine word that solves everything because it solves nothing, that old warhorse of a word used by all the quacks, who nowadays are all that is left of the old sorcerers who used to have such a hold on the popular imagination. This ex-Abbé Reniant—"for," he would say angrily, "that damnable title of Abbé was like a case of ringworm on his name, and all the resin plasters in the world couldn't make it come off!"—was not motivated by the lust for money in his practice of making up remedies that might turn out to be poisonous: he already had enough to live on. But he was a follower of that dangerous demon of experiment, which begins by treating human life as merely something to work upon and ends up creating people like Sainte-Croix and Brinvilliers![34] Not wanting to be involved with "patent medicines," as he sneeringly called them, he mixed his own drugs, and he sold or gave them away—and indeed, he often did give them away—on the condition that people return the bottles to him. This rogue was no fool and knew how to make his patients into accomplices in his medicine. He gave white wine mixed with who knows what herbs to patients whose heavy drinking had led to dropsy, and to girls who were "in trouble"—as the peasants put it, with a wink—he gave tisanes that "took their trouble away." He was of medium height, with a frigid, inexpressive face, dressed in the same style as old Monsieur de Mesnilgrand (though in blue rather than black); his face was the color of unbleached linen, and his hair, cut in a round shape around his head (the only remnant of his time as a priest), was an ugly dirty blond, hanging down straight and heavy like candle wax. He spoke little; when he did speak, he was direct and to the point. Cold, and as neat as the chimney hook in a Dutch fireplace, at these dinners where people said whatever was on their minds, he sat at a corner of the table and sipped his wine affectedly while the others were gulping theirs, and as a result he wasn't much liked by those hot-blooded types, who compared him to the soured wine of Saint Nitouche (a vineyard of their own invention).[35] But that air of his only added flavor to the story he was modestly telling, saying that the only blow he had ever struck against what Monsieur de Voltaire called *l'infâme* was when—damn it, I'm sorry, but one does what one can—one day, he gave a packet of consecrated communion wafers to some pigs.[36]

This announcement was met with a round of triumphant approval. But then old Monsieur de Mesnilgrand broke through the noise with his incisive, shrill voice:

"That must have been," he said, "the last time, Abbé, that you gave communion?"

And the sly wit put his white, dry hand up to shade his eyes so as to be able to look directly at Reniant, half-hidden behind his wine glass and sitting between two barrel-chested neighbors, Captain Rançonnet, red-faced and fiery as a torch, and the Captain Travers de Mautravers of the 6th Cuirassers, a man the size of a wagon.

"I'd stopped giving it long before that," replied the ex-priest. "I had thrown my cassock into the trash long before. This was when the Revolution was at its height, when you were here, Citizen

Le Carpentier, on your tour through this region representing the people.[37] Do you remember a young girl in Hémèves whom you had imprisoned—a mad girl, an epileptic?"

"Oh-ho!" exclaimed Mautravers. "So there was a woman mixed up with the communion hosts! Did you feed her to the pigs, too?"

"Now you're becoming a wit, Mautravers?" said Rançonnet. "Don't interrupt the abbé. Abbé, finish your story."

"Oh! Well, the story is a short one," said Reniant. "I was saying, Monsieur Le Carpentier, do you remember that girl from Hémèves? Her name was Tesson . . . Josephine Tesson, if I remember correctly, a big, fat girl—calm, tranquil personality, like Marie Alacoque[38]—she was a sort of plaything for the *chouans* and the priests, who set her blood on fire with fantasies and ended up driving her mad. . . . And she spent her life finding hiding places for them, the priests, I mean. . . . She would have defied twenty guillotines if it meant saving just one of them. Oh, the ministers of the Lord!—as she called them, hiding them in her home and anywhere else she could. She would have hidden them under her bed, or in her bed, or under her skirts, and if she could have, she would have rolled them up and stuffed them—Devil take me!—right where she hid the communion hosts—right between her tits!"

"A thousand cannon balls!" exclaimed Rançonnet, exalted with the story.

"No, not a thousand, only two, Monsieur Rançonnet," said the old apostate libertine Mesnilgrand, laughing at his own joke. "But those two were of the finest caliber!"

Everyone repeated his pun. The laughter rose to gale force.

"A strange ciborium, a woman's breasts," said Doctor Bleny pensively.

"Oh, the ciborium of necessity!" replied Reniant, who had recovered his phlegmatic air. "All those priests she had hidden—persecuted, pursued, tracked, and hunted, without a church of their own, with no sanctuary, no safe haven anywhere—they had her guard their Holy Sacrament, and she hid them in her cleavage, believing no one would ever look there! . . . Oh, the faith they had in her. . . . They called her a saint. They had her believing that she was one. They gave her a big head and instilled a desire in her to be a martyr. She was courageous, ardent, coming and going bravely with her little box of hosts beneath her bib. She carried it at night, in all kinds of weather, in rain and wind, snow, fog, over hellish roads, to get it to the hidden priests who used it to give communion to the dying, in secret. . . . One evening, we surprised her, at a farm where a *chouan* was dying, some good men from Rossignol's Infernal Column and I.[39] One of them was tempted by her superb jutting outposts of warm flesh and tried to take liberties with her; but it wasn't such a good idea, as she used all ten of her nails on his face and left a deep decoration there that will last the rest of his life! But now his blood was up and he wouldn't let go of her, and he pulled out the little box of gods he'd found in her bosom,[40] and I counted a good dozen hosts in it, and even though she screamed and struggled and tried to get at me like some kind of Fury, I threw them all straight into the trough for the pigs."

And he stopped there, clearly preening himself with pride for having managed so fine a thing—a feeling of being impressed with himself, rather like the way a flea feels when perched on top of a boil.

"You've avenged the pigs in the Gospel very well—the ones into which Jesus Christ sent the demons," said old Monsieur de Mesnilgrand in his sarcastic presider's voice. "You've put the good Lord into them instead of the Devil. A fine turnabout!"

"And did they get indigestion, Monsieur Reniant, or did the people who ate them?" asked a hideous little bourgeois named Le Hay in a serious voice. He was a usurer charging 50 percent interest, and he had a habit of saying, "Always ask whether the end justifies the means."

There was a pause in the ongoing tide of blasphemy.

"But you, Mesnil, you haven't said a thing about the Abbé Reniant's story. Why not?" asked Captain Rançonnet, who had been on the alert for the right moment to tell everyone the story about seeing Mesnilgrand going into the church.

And in fact Mesnil had not said a thing. He was leaning his elbows against the table, his cheek resting on his hand, listening without disgust but also without relish to all these horrors being reeled off by the hardened atheists; he was so accustomed to them that they left him uninterested. And he had had to listen to so many stories like this in the course of his life! For a man, his environment is practically his destiny. In the Middle Ages, the Chevalier de Mesnilgrand would have been a crusader, on fire with his faith. In the nineteenth century, he was a soldier under Bonaparte, a man to whom his infidel father had never once spoken about God, and a man who, especially in Spain, had lived with an army that permitted everything and that committed as many sacrileges as the soldiers of the Commander of Bourbon had at the sack of Rome.[41] Fortunately, though, one's surroundings are only truly fatal in the case of vulgar souls and minds. In the case of truly strong personalities, there is something, even if it's only an atom or so, that manages to escape the environment and transcend its otherwise all-powerful action. That atom was lying dormant, but invincible, within Mesnilgrand. On this particular day, he would have preferred to say nothing at all; he would have listened with indifference to the torrent of impious muck that was rolling and boiling over all around him like the sulfurs of Hell. But now, since Rançonnet had drawn him out:

"What do you want me to say?" he asked in a bored, almost melancholy voice. "Monsieur Reniant did not do anything so wonderfully brave and heroic that you all ought to be applauding him so! If he really believed it was God, the living God, the avenging God that he was throwing to the pigs and risking an immediate thunderbolt or eventual hellfire, well, that surely would have required a little bravery, a contempt for a fate worse than death, as they say, for if there is a God, he can make your torture last for eternity. That would have involved some courage—stupid courage, true, but courageous enough to appeal to courageous people like yourselves. But the thing wasn't quite that splendid, my friend. Monsieur Reniant didn't believe that the hosts were God. He didn't have the slightest doubt about that. For him, they were nothing more than little bits of bread, consecrated out of some imbecilic superstition, and for him as for you, my poor Rançonnet, to empty a box of hosts into a pig trough is no more heroic than emptying a snuffbox or a packet of sealing wafers."

"Eh! Eh!" grunted old Monsieur de Mesnilgrand, leaning himself back in his chair and shading his eyes with his hand to be able to bring his son into focus, the same way he would have stared at a pistol target to see where his shot had ended up; he was always interested in what his son said, even if he didn't agree with him, and in this case he did. And so he repeated, and louder: "Eh! Eh!"

Mesnil continued. "So there's really nothing here, my poor Rançonnet, but . . . well, let's call it what it is—the actions of a swine. But one thing does seem fine to me, gentlemen, very fine, something I must permit myself to admire, though I know it's not a great thing, and that's this girl Tesson, as you called her, Monsieur Reniant, the one who carried her God over her heart, who made a pure tabernacle for that God out of her two virgin breasts, and who breathed, and lived, and calmly passed through all the vulgarities and all the dangers of life with that bosom of hers, fearless, ardent, weighted down with a God, a tabernacle, and an altar combined, and one that at any time could be spattered with her own blood! . . . You, Rançonnet, and you, Mautravers, and Sélune, and myself, too, we've all carried the Emperor on our chests, because we've all been awarded the Legion of Honor, and sometimes that's given us more courage under fire because it was there. But for her, this wasn't just some image of her God that she carried on her person, some symbol; it was God for her, it was real. It was the substantial, literal God who can be touched, who can be given, who can be eaten, that she was carrying, and at the risk of her own life! Well, I swear to you! I find that simply sublime. . . . I see this girl the way her priests did, the ones who gave her their God to carry. I'd like to know what happened to her. Maybe she's dead, or maybe she's still alive, impoverished, and stuck in some corner of the countryside, but I can tell you this: if I were the Field Marshal of the entire French army, and I encountered her out trying to find some bread to eat, walking barefoot through the muck, I would get down off my horse and take my hat off to her with the deepest respect, that noble girl, just as if it had truly been God whom she'd carried on her heart! Henri IV, on

that day when he got down and knelt in the mud before the Holy
Sacrament when it was being carried past him on its way to some
poor person: he wouldn't have knelt with more emotion than I
would have, if I encountered that girl."

He was no longer resting his cheek on his hand. He had thrown
his head back. And while he spoke about kneeling down, he
seemed to grow before them, like the Bride of Corinth in the
poem by Goethe, who grew until she reached the ceiling.[42]

"It must be the end of the world!" exclaimed Mautravers, crush-
ing a peach pit beneath his clenched fist as if it were a hammer.
"A captain of the Hussars going down on his knees in front of a
Christian girl!"

"But still," said Rançonnet, "still it wouldn't be so bad if it were
like the infantry going in ahead of the cavalry, in order to soften
up the enemy! Because after all, they didn't make bad mistresses, those girls with an *oremus* forever on their lips, all those girls
who like eating their God, the kind who think they're going to
be damned for every little pleasure they give us or that we give
them. But Captain Mautravers, there are worse things a soldier
can do than ruin a few female bigots, and one of them is to become a bigot himself, like some weakling of a civilian, dragging
along a bent saber! . . . Now, just this past Sunday, gentlemen,
where do you think I surprised this Commandant Mesnilgrand,
the one you see before you here?"

No one replied. Everyone was wondering, and all eyes were
fixed on Captain Rançonnet.

"I swear on my saber!" Rançonnet said. "I met him. . . . No, I
didn't meet him, because I have too much respect for my boots to
dirty them by walking into one of their filthy chapels—but, rather, I saw him, from behind, slipping into a church, bending down
to get under the little low door on the corner of the square. Surprised, shocked—'Damn!' I said to myself. 'Am I seeing things?'
But it was definitely Mesnilgrand's shape and size! . . . But what
could he be doing in a church? . . . The idea popped into my head
that maybe he was still playing those little games we used to play
with the nuns in the churches in Spain. 'What,' I said to myself,
'can he still be playing at that? It must be some skirt pulling him

in. But I'm going to see what this one looks like, or the Devil himself can pull out my eyes!' So I went into their Mass shop. . . . Unfortunately, it was as dark as the throat of Hell in there. You walk along and stumble over old women down on their knees, muttering their Our Fathers. You can't make out a thing, even right in front of you, so I was feeling my way along in that infernal mélange of darkness and kneeling carcasses when what does my hand encounter but my old friend Mesnil, who was threading his way down the same side aisle as I. But, can you believe it, he wouldn't tell me what he was doing in that miserable church? . . . And that, gentlemen, is why I'm denouncing him today, to force him to explain himself to us."

The cry went up from all around the table: "Go on, Mesnil. Justify yourself. Answer Rançonnet!"

"Justify myself!" said Mesnil with a smile. "I don't have to justify doing whatever I want to do. You men, who bark and bay all day long against the Inquisition, are you going to turn inquisitors now yourselves? I went into a church on Sunday evening because I wanted to."

"And why did you want to?" asked Mautravers—for, if the Devil is a logician, a captain of the cuirassiers can be, too.

"Ah, there it is!" laughed Mesnilgrand. "I went in . . . who knows? Maybe to confess. I did, at least, open the door of a confessional. But Rançonnet, you can't say, can you, that my confession took very long?"

They could see that he was toying with them. . . . But there was something mysterious in all this that bothered them.

"Your confession! Hellfire! Have you taken the plunge, then?" said Rançonnet sadly, with something almost tragic in his voice. But then, throwing off his thoughts and righting himself, like a horse rearing up, he went on: "No!" he cried. "Damnation! It isn't possible! Look, all of you: can you picture it, the squadron leader Mesnilgrand at confession, on his knees on some rickety kneeler like an old woman, his nose stuck into the grill of the priest's box? No, that's an image that I just can't accept! I'd rather be shot by thirty thousand bullets!"

"That's very kind of you; I thank you," said Mesnilgrand with a comical sweetness in his voice, sounding like a little lamb.

"Let's talk seriously," said Mautravers. "I'm with Rançonnet on this. I'll never believe that a man of your caliber, my brave Mesnil, would descend to that kind of mummery. Even at the hour of death, men like you don't flop around like a frightened frog and jump into a bucket of holy water."

"At the hour of death, I don't know what you'll all be doing, gentlemen," Mesnilgrand replied slowly, "but as for me, before leaving for the other world, I intend to have my bags packed."

And that sentiment from a cavalry officer was stated with such seriousness that it was followed by a silence, like the kind that comes just after a pistol has been fired.

"But never mind all that," Mesnilgrand went on. "It would appear that all of you have been even more brutalized than I have by war and by all that we've been through. . . . I've got no comment to make on your disbelieving souls. But since you, Rançonnet, are so bound and determined to learn why your comrade Mesnilgrand, whom you are sure of being just as atheistic as yourself, went into a church the other evening, I'm perfectly willing to tell you, and I will. There's a story behind it. . . . When you've heard it, you'll understand, maybe, even without believing in God, why your friend went in that place."

He paused, as if he wanted to give what he was about to say even more solemnity, and then he continued.

"You mentioned Spain, Rançonnet. That's exactly where my story takes place. Many of you here today were there then, in that fateful war of 1808 that began the decline of the Empire and led to all our troubles. Nobody who took part in it will ever forget it, and, incidentally, that applies especially to you, Commandant Sélune! You have the memory of it graven right on your face, and you'll never be able to erase it."

Commandant Sélune was sitting next to old Monsieur de Mesnilgrand, and hence directly across from Mesnil. He was a big man with a stiff military bearing, who deserved the nickname Scarface even more than the Duke of Guise, for in a skirmish at an outpost in Spain, he had received a powerful saber slash that split his face, nose and all, from his left temple to his right ear.[43] In normal circumstances, this would have been no more than a serious wound that left a scar, a rather noble one, on a brave soldier's face; but the surgeon who sewed together the two gaping lips of the wound, whether out of haste or incompetence, did it badly, and, well, such is war! The army had to be on the march, and in order to finish up more quickly, he actually cut away some of the flesh with scissors, the part, about two fingers' width, that would have overlapped the wound; and the result was not just a kind of furrow across Sélune's face but a downright frightening-looking ravine. It was horrible—but, in its way, rather spectacular, too. Whenever the blood rose to Sélune's face in anger—which was often, as he was a violent man—the scar reddened and looked like a big red ribbon running across his bronzed face. Back in the days when they shared the same ambitions, Mesnil would say to him, "You're wearing the cross of the Grand Officer of the Legion of Honor on your face before they've given it to you to wear on your chest. But don't worry: it will get down there."

It had not gotten down there; the Empire was finished before it could. Sélune remained only a chevalier.

"Well, gentlemen," Mesnilgrand went on, "we saw some atrocious things in Spain, didn't we? And we did a few of them ourselves. But I don't recall ever seeing anything as hideous as what I have the honor of telling you about today."

"For my part," said Sélune nonchalantly, with the stolidity of an old hand who refuses to let anything impress him, "I remember one day seeing eighty nuns thrown into a well, half-alive, thrown in one after the other, on top of each other, after every one of them had been raped by two squadrons."

"That's just common soldiers' brutality!" said Mesnilgrand, coldly. "The story I'm about to tell involves the refined cruelty of an officer."

He took a sip of wine and then looked slowly at each of them, his gaze traveling all the way around the table.

He asked, "Did any of you gentlemen happen to know Major Ydow?"

No one replied except Rançonnet.

"I did," he said. "Major Ydow! I sure did know him! Eh! Damn right! He was with me in the 8ᵗʰ Dragoons."

"Since you know him," Mesnilgrand went on, "you must have known who he was with. He had come to the 8ᵗʰ Dragoons sporting a woman at his side . . ."

"La Rosalba, also called La Pudica," said Rançonnet, "his well-known . . ." (And here he crudely pronounced a crude word.)

"Yes," Mesnilgrand replied, pensively. "Yes, a woman like that doesn't really deserve the title of mistress, even the mistress of a man like Ydow. . . . The Major had brought her with him from Italy, where he had served at the rank of captain in a reserve corps. Since you're the only one here who knew him, Rançonnet, this Major Ydow, you won't mind if I describe him so as to give the others some idea of this devil of a man, whose arrival made such a fuss when he appeared, toting this woman along with him. . . . He was not a Frenchman, apparently. And France is none the worse for it. He was born I don't know where and I don't know to what family, maybe in Illyria or Bohemia, I'm really not sure. . . . But it didn't matter where he was born, because he seemed to be a stranger wherever he was. To look at him, you'd assume he was the product of an interracial parentage. He insisted that you had to pronounce his name in the Greek way, *Ai-dov,* not Ydow, because he came from Greek stock, and he did look it, for he was a good-looking man—Devil take me, maybe too good-looking for a soldier. Who knows if a man that handsome will take extra care to protect his looks? And people around him treated him the way you'd treat a masterpiece. Masterpiece or not, though, he went into battle the same as everyone else, and when you've said that, you've said all you need to say about Major Ydow. He did his duty, but then he never did more than his duty. He didn't have what the Emperor called 'the sacred fire.' Despite his beauty, which I fully admit, I found him to be an ugly man underneath that fine exterior. I've spent time wandering around in museums, places you men never go, and I've come across the likeness of the Major. I saw a striking resemblance to him in some of the busts of Antinous. . . .⁴⁴ There's one where the sculptor, either out of whimsy or out of bad taste, has inserted two emeralds where the pupils should be. But instead of a marble face, the Major's emerald eyes illuminated a flawless olive-skinned one; those eyes seemed at first to be like the melancholy evening stars, voluptuous, peaceful, but this was no Endymion: beneath that exterior, there was a sleeping tiger, and one day I saw the tiger awake! . . . Major Ydow was both dark and fair at the same time. The curls of his hair around his forehead were very black and clung tightly to his temples, but his long, silky mustache was the light, almost yellow-blond of a sable. . . . Some people say that it's a sign of treason or treachery when the hair and the beard are two different colors. A traitor? The Major might have gone on to become one later on. He might have betrayed the Emperor, like so many others, but as it turned out, he was not going to live long enough to do so. When he joined the 8th Dragoons, he was probably only a liar, but not liar enough to look like one, as that cunning old rogue Suvarov put it, and Suvarov did know him. . . . Was it something about the way he looked, the air he had about him, that made his comrades dislike him? In any case, it wasn't long before he was despised by everybody in the regiment. Terribly vain of that beauty of his—though I would have chosen, myself, the ugliness of the other men I knew—he seemed to be nothing more than, to use the term the soldiers used, a mirror for a . . . for that term you used a moment ago, Rançonnet, to describe Rosalba. Major Ydow was thirty-five. Now, you know that with that kind of beauty that appeals to all women, even the proudest of them—it's their universal weakness—Major Ydow must have been horribly spoiled by them and must have been initiated into all the vices they can teach a man; but he was also possessed of some that they didn't have, and which are no ornament to a man. . . . We were, as you say, Rançonnet, not exactly monks ourselves at the time. We were bad enough, gamblers, libertines, skirt-chasers, brawlers and duelists, drunk when necessary, eating through money like so many moths. We had no right to be morally superior. Well, compared to what we were, he appeared to be much worse. For us, there were things—not many, but some!— some things of which, demons though we were, we would not have been capable. But he, they say—he was capable of anything. I was not in the 8th Dragoons. I only knew some of the officers. They spoke about him bitterly. They accused him of bootlicking with the higher officers and of base ambition. They had doubts about his character. They went so far as to suspect him of espionage, and in fact he fought two duels over such accusations, and he fought them bravely; but their opinions of him did not change. There was always a certain cloud over him, and nothing could dissipate it. It is rare enough for a man to be both dark and fair, but what's just as rare is a man being lucky with both women and cards, and that was also true of Ydow. But he had to pay, and pay dearly, for these double successes, for his Lauzun-like airs,[45] and for the jealousies that his good looks inspired—for men like to pretend that they're indifferent to good looks, and to repeat the soothing saying that a man is good-looking enough if he doesn't frighten his horse, but for all that they are as petty-minded and jealous of each other's looks as any group of women. All these advantages of his, no doubt, explain why Major Ydow inspired such widespread antipathy—an antipathy that took on the form of contempt, not hatred, for contempt is more painful than hatred, and the men knew that very well! . . . How many times did I hear someone call him—sometimes in a whisper, sometimes aloud— a 'dangerous scoundrel,' though proving it definitively would be a different matter. . . . And in fact, gentlemen, even now as I'm speaking to you, I'm not sure that the Major was what they said he was. . . . But, good God!" exclaimed Mesnilgrand in a voice that mingled vigor and horror. "What they didn't say, and what he became one day, that I do know, and that's enough for me!"

"And it would probably be enough for us, too," Rançonnet said gaily, "but for God's sake, what the devil does all this have to do with my seeing you go into a church last Sunday evening and this damned Major from the 8th Dragoons—a man who would have pillaged every last church and cathedral in Spain and Christendom to get the precious stones from the Holy Sacrament chalices to give to his little minx of a woman?"

"Stay in your ranks, Rançonnet!" said Mesnil, as if he were commanding a squadron. "And be quiet! Do you always have to be the hothead and be as impatient as if we were about to face the enemy? Let me maneuver my story the way I see fit."

"Well, then—forward march!" said the ebullient Captain, who poured himself a new glass of wine to settle himself down.

Mesnilgrand continued. "It's likely that if it weren't for this woman who followed him there, whom he called his wife though she was only his mistress and did not bear his name, he would have been ostracized by the officers of the 8th Dragoons. But that woman, who was indeed everything they said about her, or she would never have got involved with such a man, kept them from isolating him the way they would have done without her. I've seen this happen in regiments. A man comes under suspicion, or becomes discredited somehow, and everyone treats him with nothing more than the most strictly necessary politeness; he's nobody's comrade anymore; nobody shakes his hand; even in the café, the main gathering place for the officers, with its warm, informal atmosphere, where every kind of coldness melts away, even there people keep their distance and remain constrained and polite until he finally leaves, and then they all begin to speak freely again. And this would have certainly happened to the Major; but a woman—she's the Devil's companion! What they wouldn't do for him, they would for her. Men who would never have offered the Major a glass of schnapps if it hadn't been for that woman, would do it thinking of her, figuring it might be the means of getting invited to his place and thus getting the chance to meet her. . . . There is a ratio of moral arithmetic, and it's written in the hearts and minds of every man without any philosopher having put it down on paper, a kind of gift from the Devil, which states that 'there is a greater distance from a woman to her first lover than there is from her first to her tenth.' And this was probably truer for the Major's woman than for any other. Since she had given herself to him, she would surely give herself to another, and, good heavens, that other could be anybody! In a very short time, everyone in the 8th Dragoons knew just how realistic that thinking was. All those who had a flair for women, who could sniff out the true scent from behind the perfumed white veils of virtue that she kept wrapped around herself, knew that Rosalba was the most corrupt of the most corrupt of women—one who had attained a kind of perfection in wickedness.

"And in saying this, I'm not libeling her at all, am I, Rançonnet? . . . Perhaps you've had her, and if you have, you know that there never was a more brilliant woman when it came to vice, nor one who was so fascinating, who crystallized all the vices within herself! Where had the Major found her? . . . Where did she come from? She was so young! No one dared to ask at first, but the hesitation didn't last long! The conflagration she lit up—and the fire wasn't limited to the 8th Dragoons, but it reached my regiment of Hussars, and you remember, Rançonnet, how it reached to the entire general staff of the expedition—the fire she lit very quickly took on enormous proportions. . . . We've all seen plenty of women, officers' mistresses following the regiment, when the officers could afford the luxury of a woman among their baggage; the colonels would turn a blind eye to the practice, and sometimes even openly permit it. But none of us ever had any idea of a woman like Rosalba. We were accustomed to pretty girls, I suppose, but almost always of a similar type—determined, assertive, almost masculine, almost insolent; most often they were pretty brunettes, either more or less passionate, that tended to look like boys, very provocative and very voluptuous when they put on the uniform that their lovers had fantasized about seeing them wear. . . . If the legitimate, decent, and honest wives of officers separate themselves from other women by some indefinable trait common to all of them, something they pick up from their military surroundings, it's even truer with the mistresses of officers. But Major Ydow's Rosalba had nothing in common with the adventuresses or the camp-followers we were all used to. To begin with, she was a tall, pale girl—but she didn't stay pale for long, as you'll see—with a thick mass of blonde hair. That was all. Nothing to get excited about. Her skin was no whiter than that of any healthy young woman whose blood is pumping beneath it. Her hair was blonde, but it was not that stunning blonde with that almost metallic gold sheen, nor was it that blonde with soft, subtle little hints of amber that I've seen in some Swedes. She had a classical face—the kind you would see on a cameo—but it was not much different from all the other monotonous faces one sees, with their invariable symmetry and unity—that kind of face that's so frustrating to a man of passion! Take her or leave her, you would have to admit that she was a good-looking woman on the whole. . . . But the love potions she made you drink had nothing to do with her beauty. . . . They came from another source . . . from a place you would never have guessed, from within this monster of shamelessness who dared to call herself Rosalba, who dared to bear the immaculate name of Rosalba, which should only be worn by innocence—and who, not content to call herself Rosalba, the Rose and the White, went further, and called herself La Pudique, La Pudica, the Modest One, to boot!"

"Virgil was also called 'le pudique,' and he's the man who wrote that *Corydon ardebat Alexim*," said Rançonnet slyly, not having forgotten his Latin.[46]

"And this wasn't ironic," Mesnilgrand continued. "We didn't invent the name Rosalba, but we all could read it in her face when we first laid eyes on her; Nature had written the name there, with all the roses available to her. Rosalba was not simply the girl with the most astonishingly modest air we had ever seen; she was modesty itself, its embodiment. If she had been as pure as the Virgins in heaven, who probably blush when even the angels look at them, she would not have been any more the incarnation of Modesty. Who was it who said—it must have been an Englishman—that the world is the work of a Devil gone mad? Surely it was that Devil who created Rosalba in a fit of madness, created her to give us pleasure . . . a Devil who could mix together, one after the other, modesty and voluptuousness, and then spice them with some celestial condiment to create the infernal ragout of all the pleasures that a woman can offer to mortal men. The modesty of Rosalba was not simply a matter of her face—disappointing as that may be to the pupils of Lavater.[47] No: with her, modesty was not merely what showed on the surface; it was also well beneath the surface, shuddering and palpitating within her like the flowing of her blood. Nor was it simple hypocrisy. The vice of Rosalba never would offer that homage to virtue. It was really true. Rosalba was just as modest as she was voluptuous, and what's so unusual is that she was both at the same time. When she was saying or doing the most . . . daring things, she had an adorable way of saying 'I'm so ashamed!' I can still hear her saying it. An unheard-of phenomenon! You were always at the beginning with her, even when you'd reached the conclusion. She would have left an orgy of Bacchantes with the air of the purest innocence having committed its first sin. Even when she was conquered, nearly fainted away, half-dead with pleasure, you would see in her the confused virgin, blushing charmingly like the fresh, new dawn itself. . . . I could never describe to you how these contrasts affected me, how they troubled my heart; language isn't sufficient for it!"

He paused. He thought about it, and they all thought about it, too. It may seem incredible, but what he had just told them had transformed them all into dreamers, those soldiers who had seen every kind of battle, those debauched monks, those old doctors, those skimmers of life's surfaces, and they all were lost in their memories now. Even the impetuous Rançonnet didn't say a word. He was remembering.

"Now, you have to realize that this phenomenon was not recognized at first," Mesnilgrand continued. "At first, when she arrived at the 8th Dragoons, all anyone saw was a very pretty, not to say beautiful, girl, of a physical type like the Princess Pauline Borghese, the Emperor's sister, whom she did resemble somewhat. Princess Pauline had that same air of ideal chastity, and you all know how she died. . . .[48] But Pauline didn't have so much as a drop of modesty, not enough to give a rosy tint to the smallest part of her body, whereas Rosalba had enough in her veins to redden every inch of hers. Consider the naïve, surprising reply the Princess made when asked how she could have posed nude for the sculptor Canova: 'But the studio was warm! There was a stove!' Rosalba would never have said that. If someone had asked her the same question, she would have rushed off in embarrassment, hiding her divinely reddened face behind her divinely pink hands. But rest assured, as she ran off, you would have been able to see a little gap in her dress, a gap in which all the temptations of Hell were lurking!

"That was Rosalba, whose virginal face had us all deceived when she first came to the regiment. Major Ydow could have introduced her to us as his legitimate wife or even his daughter, and we would have believed him. And beautiful as those limpid blue eyes of hers were, they were never more beautiful than when they were cast down. Her eyelids seemed more expressive than her direct gaze. To men like us, men who had had experience of war and of women—and what sort of women!—this creature was a new sensation; she was the sort, to use a vulgar expression, to whom you would have given communion without confession. 'What a damnably pretty girl!' whispered the old veterans. 'But look how proper she is! How can she possibly make the Major happy?' . . . He knew how, but he said nothing. . . . He drank his bliss in silence, like the real drunkards, who drink alone. He told no one about the secret happiness that made him discreet and faithful for the first time in his life, that garrison Lauzun, the most egotistical, pompous man there was; when he was in Naples, some officer who knew him there said, they called him the drum major of seduction! And now, if his beauty, of which he was so proud, had caused every girl in Spain to hurl herself at his feet, he wouldn't have stooped down to pick up a one of them. At the time, we were on the border between Spain and Portugal, with the English in front of us, and we occupied the towns that were least hostile to King Joseph.[49] Major Ydow and Rosalba lived together, much as they would have done in a garrison town in peacetime. You all remember that slow, furious, dogged war in Spain that was unlike any other, because we were fighting not just for victory but to establish a new dynasty in a country that we hadn't yet really conquered. And none of you will have forgotten that there were occasionally pauses in that war between terrible battles, when we would amuse ourselves by holding parties to which we invited the most *afrancesadas* of the women in the towns we occupied.[50] It was at these gatherings that Major Ydow's wife, who had already been the subject of considerable notice, now became celebrated. She sparkled among those dark daughters of Spain like a diamond on a fringe of jet. It was then that she first started arousing that fascination in men, which came no doubt

from the diabolical composition of her nature, and which made
her the most depraved of courtesans, with the look of one of the
most celestial Madonnas of Raphael.

"Then the passions that she aroused began to burn and spread,
like fire in the darkness. Within a short time the fire had touched
everyone, even the older men, even the generals with a reputation for wisdom, they were all on fire for La Pudica, the name
they delighted in calling her. At every level, men began feeling
they had some claim to her; first there were flirtations, and then
came duels, and soon everything began to revolve around her; she
was the trembling, pulsating center of life for these proud men
who always carried a saber at the ready. She was the sultan, and
they were the harem, and she tossed her handkerchief to whichever one pleased her—and many pleased her. As for Major Ydow,
he let people do and say as they wished. . . . Was he too vain to feel
jealousy, or was it, rather, that he knew how hated and despised
he was, and he took pleasure in possessing this woman who had
infatuated all his enemies? It can't be possible that he saw nothing.
I sometimes observed his emerald eyes turn dark as garnets when
his gaze fell upon one of us whom he suspected of being his better
half's lover; but he said nothing. . . . And since everyone always
thought the worst of him, his calm indifference, his willed blind-
ness, was imputed to the most abject motives. People thought
that his mistress was less a pedestal for his vanity and more a
ladder for his ambitions. People always say things like that, and
he didn't listen. As for me, I had my reasons for observing him,
and I found the hatred and the contempt others felt for him to
be unfounded and unjust, so I asked myself if this was a weakness
in him, or perhaps a kind of strength, that utter impassivity in a
man betrayed on a daily basis by his mistress, never revealing the
slightest effects of any gnawing jealousy. Good God, gentlemen!
We've all known men who were obsessive enough about some
woman to believe in her even when everyone else accuses her,
and who, instead of taking vengeance when the absolute certainty
of infidelity is finally driven into their skulls, prefer to hide themselves in their cowardly happiness, and to draw humiliation up
over their heads like a blanket!

"Was Major Ydow one of that type? Perhaps. But I can assure you, La Pudica was perfectly capable of arousing the most degrading obsession. Circe in ancient times, the woman who changed men into animals, was nothing in comparison to this Pudica, this woman who was both Messalina and Virgin before, during, and after.[51] With the passions that burned in her heart, and the ones she communicated to the officers, who were hardly delicate when it came to women, she was very quickly compromised, but she never compromised herself. This is an important distinction. She never did anything that allowed anyone to have a hold over her. If she took a lover, it remained a secret between her and her bed. She never gave Major Ydow the slightest evidence on which to make a scene. Did she, perhaps, actually love him? . . . She stayed with him, and she could very easily have hitched her chances to some other man. I knew of one, a Maréchal of the Empire, who was so mad about her that he had his baton, the symbol of his rank, made into an umbrella handle for her. But I'm speaking to you today as one of those men. There are women who love . . . not their lover exactly, though they love him well enough, too. Madame de Maintenon said it well: carp feel nostalgic for their mud.[52] Rosalba didn't want to feel any regrets over hers. She never left it. I entered into it."

"Now there's a sudden saber thrust! What a transition!" exclaimed Captain Mautravers.

"For God's sake, why should I be delicate about it?" said Mesnilgrand. "You know the song they sang in the eighteenth century:

When Boufflers arrived, as from above,[53]
Everyone thought her the Queen of Love;
Every man with passion burned,
And each one had her, in his turn!

"And I had my turn. Now, I had had women before, by the batch! But I never thought there was one like Rosalba. The mud with her was a paradise. I am not going to provide you with an elaborate analysis of my feelings, like some kind of novelist. I was a man of action, brutal enough when it came to the point, like Count Almaviva, and I wasn't in love with her in the grand, poetic sense of the phrase that a novelist would use. . . .[54] The kind of happiness she bathed me in had nothing to do with the soul, or the mind, or even the vanity; but that happiness was no light, trivial thing either. I had never suspected that sensuality could be so profound, and this was the most profound of sensualities. Look—picture to yourself one of these beautiful peaches, with its red flesh into which you sink your teeth, or maybe it's better not to try to imagine anything. There is no metaphor or image to express the pleasure that this human peach produced, blushing under your slightest glance, as if you had bitten into her. And then, imagine what it would have been like not just to glance at her but to press your lips against her or bite into that passionate, rosy flesh. Oh, the body of that woman *was* her soul, her only soul! And she used that body, one night, to give me a particular pleasure that will give you a better idea of her than all my words can: one night, she had the audacity, and the indecency, to greet me wearing nothing but a transparent Indian muslin, so that you seemed to glimpse her body through a mist or a vapor; the shape of her body was the only thing pure about it all, and her flesh had that double vermillion blush of both modesty and voluptuousness! . . . Devil take me, she seemed like a statue of living coral under that white cloud! Ever since that night, the whiteness of other women hasn't meant any more to me than *this*."

Mesnilgrand paused and flicked up toward the ceiling a little piece of orange peeling; it shot up over the head of Le Carpentier, the man who had helped remove the king's head.

"Our affair lasted some time," he continued, "but don't infer that I eventually got tired of her. You don't get tired of something like that. The philosophers with their ugly jargon tell us that sensation is finite. Well, she brought the infinite into it! No, if I left her, it was because of a sense of moral disgust, or out of a sense of my own basic pride, and of contempt for her, this woman who, even during the most intense and most sensuous caresses, never made me feel that she actually loved me. . . . When I would ask her, 'Do you love me?'—using that word that's impossible to avoid eventually—even when I would ask her at a moment when she was giving me the most convincing proofs of her love, she would reply, 'No!' or shake her head enigmatically. She rolled and wallowed in her combination of modesty and shame, and she stayed there, despite all the disorder of her aroused senses, as impenetrable as a sphinx. The only difference is that the sphinx was cold, and she was not. . . . Well! That impenetrability frustrated me, irritated me, as did my certainty that she was indulging in as many men as Catherine II did,[55] and for those reasons I pulled up short on the reins and forced myself out of the all-powerful grasp of that woman, the trough of all desires! I left her, or, rather, I never went back to her. But I couldn't shake the idea that there would never be a second woman like her; and that thought ended up calming me and making me indifferent to all women. Ah, she put the finishing touches on my education as an office. After her, I henceforth thought of nothing but my military service. She dipped me in the Styx."[56]

"And you've turned into a real Achilles!" said old Monsieur de Mesnilgrand, beaming.

"I don't know what I've turned into," replied Mesnilgrand, "but I do know that some time after we separated, Major Ydow—who was on the same terms with me that he was with all the other Division's officers—told us one day in the café that his wife was pregnant, and that he would soon have the joy of becoming a father. At this unexpected news, some of us looked at each other, and some others smiled; but he saw nothing or, if he did see, he deliberately didn't notice, probably having resolved to ignore everything short of a direct insult. But when he had left, one of my comrades whispered to me, 'Is the child yours, Mesnil?' And an even more emphatic voice was whispering the same question in my conscience. I dared not reply. When we had been alone together, Rosalba had never said a word about any baby, which might be mine, or the Major's, or somebody else's . . ."

"The Regiment's baby!" interrupted Mautravers, his booming voice cutting through like a saber thrust.

"Never," continued Mesnilgrand, "had she made the remotest allusion to a pregnancy; but what was surprising about that? As I've told you, this Pudica was a real sphinx, a sphinx who devoured her pleasures in silence and kept her secrets. Nothing from the heart, no deeper feelings ever passed outward through the barrier of her body; and that body was open only to pleasure . . . and it was that modesty of hers that produced the first fear, the first shiver of pleasure! Knowing she was pregnant had a singular effect on me. Let's admit, gentlemen, now that we're all past the bestial period of passions—that mess kit we all ate from!—that a shared parentage like this is wrong, that it's the end of all fatherly sentiment; this horrible anxiety about parentage keeps us from hearing the voice of nature, and it plunges us into a state of doubt from which we can't ever quite extricate ourselves. We say to ourselves, 'Is it mine, this child?' . . . Your uncertainty hunts you, pursues you like the punishment for your share in the deed, in that shameful partnership to which you had submitted! A man with any feelings, if he thinks about it for long, will go mad; but then life, pulsing, volatile life picks you up and carries you along on its wave, bobbing along like a cork on a broken fishing line. After that declaration that Major Ydow made to us, the little shudder of paternal feeling that at first coursed through me died down. Nothing else happened at first. . . . And it's true that just a few days later, I had something else to think about besides Pudica's baby. We were off to battle at Talavera, where Commandant Titan of the 9th Hussars was killed in the first charge, and I was put in command of the squadron.[57]

"The nasty beating we took at Talavera made the war even more bitter for us. We found ourselves on the march more often, more crowded together, more harassed by the enemy, and so inevitably we had less leisure to think about Pudica, who was in fact not among us. She followed the Regiment in a wagon, and it was in the wagon, they say, that she gave birth to a baby that Major Ydow, thinking it was his, loved as much as if it really had been his own. In any case, when the child died—for it did die just a few months later—the Major nearly went out of his mind with grief, and no one in the Regiment mocked him for it. For the first time, the general antipathy toward him died out. People felt a great deal more pity for him than they did for the mother who, if she did grieve for her offspring, nonetheless went back to being the same Rosalba we all knew, that bizarre whore whom the Devil steeped in modesty, that woman who, despite her behavior, retained the ability to blush all the way down her backbone a hundred times a day! Her beauty had not diminished. It resisted all the attacks of time. But yet the life she led was one that should have left her, as we say in the cavalry, as worn out as an old saddle cloth—if that life of hers had gone on much longer."

"It didn't last? She died? So you know, do you, what became of that bitch of a woman?" asked Rançonnet, practically panting with interest and seeming to have forgotten the visit to the church that so obsessed him.

"Yes," said Mesnilgrand, concentrating his voice now as if he were approaching the most profound part of the story. "You thought, as everybody else did, too, that she had been pulled down into the whirlpool of war we were all caught up in, along with Ydow, the whirlpool that drowned and scattered so many of us. But today, I am going to tell you what really happened to Rosalba."

Captain Rançonnet leaned forward, his elbows on the table, holding his glass in his big hand as tightly as if it had been a saber, listening intently.

"The war did not end," Mesnilgrand went on. "Those Spaniards had had the patience to battle the Moors for five hundred years, and they had the patience to deal with us, however long it would take. As we advanced through the country, we had to watch every step we took. When we invaded a village, we immediately fortified it and turned it into a weapon against the enemy. We made our garrison for quite a while in a little town called Alcudia. We made a big convent there into our barracks; but the staff were billeted in private houses, and Major Ydow was in that of the *alcalde,* the mayor. Since that was the most spacious house, Major Ydow often hosted the officer corps in the evenings, for we only socialized with each other then. We had broken off with the *afrancesados* out of mistrust, because hatred of the French was spreading everywhere! These get-togethers, which were often punctuated by outbursts of enemy fire around our outposts, were always hosted by Rosalba, who served us punch with that incomparably chaste air that was one of the Devil's finest jokes. She chose her next victims; but I paid no attention to my successors. I had wrenched my soul back to myself from that liaison, and I was not dragging the chain of lost hopes behind me, as someone has put it. I felt no spite, no jealousy, no resentment. I watched that woman as she lived on and maneuvered, for I found her interesting, as a spectator, the way she could hide the most impudent acts of vice under the most charmingly abashed innocence. So I would go to her place, and in front of others she would speak to me with that almost timid simplicity of a young girl you encounter by chance at a public well or in a forest. That intoxication, that sense of being swept away, that fury she used to ignite in me—all those terrible things were in the past now. I thought of them as dissipated, vanished, impossible! Only, when I saw that little nuance of redness spreading over her face due to some word or some glance, I felt like the man who sees one last drop of champagne in his glass and is tempted to pour it out onto his thumbnail in order to get at that one last droplet.

"I said that to her, one evening. That particular evening, I was alone with her at her place.

"I had left the café early, where the officers were all playing cards or billiards and betting heavily. It was night, but it was a Spanish night, in which the hot sun had just barely torn itself away from the sky. I found her only partly dressed, her shoulders bare, wearing an African shawl that left her arms exposed, those beautiful arms I had so often bitten in passion and that, in certain moments of emotion that I knew how to arouse, would change their shade to what painters would call the 'tone' of the interior of a strawberry. Her hair, made heavy by the heat, curled thickly around her golden neck, and she was beautiful thus, disheveled, negligent, languid—beautiful enough to tempt Satan and avenge Eve! She was half-reclined on a couch, writing something. . . . Now, whenever Pudica was writing something, you could be assured it was a message to a lover setting up some rendezvous for some new infidelity to Major Ydow, who continued to swallow everything in silence, the same way she swallowed her pleasures. When I came in, her letter was finished, and she was in the act of sealing it by melting wax in a candle flame—a blue wax, spangled with silver. I can still see it, and in a moment you'll understand why the memory of that blue wax with silver spangles remains so clear to me.

"'Where is the Major?' she said when I came in, appearing troubled already—but then she always seemed troubled, this woman who knew how to flatter men's sense of themselves by appearing to tremble before them.

"'He's gambling like a madman this evening,' I said with a laugh, meanwhile gazing with desire at that delicate hint of pink that was rising up over her face. 'As for myself, I felt a different kind of madness tonight.'

"She understood me. Nothing surprised her. She was born for the desires that she made flare up in men, desires that would have brought them back to her from the ends of the earth.

"'Bah!' she said slowly, though that carnation tint that I so desired was growing deeper at the idea I had given her. 'Bah! Your madness has been cured. It's over.' And she pressed her seal onto the boiling wax on the envelope; the boiling ended, and the wax hardened.

"'Look!' she said, insolent and provocative. 'This is you! It was burning just a second ago, and now it's cold.'

"And she bent down to write the address on the letter.

"Must I repeat it—have I made myself clear?—that I was not jealous of this woman? But we are all made the same way. Despite myself, I wanted to see who she was writing to, and in order to do that, since I was still standing, I had to bend down over her head, but her shoulders blocked my view, and I gazed upon that intoxicating downy cleft where I had showered so many kisses, and—my God!—mesmerized by the sight, I placed one more kiss there, and the sensation prevented her from writing. . . . She lifted up her head, which had been bent down over the table, as if she had been pricked by a firebrand, and she threw herself back against her easy chair; she gazed at me with that mixture of desire and confusion that was her particular charm, her eyes looking upward and turned toward me, standing behind her, and I bent down to place a kiss into that pink, moist, half-open mouth, a kiss to match the one I had just bestowed between her shoulders.

"Sensitive as she was, she nonetheless had the nerves of a tiger. She started suddenly. 'The Major is coming up,' she said. 'He must have lost at his betting, and he's jealous when he loses. He'll make a hideous scene. Here! Hide over here: I'll make him leave soon.' And standing up, she opened up a large armoire in which she kept her dresses and pushed me in. I suspect there aren't many men who haven't been pushed in there at one time or another, when the husband or some other lover showed up . . ."

"I call it good luck to have an armoire!" said Sélune. "Once, I had to hide in a coal sack—me! Of course, that was before this damned wound of mine. I was in the White Hussars then. You can just imagine the state I was in when I finally got out of my coal sack!"

"Yes," Mesnilgrand replied with some bitterness. "This is one of the prices of adultery and of sharing a woman! At moments like these, even the proudest men lose all their dignity out of sympathy for the frightened woman, and they become as cowardly as she is, cowardly enough to run and hide. I still feel sick at heart at having been in that armoire, in my uniform, my saber at my side, and, just to take it all to the very height of ridiculousness, all for a woman who had no honor to lose, a woman I did not love!

"But I had no time to dwell on the baseness of being there like some schoolboy, in that dark armoire where my face brushed against her dresses—which still smelled of her body, and that scent intoxicated me. But what I heard quickly put an end to any sensual sensations. The Major had come in. As she had guessed, he was in a murderous mood and, just as she had predicted, burst out in a fit of jealousy, a jealousy all the more explosive because he had hidden it from us all so thoroughly. Inclined to be suspicious and already in a rage, his gaze fell upon the letter lying on the table, the one that my two kisses had prevented Pudica from addressing.

"'What's this letter?' he asked rudely.

"'It's a letter for Italy,' said Pudica calmly.

"But that placid response did not fool him.

"'That's a lie!' he exclaimed harshly, for you didn't have to scratch very deeply into the Lauzun of this man to discover the boor beneath; and his exclamation made me understand what the domestic life of these two creatures was like, and the kinds of scenes that they must have kept hidden away from the rest of the world, an example of which I was, apparently, going to witness. I was deep inside the armoire. I couldn't see them, but I could hear everything, and hearing was just as good as seeing. Their words and the intonations of their voices implied their gestures, and I heard them quickly rising up to the height of fury. The Major insisted on her showing him the unaddressed letter, and La Pudica, who had seized hold of it, stubbornly refused to give it to him. That was when he decided to take it by force. I could hear the rustling and the trampling of a struggle between them, but as you would assume, the Major was stronger than the woman. He got hold of the letter, and he read it. It was to set up a lover's rendezvous, and it was clear that the man had already enjoyed her before. . . . But the man was not named. Absurdly curious, like all jealous people, the Major sought in vain for the name of the man who was cuckolding him. . . . And La Pudica had her vengeance on him for tearing the letter away from her, for she cried out during the struggle, 'You've hurt my hand, you beast!' Out of his mind with fury at knowing nothing, defied and mocked by that letter, which only revealed one thing to him, that she had a lover—yet one more lover—Major Ydow flew into one of those rages that dishonor a man, heaping foul insults on La Pudica, in language worthy of a coach driver. I believed he would soon turn to blows. Blows were coming, but a bit later. He reproached her—and in what language!—for being . . . well, all that she was. He was brutal, abject, revolting; and to all this fury she replied like a woman who no longer has anything to fear, who knows the man she is yoked with through and through, and who knows that eternal battles like this one are the norm in their pigsty of a life. She was less base than he was, but she was more atrocious, more insulting, and more cruel in her coldness than he was in his hot anger. She was insolent, sarcastic, laughing with the hysterical laughter of hatred at his worst paroxysms, responding to the stream of insults that the Major was vomiting at her with the kinds of words that women know, the words they can use to drive us mad, the words that they can drop into our violent rages like a hand grenade into a heap of gunpowder. Out of all the outrageous, cold, sharp things she said, the one she hurled at him the most often was that she didn't love him—that she had never loved him: 'Never! Never! Never!' she repeated with a kind of joyous fury, as if she wanted to trample his heart and dance on it! Now, this idea—that she had never loved him—was the fiercest, bitterest thing that this happy egotist could hear, this man whose good looks had won over so many women, this man whose vanity was greater than his love for her! So he soon found, hearing this thing, that she had never loved him, so pitilessly repeated, unbearable; he refused to believe it, and he rejected it:

"'And what about our child?' he objected, the idiot, as if the fact of the child would be some kind of proof against what she said, and as if invoking the memory would help.

"'Ah, our child!' she exclaimed, breaking into laughter. 'It wasn't yours!'

"I could imagine the look in the Major's green eyes, as I heard him moan, making a kind of strangled cry like that of a wildcat. He spat out a hideous oath.

"'Whose was it, then, you cursed whore?' he asked, with a tone in his voice I can't describe.

"But she only kept on laughing, making a sound like a hyena.

"'You'll never know!' she said, taunting him. And she lashed him with that 'You'll never know!' repeating it over and over, inflicting him with it again and again; and when she grew tired of saying it, she—would you believe it?—she started singing it like some kind of chant! Then, when she had whipped him long enough with the phrase, when she had used the phrase to make him spin like a top long enough, when she had roped and tied him in knots of anxiety with the phrase long enough, when she had reduced the man, out of his mind with wrath, to little more than a marionette in her hands, a doll she was ready to break, when, in the cynicism of pure hatred she named off all her lovers one by one, when the list had finally included the entire officers' corps, then:

"'I've had them all!' she cried. 'But they haven't had me! And that child you're stupid enough to believe was yours was made by the only man that I ever loved! The only man I've ever idolized! And you never guessed who? And you still can't guess?'

"She was lying. She had never loved any man. But she knew that the final sword thrust for the Major resided in this lie, and she stabbed, twisted, hacked with it, and when she had finally had enough of playing the executioner to this victim, to finish him off, as if to plunge the sword in up to the hilt, she aimed one last blow at his heart:

"'Well then,' she said, 'since you can't guess, don't vex your little mind any longer about it, imbecile! It was Captain Mesnilgrand.'

"Probably she was still lying. But I've never been sure, and hearing her pronounce my name like that struck me like a bullet coming right through the armoire. After the name was spoken, there was silence, and everything seemed to stop. I asked myself, had he killed her instead of replying? But just then I heard the splintering sound of a glass that had been thrown to the floor, shattering into a thousand pieces.

"I've told you that Major Ydow had felt an immense paternal love for the child he believed was his own, and when he lost the child, his grief almost drove him mad; it was the kind of grief that, when we feel it, we actually want to eternize it, we want to give it a permanent material expression. Because of our military situation, though, he could not erect a tomb for his son and visit it every day—yes, that idolatry of the tomb!—and so Major Ydow had had his dead son's heart embalmed so as to be able to carry it with him everywhere, and he had piously had it put inside a little crystal urn, which he in turn placed on a shelf in his bedroom. This urn was the glass that I had heard shatter into bits.

"'Oh, it wasn't mine, you abominable whore!' he cried. And I heard his dragoons boot heel grinding and crushing the crystal urn, stomping on the heart of the boy he had believed to be his son!

"Evidently she tried to get it away from him and tried to pick it up, as I heard her hurling herself toward him, and then the sounds of fighting started up again, along with the sounds of blows being landed.

"'Well, since you want it, there it is, your little bastard's heart, you shameless slut!' said the Major. And he hit her in the face with the heart that he had adored and threw it at her head like a missile. Deep calleth unto deep, they say.[58] And sacrilege leads to more sacrilege. La Pudica, insane with rage, did as the Major had done. She threw the child's heart back at his head, that heart that she might have preserved if it hadn't come from him, that hated man whose torture of her she wanted to repay with more torture, ignominy for ignominy! It had to have been the first time something so hideous has ever taken place! A father and a mother hurling the heart of their dead child into each other's faces!

"It went on for some minutes, this evil combat. . . . And it was so shockingly tragic to me that I never even thought of putting my shoulder to the door and bursting out of the armoire to intervene and stop it. . . . And then came a cry such as I've never heard before, gentlemen, and such as you've never heard either, even on the field of battle—and that cry gave me the strength to force open the door, and I saw . . . what I'll never see again. La Pudica had been knocked down and was stretched out on the writing table, and the Major was holding her down by one hand, with an iron grip; her skirts had all been torn off, and her beautiful nude body twisted beneath his grip like an injured snake. But what do you think he was doing with his other hand, gentlemen? . . . That writing table, the lit candle, the sealing wax that was right next to it had combined to give the Major an infernal idea—the idea of sealing up that woman, the way she had sealed up the letter— and he was in that monstrous act, the horrifying vengeance of a perversely jealous lover!

"'Let your punishment fall right where you committed the sin, you infamous creature!' he cried.

"He did not see me. He was bent over his victim, who cried out no longer, and was dipping the pommel of his saber into the boiling wax to use as the seal!

"I leapt at him; I didn't even tell him to defend himself, and I plunged my saber up to the hilt into his back, right between his shoulders, and if I could have, I would have plunged my hand in, too, to kill him all the more!"

"Well done, Mesnil," said Commandant Sélune. "He wasn't worthy of being killed face to face like one of us, the scoundrel."

"Ah, but this is the Abelard story, just transferred to Heloise!" exclaimed the Abbé Reniant.

"Quite a job of surgery," said Doctor Bleny, "and quite a rare one!"

But Mesnil seemed not to hear them, and he continued.

"He fell dead across the body of his fainting wife. I pulled him off, threw him onto the floor, and kicked his corpse with my foot. That scream of La Pudica's had been so savage, it sounded like something torn from the womb of a she-wolf. I could still feel it in my guts, and in fact it had been heard below, too, as a chamber-maid came up into the room.

"'Go fetch the surgeon from the 8th Dragoons; he's needed here, right now!'

"But I didn't have time to wait for the surgeon. Suddenly the bugles began to blow, calling us all to arms. It was a surprise attack by the enemy, who had silently crept up and slit the throats of our sentinels. We had to get to our horses. I took one last look at that superb, mutilated body, immobile now and pale for the first time under the gaze of a man. But before I left, I picked up that poor heart that lay on the floor in the dirt and that they had used to hit and tear at each other, and I carried it away, the heart of that infant she had said was mine, tucked into my Hussar's belt."

The Chevalier de Mesnilgrand paused here, overcome with an emotion that all the others respected, materialists and debauch-ees though they were.

"And La Pudica?" asked Rançonnet almost timidly, no longer caressing his wine glass.

"I never heard any news of Rosalba, whom they called La Pu-dica," Mesnilgrand replied. "Is she dead? Is she still living? Was the surgeon able to go to her? After the surprise attack on Alcudia, which was so fatal to us, I looked for him. I never found him. He had disappeared, like so many others, and never rejoined the de-bris that was all that remained of our regiment."

"Is that all?" asked Mautravers. "If that's all, this is some story! You were right, Mesnil, when you told Sélune that you'd outdo his eighty nuns raped and tossed in a well. But since Rançonnet seems to be daydreaming over there, I'll bring up the question he started with: what does all this have to do with your devotions in that church the other day?"

"You're right," said Mesnilgrand. "I had almost forgotten. Here's the last part I have to relate, to you, Rançonnet, and to all of you: for several years, I carried the heart of that child that might have been mine with me everywhere; but after the catastrophe of Waterloo, I've had to take off that officer's belt, part of the uniform in which I had hoped to die, where I carried that heart for those years—and I can assure you, Mautravers, that it was heavy, though it appeared light enough. Reflection came with age, and I didn't want to profane any further that heart that had already been so profaned, and I decided to put it to rest in Christian ground. So without going into all the details that I've given you today, I spoke to one of the priests in this town about this heart that weighed so heavily on my own, and I had just given it to him in the chapel's confessional when Rançonnet grabbed me by the arm in the side aisle."

Captain Rançonnet was probably satisfied. He didn't say a word, nor did the others. No one risked any reflections. A silence more expressive than any remarks they might have made weighed upon the lips of all.

Did they finally understand then, these atheists, that if the Church had been instituted for no other purpose than to receive the hearts, whether living or dead, that are no longer wanted, that would have been a beautiful enough mission?

"Bring the coffee!" ordered the old Monsieur de Mesnilgrand, in his booming host's voice. "If it's as strong as your story, Mesnil, it'll be good."

A WOMAN'S VENGEANCE

Fortiter.[1]

I have often heard people say that modern literature is too "bold"; but for my part, I just don't see it. Calling it bold is nothing more than moral snobbery. Literature has always been called the expression of society, but in fact it expresses nothing of the kind; and when this or that person with a bit more intelligence than the norm is tempted to be a little bolder than the norm, God knows what shrieks of protest result! Indeed, if one looks into the matter, literature doesn't express even half of the crimes that society commits behind closed doors, and with impunity, every single day, with its own charming facility and frequency. Ask the confessors—who would become the world's greatest novelists if they were free to tell the stories that are poured out to them in the confessional. Ask them, for instance, to number the cases of incest they know to be veiled in secrecy in the proudest, most prominent families, and then see if literature, so widely accused of immoral boldness, has dared to tell such stories, even with the intent of frightening the reader! Except for just a hint—and it really was just a passing hint—in the *René* of Chateaubriand, the religious Chateaubriand—I don't know of any book in which incest, so common in our time—at the highest as well as the lowest levels of society, though maybe a bit more common at the lowest—was made the central, frankly treated subject of a story in such a way as to draw from it the picture of a genuinely tragic morality. Modern literature, at which prudishness aims its little stones, has never dared stories like those of Myrrha, Agrippina, and Oedipus, stories that, believe me, are being played out today, because the only Hell I know (at least so far) is the social hell, and in it I've known and rubbed shoulders with plenty of Myrrhas, Agrippinas, and Oedipuses in private life and, as the phrase goes, in the very best society.[2] But Good Lord! It doesn't happen in the same way as it does on the stage, or in the history books. But beneath the social surfaces, the precautions, the fears, and the hypocrisies, you can just catch glimmerings of it. . . . I know— and all of Paris knows, as well—a certain Madame Henri III, who wears around her waist a rosary of little skulls, engraved in gold, over her blue velvet dresses, and who indulges in self-flagellation, thus mixing together her particular ragout of penances with the ragout of Henri III's other pleasures.[3] Now, who would write down the story of such a woman, who also writes pious books and whom the Jesuits believe to be a man (a nice detail!) and even a saint? . . . It is not all that many years ago that everyone in Paris watched a woman of the Faubourg Saint-Germain steal her mother's lover and then, furious at seeing the lover return to her mother, who, being older, knew better than the daughter how to make a man love her, stole some of the letters her mother had written to the man, had them printed off, and threw them, by the thousands, from the top gallery of the *Paradise* at the Opera (*paradise* being an apt name for a scene such as that) on a first night.[4] Who has written the story of a woman like that? . . . Poor literature would not know where to begin with such material.

But if literature were truly "bold," that is what it would have to present. History has its Tacitus and its Suetonius, but literature does not—at least not one on the higher levels of morality and talent. It is true that the Latin language dares to be honest, pagan that it is, while our language was baptized with Clovis in the font of Saint Rémy and contracted an imperishable modesty there, wearing its old woman's blush to this day.[5] Nevertheless, if one *dared to dare,* a Suetonius or a Tacitus could arise among the novelists, for a novel is simply a description of manners and customs put into a dramatic or narrative form, just as history itself often is. And the only difference between them is this: the one (the novel) attaches its manners and customs to fictional characters, while the other (history) provides names and addresses. Yet the novel goes well beyond history. It has the sense of an ideal, while history has none; it's confined to reality. The novel, also, holds the stage a great deal longer. The Lovelace of Richardson will live longer than the Tiberius of Tacitus.[6] But if Tacitus had given his Tiberius as much detail and development as Richardson gave his Lovelace, wouldn't history have made real gains, and wouldn't Tacitus be even more frightening? . . . Certainly, I have no fear in saying that Tacitus, as painter, is inferior to Tiberius, as model, and that in this case the painter, despite all his genius, is outweighed, even crushed beneath the weight of that model.

And that is not all. To this inexplicable yet stunning failure of literature—when one compares it as it really is with its reputation—we must add the face that crime has taken on in this delicious, modern era of progress! Our extreme civilization has effaced the fearful poetry that crime once had, and the writer is forbidden to restore it. That would be just too horrible, say those today who want everything to be made pretty, even the hideous. Oh, the advantages of the philanthropic spirit! Half-witted criminologists diminish the penalties, and inept moralists diminish the crime, and in fact do so specifically in order to reduce the penalties. However, crimes in our advanced civilization are certainly more ghastly than those of barbaric eras by virtue of their very refinement, the level of corruption they imply, and the superior level of the criminal intellect. The Inquisition knew all this very well. In an era when religious faith and public morality were stronger, the Inquisition, that tribunal that passed judgment on thoughts, that great institution that twists our modern nerves into knots and causes such alarm to our little birdbrained minds—the Inquisition knew that spiritual crimes were the worst ones, and it attacked them as such. . . . And it's a fact that these crimes appeal less to our senses and more to our intellects, and in the final analysis, the intellect is the deepest part of us. So, for the novelist, there is a whole unknown body of tragic material he can derive from these crimes, more intellectual than physical, though they will seem less tragic to a superannuated, materialistic society because no blood is spilled, and the massacre is confined to the realm of feelings and manners. . . . This is the kind of tragedy of which I wish to present a specimen, by telling the story of a revenge of the most terrifying originality, one in which no blood was spilled, and in which neither the sword nor poison play any part: it is, in short, a *civilized* crime, to which the writer's invention has added nothing, except for his manner of telling it.

One evening toward the end of the reign of Louis-Philippe, a young man was walking along on the Rue Basse-du-Rempart, which in those days well merited its name of Basse because it was lower than the level of the Boulevard, forming a sort of poorly lit, somber excavation into which you descended from the boulevard via two sets of stairs that had their backs to each other—if one can say that of stairs.[7] This excavation, which is no longer there, ran from the Rue Chaussée-d'Antin to Rue Caumartin, at which point it rose up again to street level. It was a kind of dark ravine into which few people would venture even during daylight, and it was much worse when night came. The Devil is the Prince of Darkness. And this was one of his territories. Now, roughly in the middle of this ravine, bordered on one side by the boulevard, which formed a terrace, and on the other by some big, silent houses with large carriage doors and by some shops selling bric-a-brac, there was a narrow, open passageway where the wind—when there was any wind—would whistle like a flute, and which led past a wall and some buildings under construction to the Rue Neuve-des-Mathurins. The young man in question, incidentally a very well-dressed young man, had just taken this pathway, which was by no means the path of virtue for him, for he was following a woman who had gone down into this dark, suspicious passage with no hesitation and no embarrassment. He was an elegant young man—one of the *gants jaunes,* as they were called in those days.[8] He had just had a lengthy, relaxed dinner at the Café de Paris, and he had been leaning on the balcony at Tortoni's (a balcony now removed), chewing on a toothpick, and looking over the women on the boulevard. This particular woman had passed before him several times, and although that fact, together with

her overly loud dress and the swagger in her walk marked her out
for what she was clearly enough, and although the young man,
whose name was Robert de Tressignies, was terribly blasé, and
was in fact just back from the Orient—where he had seen the
female animal in all of her varieties and all her races—despite
all that, the fifth time this night walker passed by, he followed
her . . . "like a dog," as he put it, mocking himself—for he had the
ability to observe himself and to judge his actions for what they
were, though such judgments had no effect on his actions, and at
the same time, his actions did not impair his judgment: a terrible
asymptote!—Tressignies was over thirty. He had lived through
that first absurd period of youth that makes a man the Jocrisse of
his own feelings, during which the first woman who passes us by
becomes positively magnetic.[9] All that was in the past now. Now
he was a cold libertine, highly complicated and highly intelligent,
of the sort we see often enough in this positivist era of ours, a
man who had thought about his feelings to the point of no longer being duped by them, a man who was afraid of nothing, and
horrified by nothing. What he had just seen, or what he believed
he had seen, had inspired a certain curiosity in him, the hint of a
new sensation to be explored. And therefore he had come down
from his balcony and given pursuit . . . entirely determined to see
this vulgar adventure through to the end. He believed the woman
walking ahead of him, swaying her hips in an undulating, wave-
like motion, was simply one of the lower class of prostitutes; but
she had a surprising kind of beauty, the kind that would make
one peg her as belonging to a higher class, the kind that made
one wonder why she hadn't found some protector, someone to
get her away from the abjection of the streets—for, in Paris,
wherever the Devil plants a pretty woman, he immediately turns
around and plants some fool nearby to keep her as a mistress.

And beyond that, Robert de Tressignies had another reason for
following her, apart from her sovereign beauty—which, probably, the Parisians didn't even recognize, as blind as they are to true
beauty; their aesthetic taste, like everything else in their lives,
has become entirely democratized, leaving them no sense of true
grandeur. This woman reminded him of someone. She was like that

mockingbird that imitates the nightingale, the one Byron spoke of in his memoirs with such melancholy.[10] She reminded him of a woman he had seen somewhere else. . . . He was absolutely certain that it was not she, and yet she looked so much like her that she could have deceived him—if such deceit had not been, finally, impossible. . . . And moreover, he was not so much surprised as attracted by this, because he had had enough experience to know that there is a great deal less variety in the human face than one imagines, for the traits are limited by a strict, inflexible geometry, which only generates a limited number of general types. Beauty is one of them. Only ugliness is multiple, and even its multiplicity is soon exhausted. God ordained infinite variety only in the expression, for the expression is the reflection of the soul through the lines, whether straight or crooked, pure or twisted, of the face. Tressignies was saying all this to himself somewhat confusedly as he matched his pace to that of the woman ahead of him, walking sinuously, cutting her way along the boulevard like a scythe, prouder than Tintoretto's Queen of Sheba, in her saffron-colored silk dress with its golden tones—that color so beloved of young Roman girls—and as she walked, she made the shiny, glittering folds of the dress sparkle, like a call to arms! She held herself exaggeratedly erect, in a posture rarely seen in France, wrapped in a magnificent Turkish shawl with broad stripes of white, scarlet, and gold; and the huge red feather in her white hat—in the most splendidly bad taste—shuddered as she walked, drooping down almost to her shoulder. As you recall, women in that era wore long feathers bending down from their hats, called "weeping willows." But there was nothing that suggested weeping about this woman, and hers hinted at something the opposite of melancholy. Tressignies, believing that she would take the Chaussée-d'Antin route, which sparkled with its thousand gleaming lights, watched with surprise as the woman with all her courtesan's luxury, with all that impudent pride suggesting a girl drunk with love of herself and all the silk she was wearing, descended instead into the Rue Basse-du-Rempart, the most shameful of streets in those days! And the elegant man with his varnished boots hesitated, less courageous than the woman, before deciding to go *down there.* . . .

But it only lasted a second. . . . The golden dress, lost to his view for a moment in the shadows of that black trench, shone again as she passed under the flicker of the only lamppost, and he hurried down to follow her. Catching up with her was not difficult: she was waiting for him, sure that he would be coming; and it was then, at the moment he drew up next to her, that she turned her face toward him, looking brazenly into his eyes with all the insolence of her profession. He was almost literally blinded by that magnificent face, plastered thick with rouge but golden brown beneath, a color like the wings of certain insects that even the wan light from the lamp could not bleach away.

"You're Spanish?" asked Tressignies, having recognized one of the most beautiful facial types of that race.

"*Sí,*" she replied.

Now, to be Spanish in those days was worth something! It commanded a good price on the market. The novels of those days, the plays of Clara Gazul, the poems of Alfred de Musset, the dances of Mariano Camprubi and Dolorès Serral meant that women of her complexion were highly prized—and though many boasted of being Spanish, they were not always telling the truth.[11] But this woman seemed to boast no more of being Spanish than of anything else, and she spoke to him in French:

"Are you coming?" she said, getting straight to the point, using the familiar *tu* that the lowest sort of prostitute on the Rue des Poulies, even today, favors.[12] Do you recall it? Filthy place!

The tone, the voice already hoarse, that premature familiarity, that divine use of the *tu*—like heaven!—on the lips of a woman who loves you, contrasted with the sound of it in the mouth of a creature to whom you're just one more passerby, should have been enough to disgust and sober up Tressignies; but he was in the grip of the Demon. A curiosity spiced with lust had bitten him upon seeing this woman, who was more to him than simply some fine flesh draped in satin, and for whom he would not only have eaten Eve's apple but would have swallowed all the toads in a pond!

"Am I coming!" he said. "Good God, yes, I am!" As if she had any doubts, he added to himself. And he thought, "I can get myself cleaned up later."

They were standing at the end of the passage by the Rue Neuve-des-Mathurins; they walked off together. Among the huge blocks of concrete scattered around and the new buildings going up, one single house still stood up from its base, with no neighboring houses, a narrow, ugly, scowling, trembling house that looked as if it had seen plenty of vice and crime on every one of its floors and between its rickety walls, and which looked as if it had been left standing so it could see even more; under a black sky, it loomed even blacker. The tall house seemed blind, for none of its windows (and windows are a house's eyes) was lit, and the place seemed to grope and reach out for you in the darkness! The horrible house had the classic half-opened door of wicked places; and at the end of a squalid corridor you could glimpse the staircase, a few of its steps lit from above, by a foul, dirty lamp. . . . The woman went into the narrow passage, filling it up with her broad shoulders and the ample, rustling material of her dress; and, with a step accustomed to such a place, lightly ascended the spiral staircase—and if that calls up the image of a spiral snail's shell, it's appropriate, for the walls were slimy. . . . But what was unusual in a dive like this was that the staircase actually was better lit the higher up you went: it was no longer the sickly light from the wretched oil lamp now that they reached the second floor, but instead the light up here was almost elegant. Two bronze candelabra were built into the walls, casting a strangely dignified light on an ordinary-looking door on which was pasted the card with her name that prostitutes typically posted there so that, if they have a certain reputation and a certain beauty, the card acts like a banner advertising the merchandise within. Surprised at this luxury in such a place, Tressignies looked more closely at the two candelabra, wrought in an almost grand style by a skillful artist, than he did at the card with the woman's name on it; he didn't need to know it, as he was with her now. As he examined them, while she was turning the key in that brilliantly illuminated door, he thought of the "surprises" that were often found in prostitutes' houses in the days of Louis XV. "This woman," he thought to himself, "must have read some novels or memoirs from those days, and she took it into her head to fix herself up a pretty little apartment filled with voluptuous, flirtatious items in a place you'd never expect to find them . . ." But what he found when she finally got the door opened only redoubled his astonishment—but this time in a very different way.

For it was in fact only the typical, banal, disorderly room of that sort of girl. . . . Dresses tossed haphazardly here and there on the furniture, and a huge bed—the field of battle—along with immoral mirrors on the walls and on the ceiling, all of which proclaimed what sort of home one found oneself in. . . . On the mantel, some perfume vials she had not thought to close before leaving for her evening's campaign mixed their scents with the warm atmosphere of the room, all calculated to deplete a man's energy by his third breath. . . . Two lit candelabra, similar to those outside the door, burned on either side of the fireplace. Here and there, animal skins were thrown down on the carpet. Every detail was right. Finally, an open door allowed one to glimpse the mysterious inner sanctuary, the dressing room of the priestess.

But Tressignies only took note of all these details later on. At first, he only had eyes for the woman whose room he had entered. Comfortable with the sort of place in which he found himself, he made himself at home on the couch, pulling the woman over to stand between his knees, after she had removed her hat and scarf and tossed them on an easy chair. He grasped her tightly at the waist, as if he wanted to encompass it with his hands, and he looked her over from top to toe, like a drinker who holds his glass of wine up to the light before sipping it. The impression he had formed of her on the street had not been a false one. From the point of view of a connoisseur of women, even that of a jaded but still potent man, she was truly splendid. The resemblance that had struck him so strongly before in the uncertain light of the boulevard was still there now in the clear candle light. But the woman she so much resembled had never had that expression on her face—a face that in other respects was practically identical to this one—that expression of a resolute and almost frightening pride that the Devil, that joyful father of all anarchies, had kept from a duchess and had given instead—but why?—to this streetwalker. With her head bare, her black hair, her yellow dress,

her broad shoulders, and her even broader hips, she recalled the
Judith of Vernet (a painting of that period), but with a body more
clearly made for love and an even more ferocious face.[13] That ferocity was perhaps an effect of a wrinkle that came between her
eyebrows and extended outward to her temples, like some that
Tressignies had seen in some Asiatic women in Turkey, a crease
that her almost frowning, intense concentration intensified. A
stunning contrast! The woman had the body of her profession, but
not the face. That body of a courtesan that so invitingly seemed to
say, "Take me!"—that rounded cup of love inviting the hands and
the lips was surmounted by a face that could have frozen one's
desire by its sheer haughtiness, a face that could have extinguished
at once the most burning, urgent sensuality. . . . Fortunately, the
supple, ready smile of the courtesan was there at once to disguise and even profane the disdainful curl of the lips, rallying back
those who had been frightened off by the face's cruel pride. Out
on the boulevard, she had promenaded that ready smile with her
shameless, red lips; but when Tressignies stood her up between
his knees, she became serious, and her face radiated something so
strangely implacable that all she would have needed was a curved
sword in her hands to make this dandy Tressignies believe he was
about to become a Holofernes.

He took her hands—which had no sword in them—and saw
how supremely beautiful they were. She silently allowed him to
carry out his complete examination of her person, and she looked
at him, too, but not with that pointless or sordid curiosity that
women like her usually look at you, as if they half-suspect your
money to turn out to be counterfeit. . . . Apparently, she had
something on her mind other than the money she was about to
gain or the pleasure she was about to give. There was something
about her flared nostrils, which were just as expressive as her
eyes, breathing out a burning passion as much as the eyes did,
some supreme decision, like that of some crime one has determined to commit. "If only the stern strength in that face reflected
the power of love and sensuality, what good luck it would be for
both her and me in these jaded, lifeless days!" thought Tressignies,
who never discarded any whim or fancy until he had examined it

as thoroughly as if it were an English racehorse. . . . He, the man of experience, the man expertly critical when it came to women, who had purchased the loveliest girls in the market of Adrianople and who knew the exact price of human flesh when it possessed this color and this firmness, threw a handful of *louis,* as the price of a couple of hours with her, into a crystal blue cup that sat at just the level of his hand on a small table, which had probably never received so much gold.[14]

"Ah! So you like me, then?" she cried impudently, immediately ready following his tossing the coins; perhaps, also, she was impatient after that long examination in which there had seemed to be more curiosity than desire and that to her, therefore, had seemed to be either a waste of time or a kind of rudeness. "Let me get all this off," she added, as if her dress weighed her down, and quickly began to undo the buttons on her breast. . . .

She removed herself from his knees to go into the dressing room. . . . What a prosaic detail! Was she trying to "save" her dress? The dress was, after all, the essential tool of women in her trade. . . . Tressignies, who had imagined that he saw the insatiability of a Messalina in her face, now felt himself being tumbled back down into banality.[15] He felt that, after all, he was only in the room of a streetwalker—just a Paris whore, despite the sublimity of that face that contrasted so dramatically with the life she was leading. "Bah!" he thought. "The poetry is only skin deep with these women; but you have to accept that, and take it for what it is."

And he promised himself that he would indeed take it, but still it was a surprise that he had found it there, of all places! Up until now, in following this woman he had only been obeying an irresistible curiosity and an ignoble impulse, but when the woman who had so rapidly inspired those feelings came out of her dressing room having removed her streetwalker's trappings, dressed in a kind of costume that was no costume, looking like a woman gladiator ready to do battle, he was utterly dumbstruck with the beauty he saw with his experienced, connoisseur's eye—that sculptor's eye that men have for women; it was a beauty far beyond what he had divined on the boulevard, despite the hints that her rustling dress and her manner of walking had given him. He would not have been more dumbfounded if lightning had shot in through the dressing room door. . . . She was not entirely naked—but somehow more extreme! She was far more indecent—much more, even repellently indecent than if she had been frankly nude. Marble statues are nude, and such nudity is chaste. Chastity in fact demonstrates its bravery thus. But this girl, wickedly shameless, who would have lit herself up like one of the human torches in the gardens of Nero in order to attract men to her like moths to burn in her flame,[16] this woman who had no doubt learned and absorbed all the lowest procedures of corruption—she had now combined the insidious transparency of veils with the daring of naked flesh and had combined them with the genius and the bad taste of a hideous libertinism (but then, who knows, perhaps bad taste is actually a positive trait when it comes to libertinism). This costume, monstrous in its provocation, reminded Tressignies of an indescribable statuette that had often made him stop and stare, one that was for sale in every shop at that time that sold bronze, on the pedestal of which were only the mysterious words, "Madame Husson."[17] A dangerous, obscene dream? The dream had now become reality. Finding himself before that galling reality, before that absolute beauty that lacked the coldness absolute beauty so often has, Tressignies—the man who had traveled in Turkey—even if he had been a three-tailed pasha, would have come to his senses, calm as a Christian or even an anchorite. Thus, when perfectly sure of how stunning her appearance had been, as it always was, she moved impetuously close to him and placed the delectable magnificence of her breasts almost against his lips, with the practiced movement of the courtesan tempting the Saint in the painting by Paul Véronese,[18] Robert de Tressignies, who was decidedly no saint, felt an overpowering hunger . . . for that which she was offering him, and he took her in his arms, that brutal temptress, with an ardor that she shared, for she pressed herself up tightly against him. Did she throw herself like that into every pair of arms that reached for her? Supreme practitioner though she might be of the prostitute's arts, she was so passionate that night that even some exceptional level of excitement or morbid desire could not explain it. Was she a newcomer to this horrific kind of work that she threw herself into it with such fury? There was something so animalistic, so fierce in it that she seemed to want to take her own life or that of the partner in her caresses. In that day in Paris, her peers who didn't like the too-pretty name of *lorettes* that literature had bestowed upon them and that Gavarni had immortalized, instead, took to giving themselves the more exotic, oriental title of *panthers.*[19] Well, none of them could have justified the term as well as this one did. . . . She had all the beast's lithe suppleness, all its coilings, its sudden leaps, its clawing, and its biting. Tressignies could testify that none of the women who had passed through his arms in the past had given him such unheard-of sensations as this creature, whose lust and bodily madness were contagious, even though he had been in love many times. But there is a fact that may be adduced either to the glory or to the shame of human nature, and it is this: in what we call sexual pleasure—and we call it that with a bit too much contempt, perhaps—there are abysses just as deep as those in love itself. Was she overwhelming him now in such abysses, the way the ocean overwhelms even the strongest swimmer in its own? She far, far surpassed the guiltiest memories of this shameless man and surpassed even his wildest fantasies, violent and corrupt as they were. He forgot everything—what she was, and why he had come there, and the house, and the apartment that had almost nauseated him when he first entered it. She positively drew his soul out of his body and into hers. . . . She intoxicated him to the point of delirium—he, a man with a strong grip on his senses. She plunged him ultimately into such depths of pleasure that the moment came when this man, this atheist in love, this universal skeptic, actually believed that she was in love with him, she, the woman who made a business out of selling her body. Yes, Robert de Tressignies, who was made of the same steely stuff as his patron saint Robert Lovelace, actually believed that he had inspired at least a whim in this prostitute, who surely could not carry on like this with her other men without burning herself out. He believed it for a full two minutes, like an imbecile, this strong, experienced man! But the vanity she had ignited within him by means of a pleasure as powerful as love suddenly, between two caresses, felt itself invaded by a shiver of doubt. . . . Then a voice from deep inside him called out to him, "It's not you she's making love to!"—for he had just caught a glimpse, while she was at her most panther-like, most tightly coiled around him, and saw that she was entirely distracted from him, and was staring instead with an utterly absorbed contemplation at a bracelet she wore, upon which Tressignies made out the portrait of a man. A few Spanish words that Tressignies, ignorant of the language, could not make out were mixed with her Bacchante-like cries, and they seemed to him to be addressed to that portrait. And then the idea dawned on him that he was substituting for some other man—that he was there simply to substitute for the other—and that fact, so miserably common in our lives, with our overheated and depraved imaginations, when our souls compensate for the absent object of desire by attaching themselves to its representation, took violent hold of his mind and turned his hot ferocity to ice. In one of those absurd fits of jealousy and tiger-like vanity when a man is not master of himself, he roughly took hold of her arm, desiring to get a look at the bracelet that she gazed upon with such passion, passion that was clearly not for him at such a moment, when a woman ought to belong entirely to the man she is with.

"Let me see that picture!" he said, with a voice even harsher than his grip on her arm.

She understood, but she replied with perfect coolness.

"You can't possibly be jealous of a girl like me," she said to him. But she didn't use the word *girl*. No, to the stupefaction of Tressignies, she referred to herself as a *whore*, using the word someone who wanted to insult her most deeply would have used. "You want to see it?" she continued. "All right—there, look!"

And she placed her beautiful arm, still hot with sweat from their pleasures, before his eyes.

It was the portrait of an ugly, scrawny-looking man with olive skin and yellowish black eyes; he looked very somber, but there was some nobility about him—he was either a bandit or a Spanish grandee. And it had to be the latter, for he wore around his neck the ribbon of the Golden Fleece.[20]

"Where did you find this?" Tressignies asked, thinking to himself, "Now she's going to tell me a story. She'll tell me about how she was first seduced, that same old tired novel, the story they all start with . . ."

"Find it!" she replied, offended. "*Por Dios,* the man you see there, he gave it to me himself!"

"Who, him? A lover of yours, I suppose?" said Tressignies. "And you betrayed him, and he threw you out, and that's how you ended up here."

"He is not my lover," she said coldly, as insensitive as bronze to his insinuation.

"Maybe not anymore," said Tressignies. "But you still love him: I saw it just now in your eyes."

She laughed bitterly.

"Ah, so you can't tell the difference between love and hate?" she cried. "Love this man? I detest him! He's my husband."

"Your husband?"

"Yes, my husband," she said, "the greatest aristocrat in Spain—three times a duke, four times a marquis, five times a count, a Grandee of Spain, along with many other grandeurs. The Golden Fleece. I am the Duchess d'Arcos de Sierra-Leone."

Tressignies was almost floored by these incredible avowals, but he had not the slightest doubt of their truth. He was sure that the woman was not lying. He had recognized her. The resemblance he had noted on the boulevard was the proof.

He had seen her, and not that long before! It had been at Saint-Jean-de-Luz, where he had gone for the bath season one year. And that year it so happened that the highest Spanish society gathered at that little French town so close to Spain that you can imagine you are actually in Spain, where even the most fanatically patriotic Spanish can come and not feel they've been unfaithful to their country. For the whole summer, the Duchess de Sierra-Leone had lived in that little town so deeply Spanish in its manners, its character, its physiognomy, its history; for everyone recalls that Louis XIV held his wedding festivities there, and he was, incidentally, the closest to a Spanish king that France has ever had, and it was there too that the great fortune of the Princess of Ursins ran aground after her shipwreck.[21] That summer, people said, the Duchess de Sierra-Leone was on her honeymoon, having married the greatest, wealthiest lord in Spain. When Tressignies in his turn arrived at the place, that nest of fishermen that has produced some of the world's most terrible pirates, she was displaying a luxurious splendor unseen since the days of Louis XIV; and among those Basque women, who fear no rivals when it comes to beauty, with their bodies like those of ancient canephores and their eyes of aquamarine, such a pale blue-green, her beauty simply obliterated theirs.[22] Drawn to that beauty, and moreover being of the kind of birth and fortune that gave him entrée into any level of society he wished, Robert de Tressignies tried to get close enough to meet her, but the little Spanish circle of which the Duchess was the sovereign was strictly closed to outsiders that year and opened itself to no Frenchmen spending the season at Saint-Jean-de-Luz. The Duchess, when glimpsed at a distance— on the dunes by the beach or in the church—always left before he was able to meet her, and for that reason she remained in his memory like a meteor, the kind that stands out in our memories because once it has passed, we never see it again! He traveled. He passed through Greece and parts of Asia; but even the most admirable girls, in those countries where beauty is held in such estimation that people are unable to conceive of a Heaven without it, could not efface the tenacious, flamboyant image of the Duchess.

Well! And now today, by some strange, incomprehensible chance, that same Duchess who had so fascinated him for that brief moment in the past and then disappeared had come back into his life, and by the most incredible of paths! She was a prostitute now, and he had bought her and had her. She was nothing more than a prostitute, and of the lowest kind, too, for there is a hierarchy even in infamy. . . . The superb Duchess de Sierra-Leone, the woman he had dreamed of, the woman he might even have loved—for dreams and love are so closely intertwined in our hearts—was nothing more than . . . was it really possible? A common Paris streetwalker! It was she, the woman who had been pulsing and throbbing in his arms just now, just as she had probably been throbbing in someone else's yesterday—the first one who came along, just like him—and she would be doing the same in someone else's tomorrow or even—who knows?—an hour from now. Ah—that ugly realization struck him in the chest like a fist of ice. The man in him, so blazing hot just a moment ago, the man who, in his delirium, imagined he saw flames running all around the ceiling of the apartment, his senses setting everything afire, was now abruptly sobered, chilled, crushed. The idea, the certainty that this was in fact the Duchess de Sierra-Leone, failed to reawaken his desire, extinguished now like a snuffed-out candle, and he felt no wish to touch his lips again to that burning flame he had so eagerly consumed before. In revealing herself, the duchess had made the courtesan disappear! There was no one before him now but the duchess, but in what a condition: soiled, ruined, a woman lost on the sea, fallen from a height greater than the Leukadian rock into a sea of mud, filthy and disgusting, beyond the power of anyone to rescue her.[23] He stared at her numbly, seeing her metamorphosed into something tragic; from Messalina, she had somehow suddenly changed into a kind of mysterious Agrippina, sitting there erect and somber on the edge of the bed where the two of them had sprawled moments ago. He didn't want to touch her even with the tip of his finger now, that creature whose flesh he had just been kneading with idolatrous hands, to prove that this was really the body of the woman who had so inflamed him—that it wasn't an illusion—that he wasn't dreaming—that he had not gone mad! The duchess, emerging from the shell of the streetwalker, had dumbfounded him.

"Yes," he said, barely able to tear the words from his throat, feeling almost strangled, "yes, I believe you." He spoke formally now, abandoning the familiar *tu* form he had been using. "I saw you three years ago, at Saint-Jean-de-Luz."

The name called up the memory of the place, and a light seemed to pass over her face, sunk as it had been in so powerful a darkness for him. "Ah," she exclaimed, in the glow of that memory, "in those days I was intoxicated with life, but now . . ."

The light was extinguished immediately, but she did not lower her head.

"But now?" asked Tressignies, like an echo.

"Now," she said, "the only thing that intoxicates me is revenge.
. . . But I'll make that revenge go so deep," she added with an
intense violence in her manner, "that I'll die in it—like the mos-
quitoes in the country I come from that die, gorged with blood,
in the wound they've created."

Reading the expression on his face, she went on: "You don't understand. But I'll make you understand. You know who I am, but
you don't know what I am. Do you want to? Do you want to hear
my story? Do you want to?" She kept repeating it with an exalted
insistence. "Me—I want to tell it, tell it to everyone who comes
here! I want to tell it to the whole world! I'll only be even more
despicable, but my revenge will be even better."

"Tell me!" exclaimed Tressignies, impassioned with a curiosity
he had never felt before, neither in life, nor in novels, nor in the
theater. It seemed to him that this woman was about to tell him
things he had never heard before. He no longer thought about her
beauty. He looked at her as if he were about to observe an autopsy
on her corpse. Would she bring it back to life for him?

"Yes," she continued, "I've often wanted to tell the story to the
men who came up here; but they didn't come here, they said,
to listen to stories. When I would start to tell them, they would
interrupt me or they would simply get up and leave, like sated animals, contented with what they'd come for! Some were indifferent, some mocked me, some insulted me, called me a liar or mad.
They wouldn't believe me, whereas you—you'll believe me. You
saw me at Saint-Jean-de-Luz, in all the glory of a happy wife at the
summit of existence, wearing like a diadem that name of Sierra-
Leone, which I trail now at the hem of my dress through every
kind of mud, the way they used to drag a dishonored knight's
shield behind, tied to a horse's tail. This name that I hate, and
that I only keep so that I can degrade it, is still the name of the
greatest lord in Spain, and the proudest of all those who have the
privilege of keeping their hats on in the presence of His Majesty
the King; he thinks of himself as ten times more noble than the
King. For the Duke d'Arcos de Sierra-Leone, what are the most
illustrious houses that have reigned over Spain—Castille, Aragon,
Transtamare, Austria, and Bourbon? He says his family is older

than theirs. He is a descendant of the medieval Goth kings, and through Brunehilde he is related to the Merovingians of France. He is proud of having nothing in his veins except the *sangre azul,* the blue blood that all the others, even the most ancient families, have allowed to become adulterated and degraded, even if only by a few drops. . . . Don Christoval d'Arcos, Duke of Sierra-Leone and *otros ducados,* by no means had to step down in marrying me. I am a Turre-Cremata, from the ancient family of Turre-Cremata in Italy, the last of the family, a lineage that comes to its end in me, the last of the Turre-Cremata—and I am well suited to the name, which means burned tower, for I have burned in all the fires of Hell. The Grand Inquisitor Torquemada, who was born a Turre-Cremata, inflicted fewer tortures in the whole of his lifetime than I have felt within my accursed breast.[24] . . . I want to stress that the Turre-Cremata family was every bit as proud as the Sierra-Leone. Divided into two equally illustrious branches, they had been all-powerful in Italy and Spain for centuries. In the fifteenth century, during the pontificate of Alexander VI, the Borgia—drunk with their good fortune at having Alexander in the papacy—wanted to appear to be connected with all the royal families in Europe and so claimed to be related to us; but the Turre-Cremata repulsed their pretension with contempt, and in fact two of them paid with their lives for that audacity. It's said that they were poisoned by Cesare Borgia.[25] My marriage with the Duke de Sierra-Leone was an affair of two entirely equal families. There was no personal feeling or sentiment on the part of either of us. It was simply a matter of a Turre-Cremata marrying a Sierra-Leone. It was perfectly simple, even for me, brought up in the terrible etiquette of the grand old Spanish families that imitated the family in the Escurial, that harsh, repressive etiquette that would choke off a beating heart—unless that heart were stronger than steel. I had a heart like that. . . . I loved Don Esteban. Before I met him, my married life had no happiness about it, and my heart was dead—I didn't even know that I had one; my marriage was the grave, somber thing that marriage had always been in ceremonious, Catholic Spain, and which it rarely is nowadays, except among a few families of the highest rank who have retained the old ways. And

the Duke de Sierra-Leone was too profoundly Spanish not to retain and practice the old ways. Everything you've heard in France
about the somberness of Spain, that haughty, grave, silent country, applied to the Duke—and even more so. . . . Too proud to
live anywhere but on his own lands, he resided in a feudal castle
on the Portuguese border, revealing himself in everything he did
to be even more feudal than the castle. I lived there with him, my
confessor, and my maids and lived a sumptuous but monotonous
and dismal existence, one that would have crushed the life out of
any heart weaker than mine. But I had been raised to be what I
was: the wife of a great Spanish lord. And I also had the religion
of a woman of my rank, and I was almost as impassive as the portraits of my ancestors that ornamented the vestibules and cham-
bers of the Sierra-Leone castle, with their great, grim faces, their
garde-infants, and their steely corsets.[26] I was to add one more
generation to those generations of irreproachable, stately wives,
whose virtue was as safely guarded by their pride as a fountain
is by a lion. The solitude in which I lived did not at all weigh on
my mind, which was as tranquil as the mountains of red marble
that surround Sierra-Leone. I never suspected that a volcano was
sleeping beneath that marble. I was in a state like limbo since my
birth, but I was about to be reborn, and to be rebaptized, this
time by fire, due to a single look from a man. Don Esteban, the
Marquis de Vasconcellos, of Portuguese descent and a cousin of
the Duke, came to Sierra-Leone; and love—of which I had only
a vague notion from some mystical books—descended upon me
like an eagle swooping down and carrying off a child, and the
child cries out. . . . I cried out, too. It was not for nothing that
I was a Spanish woman of an ancient family. My pride revolted
against what I felt in the presence of that dangerous Esteban, who
took such a terrible, powerful possession of my heart. I told the
Duke to get rid of him on some pretext or another, to get him
out of the castle as soon as possible . . . when I saw that he was
in love with me, which struck me as offensive and insolent. But
Don Christoval replied like the Duke of Guise when he heard the
news that Henri III was going to have him killed: 'He wouldn't

dare!' That showed a lack of respect for Fate, which would have its vengeance. That phrase threw me into the arms of Esteban . . ."

She stopped for a moment, and as he listened, he knew by her elevated language that she was who she had claimed to be, and that there was no doubt that this was the Duchess de Sierra-Leone. Ah—by now, the streetwalker had disappeared entirely. One would have sworn that a mask had been removed, and that the real face, the real person, was now revealed. That wild, unbridled body was now still and chaste. As she spoke, she picked up a shawl that had been tossed on the chair and wrapped it around herself. . . . She had wrapped its folds over that "accursed" breast— as she had called it—but prostitution had done no harm to the perfect roundness and virgin firmness of those breasts. Her voice, too, had lost the harsh quality he had heard out in the street. . . . Was it some illusion produced by what she was telling him? Tressignies thought he heard a purer tone in her voice—as if she had put her nobility back on.

"I don't know," she continued, "if other women are like me. But that incredible arrogance of Don Christoval, that calm, disdainful 'He wouldn't dare!' in speaking of the man I loved—it seemed like an insult to the man who had taken possession of the deepest part of my being, like some god. 'Prove that you *would* dare it!' I said to him that evening, declaring my love to him. I didn't have to say it. Esteban had adored me from the first time he saw me. Our love sprang into being simultaneously, like two pistols being fired off at exactly the same time—two pistols that killed what they aimed at. . . . I had done my duty as a Spanish wife in warning Don Christoval. I owed him my life, but nothing more, for the heart is not free to love where it will; and he certainly would have taken my life, had he shown Don Esteban to the door, as I had asked. My newly born heart, in its madness, would have stopped beating if I had been forced to see him no longer, but that is the terrible chance I had taken. But since the Duke, my husband, had not understood that, since he believed himself to be so far above Vasconcellos that the man would find it impossible even to lift his eyes up toward me, I was not going to be heroic and fight any longer against a love that had already mastered me. . . . I won't try to give you an exact depiction of our love. Maybe you wouldn't believe me, you either . . . But what does it matter anyway, what you think? Believe me, or don't believe me! Our love was both fiery and chaste, a chivalric love, a romantic love, almost an ideal love, almost mystical. True, we were both barely twenty, and we were living in the country of Bivar, Ignatius of Loyola, and Saint Teresa. Ignatius, that knight devoted to the Virgin, loved the Queen of the Heavens no more purely than Vasconcellos loved me; and I felt something for him like that ecstatic love that Saint Teresa had for the Divine Spouse. Adultery!—not a bit of it! Could we even have imagined ourselves being adulterous? The heart beat so high up in our chests, we lived in an atmosphere of such transcendent, such elevated feelings that we felt no wicked desires and felt none of the sensuality of vulgar lovers. We lived up in the pure blue sky; but it was an African sky, and the blue was the blue of fire. Could such a state of soul endure for long? Weren't we in fact playing the most dangerous game that two weak creatures could play, without knowing it, without any doubts in ourselves, and wasn't it only a matter of time before we would find ourselves hurled down from those immaculate heights? . . . Esteban was as pious as a priest, like a Portuguese knight in the time of Albuquerque; I was by no means as worthy as he was, but I had in him and in the purity of his love a faith that kindled and inflamed the purity of mine.[27] He kept me in his heart, like a Madonna in a golden niche—with a lamp at her feet—an inextinguishable lamp. He loved my soul, and for my soul's sake. He was one of those rare lovers who want to make the woman they adore even grander. He wanted me to be noble, pious, heroic, a great lady from the era when Spain herself was great. He would rather have seen me perform a great, noble action than to waltz with me, his lips on mine! If angels before the throne of God could fall in love with each other, they would have to love the way we loved each other. . . . We two had become so entirely one that we would pass long hours alone together, hand in hand, eyes gazing into eyes, capable of anything, since we were alone, but so happy that we desired nothing more. Some-times the immense happiness flooded into us so that we were overcome with it and wanted to die, but to die with each other and for each other, and at such times we understood Saint Teresa when she said, 'I'm dying for being unable to die!' It's the desire of a finite creature succumbing to an infinite love, of a creature believing it can make room for that torrent of infinity to pour in by breaking up its body, by dying. Today, I am one of the foulest of creatures; but in those days, would you believe it, the lips of Esteban never touched mine, and once, when he kissed a rose, and I put it up to my lips, it made me faint? From the depths of this horror into which I've deliberately plunged myself, I can recall, and doing so is my torture, those divine moments of pure love we lived together, lost, overwhelmed, and, in the sheer innocence of that sublime love, so obvious that Don Christoval could not help but see how we adored each other. We lived with our heads in the clouds. How could we possibly see that he was jealous—and what kind of jealousy? The only kind of which he was capable, the jealousy that grows out of pride. He did not catch us or find us out. You can't find someone out who isn't hiding anything. We did not hide. Why should we have hidden? We had all the candor of a flame that burns in full daylight, visible even in the daylight, and our happiness so overspilled itself that it could not help but be observed, and the Duke observed it! That splendor of our love broke through his pride and opened his eyes! Ah, so Esteban had *dared*! And I had, too! One evening, we were together the way we always were, since we had fallen in love with each other, sitting alone together, gazing at one another; he knelt at my feet, as at the feet of the Virgin Mary, in a state of contemplation so profound that we needed no other caress. Suddenly, the Duke entered with two blacks he had brought back from the Spanish colonies, where he had held a governorship for many years. We didn't see them come in, united as we were in a celestial contemplation that elevated both our souls, when Esteban's head fell abruptly on my knees. He had been strangled! The two blacks had thrown around his neck that terrible lasso they use in Mexico to strangle wild bulls. It happened as swiftly as lightning! But the lightning didn't kill me. I did not faint, and I did not cry out. No tear came to my eyes. I sat there mute, rigid, in a state of nameless horror, from which I only emerged by a violent wrenching of my whole spirit. I felt as if they had torn open my breast and were tearing out my heart. Alas, it was not my heart they tore out: it was Esteban's, Esteban's corpse, lying at my feet, strangled, his chest cut open and rifled by the hands of those monsters! My love for him had been so strong that I felt what he would have felt had he still been alive. I felt all the pain that his dead body could not feel, and that is what tore me out of the frozen horror I'd been in when I saw them strangle him. I threw myself upon them: 'Kill me, too!' I cried. I wanted to die the same death, and I stretched out my neck for the hideous cord. They were about to do it. *'No one touches the queen!'* exclaimed the Duke, that proud Duke who thought himself above the King, and he lashed them both back with his whip. 'No! You're going to live, Madame,' he said to me, 'so that you can remember, every single day, what you're about to see . . .' And at that he whistled. In raced two enormous savage dogs. 'Let them eat,' he said. 'Give the dogs this traitor's heart!' Oh, at that, I don't know what came over me:

"'You can have a better revenge than that!' I said to him. 'Don't give it to the dogs—make me eat it!'

"He stopped, stunned at the idea . . .

"'You love him that insanely?' he asked. Oh, I loved him with a love that my husband had only increased. I loved him so that I felt no fear and no disgust at that bloody heart, that heart filled with me, still warm with me, and I wanted to put it into my own heart. . . . I asked for it kneeling down, with folded hands! I wanted to spare that noble, adored heart from the unholy sacrilege. . . . I had communed with that heart, as with the sacred Host. Was it not my God? . . . The philosophy of Gabrielle de Vergy, whom we had read, Esteban and I, so many times together came back to me now.[28] I envied her! I thought she had been lucky, to have been able to turn her body into a living tomb for the man she had loved. But seeing such love in my face only made the Duke more implacable. His dogs ate Esteban's heart in front of me. I tried to fight them for it, but I couldn't tear it away from them. They bit me, hideously, over and over, and they pulled at my dress, wiping their bloody jaws on it."

She paused. She had grown livid at these memories . . . and panting for breath, she stood up violently, and opening a drawer by its bronze handle, she showed Tressignies a dress in tatters, stained with blood in many places.

"Look!" she said. "This is the heart's blood of the man I loved, which I couldn't tear away from the dogs! Whenever I find myself alone today in this wretched life I'm leading, whenever I feel overwhelmed by disgust, when the filth of it rises up in my gorge and begins to suffocate me, when the spirit of vengeance begins to weaken in me, when the Duchess reasserts herself and the streetwalker pales in fear, then I wrap myself in this dress, and I let my befouled body wallow in these bloody folds that still burn me, and that heat ignites my vengeance again. These bloody rags are like a talisman! When I wrap my body in them, the rage for revenge possesses me again, body and soul, and I regain my strength, and that strength seems as if it will last for all eternity!"

Tressignies shuddered, listening to that frightening woman. He shuddered at her gestures, her words, her head, which had become like the Gorgon's: he imagined he could see the serpents curling and twining around her head, the serpents that in fact entwined her heart. He now began to understand—the veil had been lifted!—what the word *vengeance* really meant, the word that flamed so often from her lips.

"Vengeance, oh yes!" she continued. "You understand what it is now, don't you, my vengeance! Oh, I've carefully chosen it from all the alternatives, the way a person would choose the dagger that would cause the most pain and suffering, the jagged blade that would best rip and tear the flesh of the hated man you wanted to kill! Just to kill that man, though, all at once—no, that's not what I wanted. Had he killed Vasconcellos with his sword, like a gentleman? No—he had his servants do it for him. He threw his heart to those dogs and perhaps threw his body into a charnel house. I didn't know. I never found out. Kill him, as a response to all that? No! That would be too gentle, and too swift! I needed to find something slower, something far more cruel. . . . Besides, the Duke was a brave man. He didn't fear death. The Sierra-Leone family had defied death for generations. But that pride of his, that immense pride turned to cowardice when it was a matter of dishonor. Therefore, I had to strike at him in his pride and crucify him there. I had to dishonor that name, of which he was so proud. Very well, then! I swore to myself that I would drag that name through the most diseased of swamps, that I would change that name to a byword for shame, for filth, for excrement! And that is why I've made myself into what I am—a common prostitute—yes, the whore Sierra-Leone whom you picked up tonight!"

As she spoke these last words, her eyes sparkled with the joy of a well-landed blow.

"But," Tressignies asked, "does he know, the Duke, what you've become?"

"If he doesn't know yet, he will eventually," she replied, with the absolute certainty of a woman who has thought of everything, calculated everything, a woman absolutely sure about what was to come. "The news about what I'm doing will get to him one day or another, and my shame will splash its filth up onto him! One of the men who comes up to this room can go up to him and spit the dishonor of his wife into his face, such that he'll never be able to wipe it off—but that's only a chance, and I won't leave my vengeance up to chance! I've resolved to die so as to be sure of it; my death will assure it and finish it off."

Tressignies was befuddled by these last words; but she went on to cast a hideous clarity on them.

"I want to die the same way other women like me die," she said. "Listen: do you remember this story? . . . There was a man back in the time of François I who sought out a woman like me in order to catch a terrible, disgusting disease so that he could pass it on to his wife, who would thereby poison the King, whose mistress she was, and that is how he avenged himself on the two of them. . . . I'll do no less with this man. With the shameful life I lead every single night, sooner or later I'll come to that putrefaction that wastes away every prostitute, killing her by degrees, and sending her ultimately to die in some shameful hospital! Oh, then, then the repayment will be complete!" she added, in a horrible, exuberant voice, expressing the most hideous hope for her future. "Then it will be the time for the Duke de Sierra-Leone to learn how his wife, the Duchess de Sierra-Leone, lived, and how she died!"

Tressignies had not imagined there could be such depths in revenge; this surpassed every story he had ever heard. Neither in the Italy of the sixteenth century nor in Corsica (at any period), two countries renowned for their implacable hatreds, was there an example that so combined cold calculation and sheer fierceness as this woman's story did, this woman who carried out her vengeance even at the cost of herself, of her own body, of her own soul! It was horrible, and it frightened him, but it was also sublime, for when the passions are pushed to such a height, the spectacle is sublime. It was, however, the sublimity of Hell.

"And if he never learns of it," she went on, illuminating her very soul even more, "I will know! I will know what I did every night—that I drink down this filth, and that to me it's nectar, because it's my revenge! Do you think I don't rejoice, every single minute, at the thought of what I am? Do you think that at the very moment I dishonor him, that arrogant Duke, that I'm not fully aware of it, intoxicated with the thought of dishonoring him? . . . Ah, passions like mine are insane, but it's the insanity that gives me such happiness! When I ran away from Sierra-Leone, I took this portrait of the Duke along with me, so that I could make him witness to the shame of my life! How many times I've said to that picture, as if it were he and as if it could hear me, 'Look! Look!' And when I'm overcome with horror in your arms—you and all the others—because the horror does overwhelm, constantly—you see, I'm not really used to it yet, this filth—at moments like that I have this bracelet . . ." And with that she held up her superb arm in a tragic posture. "I have this circle of fire that burns me right down to the marrow and that I keep wearing on my wrist, despite the torture of it, because I can never let myself forget Esteban's executioner, and I need his image to goad me into that ecstasy—that ecstasy that men are stupid and vain enough to believe they're giving me! I don't know who you are, but you're certainly not the most naïve of those men, and yet you believed, just a moment ago, that I was still a human being, that there was still some chord that vibrated within me: but the only thing left inside me is the thought of taking my revenge for Esteban on that monster whose image is on this bracelet! Oh, that image is like a spur to me, one of those spurs the Arabs use, big as a saber, pounding it into their horses' flanks to goad them across the desert. But I have even greater distances of shame to cover, and I pound that hateful image into my eyes, into my heart in order to be better able to flex and writhe under you while you hold me. . . . It's as if this portrait were really he! It's as if he could watch us with those painted eyes! . . . Oh, now I understand the witches of past ages, and the spells they cast! Now I understand the insane bliss of sticking a pin into the heart of the image of the man you wanted to kill! In the past, when I was religious, before I loved Esteban and he took the place of God for me, I needed to have a crucifix in order to think more deeply about the Crucified One and to love Him better; but if instead of loving I had hated Him, if I had been impious, I would still have needed the crucifix in order to blaspheme and insult Him the better! Oh . . ." she paused, her tone changing, slipping from the bitterest and the cruelest of feelings to the heartrending softness of an incredible melancholy. "I never had a portrait of Esteban. I can only see him in my imagination . . . and that might be for the best," she added. "If I could look at him, he would raise up my poor heart, and he would make me blush at the unworthy humiliation that my life has become. I would repent, and then I wouldn't be able to avenge him!"

The Gorgon had become a woman of feeling, but her eyes remained dry. Tressignies, moved by feelings very different from the ones she had just passed through, took her hand—the hand of a woman he had every right to despise—and kissed it with a mixture of pity and respect. All that suffering and all that energy had given her grandeur in his eyes. "What a woman!" he thought. "If, instead of having been the Duchess de Sierra-Leone she had been the Marquise de Vasconcellos, with that purity of love for Esteban, she would have been a kind of example for all humankind, something approaching the greatness of the Marquise de Pescaire.[29] But the difference is," he thought, "that she would not have shown it openly, and no one would ever have known what profound depths of will lay within her." Despite the skepticism of the era in which he lived, and his habit of self-mockery, Robert de Tressignies did not at all feel ridiculous in kissing the hand of this lost woman; but he did not know what to say to her. His standing with her was an awkward one. By putting her story between the two of them, she had cut, as effectively as if with an axe, any ties that might have developed. He felt an inexpressible mixture of admiration, horror, and contempt; but he would have found it in horrible taste to try to talk about feelings or morality with this woman. He had often mocked those moralists who, without mandate and without authority, swarmed everywhere in those days, under the influence of certain plays and certain novels, affecting to find and redeem fallen women, as if they were straightening up so many overturned flowerpots. Skeptic as he was, he had been born with enough common sense to know that only a real priest—a priest of the Redeemer God—could raise up such fallen women . . . and moreover, he thought, even a real priest would break down in trying to soften the soul of this woman. He felt the deep, sorrowful implications of it all, and he maintained a silence that weighed more on him than on her. But she, returning to all the violence of her thoughts and memories, continued.

"The idea of dishonoring him rather than killing him, that man for whom what society calls 'honor' is more precious than life, didn't come to me right away. . . . It took me quite a while to think of it. After the death of Vasconcellos, who was probably not even known to have been in the castle, and whose body was no doubt thrown into some cell along with the blacks who had strangled him, the Duke never said another word to me, except for necessary brief, ceremonial phrases when his servants were present, for Caesar's wife must always be above suspicion, and I had to remain the impeccable Duchess d'Arcos de Sierra-Leone in the eyes of the world. But whenever we were alone, not a word, not a gesture: silence, the silence of hatred, which feeds on itself and has no need of words. Don Christoval and I fought each other only with resolution and pride. I swallowed my tears. I am a Turre-Cremata. I am Italian, and I have all the dissimulation of my race, and I hardened myself to bronze, even my gaze, so he could not guess what was simmering behind that mask of bronze

where the idea of my vengeance was slowly gestating. I was absolutely impenetrable. Thanks to that dissimulation, which blocked
up every opening through which my secret might have filtered
out, I was able to plan my flight from the castle, whose walls
were crushing me, and where I could not carry out my vengeance
without the Duke quickly finding out and putting an end to it.
I confided in no one. Not a single one of my duennas or maid-
servants dared to raise her eyes to try to discover my thoughts.
My first plan was to go to Madrid; but the Duke was all-powerful
in Madrid, and the net of the police would have closed around
me at the first move I made. He would have easily apprehended
me, and once he had brought me back, he would have thrown
me into the *in-pace* of some convent, suffocated there, killed quietly behind high walls, hidden away from the world, the world I
needed in order to have my revenge! . . .[30] Paris was the better
choice. I preferred Paris. It was the best setting for the growth
of my infamy and my vengeance; and since my plan was for it to
become widely known, for my shame to resound in the world
like thunder, what better place could there be than this city, the
center point of every echo, the crossroads of the world! I resolved
to live this life of a prostitute, which did not frighten me, and to
descend shamelessly down to the lowest rank of those lost women
who sell themselves for money, even to the worst of men! Pious as I had been before I knew Esteban and before he pulled
God out of my heart so as to put himself there instead, I often
got up in the night without my servants, to go pray to the black
Virgin in the chapel.[31] It was from there that I made my escape
one night and audaciously made my way to the Sierra gorges. I
took as many jewels and as much money from my moneybox as
I could carry. I hid myself in the home of some peasants who
conducted me to the border. I came to Paris. Without fear, I set
to carrying out my vengeance, which is my life. I hunger for it so
much, feel the fury of vengeance so much, that I've sometimes
thought of dazzling some impressionable, energetic young man,
and then having him go to the Duke to tell him about my shame;
but in the end I repress the idea, because I don't want to heap a
few feet of dung onto *his* name and onto my memory: no, I want a

dung heap the size of a pyramid atop it! The longer it takes for my vengeance to be complete, the better my vengeance will be. . . ."

Her voice trailed off. She was no longer livid; her complexion had turned dark, almost purple, and sweat stood on her temples. She had made herself hoarse. Was this the illness of shame? . . . She feverishly seized a carafe of water from the dresser and poured a large glass of water, which she rapidly swallowed.

"It's not easy to swallow it, this sense of shame!" she said. "But I have to! I've swallowed enough of it these past few months, so I can get it down!"

"So this has been going on for three months?" asked Tressignies—not daring to specify what *this* referred to; his vagueness was in fact more horrible than precision would have been.

"Yes," she said, "three months." Then she added, "But what's three months? It takes time to cook and cook some more this dish of vengeance I'm preparing for him, to pay him back for that heart of Esteban's that he wouldn't let me eat . . ."

She said this with an atrocious passion and a wild, savage melancholy. Tressignies had no doubt that this woman contained within herself a sufficient mixture of idolatrous love and cruelty. No one has ever looked at a work of art with the attention with which he gazed upon this singular, all-powerful artist of revenge standing before him. . . . But something else figured in his observation, something he was surprised to feel. He, who thought he was finished once and for all with involuntary feelings, he who laughed a terrible, satiric laugh at such feelings, whipping and beating them the way I've seen cart drivers whip their horses to force them into obedience—he felt he was breathing something dangerous in the air surrounding this woman. This room, filled with so much physical, barbarous passion, was asphyxiating the ultra-civilized man. He felt the need for some fresh air, and he thought of leaving, and perhaps coming back later.

She thought he was leaving. But there were still some aspects of the masterpiece that he had not quite seen.

"What about this?" she said, with all the disdain of a duchess, pointing with her finger at the blue cup that he had filled with gold coins.

"Take your money back," she said. "Who knows? It could be that I'm richer than you are. Gold doesn't enter into this room. I won't accept it from anyone."

And then she added, with the deep pride in the shame that comprised her vengeance: "I'm only a hundred-sou whore."

She spoke the sentence calmly. This was the final touch of her inverted sublimity, of the Hellish sublimity that she had displayed to him, something that even the great Corneille, in the depths of his tragic soul, had never felt! The contempt in this last statement gave Tressignies the strength he needed to get up and leave. He poured the gold pieces out of the cup, leaving only the price she had asked for. "Since she wants it this way, I'll push the dagger in a bit further, and I'll add my touch of mud, since she so wants to be stained with mud." And he left in a state of extreme agitation. The candelabra still bathed the door in their light, that door that had seemed so ordinary when he first entered it. Now he understood why she had had those lights put up there, now that he saw the card pasted onto the door, like a neon sign on this boutique of flesh. The card read, in large letters:

THE DUCHESS D'ARCOS
DE SIERRA-LEONE

And below that was a single, ugly word that indicated the profession she followed.

Tressignies went back home that night, after that incredible adventure, so disturbed that he almost felt ashamed of himself. The imbeciles—that is to say, pretty much everyone in society— always think it would be a charming thing if we could recover our lost youth; but those who know something about life know how little we would benefit from it. Tressignies felt fear as he said to himself that he felt too young now . . . and therefore he swore he would never again set foot in the Duchess's room, despite the interest he felt or, rather, because of the intensity of interest that this astounding woman had inflicted upon him. "Why," he asked himself, "should I return to the unhealthy place of infection, that abyss into which that creature of such high origins has hurled herself? She's told me her entire life story, and I can easily imagine the daily details of her horrible current existence, which must be always the same." Such was the firm resolution Tressignies made, sitting alone by the fireside in his room. He shut himself away for a time from the distractions of things and the world outside, remaining alone with his impressions and memories of a night that something inside him could not help but savor, like some strange and all-powerful poem, the likes of which he had never read in Byron or Shakespeare, his two favorite poets. He passed many hours like this, his elbows resting on the arms of his easy chair, leafing through the always-open pages of that outrageously powerful poem. It was like a lotus, to make him forget about his native land—the salons of Paris. He had to gather all his strength to go back to those places. And the irreproachable duchesses that he met there seemed a bit colorless to him. . . . Though this Tressignies was no prude, nor were his friends, he didn't speak a word about his adventure to them out of a sense of delicacy, though it struck him as absurd; after all, hadn't the Duchess asked him to tell her story to anyone who would listen, and to spread it as far and wide as he possibly could? But on the contrary, he kept it to himself. He held on to it, sealing it up in the deepest, most mysterious corner of his being, the way one tightens the stopper on a vial of very rare perfume, a scent that will lose something of itself if it's allowed to breathe. And another thing, very surprising in a man like him: neither at the Café de Paris, nor at his club, nor in the theater, nor anywhere that men gather and speak freely to each other did he encounter one of his friends without fearing to hear him narrate the same adventure he had had; and his fear of this thing that could possibly happen actually caused him to tremble slightly for the first ten minutes of any conversation. Nevertheless, he kept his promise, and he not only never returned to the Rue Basse-du-Rempart, but he even avoided the Boulevard as well. He no longer lounged, with the other *gants jaunes,* the young lions of the day, on the balcony at Tortoni's. "If I were to see that yellow silk dress again," he said to himself, "I would probably be fool enough to follow again." Every yellow dress he passed sent him into a reverie. . . . He loved yellow dresses now, though he used to loathe them. "She's depraved my taste," he said to himself, and thus the dandy mocked the man. But what Madame de Staël, who knew them well, called the thoughts of the Demon were stronger than either the man or the dandy.[32] Tressignies became somber. He had been a man with a lively, sometimes fearsome, wit in society—for, indeed, all humor in the social world needs to be a bit frightening, for otherwise people will despise you while you are amusing them. He no longer conversed with the same energy. . . . "Was he in love?" asked the gossips. The old Marquise de Clérembault, believing he was interested in her granddaughter, who had just come out in society, all romantic and hot and fresh from the Sacré Coeur convent school, said to him with some annoyance: "I can't stand it when you put on these Hamlet airs of yours." From being somber, he evolved to being sickly. His complexion paled. "What's wrong with Monsieur de Tressignies?" people asked, and they might have gone on to conclude that he was suffering from a cancer in his stomach, like Bonaparte, if it hadn't happened that one day he put an end to all the questions and interrogations by packing up his trunks in a flash, the way an officer does, and disappearing so entirely that he might have slipped down a hole.

Where did he go? What was he doing? He stayed away for more than a year, and then he returned to Paris and put himself back in the yoke of his social life. One evening, he was at the home of the Spanish ambassador, which was aswarm with the most sparkling, highest Parisian society. . . . It was late. They were going into supper. The crush around the buffet had emptied the salons. A few men remained stubbornly playing whist in the card room. Suddenly, the partner of Tressignies, who was turning the pages of a little tortoiseshell book in which the bets of each rubber were entered, perceived something that made him exclaim "Ah!" the way one does when one remembers something that had been forgotten . . .

"Monsieur Ambassador," he said to the master of the house, who was standing with his hands clasped behind his back, watching them play: "Are there still any members of the Sierra-Leone family living?"

"But of course!" said the ambassador. "To begin with, there's the Duke, who is the peer of the very noblest families among the grandees."

"Then who is this Duchess de Sierra-Leone, who just died here in Paris, and what is she to the Duke?" he asked.

"She could only be his wife," replied the ambassador calmly. "But for two years now, the Duchess has been essentially dead. She disappeared, with no one knowing where she went or why: the truth is a complete mystery! Consider that this imposing Duchess d'Arcos de Sierra-Leone was not like some modern woman having an adventure, who would let herself be carried off by some lover. She is a woman every bit the equal of the Duke her husband, who is one of the proudest of the *Ricos hombres* in all Spain. Moreover, she was religious, with an almost monastic piety. She had never lived anywhere but Sierra-Leone, a desert of red marble where the eagles—if there are any!—must drop down dead of boredom from their heights! One day she disappeared, and no one has seen a trace of her since. Since then, the Duke, a man of the Charles V era, has moved to Madrid, and he speaks no more of his wife and her disappearance than if she had never existed. She was a Turre-Cremata, the last of the Italian branch of the family."

"That's the one," the card player interrupted. He looked down at what he had written on a page of the tortoiseshell notebook. "Well, then!" he began solemnly. "Monsieur Ambassador, I have the honor of informing you that the Duchess de Sierra-Leone was buried this morning, and in a detail you would never have suspected, she was buried at the church of the Salpêtrière, having been a patient there!"[33]

At this, all the players glanced down at their cards, placed them facedown on the table, and then looked over with alarm at the man who had spoken thus to the Ambassador.

"Oh, yes!" he went on, happy to be making such a splash— that effect so irresistible to a Frenchman! "I was walking by the place this morning, passing along the wall of the church, and I heard such majestic, thunderous religious music that I had to go

in, the place not being accustomed to such splendor . . . and as I
came in I was astonished to see that the portal was draped with
black cloth, decorated with coats of arms with double escutcheons, and to see in the choir the most resplendent catafalque.
The church itself was almost empty. Some beggars knelt in the
paupers' pews, and here and there were a few women, some of
the horrible lepers from the hospital next door, at any rate some
of those who aren't entirely insane and who can still keep themselves upright. Surprised to see people like that around such a
catafalque, I walked up to it and read, in big letters—silver letters
on a black background—this inscription, which, I swear, I copied
out exactly so as not to forget it:

HERE LIES

SANZIA-FLORINDA-CONCEPCION

DE TURRE-CREMATA,

DUCHESS D'ARCOS DE SIERRA-LEONE,

A REPENTANT WHORE,

WHO DIED AT THE SALPÊTRIÈRE ON THE . . . OF . . . 18 . . .

REQUIESCAT IN PACE!

The players had completely forgotten about their game. As for
the Ambassador, knowing that a diplomat must show surprise
no more than an officer must show fear, and sensing that his
astonishment might compromise him in the eyes of his guests,
he said:

"And you made no inquiries?" His tone was that of a master
speaking to his inferiors.

"Not at all, your Excellency," the player replied. "There were
only the paupers there; and the priests, who might have been
able to tell me something, were all chanting the funeral hymns.
And I remembered that I would have the honor of seeing you this
evening."

"I'll have the information tomorrow," said the ambassador. And
the game started up again, but it was broken up by many exclamations, and each player was so preoccupied with his thoughts that
this group of master whist players made mistake after mistake,
and none of them noticed how pale Tressignies had gone, nor how

quickly he picked up his hat and departed without saying good-bye to anyone.

Early the next morning, he went to the Salpêtrière. He asked for the chaplain—a friendly, elderly priest—who told him every-thing he wanted to know about patient no. 119, who had become the Duchess d'Arcos de Sierra-Leone. The unhappy woman had come to exactly the end she had predicted for herself. . . . Play-ing the terrible game that she had chosen to play, she caught the most terrible of diseases. In a matter of months—said the old priest—she had rotted to the bone. . . . One of her eyeballs had burst abruptly out of its socket one day, falling at her feet like a thick coin. . . . The other one liquefied, melting away. . . . She died—but she died stoically—in the midst of utterly intolerable tortures. . . . Still wealthy, with money and jewels, she left ev-erything to the other patients like her in the hospital that had taken her in and ordered a solemn funeral. "The only thing was," said the old priest, who had understood nothing at all about the woman, "that she had demanded, out of penitence and humility, that we inscribe on her coffin and on her tombstone, following her titles, the fact that she was a 'REPENTANT WHORE.'

"And then," the old chaplain added, duped by the confession of such a woman, "out of humility, she wanted us to omit the word *repentant*."

Tressignies could not help but smile bitterly at the good old priest, but he left intact the naïve man's illusions.

For he knew perfectly well that she had not repented, and that this touching humility was only her vengeance from beyond the grave.

APPENDIXES

A Page from History—*1606*

Preface to The Last Mistress *(1865)*

A PAGE FROM HISTORY—1606

This story was first published in the feuilleton Gil Blas, *on December 26, 1882. It was given pride of place on the front page, introduced as a "remarquable article de Barbey d'Aurevilly," and titled "Retour de Valognes. Un poème inédit de Lord Byron" (Return to Valognes: an unpublished poem by Lord Byron). The subtitle signaled Barbey's lifelong fascination with Byron, and this piece, dealing with brother-sister incest, shares that theme with the English poet's work. It was reprinted by itself in book form for the first time in 1886, with two illustrations, this time given its final title,* Une page d'histoire (1606).

I

Over the years I've returned to Normandy, the land of my birth, many times in search of impressions.[1] But I've encountered only one impression this year that, in its profundity, can be said to have molded itself to my personal memories, memories that have what I would have called a power—but perhaps this is mad—memories that, I was about to write, have the real power of specters. . . . The town I live in here in this Western land is bereft now of everything that made it so glittering in my early youth, and empty and sad like an abandoned sarcophagus: I've called it "the town of my ghosts" for a long time, in order to justify a love for the place that my friends consider incomprehensible; they say they are surprised at me, and they reproach me for coming here. But it is in fact the specters of my vanished past that attach me so strangely to the place. Without these ghosts, I would never come back!

When I walk down these deserted streets with their light-colored cobblestones, I am always accompanied by those phantoms, which are not the kind that only haunt us by night, drawing back our bed curtains and bending down to touch our lips with *what used to be their lips,* the breath that once intoxicated us now gone forever. . . . No, for me, my determined, insistent specters return at all times, even in the daytime, even in these streets where the sunlight fails to chase them away, and they rise up next to me in the brightest glare of day just as if it were night, the all-enveloping night that they love so much, that night that eventually comes; but even when it comes and they stand pale against the backdrop of darkness, they are no more vivid than they are during the day. . . . How many times has a rare passerby encountered me making my melancholy circuit of the dead streets in this dead town, its beauty the pale beauty of sepulchers, and mistakenly assumed I was walking all alone! A whole society has been walking along with me—an entire deceased society arising up out of the paving stones as out of so many tombs while I walk along, a funereal group forming an obstinate procession around me. They elbow up against me, and I see them, recognize their faces and their shapes just as definitely and just as clearly as Hamlet recognized the phantom of his father on the battlements of Elsinore.

But it isn't them—those familiar, intimate ghosts of mine—that I want to speak about today. There are two others. Two who have also appeared to me this year, looming up across three centuries of History and who have, so to speak, burrowed their way into my consciousness as if I had known them when they were visible flesh and blood—when they were living substances whose hands and eyes you would have had to touch to assure yourself that they really existed under the conditions of this accursed life, in which the body is not transparent, in which the creatures whom we have loved the most retain no more of us than the embraces in our dreams, who must eternally remain mysteries to our hearts, objects of doubt, of regret, of despair! . . . The history of these two beings who have, probably, come to join permanently that procession that always accompanies me—the history that I've put together as best as I could from the fragments and traces that time has allowed to survive, the history of two beings who were both the shame and the end of their family: their history is now attached to my own, like a horsefly stubbornly clinging to the mane of the horse that carries it along, and their story has precisely that same fascinating, mysterious character that the greatest poetry has, and through which it affects our imagination—and perhaps, given the narrow range of knowledge allowed to us, the ignorant Damned, such poetry may be our only truth!

In any case, this mystery played out in the very country least made for such a thing, the place where it was the easiest to hide it! And indeed it was hidden there. . . . And even now, in the present day, despite the impassioned efforts of later researchers, it remains largely hidden! Getting to the depths, the inmost depths of the story is impossible now; the only light shed on it is the lurid gleam of the executioner's axe, which both opened up and closed off the story, which was the story of a love and a happiness of so guilty a kind that its very idea is horrifying. . . . Horrifying, but also enthralling (may God forgive us!), with that disturbing, dangerous sort of charm that makes the soul who responds to it feel almost guilty in itself, makes the soul who contemplates it almost an accomplice in the crime, almost—who can say?—envious, wishing to have been able to have been a part of it . . .

I I

In the days when that love, that happiness, that had to remain silent due to its guilty nature, wrapped itself in shadows but was then betrayed—as such love always is—by emotions that would not remain repressed, people's hearts were marked by a proud energy. The passions, more virile than in the eras to follow, had arisen to a kind of crescendo from which they have altogether fallen since, a height to which they will probably never return. It was toward the end of the sixteenth century—the century of Italianate fanaticism that gave us Catherine de Medici and the race of the Valois, the Borgias of France. In those days, in Normandy—solid Normandy, where the people, sturdy and methodical, keep their own counsel better than anywhere else—there was an aristocratic family that had come from Brittany around 1400 and had become, over the course of several generations, Norman by virtue of the lands they owned. They lived near the Channel coast, to the east, not far from Cherbourg, in a chateau fortified with a tower; the place thus came to be called Tourlaville.[2] Like all medieval chateaux, it had been essentially a fortification designed for warfare, but the softening genius of the Renaissance had transformed it, preparing it to hide within its walls passions and criminal pleasures, readying it for those destinies that would ultimately be fulfilled there.

The family that lived there did not know it, but theirs was a fateful name: the Ravalet family. . . . And in fact that sinister name was about to be swallowed up![3] Following the crime of its two final descendants, the family excommunicated itself from its own name. It tried to wipe off the stain and thus killed itself off before actually dying.

In any case, it well deserved dying. But it didn't die the way other guilty and condemned families have done. God made a sad exception in this case. The family, an *outlaw* of God,[4] had violated all His laws before coming ultimately to violate the very law of Providence, that of divine expiation. It would not be the guiltiest ones in this depraved, ferocious, and sacrilegious family who would pay for the longstanding crimes of their race. But it would not be innocents either—innocents, who might have redeemed everything by their innocence! There were no innocents among the Ravalets. But the ones who paid were guilty of a far different sort of crime from that of their forefathers, far different from that unholy tradition; they added their own sins to those of their ancestors, sins those ancestors had never committed. And it was in this fact, at least, that we detect a sudden outburst—a wild one, and one contaminated, it is true, by the inherited vices of that damned race—yet an outburst of genuine, recovered human nature, which one would have supposed had long been extinguished in the breasts of the Ravalets!

III

All of them, from one generation down to the next, had been exceptionally ruthless men. Every one of them, without exception, had killed off any human feeling in his heart, just as they had literally killed human beings. The most pronounced trait of that terrible race was a horrific ruthlessness. With ungovernable, uncompromising temperaments, with passions as raw as those of tigers, they were men who believed the world had been created for them, and if they thought it were necessary in order to cook an egg for their meal, they would have burned down an entire city. When they took it into their heads to indulge in vice, it was the kind of vice that involved blood, and even death. . . . Once, one of them stole away the daughter of one of his equerries, and when he was done violating her, he threw her into a ditch and beat her to death with a skittle ball. For him, she was just one more pin added to his score! Another one, drunk and leaving one of the orgies with which his accursed chateau was so familiar, wandered into the local church the following morning and presented himself at the railing for Communion. When the priest refused it to him, he ran the man through with his sword, butchering him while he stood there holding the sacred Host, leaving him dead on the altar steps. A third one had killed his brother with his bare hands, marking his race with the sign of Cain for all time. . . . Everyone shuddered—in Normandy, a land where men are brave and proud—everyone shuddered when they thought of the Ravalet family, and the general horror people felt had become so powerful that everyone expected them eventually to breed not people but some kind of monster, beings of some unknown species, some unknown form, and people would say, when they heard that a Ravalet woman was pregnant, "What thing will be tumbling out of that womb? What hideous thing is about to be vomited out onto our countryside?" But such fears were unfounded. The monsters they all feared turned out to be two infants of the purest beauty who sprang up suddenly one day, like a pair of roses, out of that pool of blood that was the Ravalets.

An extraordinary—and melancholy—analogy is in the fact that

the Ravalet escutcheon featured a blooming rose *en pointe*.[5] And in fact there were two of them who appeared at the very extremity of the race, but these two carried within their double corolla the cantharides that was going to consume their lives. . . .[6] Julien and Marguerite de Ravalet, those two children who were as beautiful as innocence itself, brought their fratricidal race to an end through their own incest. Their forebears had been the Cains of hatred. These two were the Cains of love, though not less fratricidal in their way, for in loving each other they killed each other willingly with the double blade of their incest.

But how could they possibly have willed this? How could they have loved each other, those two, in such a way that the society of their day could level no other reproach at them save the very fact of their love? What makes this particular crime of incest so rare is the fact that they seemed to have grown habituated to it. In that solitary chateau where they were raised, it would seem that Julien and Marguerite de Ravalet must have grown so accustomed, so immunized to their love that its dangerous beauty ceased to be lethal to their souls; but then, they were the last drops of the Ravalet blood, and their mortal love was perhaps their inalienable birthright. . . . Who could ever know the origin of that fateful love, which was probably already too great to stop when they first perceived its existence? At what particular moment in their childhood or their youth did they gaze down into their hearts and see the cantharides of incest living there, half-asleep, just below the surface—and which of the two was it who told the other about it first? . . . How long did it take for the suspicions and the whispers to grow up around their breathless happiness—whispers that were cut short by remorse and by shame, but whispers that always started up again, eventually becoming powerful enough to suffocate them? . . . And then they were forcefully separated, the brother sent into exile and the sister married off by the imperious father—but then the brother returned, as sudden as lightning, and carried off his sister like a whirlwind. Where did they go to be together and wallow in their happiness and in their crime, these two beings who found their earthly paradise in a satanic passion? All vain questions! No one knows. All trace of the pair was lost for a year, until they finally come back into view in Paris on a sad December day—but the sight of them is a bloody one now, for they met their ends there on the scaffold. The image is a silent one, telling us nothing of the inward, profound drama of that love whose only witnesses were the walls of this chateau, the stones of which seem to us still sweating with incest—and the neighboring woods and ponds that saw the pair so deliciously, so horribly happy in their shadows or on their surfaces, they reveal nothing of what they have seen either. Only Tradition speaks, coarse, crude Tradition, which never gazes into people's souls, and it has written the scandalous word *incest* on their memory, pointing its finger at the chopping block where the beautiful heads of the incestuous lovers were decapitated by the axe; even brutal Tradition admits they were beautiful, and in fact this is the only detail Tradition has retained of the whole psychologically impenetrable story: their stunning, shocking beauty. Marguerite's beauty was so great that when she mounted the steps to the scaffold on which she was to die, she lifted her skirts slightly so as not to entangle her red silk stockings in their folds and so as to be able to mount the steps with a firmer step; her beauty acted upon the executioner like sunstroke, leaving him dumbstruck, his axe hanging at his side, and she punished him for his mad insolence by slapping him sharply across the face.

All this took place on the Place de Grève on December 2, 1603, during the reign of Henri IV. That king, to whose name the epithets of *good* and *great* have long been added and who deserved those epithets as much as any sovereign who ever existed, hesitated, it appears, before sentencing them to the axe. But his wife, Marguerite de Valois (with that same name of Marguerite, and guilty in the same way!), pushed him to the decision. She had the crime of incest on her conscience, and perhaps she was punishing herself in demanding the death of Marguerite de Ravalet.[7]

I V

And that is all that we know about this sad, cruel story. But the truly enthralling aspects are the ones we know nothing about!

. . . Now, when the historians come to a stop at the limits of what they know, the poets step in and hazard some guesses. They continue to see when the historians have stopped seeing. The poets' imagination pierces through the thick shadows of the historical tapestry or turns it and examines the other side, always fascinated by the part that is hidden from us. . . . The incest of Julien and Marguerite de Ravalet, that poem that perhaps has to remain unpublished, has not yet found its poet with the daring to write it—as if poets didn't love difficulty, and the more impossible the better! This story would require a poet like the Chateaubriand who wrote *René,* or like the Lord Byron who wrote *Parisina* and *Manfred*— two sublime, chaste geniuses, both of whom melded together their chastity with their passion the better to set both ablaze!

It is Lord Byron, above all, who boasted of his own Norman ancestry, who should have been the one to use his poet's imagination to write this Norman chronicle, as full of passion as an Italian chronicle; the memory of the story, once so powerful, now hovers only dimly in the air of modern, placid Normandy.

Those in these latter times who did remember the beautiful Incestuous Lovers of Tourlaville have made a point of examining not their dust but the dust of their chateau. These were people with the souls of architects. They have meticulously delineated this old castle that the Renaissance, like Armida herself, changed into an Armida's castle.[8] But all they have really understood is the rocks. Come now! The two specters of the two last Ravalets, who lived and breathed among these rocks, have never yet come back upon the midnight to haunt the imaginations of these tranquil gentlemen. . . . One of them, though, did say somewhere that he believed he saw the white robe of a Ravalet flutter in the air ahead of him as he walked down a path in the woods, and that it melted away immediately into the shadows of dusk. But he chose not to pursue. . . . If you want to follow ghosts, you need to have more faith in them than in rhetorical figures. Less of a rhetorician myself, I've been luckier. . . . I've never needed to chase what I came to seek. I've found them again, the specters who made me come there, found them everywhere in the castle, their arms around each other after death just as they were during life. I've found them again, wandering together below the moldings marked by those tragic lovers' inscriptions, which still breathe the pride of a boldly accepted fatalism. I've found them again in the boudoir of the octagonal tower, where I sat down next to them, as I sought for their absent warmth on the little bed in that pale-blue boudoir, where the icy satin coverlet was as cold as a bench in a cemetery under the moonlight. I've found them again in the oblong mirror by the mantel, with their great, doleful, phantom eyes gazing out at me from the depths of the glass; when I was gone, their image disappeared! And finally, I've found them again standing in front of Marguerite's portrait, where the brother was asking his sister in a passionate but melancholy voice, "Why couldn't it have been a better resemblance?" For no depiction of the beloved woman will ever be fully satisfying to the lover!

The authenticity of both the inscriptions and the portrait has been contested. As for the inscriptions, even I must admit that they could not have been made by them, the poor, unhappy lovers! And I cannot believe that two lovers who knew how guilty their love was, and whose lives were spent in concealing their bliss from the watchful eye of a father who had every right to be tyrannical—that such lovers would have had the mad imprudence to tack up on the walls the secrets of their hearts and the fury of their incest. Those inscriptions—some of which are quite beautiful—must have been put there after the fact.* They reflect the spirit of the time, an age of intense passion. In Marguerite's portrait, there is a suspect detail, involving the Cupids with white wings that are surrounding her—a pagan inspiration for a pagan era. Now among these Cupids there is one with bloody wings. This must certainly have been put in after Marguerite's death. But I do believe with all my heart in the portrait, apart from the Cupids. If she did not pose during her lifetime for this unknown painter, she surely posed in his memory, a memory reanimated by the hideous catastrophe of her death.

---

*And here are a few of them: "One only is all I need." "That which gives me life is killing me." "His [or her] coldness freezes my veins, and his [or her] ardor burns my heart." "Two are but one." "Thus I could die!"

In the portrait, she is standing upright—looking directly outward—and she does not look at the Cupids who surround her (more proof that they were added to the portrait) but, rather, at the spectator. She is in the castle's courtyard, and she seems to be welcoming the viewer to the chateau, her lovely right hand open in a gesture of hospitality. The painting emphasizes her in the role of chatelaine, with a simple, almost majestic nobility, and it depicts her also as the *Norman,* with her pure eyes untouched by any reverie or morbidity, with no trace of languor, no trace of that weight that lay so heavily, so fearfully on her heart. Her head is held erect, her face fresh with youth, the youth that she would not shed until her magnificent Norman blood was shed by the axe on the scaffold. Her hair is blonde—that blonde common among the girls of Normandy, the color of ripe wheat darkened by the harsh heat of the August sun, ready for the sickle. Her hair was awaiting its sickle, too, and the wait would not be a long one! The hair is short, cut straight across the forehead, separated into two thick bunches, with no curls—a bit like the children of Edward in the celebrated painting.[9] She is tall and slender, though she wears her waistband high; she is dressed in a white and pink ceremonial gown, the material of which appears woven, the colors of which are *one in the other,* as they say in the language of heraldry.[10] Looking at this portrait, no one would ever guess that this rosy young lady, so calm, so imposing, was led astray into incest, indeed abandoned herself to it madly. . . . Except for her left hand, falling naturally along the side of her skirt but clutching a handkerchief, as if crumpling up some secret there, something she wished to hide, something she was agonizingly, desperately trying to suppress—except for that detail, no passion whatsoever is visible in the portrait. Nothing is there to make one think of the great Incestuous Lovers from History and Poetry, nothing there that would reveal her as one of those accursed by men. She expresses none of the delirious horror of Phaedra, and none of the dazed rigidity of Parisina after her sin. The sin of this woman, that sin that occupied her entire life and dated practically from the cradle—she carries that sin without remorse, without sorrow, even without pride, with an indifference to that fate of hers against which she had never rebelled. Even on the scaffold she must not have felt any regret, this Marguerite who was also called Madeleine, and she did not repent for her crime of love, a sin so profound that it sweeps away before it all the sins of the daughter of Jerusalem. . . . The Chronicle, which tells us so little, simply notes that she stated that she was the one who seduced her brother into incest. She accepted the scaffold without lamentation and without protest, just as she had accepted the incest, and quite rightly, for the consequence of incest was, in those days, the scaffold.

V

A few rare letters between her and her brother survive and have been printed, though I have not been able to see the originals. Those from the brother are what one would expect from a young nobleman of the era, living in Paris. He calls her "Marguite" instead of Marguerite—a charming, almost tender abbreviation; but one cannot find a single word in these letters suggesting the kind of intimacy one is seeking. Did he feel a kind of terrified anxiety lest his letters fall into the hands of someone who could doom them both, and did that icy fear hide itself beneath the hypocrisy of frivolities and meaningless chatter? . . . She was freer, and on a page that I will cite in a moment dared to let her passion overflow her words, the way a scent can somehow escape from a hermetically sealed vial: "My friend," she wrote, "I received a letter of yours from Paris which contained many things that deserve my consideration, each of which aroused memories in me; your letter, which I have *burned*, reawakened a memory and gave me reason to cherish anew *your passion for my good,* the BLISS of which still lives in my heart. . . . Since your departure, the pilgrimage that is my life has grown sorrowful and *languid,* but do not fear that I haven't received your *propositions* and given them the thought that they deserve, and be assured that, with regard to the parts that depend on me, I can promise you entire satisfaction in *what you desire,* and that whenever your thoughts turn to me I will remain, my friend, your faithful sister and friend, Marguerite." Elsewhere, she says:

"Your letters from Paris gave me joy, for they contained those *sure tokens of your passion that for me is dearer than life itself. . . .*" These letters are dated from Valognes where, during one of her father's absences, she was sent to stay with Madame d'Esmondeville, who must have been the one to decide on marrying her to Monsieur Jean Le Fauconnier, an old man, rich, owner of many estates. "We have found her"—Marguerite says, picturesquely—"half covered up in a sort of litter. She embraced me in such a cold and disdainful manner that I remained firm in my inner rage, determined to reject her entirely. . . . She was almost always lying down, busy fingering a rosary or taking snuff in a most artificial, precious way. During all this, I remained standing before this d'Esmondeville, who was casting such severe glances at me that you'd think she wanted to kill me. [The horror that came with the suspicions of incest was beginning!] A little later, an old woman *came and pulled me by my shawl,* escorting me whether I would or not up to a higher room, and leaving me all alone there until nightfall." Later, they forced her to marry the man Le Fauconnier, and that is how she came to introduce adultery into incest; but the incest devoured the adultery, and of the two crimes was by far the stronger. She had children by both crimes, but they did not live, and she was able to mount the scaffold without looking back on anything in her life, her eyes fixed instead on the brother who had mounted before her, and who preceded her in death. After the execution, the King ordered the corpses returned to the family, who had them buried in the church of Saint Julien-en-Grève, with the following epitaph:

"Here lie both brother and sister. Traveler, do not ask the cause of their death, but pass by and pray to God for their souls."

The church of Saint Julien-en-Grève became the church of Saint-Julien-le-Pauvre, since abandoned, and those who do pass by no longer pray before the effaced epitaph. But the place where the passerby must pray for them—that is, if he prays—is in the castle; they are far more present there than in their tomb. I visited there this year during a tearful autumn, and I have never seen nor felt such melancholy. The castle's ruins were in the process of being restored, though if it were up to me I would have left them in the poetry of their ruins, because death cannot be whitewashed away, and it is often more beautiful than life—that castle with its base standing in a greenish lake, the evening winds rippling it into a thousand folds. . . . It was the twilight hour. Two swans were swimming on that lake, where nothing else but them was to be seen, not at a distance from each other but quite close, the one pressing up against the other as if they had been brother and sister, trembling together there on the trembling water. They made me think of the two souls of those last Ravalets, passed on and now returned to life in this charming shape; but then they were too white to have been the souls of that guilty brother and sister. To believe that they were, they would have had to be black swans, and their long, superb necks would have had to be bloodied . . .

PREFACE TO
THE LAST MISTRESS
(1865)

The novel that follows was published first in 1851.

At that time, the author had not yet entered onto the path of beliefs and ideas to which he has since dedicated his life. He had never been an enemy of the Church. On the contrary, he had always admired it and thought of it as the most beautiful, the grandest thing on earth, *even if only in human terms.* But, though a Christian by baptism and out of a sense of respect, he was not yet one out of faith and practice, as he has since become, through the grace of God.

And because he then did not simply turn away from the philosophies to which he had, passingly, adhered, but instead battled against them with all the power he could, and will continue to battle thus until his final breath—because of this, the Freethinkers, with that breadth of mind and the kind of loyalty one expects of them, have not hesitated to draw a contrast between his recent Catholicism and his earlier novel, with its bold title of *The Last Mistress,* the aim of which was to depict not only the intoxication of passion but also the enslavement it entails.

Well! It is this opposition between such a book and his faith that the author of *The Last Mistress* wishes to refute now. He in no way accepts the charge, however much it pleases the Freethinkers to make it, that his book—for which he takes full responsibility, as he republishes it now—is genuinely inconsistent with those doctrines that in his eyes are truth itself. With the exception of one libertine detail of which he is guilty, *a detail of three lines,* and which he has suppressed in the edition he now offers to the public, *The Last Mistress,* when he wrote it, deserved to be placed in that category of all those literary and artistic compositions whose object it is to depict passion, without which there would be no art, no literature, and no moral life, since passion in excess is the abuse of our freedom.

The author of *The Last Mistress,* therefore, was then, as he is today, only a novelist who painted passion such as it is and such as he has seen it, but one who, in painting it, condemned it on every page of his book. He neither advocated for it nor with it. He did not, like the Freethinking novelists, make passion and its pleasures into the rights due to man and woman, nor into the religion of the future. He gave it expression, true, as energetically as he could, but is this something deserving reproach? . . . Must he reproach himself in *Catholic* terms for the warmth of his coloring as a painter of passion? . . . But in other terms, isn't the question posed to him about *The Last Mistress* a larger and more general one, larger than that of a particular book that they would never even talk about if it didn't offer them the opportunity of throwing the issue in his face? And this question, is it not in fact the question of *the novel* itself, a topic that the enemies of Catholicism forbid us Catholics from discussing?

Yes, here we have the question! And posed thus, it is both impertinent and comic. Look: from the moral viewpoint of the Freethinkers, Catholics have no right to approach the novel and the passions, because their hands must be too pure—as if all the wounds oozing blood and poison had nothing to do with pure hands! We mustn't discuss the theater either, because that's passion again. We mustn't touch art, nor literature, nor anything, but stay kneeling in a corner praying and leaving the world and Free Thought undisturbed. Yes, I really believe this is what the Freethinkers want! While from one angle this is farcical, from another it's an idea with a certain profundity. I do believe they'd like to be rid of us, ostracize us, bar us from every avenue of thought, in order to be able to say: "Those miserable Catholics? They're utterly distant from all the pathways of the human spirit!" But frankly, we need some other reason to accept, with a humble and docile heart, the lesson that the enemies of Catholicism have the goodness to be teaching us regarding the Catholic consequences of our acts and the accomplishments of our duties.

But when we really come to the point, what do they know about Catholicism? They don't know the first thing about it. They despise it too much to have spent any time studying it. Has their hatred somehow revealed to them the spirit behind the letter? What is morally and intellectually magnificent about Catholicism is that it is large, comprehensive, immense; that it embraces human nature in its entirety, in all its diverse spheres of activity, and, above and beyond all it embraces, it deploys always this great axiom: "Shame to anyone who lets himself be shocked!" Catholicism has nothing in it of the prude, the pedant, the worrywart. It leaves all that to the hypocrites, the carefully clipped puritans. Catholicism loves the arts and accepts their audacities without trembling. It admits their passions and their depictions, because it knows it can learn something from them, even when the artist in question seems not to have done so.

For the impure soul, there are frightening indecencies in the painting of Michelangelo (*The Last Judgment*), and one can find in more than one cathedral things that will make the Protestant shield his eyes with the handkerchief of Tartuffe. Was it Catholicism that condemned these things, rejected them, effaced them? Didn't the greatest and holiest Popes protect the artists who made these things, things that Protestants would have seen, *and have seen,* as horrible sacrilege? When has Catholicism forbidden the depiction of a passion, no matter how hideous or criminal, when it could move the viewer, when it could shed some light into the abyss of the human heart, even when that light reveals only blood or muck; or the writing of a novel, which is to say a story of the *possible* if not the *real,* which is to say, in short, a human story? Never! On the contrary, it has permitted everything, but with this one absolute reservation—that the novel can never be propaganda in the service of vice, or the preaching of error; that it is never permissible to say that evil is good or good evil, and that it must not sophisticate itself into abject and perverse doctrine, like the novels of Madame Sand and Jean-Jacques Rousseau. With this sole reservation, Catholicism permits the depiction of vice and error, in act and gesture, and permits accurate depictions of them. It does not clip the wings of genius, when there is genius. . . .

Catholicism would certainly not have prevented Shakespeare, had he been a Catholic, from writing the sublime scene toward the beginning of *Richard III,* in which the grieving woman who follows her husband's coffin, poisoned by his brother, after having spewed forth horrific curses against the assassin, ends by giving him her wedding ring, and abandons herself to his false and incestuous love. It is abominable, it is hideous, and the simpletons would even say it is *improbable* because this grotesque about-face of the woman takes place within the brief duration of a single scene—which makes it, to me, even more truthful; yes, it is abominable and hideous, but it is beautiful with human truth, profoundly, cruelly, terrifyingly beautiful, and truth and beauty, whatever form they may take, are never cut out or abolished by Catholicism—which is absolute Truth. And, notice this, Shakespeare does not dogmatize. He exposes. He does not say or have it said to the spectator: "Richard III is right. This woman, whom he has seduced over the still-warm corpse of her murdered husband, is right to give herself to the brother-in-law murderer who is now king." No. He says, "This is," and with the superb impassivity of the artist, who is sometimes impassive, he lets it be seen, and in so powerful a way that one's heart shrinks in one's chest, and one's mind is struck as if by a bolt of lightning.

Well! Let us step down from Shakespeare to all the other artists, and we can see the artistic technique that Catholicism absolves, a technique consisting in never diminishing any sin or crime that it seeks to depict.

But there is more, and Catholicism goes yet further. Sometimes vice is attractive. Sometimes passion has its eloquent ways of speaking about itself, which can become fascinations. The Catholic artist turns away from the seductions of vice. Will he stifle the eloquence of passion? Must he refrain from depicting the one or the other, because they are so powerful? God gave these as possibilities, open to human free choice—will God deny the artist, in turn, the freedom to put them into his works? No! God, creator of all realities, forbids none of them to the artist, provided, as I said, that the artist doesn't make an instrument of perdition out of them. Catholicism doesn't cripple art out of fear of scandal. It is beautiful even when there is scandal.

There is something, if I may put it this way, more Catholic than one would think in the inspiration of all those painters who wanted to depict the beauty of Hérodias, splendid as gold, as imperial purple, or as snow, of the butcher, the executioner, the *murderer* of St. John. They did not omit a single one of her charms. They painted the divinity of beauty, gazing at the decapitated head being offered to her, and she is all the more infernal for that divine beauty! Here is precisely the task art must set itself. To depict what really is, to seize human reality, whether criminal or virtuous, and give it life through the omnipotence of inspiration and form, to show reality, to vivify it up to the level of the ideal— this is the artist's mission. In Catholic terms, artists are below ascetics, for they are decidedly not ascetics; they are artists. Catholicism makes a hierarchy of merit, but it does not mutilate the person. Each of us has a vocation according to our own abilities. The artist is by no means a *policeman of ideas.* When he has *created* a reality, in depicting it, he has accomplished his work. Ask nothing more of him!

But I can already hear the objection, and I am familiar with it. . . . But the morality of his work! But the influence of his work on an already weakened public morality! Etc., etc., etc.

To all that, I reply with complete confidence: the morality of the artist resides in the force and truth of his depictions. In depicting reality, infiltrating it, breathing life into it, he has been moral enough; he has been true. Truth can never be a sin or a crime. If someone abuses a truth, so much the worse for him! If someone deduces wicked things from a *living* and true work of art, so much the worse for that guilty reasoner! The artist plays no part in such deductions. You may object, "He gave rise to them." Did God *give rise to* the crimes and sins of humankind when He created the free soul of the human being? Did He *give rise to* the evil men can do, in giving them all the gifts they abuse, in placing His magnificent, calm, and good creation in their hands, beneath their feet, in their arms? Come! I have known imaginations so disordered and carnal that they felt the lashings of desire in gazing at the lowered eyes of Raphael's virgins. Should Raphael have stopped himself to avoid this danger and thrown into the fire his *Vierge d'Albe,* his *Vierge à la Chaise,* and all those masterpieces of purity, those apotheoses springing up twenty times out of human virginity? To some people, isn't everything a stumbling block, an occasion for sin? Must art expire, vanquished by having to take into account every possible weakness? Must art be replaced by a preventive system of prudence that permits nothing at all that might turn out to be dangerous, which is to say, which permits nothing at all?

The artist creates, in reproducing the things that God has made and that man falsifies and perverts. When he has reproduced them exactly, luminously, he has, and this is certain, as an artist all the morality he should have. If one has a sharp, penetrating mind, one will always be able to draw from the work, detaching from everything that is not true, some lesson, sometimes hidden, which it embodies. I am aware that sometimes one must dig a bit to find it, but artists write for their peers, or at least for those who understand them. And anyway, is profundity a crime? Assuredly, Catholic wisdom is vaster, more open, and more robust than the gentlemen moralists of Free Thought imagine. Let them inquire of the Jesuits, those stunning politicians of the human heart, with their grand understanding of morality, who see things from so great a height, as opposed to the Jansenists who shrink morality down and see everything from the lowest point, turning morality into something so narrow, so brutish, and so hardened! Let them inquire of one of those casuists of discerning and healing minds, of whom the Church has produced so many, especially in Italy, and they will learn, since they don't know it, that there is no proscription snatching out of our hands the passion described in the novel, and that the narrow, embarrassed, and overscrupulous

Catholicizing that they invent to hold against us is not the one that has always formed the Civilization of this world, both in the realm of thought and that of morality.

And this is no merely pleasing theory invented to advance a cause but is instead the very spirit of Catholicism. The author of *The Last Mistress* asks to be judged in that light. Catholicism is the science of Good and Evil. It surveys the loins and the heart, two cesspits, filled like all cesspits with inflammable phosphorous; it gazes into the soul: this is what the author of *The Last Mistress* has done. Is what he has depicted actually found there? He depicted passion and its errors, but has he glorified them? He described their power, their charms, the sort of bar they place in our free will, like a falsified coat of arms. He did not narrow down either passion or Catholicism in depicting them. Either *The Last Mistress* must be absolved for being what it is, or we must renounce that thing we call the novel. Either we must renounce depictions of the human heart, or we must depict it as it is.

It is only the gentlemen of Free Thought, so devoted to social interests, as we all know, who have been able to find *The Last Mistress* subversive. Subversive! But the author, in recounting this sad tale, ought to have been impassive, and he hasn't been! He has condemned Marigny, the guilty husband! He gave him remorse and even shame! He caused him to confess to his grandmother and to condemn himself. But his wife, of whom Marigny ultimately begs pardon, does not pardon him! No novelist has ever been such a Torquemada to his characters as the author of *The Last Mistress*! Subversive, his book! So nothing remains we can safely depict except Grandisons? Yes, passion is revolutionary, but it is precisely for that reason that it must be depicted in all its strange and abominable power. From the viewpoint of Order, it is a good thing to write the history of Revolutions.

This, then, is our response to the gentlemen of Free Thought! Let us conclude with a word from their Master: "There is such a thing as a vile decency," said Rousseau.

But Catholicism does not recognize it.

1 October 1865

TRANSLATOR'S NOTES

INTRODUCTION

1 Rémy de Gourmont, "La Vie de Barbey d'Aurevilly," in *Promenades Littéraires* (1905; Paris: Mercure de France, 1919 [reprint]).

2 Luc Fraisse teases out the specifics of Barbey's influence in *La Petite Musique du style: Proust et ses sources littéraires* (Paris: Classiques Garnier, 2011), 203–28. See also Brian Rogers, *Proust et Barbey d'Aurevilly: Le dessous des cartes* (Paris: Honoré Champion, 2000).

3 Praz, cited in Pascale Auraix-Jonchière, "Barbey d'Aurevilly et *La Belle Dame sans merci,*" in *Barbey d'Aurevilly et l'esthétique: Les paradoxes de l'écriture* (Besançon: Presses universitaires de Franche-Comté, 2011), 257; Gilles Deleuze and Félix Guattari, *A Thousand Plateaus: Capitalism and Schizophrenia,* trans. Brian Massumi (Minneapolis: University of Minnesota Press, 1987), 193–94.

4 The best biographies of Barbey are Michel Lécureur, *Barbey d'Aurevilly: Le Sagittaire* (Paris: Fayard, 2008); Arnould de Liedekerke, *Talon Rouge: Barbey d'Aurevilly, le dandy absolu* (Paris: Olivier Orban, 1986); and Sylvie Girard, *Le Parfum du démon: Un écrivain nommé Barbey d'Aurevilly* (Paris: Hermé, 1986). In English, there is a good brief treatment in Armand B. Chartier, *Barbey d'Aurevilly* (Boston: Twayne, 1977), 17–40.

5 A new, fully annotated edition of the letters is Philippe Berthier, ed., *Barbey d'Aurevilly: Lettres à Trebutien, 1832–1858* (Paris: Bartillat, 2013). Barbey's extravagances often pushed the more conventional Trebutien's tolerance to the limits, and the friendship and correspondence came to an end in 1858.

6 One index of how much Barbey had changed is in the fact that he was briefly arrested and jailed in 1851 for refusing to serve his required term in *La Garde Nationale*—and this from the person who had hoped to make a military career for himself.

7 Jessica R. Feldman, *Gender on the Divide: The Dandy in Modernist Literature* (Ithaca, N.Y.: Cornell University Press, 1993), 85.

8 *Dandyism,* trans. Douglas Ainslie (1897; New York: PAJ, 1988 [reprint]), 33.

9 Patrick Avrane, *Barbey d'Aurevilly, solitaire et singulier* (Paris: Campagne Première, 2005), 59–60.

10 Isaiah Berlin's is the traditional view of Maistre, seeing him as a kind of protofascist; see Berlin's "Joseph de Maistre and the Origins of Fascism" in his *The Crooked Timber of Humanity: Chapters in the History of Ideas,* ed. Henry Hardy (New York: Knopf, 1991). Some more recent scholars are questioning that view and rehabilitating Maistre, notably Carolina Armenteros, *The French Idea of History: Joseph de Maistre and His Heirs, 1794–1854* (Ithaca, N.Y.: Cornell University Press, 2011).

11 The critic was Francis Lacombe, cited in David Cocksey's edition of *Les Prophètes du passé* (Paris: Éditions du Sandre, 2009), v.

12 Letter of 1 June 1851, in Berthier, *Barbey d'Aurevilly: Lettres à Trebutien,* 423.

13 Quoted in Chartier, *Barbey d'Aurevilly,* 30.

14 Georges Rodenbach, *L'Élite* (Paris: Charpentier, 1899).

15 The story first appeared in serial form in the periodical *La Mode* for May 5, 15, and 25, 1850.

16 Baudelaire seems to have been moving in a similar direction when he began turning from verse to the prose poems that dominated his last years. In the dedication to the volume we now call *Paris Spleen,* he lays out an ideal prose that would be "supple enough and jarring enough to be adapted to the soul's lyrical movements, to the undulations of reverie, to the twists and turns that consciousness takes" (translation mine); see *"Paris Spleen and La Fanfarlo"* (Indianapolis/Cambridge: Hackett, 2008), 3. Those "twists and turns" are quite similar to what Barbey was thinking of as "ricochets."

17 Huysmans makes the point in a letter of 21 April 1892, printed in *The Road from Decadence, from Brothel to Cloister: Selected Letters of J. K. Huysmans,* ed. and trans. Barbara Beaumont (Columbus: Ohio State University Press, 1989), 94.

18 The title of the story employs the French idiom *le dessous des cartes,* a phrase that promises the real story, the hidden side of things. That we never quite get that *dessous,* no matter how deeply we delve, is one of the story's great ironies.

19 He wrote to Trebutien that he was engaged in the long-term project of an *"epopée chouanne,"* a Chouan epic (letter of 22 November 1851); Berthier, *Barbey d'Aurevilly: Lettres à Trebutien,* 482.

20 See the discussion in Pierre Glaudes, *Esthétique de Barbey d'Aurevilly* (Paris: Garnier, 2009), 58–69.

21 The concept is sometimes called the reversibility of merits. On de Maistre's development of the idea as part of his philosophy of history, see Amenteros, *The French Idea of History,* but of course the idea is as old as Christianity itself— and older than that, as it is implicit in the ancient concept of sacrifice.

22 Letter to Trebutien of 17 November 1855—a full ten years before the finished novel saw publication.

23 Francesco Manzini includes a chapter on it in his well-titled study *The Fevered Novel from Balzac to Bernanos: Frenetic Catholicism in Crisis, Delirium, and Revolution* (London: IGRS, 2010).

24 Both Dentu and some bookshops seem to have attempted to hide copies from the police. Details are in Lécureur, *Barbey d'Aurevilly: Le Sagittaire*, 408–11.

25 Ibid., 410.

26 Ironically, Lemerre and Rops quarreled over payment for the illustrations, and this nearly led to the book figuring in a second court appearance; an agreement was reached before that stage, however. Details are in Jacques-Henry Bornecque's edition of *Les Diaboliques* (Paris: Classiques Garnier, 1963), cxl–cxliii.

27 *The Story without a Name* (New York: Brentano's, 1919) was translated by Edgar Saltus, an American who had fallen under the spell of Barbey and Huysmans.

28 Did Wilde actually translate *Ce qui ne meurt pas?* Richard Ellman's biography notes that Wilde announced that he was planning to translate the book, but his close friend Robert Ross later said he never did it; Ellman, *Oscar Wilde* (New York: Knopf, 1988), 561. The translation was nonetheless published in 1902 by Charles Carrington, the title page attributing it to Sebastian Melmoth, the name Wilde used after his release from prison. However, in 1909, Carrington said that the translation had been erroneously attributed to Wilde. That would seem to settle the issue, but if the translation is not by Wilde, it is a remarkable job of deception and mimicry, for it reads much more like Wilde—like the languid style of the Wilde of *The Picture of Dorian Gray*—than it does Barbey.

29 Quoted in Lecureur, *Barbey d'Aurevilly: Le Sagittaire*, 367. The article is dated 1 December 1869.

30 Malcolm Scott, *The Struggle for the Soul of the French Novel: French Catholic and Realist Novelists, 1850–1970* (Washington, D.C.: Catholic University of America Press, 1990), 54.

31 Léon Bloy, *Les Funérailles du naturalism*, ed. Pierre Glaudes (1891; Paris: Les Belles Lettres, 2001), 169.

PREFACE TO *LES DIABOLIQUES*

1 The later six stories were evidently projected but never actually written. Barbey puns here in a way that eludes English translation: the stories are like a dozen peaches (*pêches*), or like a dozen sinners (*pécheresses*). The same pun occurs later in one of the stories.

THE CRIMSON CURTAIN

1 The epigraph is in English in the original.

2 On Barbey's concept of the dandy, see the introduction. His two great exemplars were Beau Brummel and the Comte d'Orsay.

3 Joachim Murat (1767–1815), brother-in-law to Napoleon, Maréchal of France, and a flamboyant dandy, was known for his daring cavalry charges in battle. Auguste de Marmont (1774–1852), also Maréchal of France and aide-de-camp to Napoleon, was known for his careful strategy rather than boldness.

4 "The Emperor" is of course Napoleon; the Hundred Days is the term for the period in 1815 between Napoleon's return from exile and his final defeat.

After that defeat, the Bourbon monarchy, under King Louis XVIII, was restored.

5 Charles X reigned from 1824 to 1830. Before he was crowned, he was referred to in higher circles simply as "Monsieur." The Duchess of Angoulême, Princess Marie-Thérèse-Charlotte, is here referred to, with exaggerated discretion, as "Madame."

6 *Permission de dix heures* (ten hours' leave) was an 1867 comic operetta by Offenbach.

7 The July Revolution of 1830, sometimes called the Three Glorious Days' Revolution, deposed King Charles X and put his cousin, Louis-Philippe, the Duc d'Orléans, on the throne. Barbey's narrator sees the Orléans branch of the Bourbon family as illegitimate upstarts—an attitude Barbey himself shared.

8 François de Bassompierre (1579–1646) was a courtier whose memoirs are still read today; this is one of several allusions linking the Vicomte with the sixteenth and seventeenth centuries.

9 The Faubourg Saint-Germain was the most aristocratic district in Paris; the term is often used as shorthand for the very highest level of French society in the early nineteenth century.

10 Maurice de Saxe (1696–1750) was a German who rose to become Maréchal of France; his posthumously published memoir, *Mes Rêveries,* is a widely studied book on the art of war. He was also, as the following exchange suggests, known for his amorous conquests.

11 The city of Bergen-op-Zoom, in the southern Netherlands, was noted for its historical ability to withstand military sieges, but it finally fell to the French army in 1747.

12 Brantôme (1540–1614), yet another sixteenth-century reference, was a soldier and memoirist.

13 Lovelace is the witty yet wicked seducer who abducts the virtuous heroine in Samuel Richardson's 1747 novel *Clarissa.*

14 Ninon de Lenclos (1620–1705), a French courtesan and author, gave much advice on how to carry on a love affair, including, as here, when to advance and when to retreat.

15 In Greek mythology, Niobe boasted of her children so much that the gods killed them all, and she was turned into a stone that wept unceasingly.

16 Saint Lawrence is said to have been martyred, c. 258 C.E., by being burned alive over a grilling iron.

17 The powerful Guise family was prominent in sixteenth-century France; the last Duke of Guise died in 1688.

18 The barons of Chamboran, or Chamborand, were illustrious military leaders, going back at least to the sixteenth century.

19 The prophet Elijah brings a dead boy back to life this way in 1 Kings 17:17–23.

20 Werther is the hero of Goethe's 1774 novel *The Sorrows of Young Werther;* unhappy in love, Werther eventually kills himself, and his suicide made a deep impression on the young generation of readers throughout Europe.

21 Napoleon's armies fought the Battle of Leipzig on October 16–19, 1813.

DON JUAN'S FINEST CONQUEST

1 The source of the epigraph has not been discovered; it is likely to be Barbey's invention.

2 The Maison d'Or was a fashionable restaurant in Paris in the 1840s.

3 Arnold of Brescia (c. 1090–1155) was an Italian monk and reformer, calling on the Church to turn away from the accumulation of wealth and the ownership of property. The Church banned his writings and, ultimately, hanged him.

4 The *mille è tré* are the 1,003 women that Don Juan (in Mozart's 1787 opera *Don Giovanni*) is said to have seduced.

5 The Comtesse is fictional, but there is a Chiffrevast chateau in Normandy; Barbey may have chosen the name because of its Norman associations.

6 The *bals des victimes,* or victims' balls, were a social phenomenon of 1790s Paris: following the Reign of Terror, dances were arranged, and the only people invited were those who had had a relative killed during the Terror.

7 The name includes Barbey's own first names, Jules Amédée. The surname, "Ravila de Ravilès," includes an untranslatable pun, suggesting the Comte is one who has ravished one woman and many (*ravi la, ravi les*).

8 Franz Mesmer (1734–1815), the prophet of curing various diseases through magnetism, pioneered what was called the *baquet,* or tub treatment: his patients would sit forming a chain around a tub with iron rods protruding from it, one for each patient; the treatment would involve the group passing the "magnetism" and, ideally, the cure from one to another.

9 Alcibiades (c. 450–404 B.C.) was an Athenian statesman and general, famed for his youthful good looks.

10 Alfred d'Orsay (1801–52) was one of the preeminent dandies of the era. He features in a number of literary texts, including Disraeli's novel *Henrietta Temple* (1837), where he is given the name Alcibiades de Mirabel.

11 Barbey alludes again to the last act of Mozart's *Don Giovanni,* in which the marble statue of the Commendatore comes to life and harries Giovanni down to Hell.

12 Molière's play about the Greek mythological character *Amphitryon* (1668) established him as the archetype of the generous host. In Barbey's text, Amphitryon's name is feminized as Amphitryonne. Sardanapalus was a semimythical Assyrian king of the seventh century B.C. His opulent funeral pyre is the subject of a remarkable painting by Delacroix (1827), which was in turn inspired by Lord Byron's play *Sardanapalus* (1821).

13 Barbey's pun, changed here to *hyacinth/higher sin,* is on the French words for peach (*pêche*) and sin (*péché*).

14 Mélusine is a character in European folklore, usually depicted as half-woman and half-serpent; sometimes she is depicted as a mermaid. She is especially associated with Barbey's native Normandy.

15 Nebuchadnezzar is driven mad in the biblical book of Daniel and goes out to eat the grass of the field like a cow. The Café Anglais was one of the most fashionable restaurants in nineteenth-century Paris.

16 The Jagiellons were a dynasty of aristocrats prominent in central Europe, especially Poland, from the fourteenth through the sixteenth centuries.

17 There was a widely repeated tale in previous centuries that the Turkish sultan would go to his harem and choose the woman he wanted for that night by throwing a handkerchief toward her.

18 The French phrase is *j'avais fini mes caravanes*, an expression dating back to the Knights of Malta, who used it to describe their sorties against the Turks. The phrase later came to mean something like the English phrase "sowing one's wild oats." Barbey uses the phrase in a number of other works.

19 To dress *en ferronnière* is to wear a jewel on a chain across the forehead, like the woman in the Renaissance painting known as *La Belle Ferronnière*, thought to be from the circle of Da Vinci.

20 Turkish pashas were distinguished in rank by the number of horse or yak tails they displayed on their standards.

21 Caryatids are the female statues that appear to support the entire structure of a temple (its entablature) in classical Greek architecture.

22 This story about Joseph is in Sura 12 of the Koran. Joseph's story is also told in Genesis, but without the detail of the women cutting themselves.

HAPPINESS IN CRIME

1 The Jardin des Plantes is the largest botanical garden in Paris, situated on the Left Bank.

2 As in several of the other stories, the town of V*** is Valognes, in Normandy.

3 Doctor Torty is modeled on Barbey's uncle, Jean-Louis Pontas-Dumeril (1753–1826). He held several positions in the region during his life, including a spell as mayor of Valognes, so he would have been quite informed, as Torty is, of the scandals and behind-the-scenes stories of the aristocratic inhabitants.

4 The *livre* was an obsolete unit of money by the nineteenth century, but the term continued to be used; a livre in this case is roughly equivalent to a franc.

5 Barbey refers to three famous doctors of the late eighteenth and early nineteenth centuries. Pierre-Georges Cabanis (1757–1808) was also a materialist philosopher, denying the existence of the soul and arguing that the mind is merely a function of the brain. François Chaussier (1746–1828) was also an anatomist. Antoine Dubois (1756–1857) was the most celebrated obstetrician of the era.

6 The story of Moses striking a rock from which water gushed is in Exodus 17.

7 The word *torte* in French means "twisted."

8 Alceste is the main character in Molière's play *The Misanthrope* (1666).

9 Armida is the beautiful pagan witch of Tasso's sixteenth-century epic *Gerusalemme Liberata* (Jerusalem delivered), who falls in love with Rinaldo, a crusading knight, and converts to Christianity. Locusta was an infamous poisoner in ancient Rome; she is said to have prepared the poison that killed the emperor Claudius, and she features in Racine's tragedy *Britannicus* (1669).

10 *Jean Sbogar* was an 1818 novel by Charles Nodier. The title character, like many in the works of Byron, is a highly romantic one, a sensitive-souled bandit with generous, even poetic sentiments.

11 Philemon and Baucis were an old married couple who, unlike all the other humans, were hospitable when the disguised Zeus and Hermes came to their cottage. When the rest of the world was flooded, the gods spared them. Their story is told in Ovid's *Metamorphoses* (Book 8), and, more recently, they had figured in Part 2 of Goethe's *Faust*.

12 The monarchy was restored after Napoleon's fall—first, briefly, from 1814 to March 1815, and then from June 1815 to July 1830.

13 The *Gardes-du-Corps* (bodyguards) were an elite unit serving the King; *Monsieur* was the commonly used term for the Prince.

14 The fleur-de-lis is the royal symbol, so letting the fencing master use it is a significant honor. The reference here is to the famous fencer Guillaume Danet, who did indeed write a book on the subject; see Egerton Castle's 1885 study *Schools and Masters of Fencing: From the Middle Ages to the Eighteenth Century* (New York: Dover Books, 2003), especially chapter 11.

15 In fencing, to "button" one's opponent is to hit him squarely with the rubber tip of the foil.

16 Haute Claire is the name of the knight Olivier's sword in the twelfth-century French epic *La Chanson de Roland* (the song of Roland).

17 The July Revolution of 1830 forced Charles X from the throne and instituted the far more liberal constitutional monarchy of Louis-Philippe. As such, it dashed the hopes of the aristocrats that France would return to its pre-Revolutionary political and social system.

18 We will meet Mesnilgrand again in the story "At a Dinner of Atheists."

19 The large statue of Pallas Athena was unearthed at Velletri during the eighteenth century and is now displayed at the Louvre. The Circassians, more often called the Adygs today, are a people of the north Caucasus.

20 Clorinda is a beautiful and pure woman warrior in, again, Tasso's *Gerusalemme Liberata*. She converts to Islam. The Christian knight Tancred is in love with her, but in Book VIII of the poem, he does not recognize her in her armor; they fight, and he kills her, only realizing his mistake when it is too late.

21 In fencing, *carte* and *tierce* are positions for the hand holding the foil. With *carte*, the nails are pointing upward; with *tierce*, downward.

22 Ahasuerus is the name of at least two ancient kings of Persia. The allusion to the twenty thousand daughters seems to be a generalized one, akin to saying "the daughters of Eve"—or, in other words, all women.

23 *The Marriage of Figaro*, the wildly popular 1784 comedy by Beaumarchais, features the character of the Count Almaviva, who is in love with the servant girl Suzanne.

24 Fulvia (83–40 B.C.), a powerful Roman aristocrat, is best remembered today for her association with her third husband, Marc Antony, but she was politically active throughout her adult life; she was the first Roman woman to have her face on coins.

25 In Genesis 39, the Egyptian Potiphar takes Joseph into his palace to be head of his household servants. Potiphar's wife tries to seduce Joseph, who rebuffs her; she takes her revenge by falsely accusing him of attempted rape.

26 Barbey evidently has in mind the *Cupid and Psyche* by Antonio Canova (1757–1822) in the Villa Carlotta on Lake Como.

27 Isabel of Bavaria (1370–1435) was Queen to King Charles VI of France. In medieval depictions of her, she wears her hair in an elaborate *hennin*, or two-horned shape.

28 In Genesis 25:19–28, the character of Esau, brother to Jacob, is called a skillful hunter. Esau's descendants, according to David Lyle Jeffrey, "are said to be nomadic desert peoples who refuse the Torah because they wish to live by the sword." See Jeffrey, *A Dictionary of Biblical Tradition in English Literature* (Grand Rapids, Mich.: Eerdmans, 1992), 239.

29 In Song of Songs 4:9, the lover says "you ravish my heart . . . with a single one of your glances, with a single link of your necklace."

30 Snuff from Macouba, in the French colony of Martinique, expensive and hence something of a status symbol in the nineteenth century, is still manufactured and sold today.

31 In Molière's play *Don Juan* (1665), Juan finds himself at the tomb of the Commendatore, a man he has killed. He mockingly invites the statue above the grave to supper and is aghast when the statue nods its head in agreement.

32 Barbey's phrase translated here as "printing ink" is *encre double*—double ink. Michéle M. Respaut glosses the phrase by noting that "nineteenth-century industrially produced inks were 'double' in combining a solid pigment with a fluid element," suggesting that the phrase fits in with a network of doublings in the story: "The Doctor's Discourse: Emblems of Science, Sexual Fantasy, and Myth in Barbey d'Aurevilly's 'Le Bonheur dans le crime,'" *French Review* 73:1 (October 1999), 79.

33 A technical fencing term, *se fendre à fond* is to lunge forward as far as possible on the attack. The implication is that all the male onlookers in the fencing school would have seen Hauteclaire's body in a very exposed position.

34 Teratology is the study of physiological abnormalities.

35 François Joseph-Victor Broussais (1772–1838) was a celebrated and controversial physician whose highly mechanistic view of the human body is suggested by the phrase Dr. Torty ascribes to him.

36 Madame de Staël's *De l'Allemagne* (on Germany, 1810) includes an idealistic section on love in marriage in its part III, chapter 29 (in the book's final form). John Milton praises "wedded love" for its moral qualities in *Paradise Lost* (IV.750–75). Both references are of course highly ironic in Barbey's context.

BENEATH THE CARDS IN A GAME OF WHIST

1 "Beneath the cards" translates the French phrase *le dessous des cartes,* which means literally the underside of the cards in one's hand—in other words, the hidden side of things, the real story. Barbey literalizes the phrase here by applying it to the card game whist.

2 Koblentz, in the German Rhineland, was the destination of many French aristocrats emigrating after the Revolution of 1789.

3   Mademoiselle Mars (1779–1847) was the leading actress of her day in France.

4   See "The Crimson Curtain," note 9.

5   The two Menaechmi are twin brothers in the play of that title by the Roman Plautus (254–184 B.C.).

6   Petit (Pléiade II: 1315) notes that while the saying is often attributed to Molière, it appears nowhere in his works.

7   See Pascal's *Pensées*: "The final act [of our lives] is a bloody one, however comic the rest of the play may have been."

8   The reference again is to Valognes, in Normandy.

9   The Holy Ampulla (*Sainte Ampoule*) is the vial that was used to anoint the kings of France from the year 1131 onward. Legends about its origin and miraculous powers circulated for centuries. As a symbol of the monarchy, it was destroyed during the Revolution.

10 As Petit notes (Pléiade II: 1316), this was the name of an actual aristocratic family in Valognes, and Barbey was acquainted with them. They, and the other families of the region, are listed in Édouard de Magny, ed., *Nobiliare de Normandie* (Lille, 1863).

11 The *Charte Constitutionelle* of 1814 allowed for the restoration of the monarchy in France; it was, however, a compromise between traditional royalism and the new liberal, republican sentiments that had dominated since the Revolution.

12 All the names—at least up to that of the Devil—are of real persons, French, Italian, and English, all more or less of the Marquis's generation, suggesting he has mixed intimately with many of the most powerful people of his day.

13 At the beginning of his great essay "Apology for Raymond Sebond" (1580), the theme of which is the fallibility of all human knowledge, Montaigne retells a story he found in Plutarch about the ancient Thracians' use of foxes to determine whether a frozen river was safe for walking. Montaigne depicts the fox as thinking it through and logically deducing that the ice is safe.

14 Richard Brinsley Sheridan (1751–1816), British playwright and wit. As we learned earlier, the Marquis had played with Sheridan during the aristocrats' emigration period.

15 Edward Bulwer-Lytton (1803–73), English novelist, playwright, and politician. In his early life he indulged in dandyism, and hence the profusion of rings mentioned here; his novel *Pelham* (1828) was a roman à clef that included among its characters the archetypal dandy Beau Brummell.

16 The Swiss writer Johann Kasper Lavater (1741–1801) was highly influential in forming nineteenth-century Europe's widely held belief in physiognomy, that one can determine a person's moral character from externals, especially the face.

17 At the Spanish court, the *camerera major* was the person entrusted with overseeing the education of the prince or princess.

18 Marmor is a form of marble.

19 Constance Chlore was Roman emperor from 293–305. Edward Gibbon (1737–94) wrote about him in *The Decline and Fall of the Roman Empire* (six

volumes, 1766–88). The *chloro* word root means "green," suggesting the complexion of the Countess. Ernestine's witticism is, to say the least, a bit labored.

20 Polycrates was ruler of Samos in the sixth century B.C. According to a story in Herodotus's *History,* Polycrates was advised to throw away whatever he valued most, as a way of warding off retribution from the jealous gods. He threw his most prized ring into the ocean, where a fish swallowed it. The fish, however, was caught by Polycrates's cook, who discovered the ring inside it and triumphantly returned it to its owner.

21 The "fiery flashing sword" (Genesis 3:24) is wielded by an angel to forbid Adam and Eve any reentry into the Garden of Eden.

22 The memoirs of the Cardinal de Retz (1613–79) describe his relative, Mademoiselle de Retz, in a cynical enough fashion, emphasizing that her wealth made up for the defects in her figure.

23 François-Henri de Montmorency, Marshal of Luxembourg (1628–95), a great general in his time, also had a hunchback.

24 Barbey's 1864 novel *Le Chevalier Destouches* describes the *chouan* uprisings against the Revolutionary government during the 1790s. In 1856, Barbey had met the historical chevalier Jacques Destouches (1780–1858), a swashbuckling romantic hero come to life.

25 Undines, in mythology, are female water spirits, usually (but not always) benign.

26 The *rois fainéants,* or "lazy kings," were kings in the Middle Ages who delegated much of their authority to others.

27 Scott's novel *The Pirate* (1822) involves the title character, Clement Cleveland, who is saved from a shipwreck and becomes the lover of the erstwhile respectable girl Minna Troil; Barbey implies that Karkoël like Cleveland sweeps in from nowhere to disrupt many lives.

28 The Maratha wars (1775–1818) were fought between the British and the Maratha Empire in India.

29 The Scottish Earls of Douglas flourished in the fourteenth and fifteenth centuries; the family is thus one of the most distinguished in the country's history. Douglas characters were featured in a number of Romantic plays and novels in the late eighteenth and early nineteenth centuries.

30 Count Alessandro Volta (1745–1827) was the inventor of the electric cell battery.

31 This is Barbey's own uncle, Jean-Louis Pontas-Dumeril, again. See note 3 to "Happiness in Crime." Pontas-Dumeril was a liberal, so he would not have observed the holiday described here.

32 The Duke of Enghien (Louis Antoine Henri de Bourbon, 1772–1804), a charismatic relative of the executed King Louis XVI, was executed by Napoleon for his role in émigré politics, making him something of a martyr for the conservative, monarchist cause, and losing any support Napoleon might have had from the émigré aristocrats.

33 The image is that of the Colossus of Rhodes, the legendary ancient statue, so huge that it straddled the harbor at Rhodes. Petit notes (Plèiade II: 1320) that

the character of de Tharsis is based on Barbey's godfather, Henri Lefebvre de Montressel; in his will, he made Barbey his heir.

34 An *Almée* is an Indian woman who improvises verses while she dances. Such figures were eroticized fantasies for many a French artist in the nineteenth century, including Bizet, Gerôme, and Toulouse-Lautrec, and hence it is a natural fantasy for our adolescent narrator to have had.

35 In July 1830, deepening resistance, protest, and rioting drove King Charles X from the throne; he escaped to England, never to return, and a constitutional monarchy was established.

36 The "only genuine statesman" was the Count de Villèle (1773–1854), an ultra royalist and prime minister under Charles X. His bill to reinstate primogeniture in 1826 was unsuccessful.

37 Barbey plays on the old proverb "No man is a hero to his valet."

AT A DINNER OF ATHEISTS

1 The setting is again Valognes.

2 The Swedish Saint Bridget (1303–73) had a series of visions that she wrote down in her book *Celestial Revelations.*

3 Petit (Pléiade II: 1286) notes that François Mesnilgrand was a real person, a cousin of Barbey's, and that the general outlines of his life are similar to those Barbey gives to the character in this story. However, his personality and character traits are fictionalized here.

4 *Turcaret,* subtitled *The Financier,* was a 1709 comedy by Alain-René Lesage. The character of Turcaret is an unscrupulous, scheming social climber who, in the end, is himself duped and cheated.

5 After his forced abdication in 1814, Napoleon was exiled to the island of Elba, and many of his officers swore allegiance to the newly restored monarchy. But in 1815 he escaped and returned to France; during the Hundred Days of his return, his officers and soldiers flocked back to him, only to face ultimate defeat at Waterloo.

6 Tabes dorsalis is a condition involving degenerating nerve cells in the spine; it results from untreated syphilis, which Barbey hints at here. The moxas treatment, originating in Chinese medicine, uses a kind of cone with dried leaves in it; these are set alight and applied to the spine.

7 Charles the Bold (*Charles le Téméraire*) lived from 1433 until 1477. Despite his bravery, his life ended in a series of ignominious military defeats at Granson, Morat, and Nancy—battles that Barbey mentions in the text that follows.

8 Vittorio Alfieri (1749–1803), Italian poet and dramatist. It is an extreme exaggeration to say he knew nothing but breaking horses at forty (for, though he was an expert horseman, he had also been writing since he was a boy), but he did in fact teach himself Greek at that age.

9 The great painter Théodore Géricault (1791–1824) spent about two years in the army at the same time as Mesnilgrand.

10 The Carbonari were a loosely affiliated grouping of revolutionaries in early

nineteenth-century Italy, flourishing especially from 1815 to 1830. Though they never had a well-organized political program, they stood in general for a unified, free Italy.

11 General Jean-Baptiste Berton was at the head of a group of conspirators—including members of the Carbonari—in a plot against the King. He was arrested and executed in 1822.

12 Barbey's reference is to the great German poet Heinrich Heine (1797–1856), but the source of the quoted phrase is uncertain.

13 Honoré Gabriel Riqueti, Count Mirabeau (1749–91), was one of the foremost Revolutionary statesmen and, as the text suggests, famous as an orator.

14 François-Joseph Talma (1763–1826) was among his generation's most famous actors. The character of Orestes figured in many French neoclassical plays, but the reference here is probably to the highly dramatic role of Orestes in Racine's 1667 tragedy *Andromaque,* the kind of drama in which Talma excelled.

15 Byron's *Lara* and *The Corsair* (both published in 1814) were extremely popular verse tales; the heroes of these and other tales tended to be described in much the same terms as Mesnilgrand is here.

16 The lavish feast of Balthazar (or Belshazzar) is described in the biblical book of Daniel (5:1–4). The phrase *Balthazar's feast* had become proverbial for any sumptuous meal and was the subject of many works of art, including a painting by Rembrandt and an oratorio by Handel.

17 Molière's 1673 comic play *Le Malade imaginaire* (sometimes translated as The Imaginary Invalid) involves an aging man, Argan, who is continually convinced he is ill; onstage he is usually portrayed in a dressing gown and headwear like that described here.

18 Two of France's greatest comic writers: Jean-François Regnard (1655–1709) and Jean-Baptiste Poquelin, known as Molière (1622–73).

19 Two Molière characters: Géronte is from *Les Fourberies de Scapin* (Scapin's tricks, 1671), and Harpagon is from *L'Avare* (the miser, 1668).

20 Bernard Le Bovier, Sieur de Fontenelle (1657–1757), one of the great polymaths of the early Enlightenment, did indeed live long enough to be a centenarian.

21 Jean de La Fontaine mentions that gardens don't speak in his 1698 fable "The Bear and the Garden Lover," book VIII, fable X. See the translation by James Michie in *Selected Fables* (New York: Viking, 1979), 203–5.

22 The great Roman historian Tacitus (56–117 A.D.) was known for his concise style. Barbey is also punning here: the French version of the name is *Tacite,* and the word *tacite,* like the English *tacit,* means implied, unspoken, silent.

23 The Baron d'Holbach (1723–89) was renowned both for the lavish food and drink served at his salon and for his atheism.

24 The reference here is to the well-known dinner held on Good Friday of 1868 involving a group of the literary elite (contemptuously called "mandarins" here). They included Sainte-Beuve, Hippolyte Taine, and Ernest Renan, all of whom Barbey regarded as enemies. The day chosen for the dinner and its extravagance caused a scandal, because Sainte-Beuve was a member of the Senate at the time, and the young prince Napoleon was present as well.

25 Petit (Plèiade II: 1324–25) notes that Cynegirus appears in Herodotus. After the battle of Marathon, Cynegirus tried to stop a Persian boat from fleeing by holding on with his bare hands. When his hands were cut off, he tried to hold on by his teeth.

26 The opening word of the Latin Mass is *oremus,* or Let us pray.

27 The revolutionary assembly known as the Convention voted to execute King Louis XVI on January 17, 1793; the excecution was carried out, by guillotine, on January 21.

28 The red caps (*bonnets rouges*) were worn during the Revolution, and the shako, a tall cylindrical military hat, was worn during the Napoleonic era and long after as well.

29 Barbey implies approval of the dandyism associated with these two: the great French Romantic writer Chateaubriand (1768–1846) and the Russian Grand Duke Constantine (though there are others by that name, Barbey probably refers to Konstantin Pavlovich [1779–1831], who had some reputation for an obsession with military dress).

30 In classical mythology, the king of the Lapiths, Pirithous, invited the Centaurs (half-men, half-horse creatures said to be related to the Lapiths) to his wedding feast. The Centaurs, not used to wine, quickly became drunk, and one of them attempted to rape Pirithous's bride; the wedding feast devolved into a violent battle, with the Centaurs eventually driven out of the region.

31 Paul-Louis Courier (1773–1825) was a classical scholar and political writer who was a fierce opponent of the Restoration.

32 The Congregation was a shadowy politico-religious group during the Restoration that was rumored to be run by radical Jesuits.

33 Regarding the prophetic name, a *reniant* is someone who renounces, who disavows—in this case, who turns his back on his faith.

34 The Marquise de Brinvilliers and her lover, the Chevalier de Sainte-Croix, were involved in a series of murders by poison in seventeenth-century France; accusations of witchcraft and Satanism were also involved in the subsequent investigations.

35 *Saint Nitouche* is a French slang term for a sanctimonious, hypocritical person.

36 Voltaire is credited with the anticlerical rallying cry of the Enlightenment, *Ecrasez l'infâme,* or crush the infamous one—the Church in some contexts, the established social system in others.

37 As Bornecque points out in his edition, Jean-Baptiste Le Carpentier was a real person, though he could not have attended this particular dinner, having been imprisoned in Mont Saint-Michel from 1820 to his death in 1828. He was, though, in fact a member of the Convention (see n. 27) and had voted for the execution of the king.

38 Saint Margaret Marie Alacoque (1647–90) was a French nun and mystic.

39 General Jean-Antoine Rossignol (1759–1802) was a Revolutionary commander who fought fiercely against counterrevolutionaries like the *chouans* in the West during the 1790s.

40 For the Roman Catholic, the consecrated host is literally the body of Christ.

Hence Reniant's phrase "the little box of gods" has an especially blasphemous tone.

41 Charles of Montpensier, Duke of Bourbon (1490–1527), led an army against Rome and Pope Clement VII; he died during the siege of the city, and his men went on to loot and pillage it.

42 Goethe's poem "The Bride of Corinth" (1816) concerns a dead woman who returns from the grave to claim the young man she loved.

43 Henri I, Duke of Guise (1550–88) was given the nickname *le balafré*, the scarred one; he received his scars at the Battle of Dormans in 1575.

44 Antinous was the lover of the Roman Emperor Hadrian. After Antinous drowned in 130 A.D., Hadrian's grief was extreme, and he insisted that Antinous from then on be worshipped as a god. There are many busts of him, all emphasizing an extraordinary beauty.

45 The Duc de Lauzun (1747–93) was haughty, colorful, and extremely successful in his military endeavors; he put together a regiment that aided the American colonists in the Revolutionary War, and his regiment still exists today.

46 Rançonnet, who would have had a classical education like all the others, partially remembers Virgil's second *Eclogue*, the first line of which is *Formosum pastor Corydon ardebat Alexim* (the handsome shepherd Corydon burned with love for Alexis). The eclogue, or simply its opening line, is often cited for its explicit homoeroticism.

47 On the physiognomist Lavater, see n. 16 in "Beneath the Cards at a Game of Whist."

48 Napoleon's sister, Pauline Bonaparte (1780–1825), was known for her often lavish and sensual lifestyle, though the rumors about her probably exaggerated this.

49 Napoleon had made his brother Joseph King of Spain in 1808; he was widely detested and was finally deposed in 1813.

50 Spaniards who sympathized with the French occupiers were called *afrancesadas*, or "Frenchified."

51 Messalina (17–48 A.D.) was the third wife of the Roman Emperor Claudius, and a byword for extreme feats of promiscuity.

52 Madame de Maintenon (1635–1719) was the second wife of King Louis XIV. In a widely reported anecdote, she was gazing into an artificial fishpond with some other people, and someone remarked how languid the fish seemed to be. "The carp are like me," she is said to have replied. "They regret their native mud."

53 The Marquise de Boufflers (1711–87), a beautiful French noblewoman, was renowned for her long line of lovers, though the verse exaggerates this; she was also a poet and painter.

54 Count Almaviva is a lecherous character in Pierre Beaumarchais's play *The Marriage of Figaro* (1784).

55 Catherine II of Russia, also known as Catherine the Great (1729–96), was renowned for her many lovers.

56 In one version of the story of Achilles, his mother Thetis dipped him in the

underworld's River Styx, thus making him invulnerable in all parts of his body that the water had touched.

57 The French fought a combined army of English and Spanish at Talavera, near Madrid, in July 1809.

58 Psalms 42:7. The quotation is of course ironic because the point in the Psalm is that the wonders of God's creation echo each other.

A WOMAN'S VENGEANCE

The title of this story in French, "La Vengeance d'une femme," could also be translated as "A Wife's Vengeance."

1 The Latin adverb *fortiter* means strongly, powerfully. Barbey is probably recalling the famous formulation of Martin Luther, *Pecca fortiter, sed fortius fide et gaude in Christ* (Sin boldly, but believe and rejoice in Christ even more). The phrase comes from a letter of Luther's dated August 1, 1521.

2 In ancient mythology, Myrrha slept with her father and gave birth to Adonis; Agrippina was the mother of the Roman emperor Nero, who had her executed; Oedipus, again in mythology, murdered his father and slept with his mother.

3 One of Barbey's projected stories for a second volume of *Diaboliques* was to be titled "Madame Henri III."

4 *Paradise* was the slang term for the highest gallery, presumably because it was so high up it was close to heaven; a first night was, then as now, the most popular night to attend.

5 Saint Rémy (c. 437–533) baptized Clovis, King of the Franks in 496, leading to the conversion of the entire Frankish tribe. It is a foundational moment in French, and European, history.

6 Regarding Lovelace, see "The Crimson Curtain," n. 13.

7 Louis-Philippe abdicated in 1848.

8 The term *gant jaune* (yellow glove) was applied to dandies in the era.

9 Jocrisse is a stock character type from traditional comedy. He is naïve, sentimental, and ignorant, easily duped.

10 The reference is unclear: Byron did write a memoir, but it was burned soon after his death and never published.

11 One of the writers who created the vogue for an exoticized Spain was Prosper Merimée, who wrote plays under the pen name of Clara Gazul (and Merimée also created the ultimate Spanish femme fatale, Carmen, in the 1847 story of that name). Musset's *Tales of Spain and Italy* was published in 1829. The dancer Mariano Camprubi was immortalized in a painting by Manet (*The Dancer*, 1860). Dolorès Serral, like Camprubi, made her dancing debut in Paris in the 1830s.

12 The Rue des Poulies, like the sinister Rue Basse-du-Rempart, no longer exists, both swept away in the huge renovation of Paris under the direction of Baron Haussmann.

13 The painting, Horace Vernet's *Judith and Holofernes* (1829), depicts the moment where the heroic Judith is just about to behead the sleeping Holofernes; in the Old Testament, see Judith 13.

14 The *louis* was a French coin worth about 20 francs.

15 On Messalina, see "At a Dinner of Atheists," n. 51.

16 The story of the Roman emperor Nero setting fire to Christian prisoners to use them as human torches is told in Tacitus, *Annals* XV: 44.

17 Scholars have not identified any statuette with this title; Barbey may have altered the name.

18 The reference is to Véronese's *The Temptation of Saint Anthony* (1552) in the Musée des Beaux-Arts, Caen.

19 Paul Gavarni (the pseudonym of Sulpice Guillaume Chevalier) was a caricaturist admired by writers as diverse as Balzac and Baudelaire; he did a series of sketches of so-called kept women that he called *lorettes*.

20 The Order of the Golden Fleece is one of Spain's oldest and most prestigious orders, founded in the fifteenth century and still in existence today.

21 The Princess of Ursins (Marie Anne de la Trémoille, 1642–1722) was a French aristocrat who became one of the most important women of the Spanish court, at one point even vying to become queen, until the tide turned against her.

22 Canephores, in ancient Greek architecture, are figures of women bearing baskets on their heads.

23 The ancient Greek poet Sappho is said to have hurled herself from the Leukadian rock (the cliffs on the island of Leukas) to escape the pain of unrequited love.

24 Tomas de Torquemada (1420–98) was one of the most fanatical leaders of the Inquisition in Spain. His family name is, as Barbey has it, simply a variant of Turre-Cremata.

25 Cesare Borgia (1475–1507) was in fact involved in many assassinations, some involving poison.

26 A *garde-infant* was a full skirt that offered a woman protection in a crowd; its name suggests that it originally was designed to protect (*garde*) the Spanish princess (the *infanta*). It could also be worn to hide a pregnancy. See the discussion in Abbey Zanger, *Scenes from the Marriage of Louis XIV: Nuptial Fictions and the Making of Absolute Power* (Stanford, Calif.: Stanford University Press, 1997), 53 ff.

27 Alfonso de Albuquerque (1453–1515) was a Portuguese nobleman, explorer, adventurer, and governor of Portuguese India.

28 *Gabrielle de Vergy* was a tragedy by Dormont de Belloy (the pen name of Pierre-Laurent Buirette) originally produced in 1777 but based on a medieval legend with strong similarities to the present story. The title character, unfaithful to her husband, is made to eat her lover's heart.

29 Vittoria Colonna, the Marquise de Pescaire (1490–1547), was a highly educated Italian woman who married a French nobleman; after his death, she devoted herself to religious and literary pursuits, becoming a kind of symbol of greatness of spirit.

30 The Latin *in pace* literally means "in peace," but the term was also a euphemism for a deeply hidden, isolated cell within or beneath a dungeon.

31 A "black Virgin" is an image or statue of Mary done in dark colors or dark wood.

32 Madame de Staël (1766–1817) uses the phrase in her 1802 novel *Delphine,* noting that we sometimes try to account for our internal contradictions by labeling some of our ideas and feelings as "the thoughts of the demon."

33 The Salpêtrière was the primary hospital for the poor in Paris.

A PAGE FROM HISTORY—1606

1 The *impression* is a key concept in Barbey's aesthetics. An impression is a powerful external stimulus that arouses something in one's personal memory; the result is both an altered, revivified self and an inspiration for the writer. In his *Quatrième Memorandum* (1858), for example, he speaks of an impression as being a kind of sudden, unexpected "slap" (*sifflet*) given to something within us (Pléiade II: 1077). Barbey visited the Ravalet chateau in October 1882 and wrote to Louise Read, "What an unimaginable impression! (*Impression inouïe!*). . . . The place is worthy of Edgar Poe! I'm going to make a poem out of the story" (OC II: 1361).

2 *Tour* in French means "tower."

3 The French verb *ravaler*—to swallow up again, or to wipe out, to cause to disappear—is pronounced the same as Ravalet. Barbey deployed a somewhat phonetically similar pun with a fictional character's name in "Don Juan's Finest Conquest."

4 The word *outlaw* is in English in the original.

5 In heraldry, the phrase *en pointe* refers to the position at the lowest part of the shield, the part that terminates in a kind of point.

6 In the nineteenth century, the substance called cantharides (sometimes called Spanish fly) was believed to have strong aphrodisiac properties. It is produced from beetles that feed on flowers and plants.

7 Barbey's history is in error here: Marguerite de Valois was divorced from Henri IV in 1599; Marie de Medici was Queen in 1603.

8 The enchantress Armida, in Tasso's *Jerusalem Delivered,* imprisoned a knight she loved, inside her castle.

9 Paul Delaroche's 1833 painting *The Children of Edward* is in the Louvre. It depicts the two young English princes who were put to death on the orders of King Richard III.

10 The term *one in the other* refers to an alternating pattern of color on the heraldic escutcheon.

JULES BARBEY D'AUREVILLY (1808–1889), aristocrat, Catholic, monarchist, and flamboyant dandy, was one of the most original writers of the Decadent movement. Born in Normandy, France, he spent most of his adult life in Paris, where he was a prolific and influential journalist, critic, poet, and novelist.

RAYMOND N. MACKENZIE has translated works by François Mauriac, Charles Baudelaire, Gustave Flaubert, and Émile Zola. He is professor of English at the University of St. Thomas in St. Paul, Minnesota.